TALES OF HEROES, GODS & MONSTERS

EGYPTIAN MYTHS & LEGENDS

FLAME TREE PUBLISHING
6 Melbray Mews, Fulham,
London SW6 3NS, United Kingdom
www.flametreepublishing.com

First published and copyright © 2022
Flame Tree Publishing Ltd

22 24 26 25 23
1 3 5 7 9 10 8 6 4 2

ISBN: 978-1-80417-326-8

Cover and pattern art was created by Flame Tree Studio, with elements courtesy of
Shutterstock.com/OlgaChernyak/chasiki/Svekloid.
Inside decoration courtesy of Shutterstock.com/Panda Vector.

Judith John (Glossary) is a writer and editor specializing in literature and history. A
former secondary school English Language and Literature teacher, she has subsequently
worked as an editor on major educational projects, including *English A: Literature* for
the Pearson International Baccalaureate series. Judith's major research interests include
Romantic and Gothic literature, and Renaissance drama.

Contributors, authors, editors and sources for this book include:
E.A. Wallis Budge, W.M. Flinders Petrie and other anonymous.

A copy of the CIP data for this book is available
from the British Library.

Designed and created in the UK | Printed and bound in China

TALES OF HEROES, GODS & MONSTERS

EGYPTIAN

MYTHS & LEGENDS

Reading List & Glossary of Terms
with a New Introduction by
PROF. JOYCE TYLDESLEY

CONTENTS

CONTENTS

TALES OF HEROES, GODS & MONSTERS

EGYPTIAN

MYTHS & LEGENDS

SERIES FOREWORD

Stretching back to the oral traditions of thousands of years ago, tales of heroes and disaster, creation and conquest have been told by many different civilizations in many different ways. Their impact sits deep within our culture even though the detail in the tales themselves are a loose mix of historical record, transformed narrative and the distortions of hundreds of storytellers.

Today the language of mythology lives with us: our mood is jovial, our countenance is saturnine, we are narcissistic and our modern life is hermetically sealed from others. The nuances of myths and legends form part of our daily routines and help us navigate the world around us, with its half truths and biased reported facts.

The nature of a myth is that its story is already known by most of those who hear it, or read it. Every generation brings a new emphasis, but the fundamentals remain the same: a desire to understand and describe the events and relationships of the world. Many of the great stories are archetypes that help us find our own place, equipping us with tools for self-understanding, both individually and as part of a broader culture.

For Western societies it is Greek mythology that speaks to us most clearly. It greatly influenced the mythological heritage of the ancient Roman civilization and is the lens through which we still see the Celts, the Norse and many of the other great peoples and religions. The Greeks themselves learned much from their neighbours, the Egyptians, an older culture that became weak with age and incestuous leadership.

It is important to understand that what we perceive now as mythology had its own origins in perceptions of the divine and the rituals of the sacred. The earliest civilizations, in the crucible of the Middle East, in the Sumer of the third millennium BCE, are the source to which many of the mythic archetypes can be traced. As humankind collected together in cities for the first time, developed writing and industrial scale agriculture, started to irrigate the rivers and attempted to control rather than be at the mercy of its environment, humanity began to write down its tentative explanations of natural events, of floods and plagues, of disease.

Early stories tell of Gods (or god-like animals in the case of tribal societies such as African, Native American or Aboriginal cultures) who are crafty and use their wits to survive, and it is reasonable to suggest that these were the first rulers of the gathering peoples of the earth, later elevated to god-like status with the distance of time. Such tales became more political as cities vied with each other for supremacy, creating new Gods, new hierarchies for their pantheons. The older Gods took on primordial roles and became the preserve of creation and destruction, leaving the new gods to deal with more current, everyday affairs. Empires rose and fell, with Babylon assuming the mantle from Sumeria in the 1800s BCE, then in turn to be swept away by the Assyrians of the 1200s BCE; then the Assyrians and the Egyptians were subjugated by the Greeks, the Greeks by the Romans and so on, leading to the spread and assimilation of common themes, ideas and stories throughout the world.

The survival of history is dependent on the telling of good tales, but each one must have the 'feeling' of truth, otherwise it will be ignored. Around the firesides, or embedded in a book or a computer, the myths and legends of the past are still the living materials of retold myth, not restricted to an exploration of origins. Now we have devices and global communications that give us unparalleled access to a diversity of traditions. We can find out about Native American, Indian, Chinese and tribal African mythology in a way that was denied to our ancestors, we can find connections, match the archaeology, religion and the mythologies of the world to build a comprehensive image of the human experience that is endlessly fascinating.

The stories in this book provide an introduction to the themes and concerns of the myths and legends of their respective cultures, with a short introduction to provide a linguistic, geographic and political context. This is where the myths have arrived today, but undoubtedly over the next millennia, they will transform again whilst retaining their essential truths and signs.

Jake Jackson
General Editor

TALES OF HEROES, GODS & MONSTERS
EGYPTIAN
MYTHS & LEGENDS

INTRODUCTION
& FURTHER READING

A NEW INTRODUCTION
TO EGYPTIAN MYTHOLOGY

'**Pharaonic Egypt**' – the time when Egypt was ruled by a king, or pharaoh – stretched from the coronation of the first king of the united land in 3100 BCE until the death of Cleopatra VII in 30 BCE. This immense timespan saw the rise and fall of empires, the building of magnificent stone monuments and the development of a complex and sophisticated series of religious beliefs which continued to evolve as the Pharaonic age progressed. Although it is traditional to talk about 'ancient Egyptian religion' as if it were a single, well-defined entity, it would be more accurate to see this 'religion' as a collection of cults. Egyptian theology had no central dogma and no single book of divine revelation. While the king was expected to serve all the state gods, ordinary people were free to worship as they wished.

There was just one – short-lived – exemption to this rule. From approximately 1352–1336 BCE the pharaoh Akhenaten expected his elite to worship the solar god known as the Aten. This religious experiment – henotheism rather than monotheism, as the Aten was not the only god in Akhenaten's world – did not last long, however, and the country quickly returned to the traditional pantheon.

Egypt's many gods and goddesses (impossible to count, but estimated at well over a thousand) generated stories that were passed down through the generations. These stories offer explanations for the mysteries of creation, existence and death. In so doing, they provide a glimpse into the ancient Egyptian mind.

THE WORLD OF THE PHARAOHS

Ancient Egypt owed its prosperity to the predictable behaviour of the River Nile, known simply as 'the river'. Having entered Egypt at the border town of Aswan, the river flowed northwards for 645 km (400 miles), passing through the hot, steep valley known as Upper Egypt. Here the distinction between the 'Black Land', the fertile soil bordering the Nile, and the 'Red Land', the infertile desert beyond, was very clear. The Black Land was the land of the living: it was here that the mud-brick dwellings and stone cult temples were built. The Red Land was the realm of the dead; it was home to wild animals, desert cemeteries and tombs. Just beyond the ancient city of Memphis, near modern Cairo, the Nile split into several branches and flowed across the broad, flat Delta (Lower Egypt) to empty into the Mediterranean Sea. With its extensive coastline, the Libyan border to the west and the Sinai land bridge to the east, the Delta was always open to foreign influences and ideas.

Recognizing the very real differences between Upper and Lower Egypt, the Egyptians viewed their country as two very different yet united lands. This idea of balanced tension appealed to them; the juxtaposition of opposites became a constant mythological theme, with the conflict between chaos (*isfet*) and order (*maat*) being fundamental to Egyptian thought.

The Inundation

Every year, in late summer, the River Nile burst its banks. Fields were flooded and settlements became islands, linked only by raised pathways. In late October the water retreated, enabling the peasants to sow their crops. Late spring would yield a copious harvest of grain, fruits, vegetables and flax from the fertile soils. The land would then bake in the hot sun before the river swelled and the cycle began again. Floods, which often bring disaster in world mythology, were in ancient Egypt regarded as a blessing.

The Nile brought other benefits too. A reliable source of fish, it ensured that no one needed to starve. It supplied the mud used to make both pottery and mud-bricks and allowed the papyrus plant to flourish in the Delta. Its waters served as both a laundry and a sewer. Last but not least, it was the highway which not only enabled people to travel, but also allowed the transport of heavy goods from quarries to building sites. In Egyptian mythology it is the boat, rather than the chariot, which carries the sun god across the sky.

Kingdoms, Intermediate Periods and Dynasties

In 3100 BCE the soldier-king Narmer sailed northwards from the ancient city of Hierakonpolis (south of modern Luxor), conquering the city-states of the Valley and Delta and creating one unified land. From this time onwards Egypt would be ruled by pharaohs. Traditionally historians have separated these monarchs into 'dynasties' – lines of kings who were connected, but not necessarily by blood. These dynasties have been grouped by historians into times of centralized rule (Kingdoms) interspersed by times of decentralized or foreign control (Intermediate Periods), as follows:

Early Dynastic Period (3100–2686 BCE): Dynasties 1–2
Old Kingdom (2686–2160 BCE): Dynasties 3–8
First Intermediate Period (2160–2055 BCE):
    Dynasties 9–11(part)
Middle Kingdom (2055–1650 BCE):
    Dynasties 11(part)–13
Second Intermediate Period (1650–1550 BCE):
    Dynasties 14–17
New Kingdom (1550–1069 BCE): Dynasties 18–20
Third Intermediate Period (1069–664 BCE):
    Dynasties 21–25
Late Period (664–332 BCE): Dynasties 26–31
Macedonian and Ptolemaic Period: (332–30 BCE)

This imposition of arbitrary cut-offs is a far from ideal way of classifying 3,000 years of complex history. It is not a dating system that the ancient Egyptians themselves would have recognized and some associated views have been proved incorrect. Archaeology has confirmed, for example, that life in the Intermediate Periods was far from the grim experience it was once assumed to be. However, this system has become so deeply embedded in the Egyptological literature that it is difficult to avoid.

THE WORLD OF THE GODS

Egypt's many gods evolved in the villages and towns of the Valley and Delta long before Narmer unified his land. These local deities developed their own independent explanations for life's mysteries. Once formed, the local stories evolved, becoming longer and more intricate as they absorbed influences from other cults and cultures. As a result, Egyptian mythology offers many solutions to the same questions. As we will see, this is particularly true of the creation stories. While the ancient Egyptians had no difficulty in accepting multiple explanations for the origins of their world, modern observers have often struggled with the idea of there being more than one valid explanation for the same phenomenon.

Divine Hierarchy

Gradually, as some towns became rich and powerful, their gods grew in status until, with Egypt a united land, a 'pyramid of gods' developed. This was topped by a select band of nationally recognized state gods, followed by a wider group of influential local gods. The bottom layer of the pyramid included an eclectic mixture of local gods, demi-gods and supernatural beings including spirits, demons, ancestors and ghosts.

Many of the gods had strong associations with particular aspects of life or the natural world, or were the personification of things, places or concepts. However, most gods had more than one sphere of influence, so it would be a mistake to try to classify them by their 'powers'. Osiris, for example, is widely recognized today as the king of the dead, but he was far more than this; the ancient Egyptians would also have recognized him as a powerful fertility god.

It was possible too for individual gods to unite to form composite deities. The falcon-headed Horus, for example, might join with the sun god Ra to form Ra-Horakhty, a manifestation of Ra as the strong rising sun. Alternatively, a god might separate into several aspects of the same being. Horus, for instance, might be worshipped as Horus-the-Child or Horus-the-Elder, as Horakhty (Horus of the two horizons) or Horemakhet (Horus in the horizon). More unusually, the mild-mannered mother goddess Hathor could, when angry, transform into an entirely different being. Her alter ego Sekhmet, the 'powerful one', was an uncompromising, fire-breathing lioness who used an arsenal of pestilence and plague to protect Egypt's pharaohs.

'Animal' Gods

While some of Egypt's gods were depicted with a human head and body, others were shown with an animal or a part-animal body. This inclusion of 'animals' within the pantheon has frequently been misinterpreted as zoolatry and taken as an indication that Egyptian religion was primitive. This is far from correct, however. The ancient Egyptians did not worship animals: they worshipped sophisticated gods whose immensely complex characters might best be represented either by a human or animal form. The fierce, nurturing mother-goddess Hathor is a good example of this. She may, with equal validity, appear as a conventional woman, as a woman with a cow's head or as a whole cow. The artist depicting her instinctively chose the form most appropriate to the context. If Hathor were to be shown seated on a throne to receive offerings from the pharaoh, it was sensible to equip her with the human body that would allow her to do this with ease. If she were to suckle the pharaoh, it made sense that she be depicted as a cow. Neither of these very different representations was intended to be a portrait. How did the Egyptians imagine Hathor? We have no way of knowing.

The cow goddess is one of Egypt's earliest deities. She appears on Predynastic painted pottery as a woman whose long, curved arms, raised above her faceless head, are reminiscent of curved cow horns. An early ceremonial carved stone palette depicts a stylized cow's head with stars on the ears, horns and top of the head; it reveals that cows are already associated with the sky. This early form of the celestial cow goddess is anonymous, however. Hathor is first named in the Giza pyramid complex built by the Fourth Dynasty pharaoh Khaefre. Her popularity and importance then increase swiftly as she absorbs the mythologies of other cow goddesses. Such a usurpation of myths is common throughout the Pharaonic age, a period in which almost all the state gods absorb the myths of lesser deities. Hathor eventually lost her own powerful status when Isis, sister-wife of Osiris, usurped her stories and her role, taking her place as Egypt's most important female deity. Isis, a goddess almost always depicted in human form, was far more acceptable to the Classical world than the bovine Hathor – a fact that allowed her cult to flourish beyond the end of the Pharaonic Age.

Communicating with the Gods

Initially gods and mortals lived together in Egypt. Then, as the gods grew disenchanted with life on earth, they separated. Some gods now occupied specific locations. Mertseger, goddess of the Theban Peak, for example, was guardian of the Theban Necropolis and so associated with the highest point in the Theban Hills, the 'Horn'; Osiris lived in an afterlife kingdom known as the Field of Reeds. Other gods might be found anywhere and everywhere. The one place where all the gods might be found was in their temple(s); here the cult statue, hidden deep within the temple sanctuary, was treated as if it were a living god.

The pharaoh served as a conduit between his people and the gods who controlled their destiny. He was therefore chief priest of every cult, with sole responsibility for the regular temple offerings of food, drink and prayers that all the gods craved. In recognition of this, scenes decorating the temple walls show the pharaoh alone, making offerings himself. In practice, as the pharaoh could not conduct every ceremony in every temple throughout Egypt, it was accepted that he could be assisted by a non-vocational priesthood, drawn from the educated elite.

Ordinary people were almost entirely excluded from participation in formal state religion; for most of the time state temples were effectively out of bounds to them. A private Egyptian would communicate with the divine via local temples and personal domestic rituals, including ancestor worship.

SOURCES

As no contemporary book of Egyptian myths has survived, our understanding of Egyptian mythology relies on a range of writings – principally funerary texts, fictional tales and the works of the Classical authors – plus the indirect information that can be gleaned from art, architecture and archaeology. Unfortunately, the archaeological bias that has seen the preservation of many of Egypt's desert cemeteries but an almost complete loss of the mud-brick domestic architecture means that this evidence is heavily skewed towards the mythology of death as expressed in the elite and royal tombs. The principal sources of written information are outlined below.

The Pyramid Texts

Funerary texts are writings designed to protect and aid the dead as they journey to the afterlife. They reflect two strong Egyptian traditions: the myths of the king of the dead, Osiris, and the myths of the creator god Atum and the sun god Ra. These very different traditions exist in parallel; both contribute to the survival of the deceased.

The earliest funerary texts are the Old Kingdom *Pyramid Texts*. This confusing and contradictory collection of spells recounts the story of the dead pharaoh as he struggles to join the sun god. The earliest known *Pyramid Texts* were carved in the Fifth Dynasty pyramid of Pharaoh Unas, who ruled 2375–2345 BCE, but analysis of their language suggests that many of the spells pre-date the pyramid age. They are intended to be read in a specific order, although no one pyramid has every spell. Unas was lucky, as it was recognized that his spirit was strong enough to leave the tomb. His people were less fortunate. Resurrected, they were trapped in their tombs until the end of time.

The Coffin Texts

At the end of the Old Kingdom, the exclusively royal afterlife was thrown open to the masses. Now anyone who could afford the correct funerary rituals could reasonably hope to escape the tomb. The First Intermediate Period and

Middle Kingdom *Coffin Texts* were a collection of spells designed to help the deceased to be reborn after death. Unlike the *Pyramid Texts*, the *Coffin Texts* were, in theory, available to everyone. Although occasionally written on tomb walls, stelae, papyri and canopic chests (the boxes that stored the canopic jars containing the preserved entrails of the deceased), these texts were principally inscribed on the rectangular wooden outer coffins that protected the mummies of the elite.

The Books of the Dead

By the New Kingdom (from approximately 1550 BCE onwards), the non-royal dead were being buried with the *Chapters of Going Forth by Day*, better known today as the *Book of the Dead*. The *Book* was a personalized guide to the afterlife; written on a papyrus scroll, it was placed either within the coffin or among the grave goods. The *Book* did not reach its finished form until the 26th Dynasty. By this time its 192 spells or chapters had been given an agreed order, although no individual *Book* included all the spells. Originally created without illustrations, the *Book* soon acquired a series of standard vignettes that sometimes replaced the spells.

The New Kingdom pharaohs were buried in rock-cut tombs in the remote Valley of the Kings at Thebes. Here the walls of their tombs were decorated with exclusively royal texts and scenes selected from a group of approximately 12 religious writings known as the *Books of the Underworld* or the *Guides to the Afterlife*. These told the story of the dangerous night-journey of the sun god Ra (*see* page 30).

Fictional Tales

Unfortunately only a few contemporary stories have survived, all dating to the Middle Kingdom and later. These, presumably a fraction of the tales once told, are fundamental to our understanding of Egyptian mythology. It is here that we can read of the fierce dispute that arose between Horus and his Uncle Seth, and of the skilful magic employed by the goddess Isis. However, we need to be careful. In most cases we have a single papyrus, giving just one version of what we can assume to have been a widely told story. It would be a mistake to accept this as the definitive version of that particular tale. Nor should we underestimate the difficulties inherent in translating a story from an ancient, long-dead language into a modern one.

The myths presented in this book have been translated by scholars who worked in the early days of Egyptology – in some cases not long after the decipherment of the hieroglyphic script. Their work forms a useful introduction to the subject and is of clear historical interest. However, we must also remember that Egyptology has made considerable advances in understanding over the past century. Readers with an interest in ancient Egyptian mythology should treat this volume as a beginning and use the 'Further Reading' list to develop their knowledge further.

The Classical Authors

Herodotus of Halicarnasus (Late Period), Diodorus of Sicily (Ptolemaic Period) and Plutarch (post-Pharaonic Roman Age) preserved versions of some of Egypt's better-known myths, written in Greek for their non-Egyptian readers. Their work is invaluable, yet we must bear in mind that it is not entirely authentic. None of the authors was fluent in the Egyptian language; as a result they could neither speak directly to the priests and storytellers nor read scrolls stored in the temple libraries. All three Classical authors had to research their myths via interpreters and tour guides; as a result their writings incorporate errors, misconceptions and their own cultural biases. Furthermore, they tell the tale that was current in their own lifetime. It needs to be remembered that Egyptian mythology was a constantly evolving phenomenon. The lengthy story of Isis and Osiris told by Plutarch, for example, would have been virtually unrecognizable to an Egyptian of the Old Kingdom.

THE CREATION OF THE LIVING WORLD

The priests who served the sun god in the temple of Heliopolis (now absorbed into modern Cairo) told a dramatic tale. At the very beginning of time, nothing existed but the waters known as Nun. Suddenly, just as Egypt's fields re-emerged each year from the Nile floods, an island emerged from Nun. Seated on this island was the god Atum, who then brought life to his new world. He coughed and spat (and in some versions of the story masturbated) to create twin children: Shu, the god of the atmosphere, and Tefnut, the goddess of moisture. Shu and Tefnut, Egypt's first sexually differentiated beings, married and produced Geb and Nut – a brother and sister whose quarrelsome marriage produced four divine children.

While Atum's creation of the gods was a deliberate act, his creation of people was a happy accident. One day the twins fell into the waters of chaos and were presumed drowned. Atum mourned his lost children deeply. When they returned to him, he cried tears of joy which, as they hit the ground, became men and women.

With the creation of the first five gods, the bubble-like organization of the Egyptian cosmos was established. The earth god Geb lay beneath the sky goddess Nut, separated from her by Shu, the atmosphere. Surrounding this bubble of life were the chaotic waters of Nun. Egypt was, naturally, the centre of the world within the bubble. It is tempting to speculate that the *Duat*, the land of the dead, lay underneath Geb, separated from him by his moist mother Tefnut.

The Sun God Ra

Atum had no need to create a sun: as a solar deity, he brought his own light with him. Later versions of the myth clarify this, and it is Ra who emerges on the mound of creation. While Ra was celebrated as the powerful midday sun, Atum became associated with the dying evening sun, while the dung beetle Khepri was revered as the morning sun.

Ra was a self-generated solar god who had the power to create all living things. Emerging from the waters of chaos, he slashed his penis to release two children, Hu and Sia. Ra then created the world. He ruled it until, growing old and tired, he retreated to the sky.

Every day the young Ra sailed his day-boat on a fairly uneventful voyage from east to west across Egypt's blue sky. As he crossed the sky, he grew older. Each evening the now elderly Ra sailed his night-boat on a hazardous voyage through the underworld. Assisted by his faithful crew, Ra spent the 12 hours of the night being attacked and battling enemies, such as the evil serpent Apophis, who threatened to extinguish his light. Eventually, if all went well, he would be reborn from Nut in the morning.

Other Creation Stories

At the Middle Egyptian site of Hermopolis Magna (modern Ashmunein) the priests of the temple of Thoth told a very different story. At the beginning of time four frog-headed gods and four snake-headed goddesses existed in the primeval waters. Suddenly the Mound of Flame emerged. What happened next is not clear. In some versions of the tale a celestial goose laid an egg on the mound. The egg cracked open and the sun god was born. In other versions the sun god landed on the mound as a falcon, or emerged from a lotus bud which opened either on the land or on the water. Six of the original Hermopolitan gods sank into relative obscurity, but Amun and his consort Amaunet continued to be revered in the southern city of Thebes. During the New Kingdom the now powerful Amun of Thebes united with Ra of Heliopolis to form the potent god-king Amun-Ra.

Memphis, just 32 km (20 miles) across the river from Heliopolis, was home to the ancient god Ptah – a deity able to create all things using his heart (believed to be the centre of the intellect) and the spoken word. Four hundred miles away at the opposite end of Egypt, the ram-headed Khnum lived on the Island of Elephantine (opposite the modern town of Aswan). Khnum controlled the waters of the inundation which poured into Egypt from Nun. He was associated both with rebirth and with Nile mud, which he used to shape human beings and their souls on his potter's wheel.

THE WORLD OF THE DEAD

The earth goddess Nut bore two sons, Osiris and Seth, and two daughters, Isis and Nephthys. Osiris inherited the Egyptian throne and ruled with his sister-wife Isis by his side. He proved to be a wise and just king, but his reign came to an abrupt end following his murder by his brother Seth. Although the death and resurrection of Osiris is one of Egypt's most important myths, it is not preserved in its full form before the Ptolemaic Age. Earlier references to the story stress the resurrection of Osiris but avoid the details of his betrayal and death. The most detailed version of the Osiris myth survives in Plutarch's *Isis and Osiris*, written in c. 120 CE. However, some elements of Plutarch's story are late additions, drawn from other mythologies.

The Murder of Osiris

Seth plotted to murder his brother Osiris. To do so he commissioned an elaborately decorated wooden chest and tricked Osiris into lying in it. Immediately Seth slammed the lid shut: the chest had become Egypt's first coffin. Seth coated the coffin in lead, threw it into the Nile and started to rule as king in his brother's place. However, he had reckoned without the determined loyalty of Isis, his brother's wife. She searched the world, found her husband still lying in his coffin and returned him to Egypt. Unfortunately Seth, hunting wild boar in the moonlight, stumbled across the remains of his brother. Furious, he hacked Osiris's corpse to pieces which he flung far and wide. Isis transformed into a bird and, assisted by her sister Nephthys, recovered her husband's body parts. Only the penis was missing: this had been eaten by the Nile fish. Isis wrapped her husband in bandages and brought him back to a form of life which allowed her to conceive a child with him.

As Isis raised her son, Horus-the-Child, in Egypt, Osiris became king of the underworld. Protected by his mother and nourished by the divine cow Hathor, Horus was raised in the papyrus marshes. His childhood was marred by an unfortunate series of accidents and illnesses, but his mother's healing magic ensured that he survived. Eventually the time came for Horus to claim his throne – a process that did not go smoothly. Seth was not prepared to surrender his crown to his nephew and many of the gods were on his side. The quarrel between Horus and Seth lasted for 80 years until Horus was eventually awarded the throne. From this time onwards, it was acknowledged that the eldest son born to the queen consort would inherit his father's crown. The living king of Egypt would now be associated with Horus, while all dead kings were associated with Osiris.

Seth: The Bad Brother

Seth had the misfortune to be the world's first second-born son. He had to watch his elder brother become king, a position for which he thought himself better suited, then was expected to stand by for a child to inherit the throne; to modern eyes it is little surprise that he rebelled. Seth's odd appearance reflects his chaotic nature. His human-form body is topped by a head that seems to combine the pronounced snout of an aardvark with straight, flat-topped, donkey-like ears. When represented in fully animal form, Seth also has a long neck, a dog-like body and an erect forked tail.

To classify Seth as pure evil would be a vast over-simplification. He is associated with chaotic things – for example, he is god of the desert and lord of foreigners – but only towards the end of the Pharaonic Age does he appear as a consummate villain. In earlier mythology he is far from irredeemable, and his bad deeds seen as no worse than the violent assaults occasionally committed by his fellow gods. At that time Seth was accepted as a maverick who, when eternal danger threatened – for example, when the sun Ra was attacked in the underworld – would always align himself on the right side. This explains why Seth, or Seti, gave his name to three New Kingdom pharaohs: the 19th Dynasty Seti I and Seti II and the 20th Dynasty Sethnakht.

Isis: The Good Wife

Isis makes her first appearance in the *Pyramid Texts* as the mother of Horus; only later does she become the sister-wife of Osiris. Her name, *Aset* in the original Egyptian, is represented by the hieroglyphic sign of the throne. Her crown too is a throne, worn either alone or in conjunction with the cow horns and solar disc that she has 'borrowed' from Hathor. As she is both the living throne and the mother and protector of Horus, Isis naturally becomes the mother and protector of all of Egypt's living kings.

Isis's story provides the blueprint for a happy domestic life. When all is well, she supports her husband within the home, attending to the running of the house. When disaster strikes and her husband vanishes, she is able to step forward and take control. Having solved the mystery of Osiris's disappearance, she is then able to deputize for her husband until her son is old enough to act independently. This pattern was repeated both in the royal family, where a queen consort might act as regent for an underage pharaoh, and in ordinary households, where a wife might take business decisions on her absent husband's behalf. The freedom experienced by Egyptian women, especially their right to live independent lives free from male control, astonished Classical visitors, accustomed to the more restricted lives of their own mothers, sisters and wives.

THE SCIENCE AND RITUAL OF MUMMIFICATION

Osiris invariably appears as a mummy swathed in white bandages. His crossed arms grasp the crook and flail which symbolize leadership and punishment, and he wears an elaborate crown on his unwrapped head. In spite of this somewhat unprepossessing appearance, his promise of life beyond death made Osiris an intensely comforting figure to many in ancient Egypt.

Osiris's myth explains the heavily bandaged mummies who lay in Egypt's elite tombs. Mummification was an art, a science and religious rite, developed in response to the belief that only those whose corpse remained in a lifelike condition had any hope of living again. It is difficult to state which came first, the myth or the mummy, but archaeological evidence indicates that experiments in mummification preceded the Osiris myth.

Preserving the Dead

The ancient Egyptians believed that death would release three spirits from the body. The weakest of these, the *ka* or life force, had to remain close to the corpse; it could never leave the grave and needed to receive regular offerings of food and drink from the living. Worryingly, if the *ka* could not recognize the corpse, it might die. If the *ka* died, there could be no hope of life beyond death. The *ba*, meaning the soul or personality of the deceased, was often depicted as a human-headed bird. The *ba* also lived in the tomb, but was able to visit the land of the living. The *akh* was an ill-understood spirit that represented immortality. The *akh* did not need to remain close to the corpse, but could survive elsewhere.

The ancient Egyptians knew that it was possible for a corpse to survive beyond death. The ancient desert pit graves held naturally preserved bodies which, when accidentally exposed by animals or grave robbers, were still recognizably human. These corpses had retained their skin, internal organs, hair, fingernails and toenails. They had been preserved by direct contact with the hot and sterile sand, which leached moisture away from the decomposing body and inhibited the growth of bacteria. As long as the Egyptians continued to bury their dead in simple desert pit graves, their bodies would survive.

Unfortunately, the elite did not want to be buried in simple sandy pits. They wanted coffins and stone tombs that offered plenty of space for grave goods, all of which separated the body from the hot sand. Burial in a coffin within a tomb made natural mummification an impossibility. Rather than abandon the tomb, however, a great deal of effort was put into developing a technology that would allow undertakers to replicate the desert's natural drying effect. Mummification would always be the privilege of an elite; most Egyptians continued to be buried, unmodified, in simple desert pit graves.

The earliest mummies conserved the shape of the body, but not the actual tissue. Layers of padded, plaster-soaked bandages allowed the undertakers to mould the facial features and the limbs, but beneath the bandages the bodies continued to rot. By the end of the Third Dynasty, evisceration, followed by a lengthy dehydration in natron salt and extensive bandaging, had become routine. Centuries of experimentation would lead to the perfection of this technique during the Third Intermediate Period (1069–664 BCE).

The Opening of the Mouth

Mummification was just the first stage in a series of rituals designed to allow the deceased to live again. The next important stage was the funeral.

The mummy travelled to the cemetery by sledge, the coffin being dragged across the desert sand. The accompanying cortege included the lector-priest who would read out the spells and the *sem*-priest who would perform the rituals, as well as family, friends, servants and professional mourners. At the tomb entrance a series of rituals was performed. The most important of these was the 'Opening of the Mouth', a ritual designed to animate the eyes, ears, nose and mouth; in so doing, it served to convert the inert mummy into a latent being with the potential for life. The mummy was propped upright as the *sem*-priest touched it with sacred objects, including the flint *pesesh-kef* knife (similar to the knife used to cut the umbilical cord from a newborn baby), an adze and the leg of an ox. Meanwhile the lector-priest recited the spells that would make the transformation complete.

Journey to the Afterlife

With the funeral ended and the tomb sealed, the mummy entered a stage somewhere between death and life. It was now time for the spirit to embark on the long and perilous journey to the afterlife – a voyage that would invariably involve some form of test. The *Coffin Texts* describe the deceased appearing before a tribunal to petition for entry into the next life, while the New Kingdom funerary texts anticipate a longer journey and a more elaborate court appearance. The *Book of the Dead* clearly emphasizes that entry to the afterlife was dependent on the knowledge that could be obtained from the *Book* itself, rather than on good behaviour in the mortal world.

Following the dying sun, the spirit travelled westwards until it reached a labyrinth guarded by a series of gateways. To progress, the spirit had to recite set text before each door. It then entered the courtroom to stand before Osiris and the 42 assessor gods. Here the spirit was required to recite the 'negative confession': a list of crimes that had not been committed. The climax of the trial was the weighing of the heart against the feather, the symbol of truth and justice. With the weighing complete, the verdict was announced and Thoth, the ibis-headed scribe of the gods, recorded it in his scroll.

Those light of heart were transfigured to become the blessed dead. They would live for ever, working in the Field of Reeds for Osiris. Those whose hearts weighed heavy faced a future of eternal chaos. During the Old Kingdom they might suffer perpetual hunger and thirst, or be required to perform chaotic behaviour such as eating excrement. In the Middle Kingdom the damned might be burned in the lake of fire, cooked in cauldrons or eaten by a monster. Finally, the New Kingdom funerary books introduce the fearsome Ammit, the 'eater of the damned'. This was a composite beast with the head of a crocodile, the foreparts and body of a lion or leopard and the hind parts of a hippopotamus.

ROYAL MYTHS

Although all Egyptians were heroes in the autobiographies carved and painted on their stone tomb walls, there was only room for one national hero – the current pharaoh – in the public sphere.

Egypt's major myths all reinforced the right of the pharaoh to rule. The creation myths stressed the need to ward off chaos while placing kings on newly created thrones;

the saga of Osiris, Isis, Seth and Horus confirmed the right of the son to inherit his father's throne; funerary mythology promoted the existence of an afterlife ruled by a divine king. It is little wonder that, for almost 3,000 years, pharaohs were regarded as crucial to Egypt's survival.

The living pharaoh was neither fully human nor fully divine. He was born to a mortal mother, just one among many princes who might succeed to the throne. His coronation then enabled him to become both the son of Ra and the living Horus. All pharaohs expected to acquire full divinity with death; some believed they were already at least partially divine. The earliest surviving royal birth myth is preserved in *Papyrus Westcar*, an anthology of fictional tales set during the Fourth Dynasty. These include the story of the Lady Redjedet, who gives birth to boy triplets fathered by the sun god Ra. The three babies are destined to rule Egypt. Clearly not an accurate historical account, this is royal propaganda designed to reinforce the rule of the three Fifth Dynasty kings Userkaf, Sahure and Niuserre.

The New Kingdom monarchs Hatshepsut, Amenhotep III and Ramesses II made their divine status more explicit. Each claimed Amen-Ra as their father and recounted the stories of their divine conception on their temple walls. These stories focus upon the moment of conception; they are romantic tales involving determined gods who visit beautiful queens in their bedrooms, intent on creating a child. In all three, the god assumes the guise of the queen's husband. These myths are very specific; they deal with named individuals rather than the origins of all pharaohs. Because of this, and because they make the physical relationship between the king's mother and the god very clear, they enhance the profile of the king's mother – one of the few mortals able to communicate directly with the gods.

THE END OF THE WORLD

In this brief introduction to Egyptian mythology we have considered myths developed to explain the mysteries of creation and of life beyond death. It seems appropriate to end by reflecting on what will happen when time itself runs out. The ancient Egyptians preferred not to commit worrying thoughts to writing, fearful that the powerful hieroglyphic script might make those concerns come true. However, several references hint at what might happen when the people and the gods have died. The *Coffin Texts* predict a bleak future. Atum will become one with Osiris and the land will return to the waters. The *Book of the Dead* expands on this, describing how at the end of time Atum and Osiris will exist as twin snakes in the endless waters of chaos.

Prof. Joyce Tyldesley

FURTHER READING

Allen, J.P., *Genesis in Egypt: The Philosophy of Ancient Egyptian Creation Accounts* (New Haven: Yale Egyptological Seminar, 1988)

Allen, J.P., *The Ancient Egyptian Pyramid Texts* (Atlanta: Society of Biblical Literature, 2015)

Assmann, J., *The Search for God in Ancient Egypt*, translated by D. Lorton (New York: Cornell University Press, 2001)

Baines, J., 'Egyptian Myth and Discourse: Myth, Gods, and the Early Written and Iconographic Record', *Journal of Near Eastern Studies* 50:2 (1991): 81–105.

Faulkner, R.O., *The Egyptian Book of the Dead: The Book of Going Forth by Day* (San Francisco: Chronicle Books, 2008 edition)

Faulkner, R.O., *The Ancient Egyptian Coffin Texts*, 3 volumes (Warminster: Aris & Phillips, 1973–8)

Griffiths, J.G., *Plutarch's De Iside et Osiride* (Cardiff: University of Wales, 1970)

Hornung, E., (1982), *Conceptions of God in Ancient Egypt: The One and the Many*, translated by J. Baines (New York: Cornell University Press, 1982)

Hornung, E., *The Ancient Egyptian Books of the Afterlife*, translated by D. Lorton (New York and London: Cornell University Press, 1999)

Kemp, B.J., *How to Read the Ancient Egyptian Book of the Dead* (London: Granta Books, 2007)

Lesko, B., *The Great Goddesses of Egypt* (Oklahoma: University of Oklahoma Press, 1999)

Pinch, G., *Egyptian Mythology: A Guide to the Gods, Goddesses and Traditions of Ancient Egypt* (Oxford: Oxford University Press, 2002)

Quirke, S., *The Cult of Ra: Sun Worship in Ancient Egypt* (London: Thames and Hudson, 2001)

Ray, J., *Reflections of Osiris* (London: Profile Books, 2002)

Redford, D.B., ed., *The Oxford Essential Guide to Egyptian Mythology* (Berkley: Berkley Publishing Group, 2002)

Shafer, B.E., ed., *Religion in Ancient Egypt: Gods, Myths and Personal Practice* (New York: Cornell University Press, 1991).

Te Velde, H., *Seth, God of Confusion: A Study of his Role in Egyptian Mythology and Religion* (Leiden: Probleme der Ägyptologie, 1977)

Tyldesley, J.A., *Myths and Legends of Ancient Egypt* (London: Viking/Penguin, 2010)

Wilkinson, R.H., *The Complete Gods and Goddesses of Ancient Egypt* (London: Thames and Hudson, 2003)

Joyce Tyldesley is Professor of Egyptology at the University of Manchester, where she teaches a suite of online courses to students worldwide. She is also an Honorary Fellow of the Manchester Museum. Joyce has extensive experience of excavating in Britain, Europe and Egypt. She is the author of many bestselling books about ancient Egypt. Her book *Cleopatra: Egypt's Last Queen* was a BBC Radio 4 Book of the Week; her book *Tutankhamun* won the Felicia A. Holton Book Award, given by the Archaeological Institute of America.

ANCIENT EGYPTIAN LITERATURE

The literature of ancient Egypt is the product of a period of about 4,000 years. It was written in three kinds of writing, which are called hieroglyphic, hieratic and demotic. In the first of these the characters were pictures of objects, in the second the forms of the characters were made as simple as possible so that they might be written quickly, and in the third many of them lost their picture form altogether and became mere symbols. Egyptian writing was believed to have been invented by the god Tehuti, or Thoth, and as this god was thought to be a form of the mind and intellect and wisdom of the god who created the heavens and the earth, the picture characters, or hieroglyphs as they are called, were held to be holy, or divine, or sacred. Certain religious texts were thought to possess special virtue when written in hieroglyphs, and the chapters and sections of books that were considered to have been composed by Thoth himself were believed to possess very great power, and to be of the utmost benefit to the dead when they were written out for them in hieroglyphs and buried with them in their coffins.

THOTH, THE SCRIBE OF THE GODS

Aside from inventing Egyptian writing, Thoth also invented the science of numbers and, as he fixed the courses of the sun, moon, and stars, and ordered the seasons, he was thought to be the first astronomer. He was the lord of wisdom and the possessor of all knowledge, both heavenly and earthly, divine and human; and he was the author of every attempt made by man to draw, paint and carve. As the lord and maker of books and as the skilled scribe, he was the clerk of the gods. He kept the registers wherein the deeds of men were written down. The deep knowledge of Thoth enabled him to find out the truth at all times. This ability caused the Egyptians to assign him to the position of Chief Judge of the dead. A very ancient legend states that Thoth acted in this capacity in the great trial that took place in heaven when Osiris was accused of certain crimes by his twin-brother Set, the god of evil. Thoth examined the evidence and proved to the gods that the charges made by Set were untrue and that Osiris had spoken the truth and that Set was a liar. For this reason, every Egyptian prayed that Thoth might act for him as he did for Osiris. That on the day of the Great Judgment Thoth might preside over the weighing of his heart in the Balance.

All the important religious works in all periods were believed to have been composed either by Thoth, or by holy scribes who were inspired by him. They were believed to be sources of the deepest wisdom, the like of which existed in no other books in the world. And it is probably to these books that Egypt owed her fame for learning and wisdom, which spread throughout all the civilized world. The 'Books of Thoth', which late popular tradition in Egypt declared to be as many as 36,525 in number, were revered by both natives and foreigners in a way which it is difficult for us in modern times to realise. The scribes who studied and copied these books were also specially honoured, for it was believed that the spirit of Thoth, the twice-great and thrice-great god, dwelt in them. The profession of the scribe was considered to be most honourable and its rewards were great, for no rank and no dignity were too high for the educated scribe. Thoth appears in the papyri and on the monuments as an ibis-headed man, and his companion is usually a dog-headed ape called Asten. In the Hall of the Great Judgment he is seen holding in one hand a reed with which he is writing on a palette the result of the weighing of the heart of the dead man in the Balance. The gods accepted the report of Thoth without question and rewarded the good soul and punished the bad according to his statement.

From the beginning to the end of the history of Egypt the position of Thoth as the 'righteous judge' and framer of the laws by which heaven and earth, and men and gods were governed, remained unchanged.

EARLIEST WRITING MATERIALS

The substances used by the Egyptians for writing on were numerous, but the most common were stone of various kinds, wood, skin and papyrus. The earliest writings were probably traced upon these substances with some fluid, coloured black or red, which served as ink. When the Egyptians became acquainted with the use of metals they began to cut their writings in stone. The text of one of the oldest chapters of the *Book of the Dead* (LXIV) is said in the Rubric to the chapter to have been 'found' cut upon a block of 'alabaster of the south' during the reign of Menkaura, a king of the fourth dynasty, about 3700 BCE ('Rubrics' often accompanied the main texts and were instructions as to how the spells or prayers should be used). As time went on and men wanted to write long texts or inscriptions, they made great use of wood as a writing material, partly on account of the labour and expense of cutting in stone. In the British Museum, many wooden coffins may be seen with their insides covered with religious texts, which were written with ink as on paper. Sheepskin, or goatskin, was used as a writing material, but its use was never general; ancient Egyptian documents written on skin or, as we should say, on parchment, are very few. At a very early period, the Egyptians learned how to make a sort of paper, which is now universally known by the name of 'papyrus'. When they made this discovery cannot be said, but the hieroglyphic inscriptions of the early dynasties contain the picture of a roll of papyrus and the antiquity of the use of papyrus must therefore be very great. Among the oldest dated examples of inscribed papyrus are some accounts which were written in the reign of King Assa (fourth dynasty, 3400 BCE). These were found at Sakkarah, about 32 km (20 miles) to the south of Cairo.

Papyrus was made from the papyrus plant that grew and flourished in the swamps and marshes of Lower Egypt, as well as in the shallow pools that were formed by the annual Nile flood. It no longer grows in Egypt, but it is found in the swamps of the Egyptian Sudan, where it sometimes grows to a height of 7.6 metres (25 feet). The roots and the stem, which is often thicker than a man's arm, are used as fuel and the head, which is large and rounded, is in some districts boiled and eaten as a vegetable. The Egyptian variety of the papyrus plant was smaller than that found in the Sudan. The Egyptians made their paper from it by cutting the inner part of the stem into thin strips, the width of which depended upon the thickness of the stem; the length of these varied, of course, with the length of the stem.

To make a sheet of papyrus, several of these strips were laid side by side lengthwise and several others were laid over them crosswise. Each sheet of papyrus contained two layers, which were joined together by means of glue and water or gum. It is believed that Nile water, which, when in a muddy state, has the peculiar qualities of glue, was used in fastening the two layers of strips together, but traces of gum have actually been found on papyri. The sheets were next pressed and then dried in the sun, and when rubbed with a hard polisher in order to remove roughnesses, were ready for use. By adding sheet to sheet, rolls of papyrus of almost any length could be made. The longest roll in the British Museum is the Harris Papyrus, No. 1, which is 40.5 metres (133 feet) long by 42 cm (16½ inches) high. The second in length is a copy of the *Book of the Dead*, which is 37.5 metres (123 feet) long and 47 cm (18½ inches) high; the latter contains 2666 lines of writing arranged in 172 columns. The rolls on which ordinary compositions were

written were much shorter and not so high. They are rarely
more than 6 metres (20 feet) long, and are only 20–25 cm (8–
10 inches) in height.

The scribe mixed on his palette the paints which he used.
This palette usually consisted of a square piece of alabaster,
wood, ivory or slate, 20–40 cm (8–16 inches) in length and 5–9
cm (2–3½ inches) in width. At one end of the palette a number
of oval or circular hollows were sunk to hold ink or paint. Down
the middle was cut a groove, square at one end and sloping at
the other, in which the writing reeds were placed. These were
kept in position by a piece of wood glued across the middle of
the palette, or by a sliding cover, which also served to protect
the reeds from damage. On the sides of this groove there are
often inscriptions that give the name of the palette's owner as
well as prayers to the gods for funerary offerings, or invocations
to Thoth, the inventor of the art of writing.

The black ink used by the scribes was made of lamp-black
or of finely-powdered charcoal mixed with water, to which a
very small quantity of gum was probably added. Red and yellow
paint were made from mineral earths or ochres, blue paint
was made from lapis-lazuli powder, green paint from sulphate
of copper and white paint from lime-white. Sometimes the
ink was placed in small wide-mouthed pots made of Egyptian
porcelain or alabaster. The scribe rubbed down his colours on
a stone slab with a small stone muller. The thin writing reed,
which served as a pen, was 20–25 cm (8–10 inches) long, and
1.5–3 mm (¹⁄₁₆–⅛ of an inch) in diameter; the end used in
writing was bruised and not cut. In later times a much thicker
reed was used and then the end was cut like a quill or steel
pen. Writing reeds of this kind were carried in boxes of wood

and metal specially made for the purpose. Many specimens of all kinds of Egyptian writing materials are to be seen in the Egyptian Rooms of the British Museum.

As papyrus was expensive, the pupils in the schools attached to the great temples of Egypt wrote their exercises and copies of standard literary compositions on slices of finely textured white limestone, or on boards whitened with lime. The 'copies' from which they worked were written by the teacher on limestone slabs of somewhat larger size. Copies of the texts that masons cut upon the walls of temples and other monuments were also written on slabs of this kind, and when figures of kings or gods were to be sculptured on the walls their proportions were indicated by perpendicular and horizontal lines drawn to scale. Portions of broken earthen-ware pots were also used for practising writing upon. In the Ptolemaic and Roman periods, lists of goods, business letters and receipts given by the tax-gatherers, were written upon potsherds. In later times, when skin or parchment was as expensive as papyrus, the Copts, or Egyptian Christians, used slices of limestone and potsherds for drafts of portions of the Scriptures and letters in much the same way as did their ancestors.

A roll of papyrus when not in use was kept in shape by a string or piece of papyrus cord, which was tied in a bow; sometimes, especially in the case of legal documents, a clay seal bearing the owner's name was stamped on the cord. Valuable rolls were kept in wooden cases or 'book boxes', which were deposited in a chamber or 'house' set apart for the purpose, which was commonly called the 'house of books', i.e. the library.

THE PYRAMID TEXTS

'**P**yramid Texts' **is the name now** commonly given to the long hieroglyphic inscriptions that are carved into the walls of the chambers and corridors of five pyramids at Sakkarah. The oldest of them was built for Unas, a king of the fifth dynasty. The remaining four were built for Teta, Pepi I, Merenra, and Pepi II, kings of the sixth dynasty. These pyrmaids were originally thought to have been built between 3300 and 3150 BCE, but more recent theories assign them to a period about 700 years later.

The *Pyramid Texts* represent the oldest religious literature known to us. They contain beliefs, dogmas and ideas that must be yousands of years older than the period of the sixth dynasty when the bulk of them was drafted for the use of the masons who cut them inside the pyramids. It is probable that certain sections of them were composed by the priests for the benefit of the dead in very primitive times in Egypt, when the art of writing was unknown, and that they were repeated each time a king died. They were first learned by heart by the funerary priests and then handed down orally to generation after generation. Eventually, after the Egyptians had learned to write and there was danger of their being forgotten, they were committed to writing. And just as these certain sections were absorbed into the great body of *Pyramid Texts* of the sixth dynasty, so portions of the Texts of the sixth dynasty were incorporated into the great Theban *Book of the Dead*, and they appear in papyri that were written more than 2,000 years later.

The *Pyramid Texts* supply us with plenty of information concerning the religious beliefs of the primitive Egyptians, and also with many isolated facts of history that are to be found nowhere else. However, it seems we must always remain ignorant to the meaning of a very large number of passages, because they describe states of civilization and conditions of life and climate, of which no modern person can form any true conception. Besides this the meanings of many words are unknown, the spelling is strange and often inexplicable, the construction of the sentence is often unlike anything known in later texts, and the ideas that they express are wholly foreign to the minds of students of today, who are in every way aliens to the primitive Egyptian African whose beliefs these words represent.

The pyramids at Sakkarah in which the *Pyramid Texts* are found were discovered by the Frenchman, Mariette, in 1880. Paper casts of the inscriptions, which are deeply cut in the walls and painted green, were made for Professor Maspero, the Director of the Service of Antiquities in Egypt. From these he printed an edition in hieroglyphic type of all five texts and added a French translation of the greater part of them. Maspero correctly recognized the true character of these ancient documents and his translation displayed an unrivalled insight into the true meaning of many sections of them. The discovery and study of other texts and the labours of recent workers have cleared up passages that offered difficulties to him, but his work will remain for a very long time the base of all investigations.

The *Pyramid Texts*, and the older texts quoted or embodied in them, were written, like every religious funerary work in Egypt, for the benefit of the king. That is to say, to effect his glorious resurrection and to secure him happiness in the Other World and life everlasting. They were intended to make him become a king in the Other World as he had been a king on earth; in other words, he was to reign over the gods and to have control of all the powers of heaven. He was to have the power to command the spirits and souls of the righteous, as his ancestors the kings of Egypt had ruled their bodies when they lived on earth.

The Egyptians found that their king, who was an incarnation of the 'Great God', died like other men and they feared that, even if they succeeded in effecting his resurrection by means of the *Pyramid Texts*, he might die a second time in the Other World. They spared no effort and left no means untried to make him not only a 'living soul' in the 'Tuat' (or Other World), but to keep him alive there. The object of every prayer, every spell, every hymn and every incantation contained in these Texts was to preserve the king's life. This might be done in many ways. In the first place it was necessary to provide a daily supply of offerings, which were offered up in the funerary temple that was attached to every pyramid. The carefully selected and duly appointed priest offered these one by one, and as he presented each to the spirit of the king he uttered a formula that was believed to convert the material food into a substance possessing a spiritual character and fit to form the food of the *ka* ('double' or 'vital power') of the dead king. The offerings helped renew his life and any failure to perform this service was counted a sin against the dead king's spirit.

It was also necessary to perform another set of ceremonies, the object of which was to 'open the mouth' of the dead king, i.e. to restore to him the power to breathe, think, speak, taste, smell and walk. At the performance of these ceremonies it was important to present articles of food, clothing, scents and ointments – in short, every object that the king was likely to require in the Other World. The spirits of all these objects passed into the Other World ready for use by the spirit of the king. It follows as a matter of course that the king in the Other World needed an entourage, a bodyguard and a host of servants, just as he needed slaves on earth. In primitive times, a large number of slaves, both male and female, were slain when a king died. Their bodies were buried in his tomb, whilst their spirits passed into the Other World to serve the spirit of the king, just as their bodies had served his body on earth.

As the king had enemies in this world, so it was thought he would have enemies in the Other World, and men feared that he would be attacked by evil gods and spirits, or by deadly animals, serpents and other noxious reptiles. To ward off the attacks of these from his tomb, and therefore his mummified body and his spirit, the priest composed spells of various kinds. The utterance of such spells was believed to render him immune from the attacks of foes of all kinds. Very often these took the form of prayers. Many of the spells were exceedingly ancient, even in the Pyramid Period; they were, in fact, so old that they were unintelligible to the scribes of the day. They date from the time when the Egyptians believed more in magic than religion; it is possible that when they were composed, religion (in our sense of the word) was still undeveloped among the Egyptians.

When the *Pyramid Texts* were written, men believed that the welfare of souls and spirits in the Other World could be secured by the prayers of the living. Hence we find in them numerous prayers for the dead and hymns addressed to the gods on their behalf, as well as in extracts from many kinds of ancient religious books. When these were recited together with offerings made both to the gods and to the dead, it was confidently believed that the souls of the dead received special consideration and help from the gods and from all the good spirits.

These prayers are very important from many points of view, but specially so from the fact that they prove that the Egyptians who lived under the sixth dynasty attached more importance to them than to magical spells and incantations. In other words, the Egyptians had begun to reject their belief in the efficacy of magic and to develop a belief of a more spiritual character. There were many reasons for this development, but the most important was the extraordinary growth of the influence of the religion of Osiris, which had spread all over Egypt by the end of the period of the sixth dynasty. This religion promised to all who followed it, high or low, rich or poor, a life in the world beyond the grave, after a resurrection that was made certain to them through the sufferings, death and resurrection of Osiris, who was the incarnation of the great primeval god who created the heavens and the earth.

Mention has already been made of the 'opening of the mouth' of the dead king: under the earliest dynasties this ceremony was performed on a statue of the king. Water was sprinkled before it, incense was burnt, the statue was anointed with seven kinds of ointments and its eyes were smeared with eye paint. After the statue had been washed and dressed, a meal of sepulchral offerings was set before it. The essential ceremony consisted in applying to the lips of the statue a curiously shaped instrument called the Pesh Kef, with which the bandages that covered the mouth of the dead king in his tomb were supposed to be cut and the mouth set free to open.

In later times, the *Liturgy of Opening the Mouth* was greatly enlarged and was called the *Book of Opening the Mouth*. The ceremonies were performed by the Kher-heb priest, the son of the deceased, the priests and ministrants called Sameref, Sem, Smer, Am-as, Am-khent, and the assistants called Mesentiu.

The *Liturgy of Funerary Offerings* was another all-important work. The oldest form of it, which is found in the *Pyramid Texts*, proves that even under the earliest dynasties the belief in the efficacy of sacrifices and offerings was an essential of the Egyptian religion.

The opening ceremonies were about the purification of the deceased by means of sprinkling with water in which salt, natron (an important preservative used in the embalming process) and other cleansing substances had been dissolved, along with the burning of incense. Then followed the presentation of about 150 offerings of food of all kinds – fruit, flowers, vegetables, various kinds of wine, seven kinds of precious ointments, clothing of the kind suitable for a king, etc.

As each object was presented to the spirit of the king, which was present in his statue in the Tuat Chamber of the tomb, the priest recited a form of words, which had the effect of transmuting the substance of the object into something which, when used or absorbed by the king's spirit, renewed the king's life and maintained his existence in the Other World. Every object was called the 'Eye of Horus', in allusion to its life-giving qualities.

THE BOOK OF THE DEAD

The 'Book of the Dead' is the name now generally given to the large collection of compositions or 'Chapters', both short and long, which the ancient Egyptians cut onto the walls of the corridors and chambers in pyramids and tombs, and cut or painted onto the insides and outsides of coffins and sarcophagi, and wrote on papyri, which were buried with the dead in their tombs.

The first modern scholar to study these Chapters was the eminent Frenchman, J. François Champollion. He rightly concluded that all of them were of a religious character, but he was wrong in calling the collection as a whole 'Funerary Ritual'. The name *Book of the Dead* is a translation of the title 'Todtenbuch', given by Dr. R. Lepsius to his edition of a papyrus at Turin, containing a very long selection of the Chapters, which he published in 1842.

'Book of the Dead' is a highly satisfactory general description of these Chapters, as they deal almost entirely with the dead, and they were written entirely for the dead.

They have nothing to do with the worship of the gods by those who live on earth, and the prayers and hymns that are incorporated within them were supposed to be said and sung by the dead for their own benefit.

The author of the Chapters of the *Book of the Dead* was the god Thoth, whose greatness we have already described earlier in this book. For this reason, they were considered to be of divine origin, and were greatly revered by Egyptians throughout their long history. They do not all belong to the same period – many of them allude to the dismemberment and burning of the dead, customs that, though common enough in very primitive times, were abandoned soon after royal dynasties became established in Egypt.

It is probable that in one form or another many of the Chapters were in existence in the predynastic period (i.e. before Menes became king of both Upper and Lower Egypt), but no copies of such primitive versions, if they ever existed, have passed down to us. One Egyptian tradition, which is at least as old as the early part of the eighteenth dynasty (c. 1600 BCE), states that Chapters XXXB and LXIV were 'discovered' during the reign of Semti, a king of the first dynasty, and another tradition assigns their discovery to the reign of Menkaura, a king of the fourth dynasty. It is certain, however, that the Egyptians possessed a *Book of the Dead* which was used for kings and other royals, at least, early under the first dynasty, and that, in a form more or less complete, it was in use down to the time of the coming of Christianity to Egypt.

The tombs of the officials of the third and fourth dynasties prove that the *Book of Opening the Mouth* and the

Liturgy of Funerary Offerings were in use when they were made, and this being so it follows as a matter of course that, at this period, the Egyptians believed in the resurrection of the dead and in their immortality. Also that the religion of Osiris was generally accepted, that the efficacy of funerary offerings was unquestioned by the religious, and that men died believing that those who were righteous on earth would be rewarded in heaven, and that the evil would be punished.

The *Pyramid Texts* also prove that a *Book of the Dead* divided into chapters was in existence when they were written, for they mention the 'Chapter of those who come forth' (i.e. appear in heaven), and the 'Chapter of those who rise up'. Whether these Chapters formed parts of the *Pyramid Texts*, or whether both they and the *Pyramid Texts* belonged to the *Book of the Dead* cannot be said, but it seems clear that the Chapters mentioned above formed part of a work belonging to a *Book of the Dead* that was older than the *Pyramid Texts*.

This *Book of the Dead* was no doubt based on the beliefs of the followers of the religion of Osiris, which began in the Delta and spread southwards into Upper Egypt. Its doctrines must have differed in many important particulars from those of the worshippers of the Sun god of Heliopolis, whose priests preached the existence of a heaven of a solar character, and taught their followers to believe in the Sun god Ra, and not in Temu, the ancient native god of Heliopolis, and not in the divine man Osiris. The exposition of the Heliopolitan creed is found in the *Pyramid Texts*, which also contain the proofs that before the close of the sixth dynasty, the cult of

Osiris had vanquished the cult of Ra, and that the religion of Osiris had triumphed.

Certain Chapters of the *Book of the Dead* (e.g. XXXB and LXIV) were written in the city of Thoth, or Khemenu, others were written in Anu, or Heliopolis, and others in Busiris and other towns of the Delta. We have no copies of the *Book of the Dead* that was in use under the fifth and sixth dynasties, but many Chapters of the Recension in use under the eleventh and twelfth dynasties are found written in cursive hieroglyphs on wooden sarcophagi, many of which may be seen in the British Museum.

At the beginning of the eighteenth dynasty, the *Book of the Dead* entered a new phase of its existence, and it became the custom to write it on rolls of papyrus, which were laid with the dead in their coffins, instead of on the coffins themselves. As the greater number of such rolls have been found in the tombs of priests and others at Thebes, the Recension that was in use from the eighteenth to the twenty-first dynasty (1600–900 BCE) is commonly called the 'Theban Recension'. This Recension, in its earliest form, is usually written with black ink in vertical columns of hieroglyphs, which are separated by black lines; the titles of the Chapters, the opening words of each section, and the Rubrics (instructions) are written with red ink. Around the middle of the eighteenth dynasty, pictures painted in bright colours (i.e. 'vignettes') were added to the Chapters; these are extremely valuable, because they sometimes explain or give a clue to the meaning of parts of the texts that are obscure.

Under the twentieth and twenty-first dynasties, the writing of copies of the *Book of the Dead* in hieroglyphs went out of fashion. Copies written in the hieratic (or cursive) character took their place. These were ornamented with vignettes drawn in outline with black ink, and although the scribes who made them wrote certain sections in hieroglyphs, it is clear that they did not possess the skill of the great scribes who flourished between 1600 and 1050 BCE. The last Recension of the *Book of the Dead* known to us in a complete form is the 'Saite Recension', which came into existence about 600 BCE and continued in use from that time to the Roman Period. In the Ptolemaic and Roman Periods the priests composed several small works such as the 'Book of Breathings' and the 'Book of Traversing Eternity', which were based on the *Book of the Dead*. They were supposed to contain (in a highly condensed form) all the texts that were necessary for salvation. At a still later period even more abbreviated texts came into use, and the *Book of the Dead* ended its existence in the form of a series of almost illegible scrawls traced onto scraps of papyrus only a few inches square. (These later substitutes are discussed in the section 'Books of the Dead of the Graeco-Roman Period', from page 48, and extracts are featured in the chapter 'Spells from the Books of the Dead', from page 76.)

Rolls of papyrus containing the *Book of the Dead* were placed either in a niche in the wall of the mummy chamber; in the coffin by the side of the deceased, or laid between the thighs or just above the ankles; or alternatively in hollow wooden figures of the god Osiris, or Ptah-Seker-Osiris, or in the hollow pedestals on which such figures stood.

The Egyptians believed that the souls of the dead on leaving this world had to travel across a vast and difficult region called the Tuat, which was inhabited by gods, devils, fiends, demons, good spirits, bad spirits, and the souls of the wicked, to say nothing of snakes, serpents, savage animals, and monsters, before they could reach the Elysian Fields and appear in the presence of Osiris. The Tuat was like the African 'bush', and had no roads through it. In primitive times the Egyptians thought that only those souls that were provided with spells, incantations, prayers, charms, words of power and amulets could ever hope to reach the Kingdom of Osiris – the *Book of the Dead* was written to furnish the dead with all these, contained in many chapters. The spells and incantations were needed for the bewitchment of hostile beings of every kind; the prayers, charms and words of power were necessary for making other kinds of beings that possessed great powers to help the soul on its journey, and to deliver it from foes. The amulets gave the soul strength, power, will and knowledge to successfully employ every means of assistance that presented itself.

The religion of the eighteenth dynasty was far higher in its spiritual character generally than that of the twelfth dynasty, but the Chapters that were used under the twelfth dynasty were used under the eighteenth, and even under the twenty-sixth dynasty. In religion, the Egyptian forgot nothing and abandoned nothing; what was good enough for his ancestors was good enough for him, and he was content to go into the next world relying for his salvation on the texts which he thought had procured their salvation. Therefore the *Book of the Dead* as a whole is a work that reflects all the religious beliefs of the Egyptians from the time when they were half savages to the period of the final downfall of their power.

The Theban Recension of the *Book of the Dead* contains about 190 Chapters, many of which have Rubrics stating what effects will be produced by their recital, and describing ceremonies that must be performed whilst they are being recited. It would be impossible to describe the contents of all the Chapters in this book, but the following is a brief summary of the most important:

Chapter 1 contains the formulas that were recited on the day of the funeral.

Chapter 151 gives a picture of the arrangement of the mummy chamber, and the texts to be said in it.

Chapter 137 describes certain magical ceremonies that were performed in the mummy chamber, and describes the objects of magical power that were placed in niches in the four walls.

Chapter 125 gives a picture of the Judgment Hall of Osiris, and supplies the declarations of innocence that the deceased made before the Forty-two Judges.

Chapters 144–47, 149 and 150 describe the Halls, Pylons, and Divisions of the Kingdom of Osiris, and supply the name of the gods who guard them, and the formulas to be said by the deceased as he comes to each.

Chapter 110 gives a picture of the Elysian Fields and a text describing all the towns and places in them.

Chapter 5 is a spell by the use of which the deceased avoided doing work.

Chapter 6 is another such spell, the recital of which made a figure to work for him.

Chapter 15 contains hymns to the rising and to the setting sun, and a Litany of Osiris.

Chapter 183 is a hymn to Osiris.

Chapters 2, 3, 12, 13, and others enabled a man to move about freely in the Other World.

Chapter 9 secured his free passage in and out of the tomb.

Chapter 11 overthrew his enemies.

Chapter 17 deals with important beliefs as to the origin of God and the gods, and of the heavens and the earth, and states the different opinions which Egyptian theologians held about many divine and mythological beings. The reason for including it in the *Book of the Dead* is not quite clear, but that it was a most important Chapter is beyond all doubt.

Chapters 21 and 22 restored his mouth to the deceased and Chapter 23 enabled him to open it.

Chapter 24 supplied him with words of power.

Chapter 25 restored to him his memory.

Chapters 26–30B gave to the deceased his heart, and supplied the spells that prevented the stealers of hearts from carrying it off, or from injuring it in any way. Two of these Chapters (29 and 30B) were cut upon amulets made in the form of a human heart.

Chapters 31 and 32 are spells for driving away crocodiles, and Chapters 33–38 and 40 are spells against snakes and serpents.

Chapters 41 and 42 preserved a man from slaughter in the Other World, Chapter 43 enabled him to avoid decapitation, and Chapter 44 preserved him from the second death.

Chapters 45, 46, and 154 protected the body from rot or decay and worms in the tomb.

Chapter 50 saved the deceased from the headsman in the Tuat, and Chapter 51 enabled him to avoid stumbling.

Chapters 38, 52–60, and 62 ensured for him a supply of air and water in the Tuat, and Chapter 63 protected him from drinking boiling water there.

Chapters 64–74 gave him the power to leave the tomb, to overthrow enemies, and to 'come forth by day'.

Chapters 76–89 enabled a man to transform himself into the Light-god, the primeval soul of God, the gods Ptah and Osiris, a golden hawk, a divine hawk, a lotus, a Bennu bird, a heron, a swallow, a serpent, a crocodile, and into any being or thing he pleased.

Chapter 89 enabled the soul of the deceased to rejoin its body at pleasure, and Chapters 91 and 92 secured the exit of his soul and spirit from the tomb.

Chapters 94–97 made the deceased an associate of Thoth, and Chapters 98 and 99 secured for him the use of the magical boat, and the services of the celestial ferryman, who would ferry him across the river in the Tuat to the Island of Fire, in which Osiris lived.

Chapters 101 and 102 provided access for him to the Boat of Ra.

Chapters 108, 109, 112, and 116 enabled him to know the Souls (i.e. gods) of the East and West, and of the towns of Pe (i.e. Pe Tep, or Buto), Nekhen (Eileiyouriaspolis), Khemenu (Hermopolis), and Anu (Heliopolis).

Chapters 117–119 enabled him to find his way through Rastau, a part of the kingdom of Seker, the god of Death.

Chapter 152 enabled him to build a house, and Chapter 132 gave him power to return to the earth and see it.

Chapter 153 provided for his escape from the fiend who went about to take souls in a net.

Chapters 155–160, 166, and 167 formed the spells that were engraved on amulets, i.e. the Tet (male), the Tet (female), the Vulture, the Collar, the Sceptre, the Pillow, the Pectoral, etc., and gave to the deceased the power of Osiris and Isis and other gods, and restored to him his heart, and lifted up his head.

Chapter 162 kept heat in the body until the day of the resurrection.

Chapters 175 and 176 gave the deceased everlasting life and enabled him to escape the second death.

Chapter 177 raised up the dead body, and Chapter 178 raised up the spirit-soul.

The remaining Chapters perfected the spirit-soul, and gave it celestial powers, and enabled it to enjoy intercourse with the gods as an equal, and enabled it to participate in all their occupations and pleasures.

BOOKS OF THE DEAD OF THE GRAECO-ROMAN PERIOD

From what has been said in the preceding section it will be clear that only wealthy people could afford to bury copies of the great *Book of the Dead* with their deceased relatives. Whether the chapters that formed it were written on coffins or on papyrus the cost of copying the work by a competent scribe must have been relatively very great. Towards the close of the twenty-sixth dynasty a feeling spread among the Egyptians that only certain parts of the *Book of the Dead* were essential for the resurrection of the body and for the salvation of the soul, and men began to bury with their dead copies of the most important chapters of it in a very much abridged form. A little later the scribes produced a number of works, in which they included only such portions of the most important chapters as were considered necessary to effect the resurrection of the body. In other words, they rejected all the old magical elements in the *Book of the Dead*, and preserved only the texts and formulae that appertained to the cult of Osiris, the first man who had risen from the dead.

One of the oldest of these later substitutes for the *Book of the Dead* is the *Shai en Sensen*, or 'Book of Breathings'. Several copies of this work are extant in the funerary papyri. Another late work of considerable interest is the 'Book of Traversing Eternity', the fullest known form of which is found on a papyrus at Vienna. This work describes how the soul of the deceased, when armed with the power which the Book of Traversing Eternity will give it, shall be able to travel from one end of Egypt to the other, and to visit all the holy places, and to assist at the festivals, and to enjoy communion not only with the gods and spirits who assemble there, but also with its kinsfolk and acquaintances whom it left behind alive on the earth. The object of the book was to secure for the deceased the resurrection of his body

Of the works that were originally composed for recitation on the days of the festivals of Osiris, and were specially connected with the cult of this god, three, which became very popular in the Graeco-Roman period, may be mentioned. These are: 'The Lamentations of Isis and Nephthys', 'The Festival Songs of Isis and Nephthys', and 'The Book of Making Splendid the Spirit of Osiris'. The first of these works was recited on the twenty-fifth day of the fourth month of the season Akhet (October-November) by two 'fair women', who personified Isis and Nephthys. One of these had the name of Isis on her shoulder, and the other the name of Nephthys, and each held a vessel of water in her right hand, and a 'Memphis cake of bread' in her left. The object of the recital was to commemorate the resurrection of Osiris, and if the book were recited on behalf of any deceased person it would make his spirit glorious, and establish his body, and cause his Ka to rejoice, and give breath to his nostrils and air to his throat. The two 'fair women' sang the sections alternately in the presence of the Kher-heb and Setem priests.

The second work, the 'Festival Songs of Isis and Nephthys', was sung during the great festival of Osiris, which took place in the fourth month of the Season of Akhet and lasted five days (from the twenty-second to the twenty-sixth day). It was sung by two virgins who wore fillets of sheep's wool on their heads, and held tambourines in their hands; one was called Isis and the other Nephthys. According to the rubrical directions given in the British Museum papyrus, the sections were sung by both women together.

The third work, 'The Book of Making Splendid the Spirit of Osiris', was also sung at the great festival of Osiris that took place during the November-December season at

Abydos and other great towns in Egypt, and if it were sung on behalf of any man, the resurrection and life, constantly renewed, of that man were secured for his soul and spirit. This book, written in hieratic, is found in a papyrus in Paris.

During the period of the occupation of Egypt by the Romans, the three last-named works were still further abridged, and eventually the texts that were considered essential for salvation were written upon small sheets of papyrus from 23–30 cm (9–12 inches) high, and from 13–25 cm (5–10 inches) wide.

TALES FROM THE PYRAMID TEXTS

The 'tales' in this chapter are based on extracts that illustrate the general content and ceremonies of the *Book of Opening the Mouth* and the *Liturgy of Funerary Offerings* – both of which are discussed in the previous section on the *Pyramid Texts*. Included here are the Hymns to Nut, the Sky goddess, and Ra, the Sun god – these are a more modern re-telling of the original Victorian translations. In 'The Power of the King in Heaven' section there are two passages. The first explains the power of the king and his joy in being there, the second portrays how the power of the king in heaven was almost as absolute as it was on earth – in a very remarkable passage in the text of Unas, there is a graphic description of the king as a mighty hunter, who chases the gods and lassoes them, and then kills and eats them in order to absorb their strength and wisdom, all their divine attributes, and their power of eternal life. The story of The Majesty of King Pepi is based on an extract of one of the later *Pyramid Texts*.

THE OPENING OF THE MOUTH CEREMONY

Incense was burnt and the priest declared, 'You are pure,' four times. Water was sprinkled over the statue and then the priest said, 'You are pure. You are pure. Your purifications are the purifications of Horus,' (Horus being a form of the Sun god). He continued, 'And the purifications of Horus are your purifications.' This formula was repeated three times, once with the name of Set (originally a benevolent god: later the great god of evil), once with the name of Thoth (the scribe of the gods and lord of wisdom), and once with the name of Sep. The priest then said, 'You have received your head, and your bones have been brought to you before Keb.' (Keb being the Earth god.)

During the performance of the next five ceremonies, in which incense of various kinds was offered, the priest once again said, 'You are pure.' He repeated this four times. He went on, 'That which is in the two eyes of Horus has been presented to you with the two vases of Thoth, and they purify you so that there may not exist in you the power of destruction that belongs to you. You are pure. You are pure. Pure is the incense that opens your mouth. Taste the taste of this in the divine dwelling. This incense is the emission of Horus; it establishes the heart of Horus-Set, it purifies the gods who are in the following of Horus. You are established among the gods, your brethren. Your mouth is like that of a sucking calf on the day of its birth. You are censed. You are censed. You are pure. You are pure. You are established among your brethren, the gods. Your head is censed. Your mouth is censed. Your bones are purified. Decay that is inherent in you shall not touch you. I have given you the Eye of Horus, and your face is filled with it. You are shrouded in incense.'

The next ceremony performed represented the rebirth of the king, who was personified by a priest. The priest, wrapped in the skin of a bull, lay on a small bed and feigned death. When the chief priest had said, 'Oh, my father,' four times, the priest representing the king rose up from the bull's skin; this act symbolized the resurrection of the king in the form of a spirit-body (or *sahu*). The chief priest then declared that the king was alive and should never be removed, and that he was similar in every way to Horus. The priest personifying the king then put on a special garment, and taking a staff or sceptre in his hand, said, 'I love my father and his transformation. I have made my father, I have made a statue of him, a large statue. Horus loves those who love him.' He then pressed the lips of the statue, and said, 'I have come to embrace you. I am your son. I am Horus. I have pressed for you your mouth.... I am your beloved son.' Finally, the chief priest declared, 'I have delivered this mine eye from his mouth, I have cut off his leg,' which means that the king was delivered from the jaws of death, and that a grievous wound had been inflicted on Set, the god of death.

Whilst these ceremonies were being performed the animals brought to be sacrificed were slain. Chief of these were two bulls, a gazelle, and many geese, and their slaughter typified the conquest and death of the enemies of the dead king. The heart and a foreleg of each bull were presented to the statue of the king. The priest then said: 'Hail, Osiris! I have come to embrace you. I am Horus. I have pressed for you your mouth. I am your beloved Son. I have opened your mouth. Your mouth has been made firm. I have made your mouth and your tes be in their proper places. Hail, Osiris! I have opened your mouth with the

Eye of Horus.' It was actually assumed that after death the king became a being with the nature of Osiris, and he was therefore addressed as 'Osiris'.

Then taking two instruments made of metal the priest went through the motion of cutting open the mouth and eyes of the statue, and said: 'I have opened your mouth. I have opened your two eyes. I have opened your mouth with the instrument of Anpu.' (Anpu, or Anubis is in fact a very ancient god who presided over embalming; he appears in the form of a man with the head of a dog or jackal.)

The priest continued, 'I have opened your mouth with the Meskha instrument by which the mouth of the gods was opened. Horus opens the mouth and eyes of the Osiris. Horus opens the mouth of the Osiris even as he opened the mouth of his father. As he opened the mouth of the god Osiris so shall he open the mouth of my father with the iron that comes out from Set, with the Meskha instrument of iron by which he opened the mouth of the gods shall the mouth of the Osiris be opened. And the Osiris shall walk and shall talk, and his body shall be with the Great Company of the Gods who dwell in the Great House of the Aged One (i.e. the Sun god) who dwells in Anu.' Anu is actually the On of the Bible, the Heliopolis of the Greeks. This city lay a few miles to the east of the modern city of Cairo.

The priest then said, 'And he shall take possession of the Urrt Crown therein before Horus, the Lord of mankind. Hail, Osiris! Horus has opened your mouth and your eyes with the instruments Sebur and An, by which the mouths of the gods of the South were opened.... All the gods bring words of power. They recite them for you. They make you live by them. You become the possessor of two-fold strength. You make the passes that give you the fluid of life, and their life fluid is about you. You are protected, and you shall not die. You shall change your form as you wish among the doubles of the gods. You shall rise up as a king of the South. You shall rise up as a king of the North. You are endowed with strength like all the gods and their Doubles. Shu (the Air god, and son of Keb and Nut) has equipped you. He has exalted you to the height of heaven. He has made you be a wonder. He has endowed you with strength.' The belief was that every living thing possessed a 'ka' or 'double', which was the vital power of the heart and could live after the death of the body.

The ceremonies that followed concerned the dressing of the statue of the king and his food. Various kinds of bandlets and a collar were presented, and the gift of each endowed the king in the Other World with special qualities. The words recited by the priest as he offered these and other gifts were highly symbolic, and were believed to possess great power, for they brought the double of the king back to this earth to live in the statue, and each time they were repeated they renewed the life of the king in the Other World.

THE PRESENTATION OF OFFERINGS

The priest began, 'This libation is for you, Osiris, this libation is for you, Unas.' (Unas being the king who is identified with Osiris). Here he offered cold water of the North, before continuing on with the words, 'It comes forth before your son, comes forth before Horus. I have come, I have brought to you the Eye of Horus, that your heart may be refreshed by it. I have brought it and have set it under your sandals, and I present to you that which flowed forth from you. There shall be no stoppage to your heart whilst it is with you, and the offerings you require shall appear at your command.' The priest recited these words four times.

Then the priest declared, 'You have taken possession of the two Eyes of Horus, the White and the Black, and when they are in your face they illumine it.' Here he offered two jugs of wine, one white, one black, before saying, 'Day has made an offering to you in the sky. The South and the North have given offerings to you. Night has made an offering to you. The South and the North have made an offering to you. An offering is brought to you, look upon it; an offering, hear it. There is an offering before you, there is an offering behind you, there is an offering with you.' Here he offered a cake for the journey.

Next the priest said, 'Osiris Unas, the white tes of Horus are presented to you so that they may fill your mouth.' Here he offered five bunches of onions. Then he said, 'Oh Ra, the worship that is paid to you, the worship of every kind, shall be paid also to Unas. Everything that is offered to your body shall be offered to the Double of Unas also, and everything that is offered to his body shall be yours.' Here the priest offered the table of holy offerings. He continueed, 'The oils, which are on the forehead of Horus, set these on the forehead of Unas, and make him smell sweet through you.' Here he offered oil of cedar of the finest quality.

Finally, the priest pleaded, 'Make him into a spirit-soul (khu) through possession of you, and grant him to have the mastery over his body, let his eyes be opened, and let all the spirit-souls see him, and let them hear his name. Behold, Osiris Unas, the Eye of Horus has been brought to you, for it has been seized for you that it may be before you.' Here he offered the finest Thehenu oil.

A HYMN TO NUT, THE SKY GODDESS

Oh Nut, *you have extended yourself*
over your son the Osiris Pepi,
You have snatched him out of the hand of
Set; join him to yourself, Nut.
Come, snatch your son; behold, you come,
form this great one like to yourself.
Oh Nut, cast yourself upon your son the Osiris Pepi.
Oh Nut, cast yourself upon your son the Osiris Pepi.
Form him, Oh Great Fashioner; this
great one is among your children.
Form him, Oh Great Fashioner; this
great one is among your children.
Keb was to Nut. You did become a spirit.
You were a mighty goddess in the
womb of your mother Tefnut
when you were not born.
Form you Pepi with life and well-being; he shall not die.
Strong was your heart,
You leapt in the womb of your mother
in your name of 'Nut'.
Oh perfect daughter, mighty one in

your mother, who is crowned
like a king of the North,
Make this Pepi a spirit-soul in you, let him not die.
Oh Great Lady, who did come into
being in the sky, who is mighty.
Who does make happy, and does fill every
place (or being), with your beauty,
The whole earth is under you, you
have taken possession of it.
You have encompassed the earth,
everything is in your two hands,
Grant that this Pepi may be in you like an imperishable star.
You have associated with Keb in your
name of 'Pet' (i.e. Sky).
You have united the earth in every place.
Oh mistress over the earth, you are above your father Shu,
you have the mastery over him.
He has loved you so much that he seated
himself under you in everything.
You have taken possession of every god for yourself.
You have made them shine like lamps,
Assuredly they shall not cease from you like the stars.
Let not this Pepi depart from you in your name of 'Hert'.

A HYMN TO RA, THE SUN GOD

Hail to you, Tem! Hail to you,
Kheprer, who created himself.
You are the High, in this your name of 'Height'.

You came into being in this your name of 'Kheprer'.
Hail to you, Eye of Horus, which he
furnishes with his hands completely.
He permits you not to be obedient to those of the West;
He permits you not to be obedient to those of the East;
He permits you not to be obedient to those of the South;
He permits you not to be obedient to those of the North;
He permits you not to be obedient to
those who are in the earth;
For you are obedient to Horus.
He it is who has furnished you, he it is who has built you,
He it is who has made you to be dwelt in.
You do for him whatever he asks of you, in every place
wherever he goes.
You lift up to him the water-fowl that are in you.
You lift up to him the water-fowl that
are about to be in you.
You lift up to him every tree that is in you.
You lift up to him every tree that is about to be in you.
You lift up to him the cakes and ale that are in you.
You lift up to him the cakes and ale
that are about to be in you.
You lift up to him the gifts that are in you.
You lift up to him the gifts that are about to be in you.
You lift up to him everything that is in you.
You lift up to him everything that is about to be in you.
You take them to him in every place
where it pleases him to be.
The doors upon you stand fast shut like the god Anmutef,
They open not to those who are in the West;

They open not to those who are in the East;
They open not to those who are in the North;
They open not to those who are in the South;
They open not to those who are in the middle of the earth;
But they open to Horus.
He it was who made them, he it was
who made them stand firm,
He it was who delivered them from every evil
attack which the god Set made upon them.
He it was who made you to be a settled
country in this your name of 'Kerkut'.
He it was who passed bowing after
you in your name of 'Nut'.
He it was who delivered you from every evil
attack which Set made upon you.

THE POWER OF THE KING IN HEAVEN

The sky has withdrawn the life of the star Septet (Sothis, the Dog star); behold Unas a living being, the son of Septet. The Eighteen Gods have purified him in Meskha (the Great Bear), he is an imperishable star. The house of Unas perishes not in the sky, the throne of Unas perishes not on the earth. Men make supplication there, the gods fly towards it. Septet has made Unas fly to heaven to be with his brethren the gods. Nut, the Great Lady, has unfolded her arms to Unas. She has made them into two divine souls at the head of the Souls of Anu, under the head of Ra. The throne of Unas is by you, Ra, he yields it to no one else.

Unas comes forth into heaven by you, Ra. The face of Unas is like the faces of the Hawks. The wings of Unas are like those of geese. The nails of Unas are like the claws of the god Tuf. There is no evil word concerning Unas on earth among men. There is no hostile speech about him with the gods. Unas has destroyed his word, he has ascended to heaven. Upuatu has made Unas fly up to heaven among his brethren the gods. Unas has drawn together his arms like the goose, he strikes his wings like a falcon, flying, flying. Oh men! Unas flies up into heaven.

'Oh gods of the West! Oh gods of the East! Oh gods of the South! Oh gods of the North! You four groups who embrace the holy lands, devote yourselves to Osiris when he appears in heaven. He shall sail into the Sky, with his son Horus by his fingers. He shall announce him, he shall make him rise up like the Great God in the Sky. They shall cry out concerning Unas: Behold Horus, the son of Osiris! Behold Unas, the firstborn son of Hathor! Behold the seed of Keb! Osiris has commanded that Unas shall rise as a second Horus, and these Four Spirit-souls in Anu have written an edict to the two great gods in the Sky. Ra set up the Ladder (by which souls ascended to heaven) in front of Osiris, Horus set up the Ladder in front of his father Osiris when he went to his spirit, one on this side and one on the other side; Unas is between them. Unas stands up – Horus! Unas sits down – Set! Ra grasps his hand, spirit to heaven, body to earth.'

'The skies lower, the Star gods tremble, the Archers quake, the bones of the Akeru gods tremble, and those who are with them are struck dumb when they see Unas rising up as a soul, in the form of the god who lives upon his fathers, and who turns his mothers into his food. Unas is the lord of wisdom, and his mother does not know his name. The adoration of Unas is in heaven, he has become mighty in the horizon like Temu, the father that gave him birth, and after Temu had given him birth Unas became stronger than his father. The Doubles (i.e. vital strength) of Unas are behind him, the soles of his feet are beneath his feet, his gods are over him, his serpents are seated upon his brow, the serpent guides of Unas are in front of him, and the spirit of the flame looks upon his soul. The powers of Unas protect him. Unas is a bull in heaven. He directs his steps where he wishes. He lives upon the form which each god takes upon himself, and he eats the flesh of those who come to fill their bellies with the magical charms in the Lake of Fire.

'Unas is equipped with power against these spirit souls, and he rises in the form of the mighty one, the lord of those who dwell in power. Unas has taken his seat with his back turned towards Keb (the Earth god). Unas has weighed his words (i.e. entered into judgement) with the hidden god who has no name, on the day of hacking into pieces the firstborn. Unas is the lord of offerings, the untier of the knot, and he himself makes the offerings of meat and drink abundant. Unas devours men, and lives upon the gods, he is the lord of envoys whom he sends forth on his missions. 'He who cuts off hairy scalps', who dwells in the fields, ties the gods with ropes. Tcheser-tep shepherds them for Unas and drives them to him; and the Cord Master has bound them for slaughter. Khensu, the slayer of the wicked, cuts their throats, and draws out their intestines, for it is he whom Unas sends to slaughter them, and Shesmu (i.e. the executioner of Osiris) cuts them in pieces, and boils their members in his blazing caldrons of the night. Unas eats their magical powers, and he swallows their spirit-souls.

'The great ones among them serve for his meal in the morning, the lesser serve for his meal in the evening, and the least among them serve for his meal in the night. The old gods and the old goddesses become fuel for his furnace. The mighty ones in heaven light the fire under the caldrons which are filled with the thighs of the firstborn; and he who makes those who live in heaven to go about for Unas lights the fire under the caldrons with the thighs of their women; he goes about the Two Heavens in their entirety, and he goes round about the two banks of the Celestial Nile. Unas is the Great Power, the Power of Powers, and Unas is the Chief of the gods in visible forms.

'Whatever he finds on his path he eats immediately, and the magical might of Unas is before that of all the spirit-bodies who dwell in the horizon. Unas is the firstborn of the firstborn gods. Unas is surrounded by yousands, and oblations are made to him by hundreds; he is made manifest as the Great Power by Saah (Orion), the father of the gods. Unas repeats his rising in heaven, and he is crowned lord of the horizon. He has reckoned up the bandlets and the arm-rings of his captives, he has taken possession of the hearts of the gods.

'Unas has eaten the Red Crown, and he has swallowed the White Crown; the food of Unas is the intestines, and his meat is hearts and their words of power. Behold, Unas eats of that which the Red Crown sends forth, he increases, and the words of power of the gods are in his belly; his attributes are not removed from him. Unas has eaten the whole of the knowledge of every god, and the period of his life is eternity, and the duration of his existence is everlasting. He is in the form of one who does what he wishes, and who does not do what he hates, and he abides on the horizon forever and ever and ever. The Soul of the gods is in Unas, their spirit-souls are with Unas, and the offerings made to him are more than those that are made to the gods. The fire of Unas is in their bones, for their soul is in Unas, and their shades are with those who belong to them. The seat of the heart of Unas is among those who live upon this earth forever and ever and ever.'

THE MAJESTY OF KING PEPI

'Pepi was brought forth by the god Nu, when there was no heaven, when there was no earth, when nothing had been established, when there was no fighting, and when the fear of the Eye of Horus did not exist.

'This Pepi is one of the Great Offspring who were brought forth in Anu (Heliopolis), who have never been conquered by a king or ruled by chiefs, who are irresistible, whose words cannot be contradicted. Therefore this Pepi is irresistible; he can neither be conquered by a king nor ruled by chiefs. The enemies of Pepi cannot triumph. Pepi lacks nothing. No debt is reckoned against Pepi. If Pepi falles into the water Osiris will lift him out, and the Two Companies of the Gods will bear him up on their shoulders, and Ra, wherever he may be, will give him his hand. If Pepi falls on the earth the Earth god (Keb) will lift him up, and the Two Companies of the Gods will bear him up on their shoulders, and Ra, wherever he may be, will give him his hand…. Pepi appears in heaven among the imperishable stars. His sister the star Sothis (the Dog star), his guide the Morning Star (Venus) lead him by the hand to the Field of Offerings. He takes his seat on the crystal throne, which has faces of fierce lions and feet in the form of the hoofs of the Bull Sma-ur. He stands up in his place between the Two Great Gods, and his sceptre and staff are in his hands. He lifts up his hand to the Henmemet spirits, and the gods come to him bowing. The Two Great Gods look on in their places, and they find Pepi acting as judge of the gods. The word of every spirit-soul is in him, and they make offerings to him among the Two Companies of the Gods.'

SPELLS FROM THE
BOOK OF THE DEAD

The object of the *Book of the Dead* was to provide the dead man with all the spells, prayers and amulets that were necessary to enable him to overcome all the dangers and difficulties of the Tuat, and to reach Sekhet Aaru and Sekhet Hetep (the Elysian Fields). Then he could take his place among the subjects of Osiris in the Land of Everlasting Life. The prayers usually consist of a string of petitions for sepulchral offerings to be offered in the tombs of the petitioners, and the fundamental idea underlying them is that by their transmutation, which was effected by the words of the priests, the spirits of the offerings became available as the food of the dead. Many prayers contain requests for the things that tend to the comfort and general wellbeing of the dead, but here and there we find a prayer for forgiveness of sins committed in the body. As time went on the beliefs of the Egyptians changed considerably about many important matters, but they never attempted to alter the Chapters of the *Book of the Dead* in order to bring them 'up-to-date'. Here we present a few extracts that will give an idea of the contents of some of the most important passages.

HYMN TO OSIRIS FROM THE
PAPYRUS OF ANI

'**Glory be to Osiris Un-Nefer**, the great god who dwells in Abydos, king of eternity, lord of everlastingness, whose existence endures for millions of years. Eldest son of the womb of Nut, begotten by Keb, the Erpat, lord of the crowns of the South and North, lord of the lofty white crown, prince of gods and men: he has received the sceptre, and the whip, and the rank of his divine fathers.

'Let your heart in Semt-Ament be content, for your son Horus is established on your throne. You are crowned lord of Tatu and ruler in Abydos. Through you the world flourishes in triumph before the power of Nebertcher. He leads on that which is and that which is not yet, in his name of 'Taherstanef'. He tows along the earth by Ma'at in his name of 'Seker'; he is exceedingly mighty and most terrible in his name of 'Osiris'; he endures forever and ever in his name of 'Un-Nefer'. Homage to you, Oh King of kings, Lord of lords, Prince of princes, who from the womb of Nut have ruled the world and Akert. Your body is [like] bright and shining metal, your head is of azure blue, and the brilliance of the turquoise encircles you. Oh you god An of millions of years, whose body pervades all things, whose face is beautiful in Ta-Tchesert, grant you to the Ka of the Osiris the scribe Ani splendour in heaven, power upon earth, and triumph in the Other World. Grant that I may sail down to Tatu in the form of a living soul, and sail up to Abydos in the form of the Benu bird; that I may go in and come out without being stopped at the pylons of the Lords of the Other World. May there be given to me bread-cakes in the house of coolness, and offerings of food in Anu (Heliopolis), and a homestead forever in Sekhet Aru, with wheat and barley therefor.'

HYMN TO OSIRIS FROM THE
PAPYRUS OF HUNEFER

'**The gods come to you**, bowing low before you, and they hold you in fear.

'They withdraw and depart when they see you endowed with the terror of Ra, and the victory of Your Majesty is over their hearts. Life is with you, and offerings of meat and drink follow you, and that which is your due is offered before your face. I have come to you holding in my hands truth, and my heart has in it no cunning (or deceit). I offer to you that which is your due, and I know that whereon you live. I have not committed any kind of sin in the land; I have defrauded no man of what is his. I am Thoth, the perfect scribe, whose hands are pure. I am the lord of purity, the destroyer of evil, the scribe of truth; what I abominate is sin.'

ADDRESS AND LITANY FROM THE
PAPYRUS OF ANI

From Chapter 15 of the Papyrus of Ani: 'Praise be to you, Oh Osiris, lord of eternity, Un-Nefer, Heru-Khuti, whose forms are manifold, whose attributes are majesty, [you who are] Ptah-Seker-Tem in Heliopolis, lord of the Sheta shrine, creator of Het-ka-Ptah (Memphis) and of the gods who dwell therein, you Guide of the Other World, whom the gods praise when you set in the sky.

'Isis embraces you contentedly, and she drives away the fiends from the mouth of your paths. You turn your face towards Amentet, and you make the earth shine like refined copper. The dead rise up to look upon you, they breathe the air, and they behold your face when [your] disk rises on the horizon. Their hearts are at peace, inasmuch as they behold you, Oh you who are Eternity and Everlastingness.'

Litany

'1. Homage to you, Oh [Lord of] the Dekans (Star-gods) in Heliopolis and of the heavenly beings in Kheraha, you god Unti, who are the most glorious of the gods hidden in Heliopolis.

Response repeated after each petition: 'Grant me a path where I may pass in peace, for I am just and true; I have not spoken lies wittingly, nor have I done anything with deceit.

'2. Homage to you, Oh An in Antes, Heru-Khuti, with long strides you stride over heaven, Oh Heru-Khuti.

'3. Homage to you, Oh Everlasting Soul, who dwell in Tatu (Busiris), Un-Nefer, son of Nut, who are the Lord of Akert.

'4. Homage to you in your rule over Tatu. The Urrt Crown is fixed upon your head. You are One, you create your protection, you dwell in peace in Tatu.

'5. Homage to you, Oh Lord of the Acacia. The Seker Boat is on its sledge; you turn back the Fiend, the worker of evil; you make the Eye of the Sun god rest upon its throne.

'6. Homage to you, mighty one in your hour, Prince great and mighty, dweller in Anrutef, lord of eternity, creator of everlastingness. You are the lord of Hensu.

'7. Homage to you, Oh you who rest upon Truth. You are the Lord of Abydos; your body is joined to Ta-Tchesert. You are he to whom fraud and deceit are abominable.

'8. Homage to you, Oh dweller in your boat. You lead the Nile from his source, the light shines upon your body; you are the dweller in Nekhen.

'9. Homage to you, Oh Creator of the gods, King of the South, King of the North, Osiris, Conqueror, Governor of the world in your gracious seasons! You are the Lord of the heaven of Egypt (Atebui).'

A FUNERARY HYMN TO RA

'**H**omage to you, Oh you who are in the form of Khepera, Khepera the creator of the gods. You rise, you shine, you illuminate your mother [the sky]. You are crowned King of the Gods. Mother Nut welcomes you with bowings. The Land of Sunset (Manu) receives you with satisfaction, and the goddess Ma'at embraces you at morn and at eve. Hail, you gods of the Temple of the Soul (i.e. heaven), who weigh heaven and earth in a balance, who provide celestial food! And hail, Tatunen (an ancient Earth-god), One, Creator of man, Maker of the gods of the south and of the north, of the west and of the east! Come and acclaim Ra, the Lord of heaven, the Prince – life, health, strength be to him! – the Creator of the gods, and adorehim in his beautiful form as he rises in his Morning Boat (Antchet).

'Those who dwell in the heights and those who dwell in the depths worship you. Thoth and the goddess Ma'at have laid down your course for you daily forever. Your Enemy the Serpent has been cast into the fire, the fiend has fallen down into it headlong. His arms have been bound in chains, and Ra has hacked off his legs; the Mesu Betshet (the associates of Set, the god of Evil) shall never more rise up. The Temple of the Aged God [in Anu] keeps festival, and the sound of those who rejoice is in the Great House. The gods shout for joy when they see Ra rising, and when his beams are filling the world with light. The Majesty of the Holy God goes forth and advances even to the Land of Sunset (Manu). He makes bright the earth at his birth daily, he journeys to the place where he was yesterday. Oh be you at peace with me, and let me behold your beauties! Let me appear on the earth. Let me smite [the Eater of] the Ass (a form of the Sun god). Let me crush the Serpent Seba. Let me destroy Aapep when he is most strong. Let me see the Abtu Fish in its season and the Ant Fish in its lake. Let me see Horus steering your boat, with Thoth and Ma'at standing one on each side of him. Let me have hold of the bows of [your] Evening Boat and the stern of your Morning Boat. Grant you to the Ka of me, the Osiris the scribe Ani, to behold the disk of the Sun, and to see the Moon-god regularly and daily. Let my soul come forth and walk hither and thither and whithersoever it pleases. Let my name be read from the list of those who are to receive offerings, and may offerings be set before me, even as they are set before the Followers of Horus. Let there be prepared for me a seat in the Boat of Ra on the day when the god goes forth. Let me be received into the presence of Osiris, in the Land where Truth is spoken.'

A PRAYER FOR FORGIVENESS OF SINS

'Hail, you four Ape-gods who sit in the bows of the Boat of Ra, who convey truth to Nebertchet, who sit in judgment on my weakness and on my strength, who make the gods rest contented by means of the flame of your mouths, who offer holy offerings to the gods, and sepulchral meals to the spirit-souls, who live upon truth, who feed upon truth of heart, who are without deceit and fraud, and to whom wickedness is an abomination, do away with my evil deeds, and put away my sin, which deserved stripes upon earth, and destroy every evil thing whatsoever that clings to me, and let there be no bar whatsoever on my part towards you.

'Grant that I may make my way through the Amhet chamber, let me enter into Rastau, and let me pass through the secret places of Amentet. Grant that cakes, and ale, and sweetmeats may be given to me as they are given to the spirit-souls, and grant that I may enter in and come forth from Rastau.' The four Ape-gods reply: 'Come, for we have done away with your wickedness, and we have put away your sin, which deserved stripes, which you did commit upon earth, and we have destroyed all the evil that clung to you. Enter, therefore, into Rastau, and pass in through the secret gates of Amentet, and cakes, and ale, and sweetmeats shall be given to you, and you shall go in and come out at your desire, even as do those whose spirit-souls are praised [by the god], and [your name] shall be proclaimed each day in the horizon.'

A PRAYER FOR THE WEIGHING OF THE HEART

This prayer is put into the mouth of the deceased when he is standing in the Hall of Judgment watching the weighing of his heart in the Great Scales by Anubis and Thoth, in the presence of the Great Company of the gods and Osiris. He says:

'My heart, my mother. My heart, my mother. My heart whereby I came into being. Let none stand up to oppose me at my judgment. May there be no opposition to me in the presence of the Tchatchau (the chief officers of Osiris, the divine Taskmasters). May you not be separated from me in the presence of the Keeper of the Balance. You are my Ka (i.e. Double, or vital power), that dwells in my body; the god Khnemu who knitted together and strengthened my limbs. May you come forth into the place of happiness to which we go. May the Shenit officers who decide the destinies of the lives of men not cause my name to stink [before Osiris]. Let it (i.e. the weighing) be satisfactory to us, and let there be joy of heart to us at the weighing of words (i.e. the Great Judgment). Let not that which is false be uttered against me before the Great God, the Lord of Amentet (i.e. Osiris). Verily you shall be great when you rise up [having been declared] a speaker of the truth.'

Rubric

In many papyri this prayer is followed by a Rubric, which orders that it is to be said over a green stone scarab set in a band of *tchamu* metal (i.e. silver-gold), which is to be hung by a ring from the neck of the deceased. Some Rubrics order it to be placed in the breast of a mummy, where it is to take the place of the heart, and say that it will 'open the mouth' of the deceased. A tradition which is as old as the twelfth dynasty says that the Chapter was discovered in the town of Khemenu (Hermopolis Magna) by Herutataf, the son of Khufu, in the reign of Menkaura, a king of the fourth dynasty. It was cut in hieroglyphs, inlaid with lapis-lazuli on a block of alabaster, which was set under the feet of Thoth, and was therefore believed to be a most powerful prayer.

A DECLARATION BEFORE JUDGMENT

Another remarkable composition in the *Book of the Dead* is the first part of Chapter CXXV, which well illustrates the lofty moral conceptions of the Egyptians of the eighteenth dynasty. The deceased is supposed to be standing in the 'Usekht Ma'ati', or Hall of the Two Ma'ati goddesses, one for Upper Egypt and one for Lower Egypt, wherein Osiris and his Forty-two Judges judge the souls of the dead. Before judgment is given the deceased is allowed to make a declaration:

'Homage to you, Oh Great God, you Lord of Ma'ati. I have come to you, Oh my Lord, and I have brought myself here so that I may behold your beauties. I know you. I know your name. I know the names of the Forty-two gods who live with you in this Hall of Truth, who keep ward over sinners, and who feed upon their blood on the day when the lives of men are taken into account in the presence of Un-Nefer (i.e. the Good Being or Osiris). ...

Verily, I have come to you, I have brought truth to you. I have destroyed wickedness for you. I have not done evil to men. I have not oppressed (or wronged) my family. I have not done wrong instead of right. I have not been a friend of worthless men. I have not wrought evil. I have not tried to make myself over-righteous. I have not put forward my name for exalted positions. I have not entreated servants evily. I have not defrauded the man who was in trouble. I have not done what is hateful (or taboo) to the gods. I have not caused a servant to be ill-treated by his master. I have not caused pain [to any man]. I have not permitted any man to go hungry. I have made none weep. I have not committed murder. I have not ordered any man to commit murder for me. I have inflicted pain on no man. I have not robbed the temples of their offerings. I have not stolen the cakes of the gods. I have not carried off the cakes offered to the spirits. I have not committed fornication. I have not committed acts of impurity in the holy places of the god of my town. I have not diminished the bushel. I have not added to or filched away land. I have not encroached upon the fields [of my neighbours]. I have not added to the weights of the scales. I have not falsified the pointer of the scales. I have not taken milk from the mouths of children. I have not driven away the cattle that were upon their pastures. I have not snared the feathered fowl in the preserves of the gods. I have not caught fish [with bait made of] fish of their kind. I have not stopped water at the time [when it should flow]. I have not breached a canal of running water. I have not extinguished a fire when it should burn. I have not violated the times [of offering] chosen meat-offerings. I have not driven off the cattle from the property of the gods. I have not repulsed the god in his manifestations. I am pure. I am pure. I am pure. I am pure.'

In the second part of the Chapter the deceased repeats many of the above declarations of his innocence, but with each declaration the name of one of the Forty-two Judges (probably each one representing a nome – i.e. a county – of Egypt) is coupled. Thus we have:

1. 'Hail, you of the long strides, who comes forth from Heliopolis, I have not committed sin.

2. 'Hail, you who are embraced by flame, who comes forth from Kheraha, I have not robbed with violence.

3. 'Hail, Nose, who comes forth from Hermopolis, I have not done violence [to any man].

4. 'Hail, Eater of shadows, who comes forth from the Qerti, I have not thieved.

5. 'Hail, Stinking Face, who comes forth from Rastau, I have not slain man or woman.

9. 'Hail, Crusher of bones, who comes forth from Hensu, I have not lied.'

Having declared his innocence of the forty-two sins or offences, 'the heart which is righteous and sinless' says:

'Homage to you, Oh gods who dwell in your Hall of Ma'ati! I know you and I know your names. Let me not fall under your knives, and bring not before the god whom you follow my wickedness, and let not evil come upon me through you. Declare me innocent in the presence of Nebertcher (Almighty God), because I have done that which is right in Tamera (Egypt), neither blaspheming God, nor imputing evil (?) to the king in his day.

'Homage to you, Oh gods, who live in your Hall of Ma'ati, who have no taint of sin in you, who live upon truth, who feed upon truth before Horus, the dweller in his disk. Deliver me from Baba, who lives upon the entrails of the mighty ones, on the day of the Great Judgment. Let me come to you, for I have not committed offences [against you]; I have not done evil, I have not borne false witness; therefore let nothing [evil] be done to me. I live upon truth. I feed upon truth. I have performed the commandments of men, and the things which make the gods contented. I have made the god be at peace [with me by doing] that which is his will. I have given bread to the hungry man, and water to the thirsty man, and apparel to the naked man, and a ferry boat to him that had none. I have made offerings to the gods, and given funerary meals to the spirits. Therefore be my deliverers, be my protectors; make no accusations against me in the presence [of the Great God]. I am clean of mouth and clean of hands; therefore let be said to me by those who shall see me: "Come in peace, come in peace" (i.e. Welcome! Welcome!).... I have testified before Herfhaf (the celestial ferryman), and he has approved me. I have seen the things over which the Persea tree spreads [its branches] in Rastau. I offer up my prayers to the gods, and I know their persons. I have come and have advanced to declare the truth and to set up the Balance on its stand in Aukert.'

Then addressing the god Osiris the deceased says: 'Hail, you who are exalted upon your standard, you lord of the Atef crown, whose name is "Lord of the Winds", deliver me from your envoys who inflict evils, who do harm, whose faces are uncovered, for I have done the right for the Lord of Truth. I have purified myself and my fore parts with holy water, and my hinder parts with the things that make clean, and my inward parts have been [immersed] in the Lake of Truth. There is not one member of mine wherein truth is lacking.

I purified myself in the Pool of the South. I rested in the northern town in the Field of the Grasshoppers, wherein the sailors of Ra bathe at the second hour of the night and at the third hour of the day.'

One would think that the moral worth of the deceased was such that he might then pass without delay into the most holy part of the Hall of Truth where Osiris was enthroned. But this is not the case, for before he went further he was obliged to repeat the magical names of various parts of the Hall of Truth; thus we find that the priest thrust his magic into the most sacred of texts. At length Thoth, the great Recorder of Egypt, being satisfied as to the good faith and veracity of the deceased, came to him and asked why he had come to the Hall of Truth, and the deceased replied that he had come in order to be 'mentioned' to the god. Thoth then asked him, 'Who is he whose heaven is fire, whose walls are serpents, and the floor of whose house is a stream of water?' The deceased replied, 'Osiris'; and he was then bidden to advance so that he might be introduced to Osiris. As a reward for his righteous life, sacred food, which proceeded from the Eye of Ra, was allotted to him, and, living on the food of the god, he became a counterpart of the god.

SPELLS FOR PRESERVATION AND EVERLASTING LIFE

From first to last the *Book of the Dead* is filled with spells and prayers for the preservation of the mummy and for everlasting life. As instances of these, the following passages are quoted from Chapters 154 and 175:

'Homage to you, Oh my divine father Osiris, you live with your members. You did not decay. You did not turn into worms. You did not waste away. You did not suffer corruption. You did not putrefy. I am the god Khepera, and my members shall have an everlasting existence. I shall not decay. I shall not rot. I shall not putrefy. I shall not turn into worms. I shall not see corruption before the eye of the god Shu. I shall have my being, I shall have my being. I shall live, I shall live. I shall flourish, I shall flourish. I shall wake up in peace. I shall not putrefy. My inward parts shall not perish. I shall not suffer injury. My eye shall not decay. The form of my visage shall not disappear. My ear shall not become deaf. My head shall not be separated from my neck. My tongue shall not be carried away. My hair shall not be cut off. My eyebrows shall not be shaved off. No baleful injury shall come upon me. My body shall be established, and it shall neither crumble away nor be destroyed on this earth.'

The passage that refers to everlasting life occurs in Chapter 175, wherein the scribe Ani is made to converse with Thoth and Temu in the Tuat, or Other World. Ani, who is supposed to have recently arrived there, says: 'What manner of country is this to which I have come? There is no water in it. There is no air. It is depth unfathomable, it is black as the blackest night, and men wander helplessly therein. In it a man may not live in quietness of heart; nor may the affections be gratified therein.' After a short address to Osiris, the deceased asks the god, 'How long shall I live?' And the god says, 'It is decreed that you shall live for millions of millions of years, a life of millions of years.'

An example of a spell that was used in connection with an amulet comes from Chapter 156. The amulet was the *tet*, which represented a portion of the body of Isis. The spell reads: 'The blood of Isis, the power of Isis, the words of power of Isis shall be strong to protect this mighty one (i.e. the mummy), and to guard him from him that would do to him anything which he abominates (or, is taboo to him).'

The object of the spell is explained in the Rubric, which reads: '[This spell] shall be said over a *tet* made of carnelian, which has been steeped in water of *ankham* flowers, and set in a frame of sycamore wood, and placed on the neck of the deceased on the day of the funeral. If these things are done for him the powers of Isis shall protect his body, and Horus, the son of Isis, shall rejoice in him when he sees him. And there shall be no places hidden from him as he journeys. And one hand of his shall be towards heaven and the other towards earth, regularly and continually. You shall not let any person who is with you see it [a few words broken away].'

SPELLS TO MAKE REPTILES POWERLESS

Away with you! Retreat! Get back, Oh you accursed Crocodile Sui. You shall not come nigh me, for I have life through the words of power that are in me. If I utter your name to the Great God he will make you come before the two divine messengers Betti and Herkemmaat. Heaven rules its seasons, and the spell has power over what it masters, and my mouth rules the spell that is inside it. My tes which bite are like flint knives, and my tes which grind are like those of the Wolf-god. Oh you who sits spellbound with your eyes fixed through my spell, you shall not carry off my spell, you Crocodile that lives on spells.'

'Get you back, you Crocodile of the West, that livet on the never-resting stars. That which is your taboo is in me. I have eaten the brow (or, skull) of Osiris. I am set.

'Get you back, you Crocodile of the West. The serpent Nau is inside me. I will set it on you, your flame shall not approach me.

'Get you back, you Crocodile of the East, that feeds upon the eaters of filth. That which is your taboo is in me. I advance. I am Osiris.

'Get you back, you Crocodile of the East. The serpent Nau is inside me. I will set it on you; your flame shall not approach me.

'Get you back, you Crocodile of the South, that feeds upon waste, garbage, and filth. That which is your taboo is in me.... I am Sept (an early local form of the Sun god).

'Get you back, you Crocodile of the South. I will fetter you. My charm is among the reeds (?). I will not yield to you.

'Get you back, you Crocodile of the North, that feeds upon what is left by the hours. That which is your taboo is in me. The emissions shall [not] fall upon my head. I am Tem (a form of Pautti, the oldest Egyptian god).

'Get you back, you Crocodile of the North, for the Scorpion-goddess (Serqet) is inside me, unborn (?). I am Uatch-Merti (?) (a green-eyed serpent-god, or goddess).

'Created things are in the hollow of my hand, and the things that are not yet made are inside me. I am clothed in and supplied with your spells, Oh Ra, which are above me and beneath me.... I am Ra, the self-protected, no evil thing whatsoever shall overthrow me.'

THE BOOK OF BREATHINGS

The following sections, translated from a papyrus in the British Museum, will give an idea of the character of this book that was one of the oldest of the later (Graeco-Roman) substitutes for the *Book of the Dead*:

'Hail, Osiris (i.e. the deceased) Kersher, son of Tashenatit! You are pure, your heart is pure. Your fore parts are pure, your hind parts are cleansed; your interior is cleansed with incense and natron, and no member of yours has any defect in it whatsoever. Kersher is washed in the waters of the Field of Offerings, that lies to the north of the Field of the Grasshoppers. The goddesses Uatchet and Nekhebet purify you at the eighth hour of the night and at the eighth hour of the day. Come then, enter the Hall of Truth, for you are free from all offence and from every defect, and 'Stone of Truth' is your name. You enter the Tuat (Other World) as one exceedingly pure. You are purified by the Goddesses of Truth in the Great Hall. Holy water has been poured over you in the Hall of Keb (i.e. the earth), and your body has been made pure in the Hall of Shu (heaven). You look upon Ra when he sets in the form of Tem at eventide. Amen is nigh to you and gives you air, and Ptah likewise, who fashioned your members for you; you enter the horizon with Ra. Your soul is received in the Neshem Boat of Osiris, your soul is made divine in the House of Keb, and you are made to be triumphant forever and ever.'

'Hail, Osiris Kersher! Your name flourishes, your earthly body is established, your spirit body germinates, and you are not repulsed either in heaven or on earth. Your face shines before Ra, your soul lives before Amen, and your earthly body is renewed before Osiris. You breath the breath of life forever and ever. Your soul makes offerings to you in the course of each day.... Your flesh is collected on your bones, and your form is even as it was on earth. You take drink into your body, you eat with your mouth, and you receive your rations in company with the souls of the gods. Anubis protects you; he is your protector, and you are not turned away from the Gates of the Tuat. Thoth, the most mighty god, the Lord of Khemenu (Hermopolis), comes to you, and he writes the 'Book of Breathings' with his own fingers. Then does your soul breathe forever and ever, and your form is renewed with life on earth; you are made divine with the souls of the gods, your heart is the heart of Ra, and your limbs are the limbs of the great god. Amen is nigh to you to make you live again. Upuat opens a prosperous road for you. You see with your eyes, you hear with your ears, you speak with your mouth, you walk with your legs. Your soul has been made divine in the Tuat, so that it may change itself into any form it pleases. You can snuff at will the odours of the holy Acacia of Anu (An, or Heliopolis). You wake each day and see the light of Ra; you appear upon the earth each day, and the 'Book of Breathings' of Thoth is your protection, for through it you draw your breath each day, and through it do your eyes behold the beams of the Sun god Aten. The Goddess of Truth vindicates you before Osiris, and her writings are upon your tongue. Ra vivifies your soul, the Soul of Shu is in your nostrils. You are even as Osiris, and 'Osiris Khenti Amenti' is your name. Your body lives in Tatu (Busiris), and your soul lives in heaven.... Your odour is that of the holy gods in Amentet, and your name is magnified like the names of the Spirits of heaven. Your soul lives through the 'Book of Breathings', and it is rejoined to your body by the 'Book of Breathings'.

These fine extracts are followed in the British Museum papyrus by the praises of Kersher by the gods, a prayer of Kersher himself for offerings, and an extract from the so-called Negative Confession, which has been already described. The work is closed by an address to the gods, in which it is said that Kersher is sinless, that he feeds and lives upon Truth, that his deeds have satisfied the hearts of the gods, and that he has fed the hungry and given water to the thirsty and clothes to the naked.

THE BOOK OF TRAVERSING ETERNITY

This late *Book of the Dead* **substitute** opens with the following words:

'Thy soul lives in heaven in the presence of Ra. Your Ka has acquired the divine nature of the gods. Your body remains in the deep house (i.e. tomb) in the presence of Osiris. Your spirit-body becomes glorious among the living. Your descendants flourish upon the earth, in the presence of Keb, upon your seat among the living, and your name is established by the utterance of those who have their being through the "Book of Traversing Eternity". You come forth by day, you are joined to the Sun god Aten.' The text goes on to state that the deceased breathes, speaks, eats, drinks, sees, hears, and walks, and that all the organs of his body are in their proper places, and that each is performing its proper functions. He floats in the air, hovers in the shadow, rises in the sky, follows the gods, travels with the stars, dekans, and planets, and moves about by night and by day on earth and in heaven at will.

THE LAMENTATIONS OF ISIS AND NEPHTHYS

The two first sections of this late *Book of the Dead* substitute (which were to be recited by two 'fair women' who personified Isis and Nephthys), as they are found on a papyrus in Berlin, read thus:

Isis says: 'Come to your house, come to your house, Oh An, come to your house. Your enemy [Set] has perished. Oh beautiful youth, come to your house. Look you upon me. I am the sister who loves you, go not far from me. Oh Beautiful Boy, come to your house, straightway, straightway. I cannot see you, and my heart weeps for you; my eyes follow you about. I am following you about so that I may see you. Lo, I wait to see you, I wait to see you; behold, Prince, I wait to see you. It is good to see you, it is good to see you; Oh An, it is good to see you. Come to your beloved one, come to your beloved one, Oh Un-Nefer, whose word is truth. Come to your wife, Oh you whose heart is still. Come to the lady of your house; I am your sister from your mother's [womb]. Go not you far from me. The faces of gods and men are turned towards you, they all weep for you together. As soon as I saw you I cried out to you, weeping with a loud voice which pierced the heavens, and you did not hear my voice. I am your sister who loved you on earth; none other loved you more than [your] sister, your sister.'

Nephthys says: 'Oh Beautiful Prince, come to your house. Let your heart rejoice and be glad, for your enemies have ceased to be. Your two Sisters are nigh to you; they guard your bier, they address you with words [full of] tears as you lie prone on your bier. Look at the young women; speak to us, Oh our Sovereign Lord. Destroy all the misery that is in our hearts; the chiefs among gods and men look upon you. Turn your face towards us, Oh our Sovereign Lord. At the sight of your face life comes to our faces; turn not your face from us. The joy of our heart is in the sight of you. Oh Beautiful Sovereign, our hearts would see you. I am your sister Nephthys who loves you. The fiend Seba has fallen, he has not being. I am with you, and I act as the protectress of your members forever and ever.'

THE FESTIVAL SONGS OF ISIS AND NEPHTHYS

The following passage illustrates the contents of this late *Book of the Dead* substitute:

'Come, come, run to me, Oh strong heart! Let me see your divine face, for I do not see you, and make clear the path that we may see you as we see Ra in heaven, when the heavens unite with the earth, and cause darkness to fall upon the earth each day. My heart burns as with fire at your escape from the Fiend, even as my heart burns with fire when you turn your side to me; Oh that you would never remove it from me! Oh you who unites the Two Domains (i.e. Egypt, North and South), and who turn back those who are on the roads, I seek to see you because of my love for you.... You fly like a living being, Oh Everlasting King; you have destroyed the fiend Anrekh. You are the King of the South and of the North, and you go forth from Tatchesert. May there never be a moment in your life when I do not fill your heart, Oh my divine brother, my lord who goes forth from Aqert.... My arms are raised to protect you, Oh you whom I love. I love you, Oh Husband, Brother, lord of love; come you in peace into your house.... Your hair is like turquoise as you come forth from the Fields of Turquoise, your hair is like the finest lapis-lazuli, and you yourself are more blue than your hair. Your skin and body are like southern alabaster, and your bones are of silver. The perfume of your hair is like new myrrh, and your skull is of lapis-lazuli.'

THE BOOK OF MAKING SPLENDID
THE SPIRIT OF OSIRIS

The following extract from this late *Book of the Dead* substitute illustrates its contents:

'Come to your house, come to your house, Oh An. Come to your house, Oh Beautiful Bull, lord of men and women, the beloved one, the lord of women. Oh Beautiful Face, Chief of Akert, Prince, Khenti Amentiu, are not all hearts drunk through the love of you, Oh Un-Nefer, whose word is truth? The hands of men and gods are lifted up and seek you, even as the hands of a babe are stretched out to his mother. Come to them, for their hearts are sad, and make them rejoice. The lands of Horus exult, the domains of Set are overthrown because of their fear of you. Hail, Osiris Khenti Amentiu!

'I am your sister Isis. No god and no goddess have done for you what I have done. I, a woman, made a man child for you, because of my desire to make your name live upon the earth. Your divine essence was in my body, I brought him forth on the ground. He pleaded your case, he healed your suffering, he decreed the destruction of him that caused it. Set fell under his knife, and the Smamiu fiends of Set followed him. The throne of the Earth-god is yours, Oh you who are his beloved son....

'There is health in your members, your wounds are healed, your sufferings are relieved, you shall never groan again in pain. Come to us your sisters, come to us; our hearts live when you come. Men shall cry out to you, and women shall weep glad tears, at your coming to them....

'The Nile appears at the command of your mouth; you make men live on the effluxes that proceed from your members, and you make every field flourish. When you come that which is dead springs into life, and the plants in the marshes put forth blossoms. You are the Lord of millions of years, the sustainer of wild creatures, and the lord of cattle; every created thing has its existence from you. What is in the earth is yours. What is in the heavens is yours.

What is in the waters is yours. You are the Lord of Truth, the hater of sinners, whom you overthrow in their sins. The Goddesses of Truth are with you; they never leave you. No sinful man can approach you in the place where you are. Whatsoever appertains to life and to death belongs to you, and to you belongs everything that concerns man.'

TALES OF ANCIENT EGYPTIAN MAGICIANS

The short stories of the wonderful deeds of ancient Egyptian magicians in this chapter are based on those found in the Westcar Papyrus, which is preserved in the Egyptian Museum of Berlin. This papyrus is believed to have been discovered in 1823 by British adventurer Henry Westcar. After later passing to Westcar's niece, it was claimed to have been given to the eminent German Egyptologist Richard Lepsius in 1839. Although exactly how Lepsius came to be in possession of the papyrus is a matter of debate, and its subsequent whereabouts were unknown until it was discovered in the attic of his home after his death. In 1886 it was purchased from Lepius's son by fellow German Egyptologist Adolf Erman, who subsequently left it to the museum.

The surviving material of the Westcar Papyrus consists of 12 columns of hieratic script written in classical Middle Egyptian. It was probably written some time between the 12th and 18th dynasties (c. 18th–16th centuries BCE). The first attempt at a complete translation was made by Erman in 1890. But as the hieretic signs were still insufficiently understood, the papyrus was first displayed as a curiosity.

Since then the text has been translated many times, resulting in numerous different outcomes.

Each of the stories is told at the royal court by the sons of King Khufu (Cheops) of the fourth dynasty. And as such, these tales have been used by historians as a literary source for piecing together the rich history of this dynastic period.

UBAANER AND THE WAX CROCODILE

The first story describes an event that happened during the reign of Nebka, a king of the third dynasty. It was told by Prince Khafra to King Khufu (Cheops). The tale tells of a magician named Ubaaner (meaning 'splitter of stones'), who was the chief Kher-heb in the temple of Ptah of Memphis, and a very learned man. He was a married man, but unfortunately his wife had fallen in love with a young man who worked in the fields.

One day, the wife sent one of her maids to deliver a box containing a supply of very fine clothes to the young man. Soon after receiving this gift, the young man suggested to the magician's wife that they should meet and talk in a certain lodge in her garden. So she instructed the steward to have the lodge made ready for her to receive her friend. When this was done, she went to the lodge and she sat there with the young man and drank beer with him until the evening, when he went on his way.

The steward, knowing what had happened, made up his mind to report the matter to his master, and as soon as morning came, he went to Ubaaner and informed him that his wife had spent the previous day drinking beer with the young man. Ubaaner then told the steward to bring him his casket made of ebony, silver and gold, which contained materials and instruments used for working magic. When it was brought him, Ubaaner took out some wax and fashioned a figure of a crocodile seven spans long. He then recited certain magical words over the crocodile and said to it, 'When the young man comes to bathe in my lake you shall seize him.' Then giving the wax crocodile to the steward, Ubaaner said to him, 'When the young man goes down to the lake to bathe according to his daily habit, you shall throw the crocodile into the water after him.' Having taken the crocodile from his master, the steward departed.

A little later the wife of Ubaaner told the steward to set the little lodge in the garden in order, because she was going to spend some time there. When the steward had furnished the lodge, she went there and the young man paid her a visit. After leaving the lodge he went and bathed in the lake. So the steward followed him and threw the wax crocodile into the water; it immediately turned into a large crocodile 7 cubits (about 3.5 metres/11 feet) long. It seized the young man and swallowed him up.

As this was unfolding, Ubaaner was visiting the king and he remained with him for seven days, during which time the young man was in the lake with no air to breathe. When the seven days were almost up, King Nebka suggested taking a walk with the magician. Whilst they were walking Ubaaner asked the king if he would like to see a wonderful thing that had happened to a young peasant. The king said he would and the pair immediately set off walking towards the lake. When they arrived Ubaaner uttered a spell over the crocodile and commanded it to come up out of the water bringing the young man with him; and the crocodile did so. When the king saw the beast he exclaimed at its hideousness and seemed to be afraid of it, but the magician stooped down fearlessly and took the crocodile up in his hand. Amazingly the living crocodile had disappeared and only a wax crocodile remained in its place.

Then Ubaaner told King Nebka the story of how this young man had spent days in the lodge of his garden talking and drinking beer with his wife. His Majesty said to the wax crocodile, 'Be gone and take what is yours with you.' The wax crocodile leaped out of the magician's hand into the lake and once more became a large, living crocodile. It swam away with the young man and no one ever knew what became of it afterwards. Then the king commanded his servants to seize Ubaaner's wife. They carried her off to the grounds on the north side of the royal palace, where they burned her and scattered her ashes in the river.

Once King Khufu had heard the story of Ubaaner and the wax crocodile he ordered many offerings to be made in the tomb of his predecessor Nebka and gifts to be presented to the magician.

TCHATCHAMANKH AND THE GOLD ORNAMENT

Prince Baiufra stood up and offered to tell King Khufu a story of a magician called Tchatchamankh, who flourished in the reign of Seneferu, the king's father. The offer having been accepted, Baiufra proceeded to relate the following tale.

One day King Seneferu was in a perplexed and gloomy state of mind. He wandered distractedly about the rooms and courts of his palace looking to find something to amuse himself with, but he failed to do so. Then he thought of the court magician Tchatchamankh and ordered his servants to summon him. When the great Kher-heb and scribe arrived, the king addressed him as 'my brother' and told him that he had been wandering around his palace seeking some amusement, but had failed to find any. The magician promptly suggested to the king that he should have a boat got ready, decorated with pretty things that would give pleasure, and should go for a row on the lake. The motions of the rowers as they rowed the boat would interest him, and the sight of the depths of the waters and the pretty fields and gardens round about the lake would give him great pleasure. 'Let me arrange the matter,' said the magician. 'Give me twenty ebony paddles inlaid with gold and silver, twenty pretty maidens with flowing hair and twenty beautiful garments to dress them in.'

The king gave orders for all these things to be provided, and when the boat was ready and the maidens who were to row had taken their places, he entered the boat and sat in his little pavilion and was rowed about on the lake. The magician's views proved to be correct. The king enjoyed himself and was greatly amused by watching the maidens row. Before long one of the maidens caught the handle of her paddle in her long hair. In trying to free it a gold ornament that she had been wearing in her hair fell into the water and disappeared.

The maiden was distressed over her loss, so she stopped rowing, as did the other maidens. After the king had asked why the rowing had ceased, one of the maidens told him what had happened. Immediately, the king promised the maiden that the precious ornament would be recovered, to which the maiden responded, 'I have no doubt that it will be returned to me.'

Straightaway King Seneferu summoned Tchatchamankh to be brought to his presence. When the magician arrived, the king told him all that had happened. Then the magician began to recite certain spells, the effect of which was to cause the water of the lake first to divide into two parts, and then the water on one side to rise up and place itself on the water on the other side. The boat sank down gently onto the ground of the lake near where the gold ornament was seen lying. The magician fetched it and returned it to its owner. As soon as the ornament was restored to the maiden, the magician recited further spells and the water lowered itself and spread over the ground of the lake. The lake soon regained its normal level.

After returning to the royal palace His Majesty, King Seneferu made a handsome gift to his clever magician. When King Khufu had heard the story he ordered a large supply of funerary offerings to be sent to the tomb of Seneferu, and bread, beer, meat and incense to be sent to the tomb of Tchatchamankh.

THE MAGICIAN TETA

Once Prince Baiufra had finished telling the story of Tchatchamankh and the gold ornament, Prince Herutataf, the son of King Khufu and a very wise man, stood up before his father and said to him, 'Up until now you have only heard tales about the wisdom of magicians who are dead and gone. It is quite impossible to know whether they are true or not. Now, I want Your Majesty to see a certain sage who is actually alive and whom you do not know.'

His Majesty Khufu said, 'Who is it, Herutataf?' The Prince replied, 'He is a certain peasant named Teta who lives in Tet-Seneferu. He is 110 years old, and up to this very day he eats 500 bread-cakes and a leg of beef, and drinks 100 pots of beer. He knows how to reunite to its body a head which has been cut off, he knows how to make a lion follow him whilst the rope with which he is tied drags behind him on the ground, and he knows the number of the Apet chambers of the shrine of Thoth.' Now for a long time His Majesty had been searching for the number of the Apet chambers of Thoth, because he had wished to make something like it for his own 'horizon' (thought to be the books and instruments which the ancient Egyptian magicians used in working magic). So King Khufu said to Herutataf, 'My son, you yourself shall go and bring the sage to me.'

A boat was made ready for Prince Herutataf, who set out on his journey to Tet-Seneferu, the home of the sage. When the prince came to the spot on the river bank that was nearest to the sage's village, he had the boat tied up and continued his journey overland seated in a sort of sedan chair made of ebony, which was carried on bearing poles made of wood inlaid with gold. When Herutataf arrived at the village, the chair was set down on the ground and he stood up ready to greet the old man, whom he found lying on a bed, with the door of his house lying on the ground. One servant stood by the bed holding the sage's head and fanning him, and another was engaged in rubbing his feet.

Herutataf addressed a highly poetical speech to Teta, the gist of which was that the old man seemed to be able to defy the usual effects of old age, and to be like one who had obtained the secret of everlasting youth, and then expressed the hope that he was well. Having paid these compliments, which were couched in dignified and archaic language, Herutataf went on to say that he had come with a message from his father Khufu, who hereby summoned Teta to his presence. 'I have come,' he said, 'a long way to invite you, so that you may eat the food, and enjoy the good things which the king bestows on those who follow him, and so that he may lead you after a happy life to your fathers who rest in the grave.' The sage replied, 'Welcome, Prince Herutataf, welcome, Oh son who loves his father. Your father shall reward you with gifts, and he shall promote you to the rank of the senior officials of his court. Your vital force shall fight successfully against your enemy. Your soul knows the ways of the Other World ... I salute you, Prince Herutataf.'

Herutataf then held out his hands to the sage and helped him to rise from the bed, and he went with him to the river bank, Teta leaning on his arm. When they arrived there Teta asked for a boat for his children and his books, and the prince put at his disposal two boats, with crews complete. Teta himself, however, was ushered to the prince's boat and sailed with him. When they came to the palace, Prince Herutataf went to the king to announce their arrival, and said to him, 'Oh king my lord, I have brought Teta'. His Majesty replied, 'Bring him in quickly.' Then the king went out into the large hall of his palace, and Teta was led into his presence. His Majesty said, 'How is it, Teta, that I have never seen you?' To this Teta answered, 'Only the man who is summoned to the presence comes; so as soon as the king summoned me, I came.'

Then His Majesty asked him, 'Is it indeed true, as is asserted, that you know how to rejoin to its body the head which has been cut off?' Teta answered, 'Most assuredly do I know how to do this, Oh king my lord.' His Majesty said, 'Let them bring in from the prison a prisoner, so that his death sentence may be carried out.' But Teta rejoined, 'Let them not bring a man, Oh king my lord. Perhaps it may be ordered that the head shall be cut off some other living creature.' So a goose was brought to him and he cut off its head. He laid the body of the goose on the west side of the hall and its head on the east side. Then Teta recited certain magical spells and the goose stood up and waddled towards its head and its head moved towards its body. When the body and the head came close together, the head leaped onto the body and the goose stood up on its legs and cackled.

Then a goose of another kind called *khetâa* was brought to Teta, and he did with it as he had done with the first goose. Next His Majesty caused an ox to be taken to Teta, and when he had cut off its head, and recited magical spells over the head and the body, the head rejoined itself to the body, and the ox stood up on its feet. A lion was next brought to Teta, and when he had recited spells over it, the lion went behind him, and followed him (like a dog), and the rope with which he had been tied up trailed on the ground behind the animal.

King Khufu then said to Teta, 'Is it true what they say that you know the number of the Apet chambers of the shrine of Thoth?' Teta replied, 'No. I do not know their number, Oh king my lord, but I do know the place where they can be found.' His Majesty asked, 'Where is that?' To this Teta replied, 'There is a box made of flint in a house called Sapti in Heliopolis.' The king asked, 'Who will bring me this box?' Teta replied, 'Oh king my lord, I cannot bring the box to you.' His Majesty asked, 'Who then can bring it to me?' Teta answered, 'The oldest of the three children of Rut-tetet can bring it to you.' His Majesty said, 'It is my wish that you tell me who this Rut-tetet is.' Teta answered, 'Rut-tetet is the wife of a priest of Ra of Sakhabu, who is about to give birth to three children of Ra. He told her that these children should attain to the highest dignities in the whole country, and that the oldest of them should become high priest of Heliopolis.'

On hearing these words the heart of the king became sad; and Teta said, 'Why are you so sad, Oh king my lord? Is it because of the three children?' His Majesty asked, 'When will these three children be born?' Teta explained that the children would be born on the fifteenth day of the first month of Pert (which in today's calendar would have been around 1 December).

The king then expressed his determination to go and visit the temple of Ra of Sakhabu, which was situated near the great canal of the Letopolite district of Lower Egypt. In reply Teta declared that he would ensure that the water in the canal should be deep enough for the royal barge to sail on the canal without difficulty. The king then returned to his palace and gave orders that Teta should have lodgings provided to him in the house of Prince Herutataf, that he should live with him, and that he should be given 1,000 bread-cakes, 100 pots of beer, one ox, and 100 bundles of vegetables. And all that the king commanded concerning Teta was done.

THE STORY OF RUT-TETET AND THE THREE SONS OF RA

The last section of the Westcar Papyrus deals with the birth of the three sons of Ra. When the day in which the three sons were to be born approached, Ra, the Sun god, ordered the god Khnemu and the four goddesses, Isis, Nephyours, Meskhenet and Heqet to go and oversee the birth of the three children. When the children grew up and were ruling throughout all of Egypt, the god and goddesses were to build temples to them and furnish the altars with adubant offerings of meat and drink.

The four goddesses changed themselves into the forms of dancing women and went to the house where the lady Rut-tetet lay ill. Finding her husband Rauser, the priest of Ra, outside, they clashed their cymbals together and rattled their sistra, and tried to make him cheerful. When Rauser objected to this and told them that his wife lay ill inside the house, they replied, 'Let us see her. We know how to help her.' So he said to them and to Khnemu who was with them, 'Go in, please.'

They went to the room where Rut-tetet lay. Isis, Nephyours and Heqet helped to bring the three boys into the world. Meskhenet prophesied for each of them sovereignty over the land, and Khnemu bestowed health upon their bodies. After the birth of the three boys, the four goddesses and Khnemu returned outside and told Rauser to rejoice because his wife had given him three children. Rauser was overjoyed. He said, 'My Ladies, what can I do for you in return for this?' Having apparently nothing else to give them, he begged them to have barley brought from his granary, so that they might accept it as a gift to their own granaries. They agreed, and the god Khnemu brought the barley. Afterwards the goddesses set off to return home.

When they arrived, Isis said to her companions, 'How is it that we, who were commanded by Ra to go to Rut-tetet, have worked no wonder for these heavenly children? Even their father allowed us to leave without begging a favour from the gods!' The goddesses decided to make divine crowns of life, strength and health, and they hid them in the barley. Then they sent rain and storms through the heavens and they returned to the house of Rauser, carrying the barley with them. They said to Rauser, 'Let the barley be housed in a sealed room until we dance our way back to the north.' So they put the barley in a sealed room.

After Rut-tetet had kept herself secluded for 14 days, she asked one of her handmaidens, 'Is the house all ready?' The handmaiden explained that it was stocked with everything except jars of barley drink, which had not been brought. Rut-tetet asked why this was so and the handmaiden replied that there was no barley in the house except that which belonged to the dancing goddesses. She went on to say that that was in a room which had been sealed with their seal. Rut-tetet told her to go and fetch some of the barley. She was quite certain that when her husband Rauser returned he would return what she took.

So the handmaiden went to the room and broke in. As she did so, she heard loud cries and shouts – the sounds of music, singing and dancing, and all the noises men make in honour of the birth of a king. She ran back to Rut-tetet to tell her what she had heard. Rut-tetet herself went to the room, and failed to find the place where the noises were coming from. But when she laid her temple against a box, she believed that the noises were coming from inside it. She took this small box and put it into another box, and then another, which she sealed, She then wrapped this in a leather covering and laid it in the room containing her jar of barley wine and sealed the door. When Rauser returned from the fields, Rut-tetet told him all that had happened.

A few days after these events, Rut-tetet had a bitter quarrel with her handmaiden. Enraged, the handmaiden screamed, 'How dare you treat me in this way? I can destroy you! She has given birth to three kings and I will go and tell the Majesty of King Khufu of this fact.' The handmaiden believed that if Khufu knew about the prophecies of the goddesses, and about the future of Rauser and Rut-tetet's three sons, he would kill the children and perhaps their parents, too.

With this in mind, the handmaiden went to her maternal uncle and told him what had happened. She announced that she was going to tell the king about the three children. But from her uncle she obtained neither support nor sympayour; on the contrary, he gathered together several strands of flax into a thick rope with which he gave her a beating. A little later the handmaiden went to the river to fetch some water, and whilst she was filling her pot a crocodile seized her and carried her away.

When the uncle went to Rut-tetet's house to tell her what had happened, he found her sitting down, with her head bowed low. She appeared sad and miserable. He asked her, 'Oh dear lady, why are you so sad?' She told him that the cause of her sorrow was the handmaiden, who had been born in the house and had grown up in it, and who had just left threatening to go and tell the king about the birth of the three kings. The uncle of the handmaiden slowly nodded his head in a consoling manner. He told Rut-tetet of how his neice had come to him and informed him what she planned to do. He told her the story of how he had beaten her, and how she had gone to the river to fetch some water and had been carried off by a crocodile.

There is reason to think that the three sons of Rut-tetet became the three kings of the fifth dynasty, who were known by the names of Khafra, Menkaura and Userkaf. The stories given above are valuable because they contain elements of history. It is well known that the immediate successors of the fourth dynasty, of which Khufu, Khafra and Menkaura, the builders of the three great pyramids at Gizah, were the most important kings, were kings who delighted to call themselves sons of Ra. They spared no effort to make the form of worship of the Sun god that was practised at Anu, or Heliopolis, universal in Egypt. It is also probable that the three magicians, Ubaaner, Tchatchamankh and Teta were notable historical figures, whose abilities and skill in working magic appealed to the imagination of the Egyptians under all dynasties. This likely ensured that their names were to be revered for numerous generations to come.

THE EGYPTIAN STORY
OF THE CREATION

If we consider for a moment the vast amount of thought which the Egyptians gave to the problems of the future life, and their deep-seated belief in resurrection and immortality, we cannot fail to conclude that they must have theorised deeply about the constitution of the heaven in which they hoped to live everlastingly, and about its Maker.

The translations given in the preceding pages prove that the theologians of Egypt were ready enough to describe heaven, and the life led by the blessed there, and the powers and the attributes of the gods, but they appear to have shrunk from writing down in a connected form their beliefs concerning the Creation and the origin of the Creator. The worshippers of each great god proclaimed him to be the Creator of All, and every great town had its own local belief on the subject. According to the Heliopolitans, Atem, or Tem, and at a later period Ra, was the Creator; according to Memphite theology he was Ptah; according to the Hermopolitans he was Thoth; and according to the Thebans he was Amen (Ammon). In only one native Egyptian work up to the present has there been discovered any connected account of the Creation, and the means by which it was effected, namely, the British Museum Papyrus, No. 10,188.

THE BRITISH MUSEUM PAPYRUS

This papyrus was written about 305 BCE, and is therefore of a comparatively late date, but the subject matter of the works contained in it is thousands of years older, and it is only their *forms* which are of a late date.

The Story of the Creation is found in the last work in the papyrus, which is called the 'Book of overthrowing Aapep, the Enemy of Ra, the Enemy of Un-Nefer' (i.e. Osiris). This work is a liturgy, which was said at certain times of the day and night in the great temple of Amen-Ra at Thebes, with the view of preventing the monster Aapep from obstructing the sunrise.

In the midst of the magical spells of this papyrus we find two copies of the 'Book of knowing how Ra came into being, and of overthrowing Aapep'. One copy is a little fuller than the other, but they agree substantially. The words of this book are said in the opening line to have been spoken by the god Nebertcher, i.e. the 'Lord to the uttermost limit,' or God Himself. The Egyptian Christians, or Copts, in their religious writings use this name as an equivalent of God Almighty, the Lord of All, the God of the Universe. The second version of the book states that the name of Nebertcher is Ausares (Osiris).

HOW RA CAME INTO BEING

Nebertcher says: 'I am the creator of what has come into being. I myself came into being under the form of the god Khepera. I came into being under the form of Pautti (or, in primeval time), I formed myself out of the primeval matter, I made myself out of the substance that was in primeval time.' Nothing existed at that time except the great primeval watery mass called Nu, but in this there were the germs of everything that came into being subsequently. There was no heaven, and no earth, and the god found no place on which to stand; nothing, in fact, existed except the god. He says, 'I was alone.'

He first created himself by uttering his own name as a word of power, and when this was uttered his visible form appeared. He then uttered another kind of word of power, and as a result of this his soul (*ba*) came into being, and it worked in connection with his heart or mind (*ab*). Before every act of creation Nebertcher, or his visible form Khepera, thought out what form the thing to be created was to take, and when he had uttered its name the thing itself appeared in heaven or earth. To fill the heaven, or place where he lived, the god next produced from his body and its shadow the two gods Shu and Tefnut. These with Nebertcher, or Khepera, formed the first triad of gods, and the 'one god became three', or, as we should say, the one god had three aspects, each of which was quite distinct from the other. The tradition of the begetting of Shu and Tefnut is as old as the time of the pyramids, for it is mentioned in the text of Pepi I.

The next act of creation resulted in the emerging of the Eye of Nebertcher (later identified with Ra) from the watery mass (Nu), and light shone upon its waters. Shu and Tefnut then united and they produced Keb, the Earth-god, and Nut, the Sky-goddess. The text then refers to some calamity which befell the Eye of Nebertcher or of Khepera, but what it was is not clear; at all events the Eye became obscured, and it ceased to give light. This period of darkness is, of course, the night, and to obviate the inconvenience caused by this recurring period of darkness, the god made a second Eye, i.e. the Moon, and set it in the heavens. The greater Eye ruled the day, and the lesser Eye the night. One of the results of the daily darkness was the descent of the Sky-goddess Nut to the Earth-god Keb each evening.

The gods and goddesses next created were five, namely, Osiris, Horus, Set, Isis, and Nephthys. Osiris married Isis, and their son was called Horus; Set married Nephthys, but their son Anpu, or Anubis, is not mentioned in our text. Osiris became the great Ancestor-god of Egypt, and was a reincarnation of his great-grandfather. Men and women were first formed from the tears that fell from the Eye of Khepera, or the Sun god, upon his body; the old Egyptian word for 'men' very closely resembles in form and sound the word for 'tears'. Plants, vegetables, herbs, and trees owe their origin to the light of the moon falling upon the earth. Our text contains no mention of a special creation of the 'beasts of the field', but the god states distinctly that he created the children of the earth, or creeping things of all kinds, and among this class quadrupeds are probably included. The men and women, and all the other living creatures that were made at that time by Nebertcher, or Khepera, reproduced their species, each in his own way, and thus the earth became filled with their descendants as we see at the present time. The elements of this Creation legend are very, very old, and the form in which they are grouped in our text suggests the influence of the priests of Heliopolis. It is interesting to note that only very ancient gods appear as Powers of creation, and these were certainly worshipped for many centuries before the priests of Heliopolis invented their cult of the Sun god, and identified their god with the older gods of the country. We may note, too, that gods like Ptah and Amen, whose reputation was so great in later times, and even when our text was copied in 305 BCE, find no mention at all.

LEGENDS OF THE GODS

The Egyptians believed that at one time all the great gods and goddesses lived upon earth, and that they ruled Egypt in much the same way as the pharaohs with whom they were more or less acquainted. They went about among men and took a real personal interest in their affairs, and, according to tradition, they spared no pains in promoting their wishes and wellbeing. Their rule was on the whole beneficent, chiefly because in addition to their divine attributes they possessed natures, and apparently bodily constitutions, that were similar to those of men.

Like men also they were believed to feel emotions and passions, and to be liable to the accidents that befell men, and to grow old, and even to die. The greatest of all the gods was Ra, and he reigned over Egypt for very many years. His reign was marked by justice and righteousness, and he was in all periods of Egyptian history regarded as the type of what a king should be. When men instead of gods reigned over Egypt they all delighted to call themselves sons of Ra, and every king believed that Ra was his true father, and regarded his mother's husband as his father only in name. This belief was always common in Egypt, and even Alexander the Great found it expedient to adopt it, for he made a journey to the sanctuary of Amen (Ammon) in the

Oasis of Siwah in order to be officially acknowledged by the god. Having obtained this recognition, he became the rightful lord of Egypt.

THE DESTRUCTION OF MANKIND

This legend was cut in hieroglyphs on the walls of a small chamber in the tomb of Seti I, about 1350 BCE.

When Ra, the self-begotten and self-formed god, had been ruling gods and men for some time, men began to complain about him, saying, 'His Majesty has become old. His bones have turned into silver, his flesh into gold, and his hair into real lapis-lazuli.' His Majesty heard these murmurings and commanded his followers to summon to his presence his Eye (i.e. the goddess Hathor), Shu, Tefnut, Keb, Nut, and the father and mother gods and goddesses who were with him in the watery abyss of Nu, and also the god of this water, Nu. They were to come to him with all their followers secretly, so that men should not suspect the reason for their coming, and take flight, and they were to assemble in the Great House in Heliopolis, where Ra would take counsel with them.

In due course all the gods assembled in the Great House, and they ranged themselves down the sides of the House, and they bowed down in homage before Ra until their heads touched the ground, and said, 'Speak, for we are listening.' Then Ra, addressing Nu, the father of the first-born gods, told him to give heed to what men were doing, for they whom he had created were murmuring against him. And he said, 'Tell me what you would do. Consider the matter, invent a plan for me, and I will not slay them until I have heard what you shall say concerning this thing.' Nu replied, 'You, Oh my son Ra, are greater than the god who made you (i.e. Nu himself), you are the king of those who were created with you, your throne is established, and the fear of you is great. Let your Eye (Hathor) attack those who blaspheme you.' And Ra said, 'Lo, they have fled to the mountains, for their hearts are afraid because of what they have said.' The gods replied, 'Let your Eye go forth and destroy those who blasphemed you, for no eye can resist you when it goes forth in the form of Hathor.' Thereupon the Eye of Ra, or Hathor, went in pursuit of the blasphemers in the mountains, and slew them all. On her return Ra welcomed her, and the goddess said that the work of vanquishing men was dear to her heart. Ra then said that he would be the master of men as their king, and that he would destroy them. For three nights the goddess Hathor-Sekhmet waded about in the blood of men, the slaughter beginning at Hensu (Herakleopolis Magna).

Then the Majesty of Ra ordered that messengers should be sent to Abu, a town at the foot of the First Cataract, to fetch mandrakes (?), and when they were brought he gave them to the god Sekti to crush. When the women slaves were bruising grain for making beer, the crushed mandrakes (?) were placed in the vessels that were to hold the beer, together with some of the blood of those who had been slain by Hathor. The beer was then made, and seven thousand vessels were filled with it. When Ra saw the beer he ordered it to be taken to the scene of slaughter, and poured out on the meadows of the four quarters of heaven. The object of putting mandrakes (?) in the beer was to make those who drank fall asleep quickly, and when the goddess Hathor came and drank the beer mixed with blood and mandrakes (?) she became very merry, and, the sleepy stage of drunkenness coming on her, she forgot all about men, and slew no more. At every festival of Hathor ever after 'sleepy beer' was made, and it was drunk by those who celebrated the feast.

Now, although the blasphemers of Ra had been put to death, the heart of the god was not satisfied, and he complained to the gods that he was smitten with the 'pain of the fire of sickness'. He said, 'My heart is weary because I have to live with men; I have slain some of them, but worthless men still live, and I did not slay as many as I ought to have done considering my power.' To this the gods replied, 'Trouble not about your lack of action, for your power is in proportion to your will.' Here the text becomes fragmentary, but it seems that the goddess Nut took the form of a cow, and that the other gods lifted Ra on to her back. When men saw that Ra was leaving the earth, they repented of their murmurings, and the next morning they went out with bows and arrows to fight the enemies of the Sun god. As a reward for this Ra forgave those men their former blasphemies, but persisted in his intention of retiring from the earth. He ascended into the heights of heaven, being still on the back of the Cow-goddess Nut, and he created there Sekhet-hetep and Sekhet-Aaru as abodes for the blessed, and the flowers that blossomed therein he turned into stars. He also created the millions of beings who lived there in order that they might praise him. The height to which Ra had ascended was now so great that the legs of the Cow-goddess on which he was enthroned trembled, and to give her strength he ordained that Nut should be held up in her position by the godhead and upraised arms of the god Shu. This is why we see pictures of the body of Nut being supported by Shu. The legs of the Cow-goddess were supported by the various gods, and thus the seat of the throne of Ra became stable.

When this was done Ra caused the Earth-god Keb to be summoned to his presence, and when he came he spoke to him about the venomous reptiles that lived in the earth and were hostile to him. Then turning to Thoth, he bade him to prepare a series of spells and words of power, which would enable those who knew them to overcome snakes and serpents and deadly reptiles of all kinds. Thoth did so, and the spells which he wrote under the direction of Ra served as a protection of the servants of Ra ever after, and secured for them the help of Keb, who became sole lord of all the beings that lived and moved on and in his body, the earth. Before finally relinquishing his active rule on earth, Ra summoned Thoth and told him of his desire to create a Light-soul in the Tuat and in the Land of the Caves. Over this region he appointed Thoth to rule, and he ordered him to keep a register of those who were there, and to mete out just punishments to them. In fact, Thoth was to be ever after the representative of Ra in the Other World.

THE LEGEND OF RA AND ISIS

This legend is found written in the hieratic character upon a papyrus preserved in Turin, and it illustrates a portion of the preceding legend. We have seen that Ra instructed Thoth to draw up a series of spells to be used against venomous reptiles of all kinds, and the reader will perceive from the following summary that Ra had good reason for doing this.

The legend opens with a list of the titles of Ra, the 'self-created god', creator of heaven, earth, breath of life, fire, gods, men, beasts, cattle, reptiles, feathered fowl, and fish, the King of gods and men, to whom cycles of 120 years are as years, whose manifold names are unknown even by the gods.

The text continues: Isis had the form of a woman, and knew words of power, but she was disgusted with men, and she yearned for the companionship of the gods and the spirits, and she meditated and asked herself whether, supposing she had the knowledge of the Name of Ra, it was not possible to make herself as great as Ra was in heaven and on the earth? Meanwhile Ra appeared in heaven each day upon his throne, but he had become old, and he dribbled at the mouth, and his spittle fell on the ground. One day Isis took some of the spittle and kneaded up dust in it, and made this paste into the form of a serpent with a forked tongue, so that if it struck anyone the person struck would find it impossible to escape death. This figure she placed on the path on which Ra walked as he came into heaven after his daily survey of the Two Lands (i.e. Egypt). Soon after this Ra rose up, and attended by his gods he came into heaven, but as he went along the serpent drove its fangs into him. As soon as he was bitten Ra felt the living fire leaving his body, and he cried out so loudly that his voice reached the uttermost parts of heaven. The gods rushed to him in great alarm, saying, 'What is the matter?' At first Ra was speechless, and found himself unable to answer, for his jaws shook, his lips trembled, and the poison continued to run through every part of his body. When he was able to regain a little strength, he told the gods that some deadly creature had bitten him, something the like of which he had never seen, something which his hand had never made. He said, 'Never before have I felt such pain; there is no pain worse than this.' Ra then went on to describe his greatness and power, and told the listening gods that his father and mother had hidden his name in his body so that no one might be able to master him by means of any spell or word of power. In spite of this something had struck him, and he knew not what it was. 'Is it fire?' he asked. 'Is it water? My heart is full of burning fire, my limbs are shivering, shooting pains are in all my members.' All the gods round about him uttered cries of lamentation, and at this moment Isis appeared. Going to Ra she said, 'What is this, Oh divine father? What is this? Has a serpent bitten you? Has something made by you lifted up its head against you? Verily my words of power shall overthrow it; I will make it depart in the sight of your light.' Ra then repeated to Isis the story of the incident, adding, 'I am colder than water, I am hotter than fire. All my members sweat. My body quakes. My eye is unsteady. I cannot look on the sky, and my face is bedewed with water as in the time of the Inundation' (i.e. in the period of summer). Then Isis said, 'Father, tell me your name, for he who can utter his own name lives.'

Ra replied, 'I am the maker of heaven and earth. I knit together the mountains and whatsoever lives on them. I made the waters. I made Mehturit (an ancient Cow-goddess of heaven) to come into being. I made Kamutef (a form of Amen-Ra). I made heaven, and the two hidden gods of the horizon, and put souls into the gods. I open my eyes, and there is light; I shut my eyes, and there is darkness. I speak the word[s], and the waters of the Nile appear. I am he whom the gods know not. I make the hours. I create the days. I open the year. I make the river [Nile]. I create the living fire whereby works in the foundries and workshops are carried out. I am Khepera in the morning, Ra at noon, and Temu in the evening.' Meanwhile the poison of the serpent was coursing through the veins of Ra, and the enumeration of his works afforded the god no relief from it. Then Isis said to Ra, 'Among all the things which you have named to me you have not named your name. Tell me your name, and the poison shall come forth from you.' Ra still hesitated, but the poison was burning in his blood, and the heat thereof was stronger than that of a fierce fire. At length he said, 'Isis shall search me through, and my name shall come forth from my body and pass into hers.' Then Ra hid himself from the gods, and for a season his throne in the Boat of Millions of Years was empty. When the time came for the heart of the god to pass into Isis, the goddess said to Horus, her son, 'The great god shall bind himself by an oath to give us his two eyes (i.e. the sun and the moon).' When the great god had yielded up his name Isis pronounced the following spell: 'Flow poison, come out of Ra. Eye of Horus, come out of the god, and sparkle as you come through his mouth. I am the worker. I make the poison fall on the ground. The poison is conquered. Truly the name of the great god has been taken from him. Ra lives! The poison dies! If the poison live Ra shall die.' These were the words which Isis spoke, Isis the great lady, the Queen of the gods, who knew Ra by his own name.

In late times magicians used to write the above legend on papyrus above figures of Temu and Heru-Hekenu, who gave Ra his secret name, and over figures of Isis and Horus, and sell the rolls as charms against snake bites.

THE LEGEND OF HORUS OF BEHUTET

The great historical fact underlying this legend is the conquest of Egypt by some very early king who invaded Egypt from the south, and who succeeded in conquering every part of it, even the northern part of the Delta. The events described are supposed to have taken place whilst Ra was still reigning on the earth.

The legend states that in the three hundred and sixty-third year of the reign of Ra-Harmakhis, the ever living, His Majesty was in Ta-sti (i.e. the Land of the Bow, or Nubia) with his soldiers; the enemy had reviled him, and for this reason the land is called 'Uauatet' to this day. From Nubia Ra sailed down the river to Apollinopolis (Edfu), and Heru-Behutet, or Horus of Edfu, was with him. On arriving there Horus told Ra that the enemy were plotting against him, and Ra told him to go out and slay them. Horus took the form of a great winged disk, which flew up into the air and pursued the enemy, and it attacked them with such terrific force that they could neither see nor hear, and they fell upon each other, and slew each other, and in a moment not a single foe was left alive. Then Horus returned to the Boat of Ra-Harmakhis, in the form of the winged disk which shone with many colours, and said, 'Advance, Oh Ra, and look upon your enemies who are lying under you in this land.' Ra set out on the journey, taking with him the goddess Ashtoreth, and he saw his enemies lying on the ground, each of them being fettered. After looking upon his slaughtered foes Ra said to the gods who were with him, 'Behold, let us sail in our boat on the water, for our hearts are glad because our enemies have been overthrown on the earth.'

So the Boat of Ra moved onwards towards the north, and the enemies of the god who were on the banks took the form of crocodiles and hippopotami, and tried to frighten the god, for as his boat came near them they opened their jaws wide, intending to swallow it up together with the gods who were in it. Among the crew were the Followers of Horus of Edfu, who were skilled workers in metal, and each of these had in his hands an iron spear and a chain. These 'Blacksmiths' threw out their chains into the river and allowed the crocodiles and hippopotami to entangle their legs in them, and then they dragged the beasts towards the bows of the Boat, and driving their spears into their bodies, slew them there. After the slaughter the bodies of six hundred and fifty-one crocodiles were brought and laid out before the town of Edfu. When Thoth saw these he said, 'Let your hearts rejoice, Oh gods of heaven, Let your hearts rejoice, Oh gods who dwell on the earth. The Young Horus comes in peace. On his way he has made manifest deeds of valour, according to the Book of slaying the Hippopotamus.' And from that day they made figures of Horus in metal.

Then Horus of Edfu took the form of the winged disk, and set himself on the prow of the Boat of Ra. He took with him Nekhebet, goddess of the South, and Uatchet, goddess of the North, in the form of serpents, so that they might make all the enemies of the Sun god to quake in the South and in the North. His foes who had fled to the north doubled back towards the south, for they were in deadly fear of the god. Horus pursued and overtook them, and he and his blacksmiths had in their hands spears and chains, and they slew large numbers of them to the south-east of the town of Thebes in Upper Egypt. Many succeeded in escaping towards the north once more, but after pursuing them for a whole day Horus overtook them, and made a great slaughter among them. Meanwhile the other foes of the god, who had heard of the defeats of their allies, fled into Lower Egypt, and took refuge among the swamps of the Delta. Horus set out after them, and came up with them, and spent four days in the water slaying his foes, who tried to escape in the forms of crocodiles and hippopotami. He captured one hundred and forty-two of the enemy and a male hippopotamus, and took them to the fore part of the Boat of Ra. There he hacked them in pieces, and gave their inward parts to his followers, and their mutilated bodies to the gods and goddesses who were in the Boat of Ra and on the river banks in the town of Heben.

Then the remnant of the enemy turned their faces towards the Lake of the North, and they attempted to sail to the Mediterranean in boats; but the terror of Horus filled their hearts, and they left their boats and fled to the district of Mertet-Ament, where they joined themselves to the worshippers of Set, the god of evil, who dwelt in the Western Delta. Horus pursued them in his boat for one day and one night without seeing them, and he arrived at the town of Per-Rehui. At length he discovered the position of the enemy, and he and his followers fell upon them, and slew a large number of them; he captured three hundred and eighty-one of them alive, and these he took to the Boat of Ra, then, having slain them, he gave their carcasses to his followers or bodyguard, who presumably devoured them. The custom of eating the bodies of enemies is very old in Egypt, and survives in some parts of Africa to this day.

Then Set, the great antagonist of Horus, came out and cursed him for the slaughter of his people, using most shameful words of abuse. Horus stood up and fought a duel with Set, the 'Stinking Face,' as the text calls him, and Horus succeeded in throwing him to the ground and spearing him. Horus smashed his mouth with a blow of his mace, and having fettered him with his chain, he brought him into the presence of Ra, who ordered that he was to be handed over to Isis and her son Horus, that they might work their will on him. Here we must note that the ancient editor of the legend has confounded Horus the ancient Sun god with Horus, son of Isis, son of Osiris. Then Horus, the son of Isis, cut off the heads of Set and his followers in the presence of Ra, and dragged Set by his feet round about throughout the district with his spear driven through his head and back, according to the order of Ra. The form which Horus of Edfu had at that time was that of a man of great strength, with the face and back of a hawk; on his head he wore the Double Crown, with feathers and serpents attached, and in his hands he held a metal spear and a metal chain. And Horus, the son of Isis, took upon himself a similar form, and the two Horuses slew all the enemies on the bank of the river to the west of the town of Per-Rehui. This slaughter took place on the seventh day of the first month of the season Pert (about the middle of November), which was ever afterwards called the 'Day of the Festival of Sailing'.

Now, although Set in the form of a man had been slain, he reappeared in the form of a great hissing serpent, and took up his abode in a hole in the ground without being noticed by Horus. Ra, however, saw him, and gave orders that Horus, the son of Isis, in the form of a hawk-headed staff, should set himself at the mouth of the hole, so that the monster might never reappear among men. This Horus did, and Isis his mother lived there with him. Once again it became known to Ra that a remnant of the followers of Set had escaped, and that under the direction of the Smait fiends, and of Set, who had reappeared, they were hiding in the swamps of the Eastern Delta. Horus of Edfu, the winged disk, pursued them, speared them, and finally slew them in the presence of Ra. For the moment, there were no more enemies of Ra to be found in the district on land, although Horus passed six days and six nights in looking for them; but it seems that several of the followers of Set in the forms of water reptiles were lying on the ground under water, and that Horus saw them there. At this time Horus had strict guard kept over the tomb of Osiris in Anrutef (a district of Herakleopolis), because he learned that the Smait fiends wanted to come and wreck both it and the body of the god. Isis, too, never ceased to recite spells and incantations in order to keep away her husband's foes from his body. Meanwhile the 'blacksmiths' of Horus, who were in charge of the 'middle regions' of Egypt, found a body of the enemy, and attacked them fiercely, slew many of them, and took one hundred and six of them prisoners. The 'blacksmiths' of the west also took one hundred and six prisoners, and both groups of prisoners were slain before Ra. In return for their services Ra bestowed dwelling-places upon the 'blacksmiths', and allowed them to have temples with images of their gods in them, and arranged for offerings and libations to be made to them by properly appointed priests of various classes.

Shortly after these events Ra discovered that a number of his enemies were still at large, and that they had sailed in boats to the swamps that lay round about the town of Tchal, or Tchar, better known as Zoan or Tanis. Once more Horus unmoored the Boat of Ra, and set out against them; some took refuge in the waters, and others landed and escaped to the hilly land on the east. For some reason, which is not quite apparent, Horus took the form of a mighty lion with a man's face, and he wore on his head the triple crown. His

claws were like flints, and he pursued the enemy on the
hills, and chased them hither and thither, and captured one
hundred and forty-two of them. He tore out their tongues,
and ripped their bodies into strips with his claws, and gave
them over to his allies in the mountains, who, no doubt,
ate them. This was the last fight in the north of Egypt, and
Ra proposed that they should sail up the river and return
to the south. They had traversed all Egypt, and sailed over
the lakes in the Delta, and down the arms of the Nile to the
Mediterranean, and as no more of the enemy were to be seen
the prow of the boat of Ra was turned southwards. Thoth
recited the spells that produced fair weather, and said the
words of power that prevented storms from rising, and in
due course the Boat reached Nubia. When it arrived, Horus
found in the country of Uauatet men who were conspiring
against him and cursing him, just as they had at one time
blasphemed Ra. Horus, taking the form of the winged disk,
and accompanied by the two serpent-goddesses, Nekhebet
and Uatchet, attacked the rebels, but there was no fierce
fighting this time, for the hearts of the enemy melted
through fear of him. His foes cast themselves before him on
the ground in submission, they offered no resistance, and
they died straightway. Horus then returned to the town of
Behutet (Edfu), and the gods acclaimed him, and praised
his prowess. Ra was so pleased with him that he ordered
Thoth to have a winged disk, with a serpent on each side
of it, placed in every temple in Egypt in which he (i.e. Ra)
was worshipped, so that it might act as a protector of the
building, and drive away any and every fiend and devil that
might wish to attack it. This is the reason why we find the

winged disk, with a serpent on each side of it, above the doors of temples and religious buildings throughout the length and breadth of Egypt.

THE LEGEND OF KHNEMU AND THE SEVEN YEARS' FAMINE

The subject of this legend is a terrible famine, which lasted for seven years, in the reign of King Tcheser, and which recalls the seven years' famine that took place in Egypt when Joseph was there. This famine was believed to have been caused by the king's neglect to worship properly the god Khnemu, who was supposed to control the springs of the Nile, which were asserted by the sages to be situated between two great rocks on the Island of Elephantine.

The legend sets forth that the Viceroy of Nubia, in the reign of Tcheser, was a nobleman called Meter, who was also the overseer of all the temple properties in the South. His residence was in Abu, or Elephantine, and in the eighteenth year of his reign the king sent him a despatch in which it was written thus:

'This is to inform you that misery has laid hold upon me as I sit upon the great throne, and I grieve for those who dwell in the Great House. My heart is grievously afflicted by reason of a very great calamity, which is due to the fact that the waters of the Nile have not risen to their proper height for seven years. Grain is exceedingly scarce, there are no garden herbs and vegetables to be had at all, and everything which men use for food has come to an end.

Every man robs his neighbour. The people wish to walk about, but are unable to move. The baby wails, the young man shuffles along on his feet through weakness. The hearts of the old men are broken down with despair, their legs give way under them, they sink down exhausted on the ground, and they lay their hands on their bellies [in pain]. The officials are powerless and have no counsel to give, and when the public granaries, which ought to contain supplies, are opened, there comes forth from them nothing but wind. Everything is in a state of ruin. I go back in my mind to the time when I had an adviser, to the time of the gods, to the Ibis-god [Thoth], and to the chief Kher-heb priest Imhetep (Imouthis), the son of Ptah of his South Wall (a part of Memphis). [Tell me, I pray you], Where is the birthplace of the Nile? What god or what goddess presides over it? What kind of form has the god? For it is he that makes my revenue, and who fills the granaries with grain. I wish to go to [consult] the Chief of Het-Sekhmet (i.e. Hermopolis, the town of Thoth), whose beneficence strengthens all men in their works. I wish to go into the House of Life (i.e. the library of the temple), and to take the rolls of the books in my own hands, so that I may examine them [and find out these things].'

Having read the royal despatch the Viceroy Meter set out to go to the king, and when he came to him he proceeded to instruct the king in the matters about which he had asked questions. The text makes the king say: '[Meter] gave me information about the rise of the Nile, and he told me all that men had written concerning it; and he made clear to me all the difficult passages [in the books], which my ancestors had consulted haveily, and which had never before been explained to any king since the time when Ra [reigned]. And he said to me: There is a town in the river wherefrom the Nile makes his appearance. 'Abu' was its name in the beginning: it is the City of the Beginning, it is the Name of the City of the Beginning. It reaches to Uauatet, which is the first land [on the south]. There is a long flight of steps there (a nilometer?), on which Ra rests when he determines to prolong life to mankind. It is called 'Netchemtchem ankh'. Here are the 'Two Qerti' (the two caverns which contained the springs of the Nile), which are the two breasts wherefrom every good thing comes. Here is the bed of the Nile, here the Nile-god renews his youth, and here he sends out the flood on the land. Here his waters rise to a height of twenty-eight cubits; at Hermopolis (in the Delta) their height is seven cubits. Here the Nile-god smites the ground with his sandals, and here he draws the bolts and throws open the two doors through which the water pours forth. In this town the Nile-god dwells in the form of Shu, and he keeps the account of the products of all Egypt, in order to give to each his due. Here are kept the cord for measuring land and the register of the estates. Here the god lives in a wooden house with a door made of reeds, and branches of trees form the roof; its entrance is to the south-east. Round about it are mountains of stone to which quarrymen come with their tools when they want stone to build temples to the gods, shrines for sacred animals, and pyramids for kings, or to make statues. Here they offer sacrifices of all kinds in the sanctuary, and here their sweet-smelling gifts are presented before the face of the god

Khnemu. In the quarries on the river bank is granite, which is called the 'stone of Abu'. The names of its gods are: Sept (Sothis, the dog-star), Anqet, Hep (the Nile-god), Shu, Keb, Nut, Osiris, Horus, Isis, and Nephthys. Here are found precious stones (a list is given), gold, silver, copper, iron, lapis-lazuli, emerald, crystal, ruby, etc., alabaster, mother-of-emerald, and seeds of plants that are used in making incense. These were the things which I learned from Meter [the Viceroy].'

Having informed the king concerning the rise of the Nile and the other matters mentioned in his despatch, Meter made arrangements for the king to visit the temple of Khnemu in person. This he did, and the legend gives us the king's own description of his visit. He says: I entered the temple, and the keepers of the rolls untied them and showed them to me. I was purified by the sprinkling of holy water, and I passed through the places that were prohibited to ordinary folk, and a great offering of cakes, ale, geese, oxen, etc., was offered up on my behalf to the gods and goddesses of Abu. Then I found the god [Khnemu] standing in front of me, and I propitiated him with the offerings that I made to him, and I made prayer and supplication before him. Then he opened his eyes (the king was standing before a statue with movable eyes), and his heart inclined to me, and in a majestic manner he said to me: 'I am Khnemu who fashioned you. My two hands grasped you and knitted together your body; I made your members sound, and I gave you your heart. Yet the stones have been lying under the ground for ages, and no man has worked them in order to build a god-house, to repair the [sacred] buildings which

are in ruins, or to make shrines for the gods of the South
and North, or to do what he ought to do for his lord,
even though I am the Lord [the Creator]. I am Nu, the
self-created, the Great God, who came into being in the
beginning. [I am] Hep [the Nile-god] who rises at will to
give health to him that works for me. I am the Governor
and Guide of all men, in all their periods, the Most Great,
the Father of the gods, Shu, the Great One, the Chief of the
earth. The two halves of heaven are my abode. The Nile is
poured out in a stream by me, and it goes round about the
tilled lands, and its embrace produces life forevery one that
breathes, according to the extent of its embrace.... I will
make the Nile rise for you, and in no year shall it fail, and it
shall spread its water out and cover every land satisfactorily.
Plants, herbs, and trees shall bend beneath [the weight of]
their produce. The goddess Rennet (the Harvest goddess)
shall be at the head of everything, and every product shall
increase a hundred thousandfold, according to the cubit of
the year. The people shall be filled, verily to their hearts'
desire, yea, everyone. Want shall cease, and the emptiness
of the granaries shall come to an end. The Land of Mera
(i.e. Egypt) shall be one cultivated land, the districts shall
be yellow with crops of grain, and the grain shall be good.
The fertility of the land shall be according to the desire [of
the husbandman], and it shall be greater than it has ever
been before.' At the sound of the word 'crops' the king
awoke, and the courage that then filled his heart was as
great as his former despair had been.

Having left the chamber of the god the king made a
decree by which he endowed the temple of Khnemu with

lands and gifts, and he drew up a code of laws under which every farmer was compelled to pay certain dues to it. Every fisherman and hunter had to pay a tithe. Of the calves cast one tenth were to be sent to the temple to be offered up as the daily offering. Gold, ivory, ebony, spices, precious stones, and woods were tithed, whether their owners were Egyptians or not, but no local tribe was to levy duty on these things on their road to Abu. Every artisan also was to pay tithe, with the exception of those who were employed in the foundry attached to the temple, and whose occupation consisted in making the images of the gods. The king further ordered that a copy of this decree, the original of which was cut in wood, should be engraved on a stele to be set up in the sanctuary, with figures of Khnemu and his companion gods cut above it. The man who spat upon the stele [if discovered] was to be 'admonished with a rope'.

THE LEGEND OF THE WANDERINGS OF ISIS

The god Osiris lived and reigned at one time upon earth in the form of a man. His twin-brother Set was jealous of his popularity, and hated him to such a degree that he contrived a plan whereby he succeeded in putting Osiris to death. Set then tried to usurp his brother's kingdom and to make himself sole lord of Egypt, and, although no text states it distinctly, it is clear that he seized his brother's wife, Isis, and shut her up in his house. Isis was, however, under the protection of the god Thoth, and she escaped with her unborn child, and the following legend describes the incidents that befell her, and the death and revivification of Horus. The legend is narrated by the goddess herself, who says:

'I am Isis. I escaped from the dwelling wherein my brother Set placed me. Thoth, the great god, the Prince of Truth in heaven and on earth, said to me: "Come, Oh goddess Isis [hearken], it is a good thing to hearken, for he who is guided by another lives. Hide yourself with your child, and these things shall happen to him. His body shall grow and flourish, and strength of every kind shall be in him. He shall sit upon his father's throne, he shall avenge him, and he shall hold the exalted position of 'Governor of the Two Lands'." I left the house of Set in the evening, and there accompanied me Seven Scorpions, that were to travel with me, and sting with their stings on my behalf. Two of them, Tefen and Befen, followed behind me, two of them, Mestet and Mestetef, went one on each side of me, and three, Petet, Thetet, and Maatet, prepared the way for me. I charged them very carefully and adjured them to make no acquaintance with any one, to speak to none of the Red Fiends, to pay no heed to a servant (?), and to keep their gaze towards the ground so that they might show me the way. And their leader brought me to Pa-Sui, the town of the Sacred Sandals, at the head of the district of the Papyrus Swamps. When I arrived at Teb I came to a quarter of the town where women dwelt. And a certain woman of quality spied me as I was journeying along the road, and she shut her door in my face, for she was afraid because of the Seven Scorpions that were with me. Then they took counsel concerning her, and they shot out their poison on the tail of Tefen. As for me, a peasant woman called Taha opened her door, and I went into the house of this humble woman. Then the scorpion Tefen crawled in under the door of the woman Usert [who had shut it in my face], and stung her son, and a fire broke out in it; there was no water to put it out, but the sky sent down rain, though it was not the time of rain. And the heart of Usert was sore within her, and she was very sad, for she knew not whether her son would live or die; and she went through the town shrieking for help, but none came out at the sound of her voice. And I was sad for the child's sake, and I wished the innocent one to live again. So I cried out to her, saying, "Come to me! Come to me! There is life in my mouth. I am a woman well known in her town. I can destroy the devil of death by a spell which my father taught me. I am his daughter, his beloved one.'"

Then Isis laid her hands on the child and recited this spell: 'Oh poison of Tefent, come forth, fall on the ground; go no further. Oh poison of Befent, come forth, fall on the ground. I am Isis, the goddess, the mistress of words of power. I am a weaver of spells, I know how to utter words so that they take effect. Hearken to me, Oh every reptile that bites (or stings), and fall on the ground. Oh poison of Mestet, go no further. Oh poison of Mestetef, rise not up in his body. Oh poison of Petet and Thetet, enter not his body. Oh poison of Maatet, fall on the ground. Ascend not into heaven, I command you by the beloved of Ra, the egg of the goose which appears from the sycamore. My words indeed rule to the uttermost limit of the night. I speak to you, Oh scorpions. I am alone and in sorrow, and our names will stink throughout the nomes.... The child shall live! The poison shall die! For Ra lives and the poison dies. Horus shall be saved through his mother Isis, and he who is stricken shall likewise be saved.'

Meanwhile the fire in the house of Usert was extinguished, and heaven was content with the utterance of Isis. Then the lady Usert was filled with sorrow because she had shut her door in the face of Isis, and she brought to the house of the peasant woman gifts for the goddess, whom she had apparently not recognised. The spells of the goddess produced, of course, the desired effect on the poison, and we may assume that the life of the child was restored to him. The second lot of gifts made to Isis represented his mother's gratitude.

Exactly when and how Isis made her way to a hiding place cannot be said, but she reached it in safety, and her son Horus was born there. The story of the death of Horus she tells in the following words: 'I am Isis. I conceived a child, Horus, and I brought him forth in a cluster of papyrus plants (or, bulrushes). I rejoiced exceedingly, for in him I saw one who would make answer for his father. I hid him, and I covered him up carefully, being afraid of that foul one [Set], and then I went to the town of Am, where the people gave thanks for me because they knew I could cause them trouble. I passed the day in collecting food for the child, and when I returned and took Horus into my arms, I found him, Horus, the beautiful one of gold, the boy, the child, lifeless! He had bedewed the ground with the water of his eye and with the foam of his lips. His body was motionless, his heart did not beat, and his muscles were relaxed.' Then Isis sent forth a bitter cry, and lamented loudly her misfortune, for now that Horus was dead she had none to protect her, or to take vengeance on Set. When the people heard her voice they went out to her, and they bewailed with her the greatness of her affliction.

But though all lamented on her behalf there was none who could bring back Horus to life. Then a 'woman who was well known in her town, a lady who was the mistress of property in her own right,' went out to Isis, and consoled her, and assured her that the child should live through his mother. And she said, 'A scorpion has stung him, the reptile Aunab has wounded him.' Then Isis bent her face over the child to find out if he breathed, and she examined the wound, and found that there was poison in it, and then taking him in her arms, 'she leaped about with him like a fish that is put upon hot coals,' uttering loud cries of lamentation.

During this outburst of grief the goddess Nephthys, her sister, arrived, and she too lamented and cried bitterly over her sister's loss; with her came the Scorpion-goddess Serqet. Nephthys at once advised Isis to cry out for help to Ra, for, said she, it is wholly impossible for the Boat of Ra to travel across the sky whilst Horus is lying dead. Then Isis cried out, and made supplication to the Boat of Millions of Years, and the Sun god stopped the Boat. Out of it came down Thoth, who was provided with powerful spells, and, going to Isis, he inquired concerning her trouble. 'What is it, what is it, Oh Isis, you goddess of spells, whose mouth has skill to utter them with supreme effect? Surely no evil thing has befallen Horus, for the Boat of Ra has him under its protection. I have come from the Boat of the Disk to heal

Horus.' Then Thoth told Isis not to fear, but to put away all anxiety from her heart, for he had come to heal her child, and he told her that Horus was fully protected because he was the Dweller in his disk, and the firstborn son of heaven, and the Great Dwarf, and the Mighty Ram, and the Great Hawk, and the Holy Beetle, and the Hidden Body, and the Governor of the Other World, and the Holy Benu Bird, and by the spells of Isis and the names of Osiris and the weeping of his mother and brethren, and by his own name and heart.

Turning towards the child Thoth began to recite his spells and said, 'Wake up, Horus! Your protection is established. Make you happy the heart of your mother Isis. The words of Horus bind up hearts and he comforts him that is in affliction. Let your hearts rejoice, Oh dwellers in the heavens. Horus who avenged his father shall make the poison retreat. That which is in the mouth of Ra shall circulate, and the tongue of the Great God shall overcome [opposition]. The Boat of Ra stands still and moves not, and the Disk (i.e. the Sun god) is in the place where it was yesterday to heal Horus for his mother Isis. Come to earth, draw nigh, Oh Boat of Ra, Oh mariners of Ra; make the boat move and convey food of the town of Sekhem (i.e. Letopolis) hither, to heal Horus for his mother Isis.... Come to earth, Oh poison! I am Thoth, the firstborn son, the son of Ra. Tem and the company of the gods have commanded me to heal Horus for his mother Isis. Oh Horus, Oh Horus, your Ka protects you, and your Image works protection for you. The poison is as the daughter of its own flame; it is destroyed because it smote the strong son. Your temples are safe, for Horus lives for his mother.' Then the child Horus returned to life, to the great joy of his mother, and Thoth went back to the Boat of Millions of Years, which at once proceeded on its majestic course, and all the gods from one end of heaven to the other rejoiced. Isis entreated either Ra or Thoth that Horus might be nursed and brought up by the goddesses of the town of Pe-Tep, or Buto, in the Delta, and at once Thoth committed the child to their care, and instructed them about his future. Horus grew up in Buto under their protection, and in due course fought a duel with Set, and vanquished him, and so avenged the wrong done to his father by Set.

THE LEGEND OF THE PRINCESS OF BEKHTEN

This is the story of the Possessed Princess of Bekhten and the driving out of the evil spirit that was in her by Khensu-Nefer-hetep. There may indeed be historical facts underlying the legend.

The text states that the king of Egypt, UsermaatRa-setepenRa Rameses-meri-Amen, i.e. Rameses II, a king of the nineteenth dynasty about 1300 BCE, was in the country of Nehern, or Mesopotamia, according to his yearly custom, and that the chiefs of the country, even those of the remotest districts from Egypt, came to do homage to him, and to bring him gifts, i.e. to pay tribute. Their gifts consisted of gold, lapis-lazuli, turquoise, and costly woods from the land of the god (Southern Arabia and a portion of the east coast of Africa near Somaliland), and each chief tried to outdo his neighbour in the magnificence of his gifts.

Among these tributary chiefs was the Prince of Bekhten, who, in addition to his usual gift, presented to the king his eldest daughter, and he spoke words of praise to the king, and prayed for his life. His daughter was beautiful, and the king thought her the most beautiful maiden in the world, and he gave her the name of Neferu-Ra and the rank of 'chief royal wife', i.e. the chief wife of Pharaoh. When His Majesty brought her to Egypt she was treated as the Queen of Egypt.

One day in the late summer, in the fifteenth year of his reign, his Majesty was in Thebes celebrating a festival in honour of Father Amen, the King of the gods, in the temple now known as the Temple of Luxor, when an official came and informed the king that 'an ambassador of the Prince of Bekhten had arrived bearing many gifts for the Royal Wife.' The ambassador was brought into the presence with his gifts, and having addressed the king in suitable words of honour, and smelt the ground before His Majesty, he told him that he had come to present a petition to him on behalf of the Queen's sister, who was called Bentresht (i.e. daughter of joy). The princess had been attacked by a disease, and the Prince of Bekhten asked His Majesty to send a skilled physician to see her. Straightway the king ordered his magicians (or medicine men) to appear before him, and also his nobles, and when they came he told them that he had sent for them to come and hear the ambassador's request. And, he added, choose one of your number who is both wise and skilful; their choice fell upon the royal scribe Tehuti-em-heb, and the king ordered him to depart to Bekhten to heal the princess. When the magician arrived in Bekhten he found that Princess Bentresht was under the influence of a malignant spirit, and that this spirit refused to be influenced in any way by him; in fact all his wisdom and skill availed nothing, for the spirit was hostile to him.

Then the Prince of Bekhten sent a second messenger to His Majesty, beseeching him to send a god to Bekhten to overcome the evil spirit, and he arrived in Egypt nine years after the arrival of the first ambassador. Again the king was celebrating a festival of Amen, and when he heard of the request of the Prince of Bekhten he went and stood before the statue of Khensu, called 'Nefer-hetep', and he said, 'Oh my fair lord, I present myself a second time before you on behalf of the daughter of the Prince of Bekhten.' He then went on to ask the god to transmit his power to Khensu, 'Pa-ari-sekher-em-Uast', the god who drives out the evil spirits which attack men, and to permit him to go to Bekhten and release the Princess from the power of the evil spirit. And the statue of Khensu Nefer-hetep bowed its head twice at each part of the petition, and this god bestowed a fourfold portion of his spirit and power on Khensu Pa-ari-sekher-em-Uast. Then the king ordered that the god should set out on his journey to Bekhten carried in a boat, which was accompanied by five smaller boats and by chariots and horses. The journey occupied seventeen months, and the god was welcomed on his arrival by the Prince of Bekhten and his nobles with suitable homage and many cries of joy. The god was taken to the place where Princess Bentresht was, and he used his magical power upon her with such good effect that she was made whole at once. The evil spirit who had possessed her came out of her and said to Khensu:

'Welcome, welcome, Oh great god, who drives away the spirits who attack men. Bekhten is yours; its people, both men and women, are your servants, and I myself am your servant. I am going to depart to the place whence I came, so that your heart may be content concerning the matter about which you have come. I beseech your Majesty to give the order that you and I and the Prince of Bekhten may celebrate a festival together.' The god Khensu bowed his head as a sign that he approved of the proposal, and told his priest to make arrangements with the Prince of Bekhten for offering up a great offering. Whilst this conversation was passing between the evil spirit and the god the soldiers stood by in a state of great fear. The Prince of Bekhten made the great offering before Khensu and the evil spirit, and the Prince and the god and the spirit rejoiced greatly. When the festival was ended the evil spirit, by the command of Khensu, 'departed to the place which he loved.' The Prince and all his people were immeasurably glad at the happy result, and he decided that he would consider the god to be a gift to him, and that he would not let him return to Egypt. So the god Khensu stayed for three years and nine months in Bekhten, but one day, whilst the Prince was sleeping on his bed, he had a vision in which he saw Khensu in the form of a hawk leave his shrine and mount up into the air, and then depart to Egypt. When he awoke he said to the priest of Khensu, 'The god who was staying with us has departed to Egypt; let his chariot also depart.' And the Prince sent off the statue of the god to Egypt, with rich gifts of all kinds and a large escort of soldiers and horses. In due course the party arrived in Egypt, and ascended to Thebes, and the god Khensu Pa-ari-sekher-em-Uast went into the temple of Khensu Nefer-hetep, and laid all the gifts which he had received from the Prince of Bekhten before him, and kept nothing for his own temple. This he did as a proper act of gratitude to Khensu Nefer-hetep, whose gift of a fourfold portion of his spirit had enabled him to overcome the power of the evil spirit that possessed the Princess of Bekhten. Thus Khensu returned from Bekhten in safety, and he re-entered his temple in the winter, in the thirty-third year of the reign of Rameses II.

The situation of Bekhten is unknown, but the name is probably not imaginary, and the country was perhaps a part of Western Asia. The time occupied by the god Khensu in getting there does not necessarily indicate that Bekhten was a very long way off, for a mission of the kind moved slowly in those leisurely days, and the priest of the god would probably be much delayed by the people in the towns and villages on the way, who would entreat him to ask the god to work cures on the diseased and afflicted that were brought to him. We must remember that when the Nubians made a treaty with Diocletian they stipulated that the goddess Isis should be allowed to leave her temple once a year, and to make a progress through the country so that men and women might ask her for boons, and receive them.

HISTORICAL LITERATURE

Of the kings of all Egypt who reigned during the historical period of Egyptian history that lasted around 3,300–4,400 years, we know the names of about two hundred, but only about one hundred and fifty have left behind them monuments that enable us to judge of their power and greatness. There is no evidence to show that the Egyptians ever wrote history in our sense of the word, and there is not in existence any surviving native work that can be regarded as a history of Egypt, other than 'the List of Kings' by Manetho, a skilled scribe and learned man who lived during the reign of Ptolemy II Philadelphus (289–246 BCE).

The reason the Egyptians did not write the history of their country from a general point of view is easily explained. Each king wished to be thought as great as possible, and each king's courtiers lost no opportunity of showing that they believed him to be the greatest king who had sat on the throne of Egypt. To magnify the deeds of his ancestors was neither politic nor safe, nor did it lead to favours or promotion. When foreign foes invaded Egypt and conquered it their followers raided the towns, burnt and destroyed all that could be got rid of and smashed the monuments recording the prowess of the king they had overthrown. The net result of all this is that the history of Egypt can only be partially constructed, and that the sources of our information are a series of texts that were written to glorify individual kings, and not to describe the history of a dynasty, or the general development of the country, or the working out of a policy. In attempting to draw up a connected account of a reign or period, the funerary inscriptions of high officials are often more useful than the royal inscriptions.

In the following pages are given extracts from annals, building inscriptions, narratives of conquests, and 'triumph inscriptions' of an official character, mostly from the twelfth dynasty (the royal historical inscriptions of the first eleven dynasties are very few, and their contents are meagre and unimportant). Specimens of the funerary inscriptions that describe military expeditions, and supply valuable information about the general history of events, will be given in the chapter on autobiographical inscriptions.

EXTRACT FROM THE PALERMO STONE

The earliest known annals are found on a stone which is preserved in the Museum at Palermo, and which for this reason is called 'The Palermo Stone'; the Egyptian text was first published by Signor A. Pellegrini in 1896. How the principal events of certain years of the reigns of kings from the Predynastic Period to the middle of the fifth dynasty are noted is shown by the following:

[Reign of] Seneferu. Year ...

The building of Tuataua ships of *mer* wood of a hundred capacity, and 60 royal boats of sixteen capacity.

Raid in the Land of the Blacks (i.e. the Sudan), and the bringing in of seven thousand prisoners, men and women, and twenty thousand cattle, sheep, and goats.

Building of the Wall of the South and North [called] House of Seneferu.

The bringing of forty ships of cedar wood (or perhaps 'laden with cedar wood').

[Height of the Nile.] Two cubits, two fingers.

[Reign of Seneferu.] Year ...

The making of thirty-five ... 122 cattle

The construction of one Tuataua ship of cedar wood of a hundred capacity, and two ships of *mer* wood of a hundred capacity.

The numbering for the seventh time.

[Height of the Nile.] Five cubits, one hand, one finger.

EDICT AGAINST THE BLACKS

This short inscription is dated in the eighth year of the reign of Usertsen III.

'The southern frontier in the eighth year under the Majesty of the King of the South and North, KhakauRa (Usertsen III), endowed with life forever. No Black whatsoever shall be permitted to pass [this stone] going down stream, whether travelling by land or sailing in a boat, with cattle, asses, goats, etc., belonging to the Blacks, with the exception of such as comes to do business in the country of Aqen or on an embassy. Such, however, shall be well entreated in every way. No boats belonging to the Blacks shall in future be permitted to pass down the river by the region of Heh (The district of Semnah and Kummah, about 64 km (40 miles) south of Wadi Halfah).'

INSCRIPTION OF USERTSEN III AT SEMNAH

The methods of Usertsen III and his opinions of the Sudanese people are illustrated by the following inscription which he set up at Semnah, a fort built by him at the foot of the Second Cataract.

'In the third month (i.e. January-February) of the season Pert His Majesty fixed the boundary of Egypt on the south at Heh (Semnah). I made my boundary and went further up the river than my fathers. I added greatly to it. I give commands [therein]. I am the king, and what is said by me is done. What my heart conceives my hand brings to pass. I am [like] the crocodile which seizes, carries off, and destroys without mercy. Words (or matters) do not remain dormant in my heart. To the coward soft talk suggests longsuffering; this I give not to my enemies. Him who attacks me I attack. I am silent in the matter that is for silence; I answer as the matter demands. Silence after an attack makes the heart of the enemy bold. The attack must be sudden like that of a crocodile. The man who hesitates is a coward, and a wretched creature is he who is defeated on his own territory and turned into a slave. The Black understands talk only. Speak to him and he falls prostrate. He fleas before a pursuer, and he pursues only him that flees. The Blacks are not bold men; on the contrary, they are timid and weak, and their hearts are cowed. My Majesty has seen them, and [what I say] is no lie.

'I seized their women, I carried off their workers in the fields, I came to their wells, I slew their bulls, I cut their corn and I burnt it. This I swear by the life of my father. I speak the truth; there is no doubt about the matter, and that which comes forth from my mouth cannot be gainsaid. Furthermore, every son of mine who shall keep intact this boundary which My Majesty has made, is indeed my son; he is the son who protects his father, if he keep intact the boundary of him that begot him. He who shall allow this boundary to be removed, and shall not fight for it, is not my son, and he has not been begotten by me. Moreover, My Majesty has caused to be made a statue of My Majesty on this my boundary, not only with the desire that you should prosper thereby, but that you should do battle for it.'

CAMPAIGN OF THOTHMES II IN THE SUDAN

The following extract illustrates the inscriptions in which the king describes an expedition into a hostile country which he has conducted with success. It is taken from an inscription of Thothmes II, which is cut in hieroglyphs on a rock by the side of the old road leading from Elephantine to Philae, and is dated in the first year of the king's reign.

The opening lines enumerate the names and titles of the king, and proclaim his sovereignty over the Haunebu, or the dwellers in the northern Delta and on the sea coast, Upper and Lower Egypt, Nubia and the Eastern Desert, including Sinai, Syria, the lands of the Fenkhu, and the countries that lie to the south of the modern town of Khartum.

The next section states: 'A messenger came in and saluted His Majesty and said: The vile people of Kash (i.e. Cush, Northern Nubia) are in revolt. The subjects of the Lord of the Two Lands (i.e. the King of Egypt) have become hostile to him, and they have begun to fight. The Egyptians [in Nubia] are driving down their cattle from the shelter of the stronghold which your father Thothmes [I] built to keep back the tribes of the South and the tribes of the Eastern Desert.' The last part of the envoy's message seems to contain a statement that some of the Egyptians who had settled in Nubia had thrown in their lot with the Sudanese folk who were in revolt.

The text continues: 'When His Majesty heard these words he became furious like a panther (or leopard), and he said: I swear by Ra, who loves me, and by my father Amen, king of the gods, lord of the thrones of the Two Lands, that I will not leave any male alive among them. Then His Majesty sent a multitude of soldiers into Nubia, now this was his first war, to effect the overthrow of all those who had rebelled against the Lord of the Two Lands, and of all those who were disaffected towards His Majesty. And the soldiers of His Majesty arrived in the miserable land of Kash, and overthrew these savages, and according to the command of His Majesty they left no male alive, except one of the sons of the miserable Prince of Kash, who was carried away alive with some of their servants to the place where His Majesty was. His Majesty took his seat on his throne, and when the prisoners whom his soldiers had captured were brought to him they were placed under the feet of the good god. Their land was reduced to its former state of subjection, and the people rejoiced and their chiefs were glad. They ascribed praise to the Lord of the Two Lands, and they glorified the god for his divine beneficence. This took place because of the bravery of His Majesty, whom his father Amen loved more than any other king of Egypt from the very beginning, the King of the South and North, AakheperenRa, the son of Ra, Thothmes (II), whose crowns are glorious, endowed with life, stability, and serenity, like Ra forever.'

CAPTURE OF MEGIDDO BY THOTHMES III

The following is the official account of the Battle of Megiddo in Syria, which was won by Thothmes III in the twenty-third year of his reign. The narrative is taken from the Annals of Thothmes III. The king set out from Thebes and marched into Syria, and received the submission of several small towns, and having made his way with difficulty through the hilly region to the south of the city of Megiddo, he camped there to prepare for the battle:

'Then the tents of His Majesty were pitched, and orders were sent out to the whole army, saying, "Arm yourselves, get your weapons ready, for we shall set out to do battle with the miserable enemy at daybreak." The king sat in his tent, the officers made their preparations, and the rations of the servants were provided. The military sentries went about crying, "Be firm of heart. Be firm of heart. Keep watch, keep watch. Keep watch over the life of the king in his tent." And a report was brought to His Majesty that the country was quiet, and that the foot soldiers of the south and north were ready.

'On the twenty-first day of the first month of the season Shemu (March-April) of the twenty-third year of the reign of His Majesty, and the day of the festival of the new moon, which was also the anniversary of the king's coronation, at dawn, behold, the order was given to set the whole army in motion. His Majesty set out in his chariot of silver-gold, and he had girded on himself the weapons of battle, like Horus the Slayer, the lord of might, and he was like Menthu [the War-god] of Thebes, and Amen his father gave strength to his arms. The southern half of the army was stationed on a hill to the south of the stream Kina, and the northern half lay to the south-west of Megiddo; His Majesty was between them, and Amen was protecting him and giving strength to his body. His Majesty at the head of his army attacked his enemies, and broke their line, and when they saw that he was overwhelming them they broke and fled to Megiddo in a panic, leaving their horses and their gold and silver chariots on the field. [The fugitives] were pulled up by the people over the walls into the city; now they let down their clothes by which to pull them up.

'If the soldiers of His Majesty had not devoted themselves to securing loot of the enemy, they would have been able to capture the city of Megiddo at the moment when the vile foes from Kadesh and the vile foes from this city were being dragged up hurriedly over the walls into this city;

for the terror of His Majesty had entered into them, and their arms dropped helplessly, and the serpent on his crown overthrew them. Their horses and their chariots [which were decorated] with gold and silver were seized as spoil, and their mighty men of war lay stretched out dead upon the ground like fishes, and the conquering soldiers of His Majesty went about counting their shares. And behold, the tent of the vile chief of the enemy, wherein was his son, was also captured. Then all the soldiers rejoiced greatly, and they glorified Amen, because he had made his son (i.e. the king) victorious on that day, and they praised His Majesty greatly, and acclaimed his triumph. And they collected the loot which they had taken, viz. hands [cut off the dead], prisoners, horses, chariots [decorated with] gold and silver,' etc.

In spite of the joy of the army Thothmes was angry with his troops for having failed to capture the city. Every rebel chief was in Megiddo, and its capture would have been worth more than the capture of a thousand other cities, for he could have slain all the rebel chiefs, and the revolt would have collapsed completely. Thothmes then laid siege to the city, and he threw up a strong wall round about it, through which none might pass, and the daily progress of the siege was recorded on a leather roll, which was subsequently preserved in the temple of Amen at Thebes. After a time the chiefs in Megiddo left their city and advanced to the gate in the siege-wall and reported that they had come to tender their submission to His Majesty, and it was accepted. They brought to him rich gifts of gold, silver, lapis-lazuli, turquoise, wheat, wine, cattle, sheep, goats, etc., and he reappointed many of the penitent chiefs to their former towns as vassals of Egypt. Among the gifts were 340 prisoners, 83 hands, 2,041 mares, 191 foals, 6 stallions, a royal chariot with a golden pole, a second royal chariot, 892 chariots, total 924 chariots; 2 royal coats of mail, 200 ordinary coats of mail, 502 bows, 7 tent poles inlaid with gold, 1929 cattle, 2000 goats, and 20,500 sheep.

SUMMARY OF THE REIGN OF RAMESES III

The reign of Rameses III is remarkable in the annals of the New Empire, and the great works which this king carried out, and his princely benefactions to the temples of Egypt, are described at great length in his famous papyrus in the British Museum (Harris, No. 1, No. 9999). The last section of the papyrus contains an excellent historical summary of the reign of Rameses III, and as it is one of the finest examples of this class of literature a translation of it is given here. The text is written in the hieratic character and reads:

King UsermaatRa-meri-Amen (Rameses III), life, strength, health [be to him!] the great god, said to the princes, and the chiefs of the land, and the soldiers, and the charioteers, and the Shartanau soldiers, and the multitudes of the bowmen, and all those who lived in the land of Ta-mera (Egypt), Hearken, and I will cause you to know the splendid deeds which I did when I was king of men. The land of Kamt was laid open to the foreigner, every man [was ejected] from his rightful holding, there was no 'chief mouth' (i.e. ruler) for many years in olden times until the new period [came]. The land of Egypt [was divided among] chiefs and governors of towns, each one slew his neighbour. ... Another period followed with years of nothingness (famine?). Arsu, a certain Syrian, was with them as governor, he made the whole land be one holding before him. He collected his vassals, and mulcted them of their possessions heavily. They treated the gods as if they were men, and they offered up no propitiatory offerings in their temples. Now when the gods turned themselves back to peace, and to the restoration of what was right in the land, according to its accustomed and proper form, they established their son who proceeded from their body to be Governor, life, strength, health [be to him!], of every land, upon their great throne, namely, UserkhaRa-setep-en-Amen-meri-Amen, life strength, health [be to him!], the son of Ra, Set-nekht-merr-Ra-meri-Amen, life, strength, health [be to him!]. He was like Khepra-Set when he is angry. He quieted the whole country which had been in rebellion. He slew the evil-hearted ones who were in Ta-mera (Egypt). He purified the great throne of Egypt. He was the Governor, life, strength, health [be to him!], of the Two Lands, on the throne of Amen. He made appear the faces that had withdrawn themselves. Of those who had been behind walls every man recognised his fellow. He endowed the temples with offerings to offer as was right to the Nine Gods, according to use and wont. He made me by a decree the Hereditary Chief in the seat of Keb. I became the 'Great High Mouth' of the lands of Egypt, I directed the affairs of the whole land, which had been made one. He set on his double horizon (i.e. he died) like the Nine Gods. There was performed for him what was performed for Osiris; sailing in his royal boat on the river, and resting [finally] in his house of eternity (i.e. the tomb) in Western Thebes.

My father Amen, the lord of the gods, Ra, Tem, and Ptah of the Beautiful Face made me to be crowned lord of the Two Lands in the place of my begetter. I received the rank of my father with cries of joy. The land had peace, being fed with offerings, and men rejoiced in seeing me, Governor, life, strength, health [be to him!], of the Two Lands, like Horus when he was made to be Governor of the Two Lands on the throne of Osiris. I was crowned with the Atef crown with the serpents, I bound on the crown with plumes, like Tatenn. I sat on the throne of Heru-Khuti (Harmakhis). I was arrayed in the ornaments [of sovereignty] like Tem. I made Ta-mera to possess many [different] kinds of men, the officers of the palace, the great chiefs, large numbers of horse and chariot soldiers, hundreds of thousands of them, the Shartanau and the Qehequ, who were numberless, soldiers of the bodyguard in tens of thousands, and the peasants belonging to Ta-mera.

I enlarged all the frontiers of Egypt, I conquered those who crossed over them in their [own] lands. I slaughtered the Tanauna in their islands; the Thakra and the Purastau were made into a holocaust. The Shartanau and the Uasheshu of the sea were made non-existent; they were seized [by me] at one time, and were brought as captives to Egypt, like the sand in the furrows. I provided fortresses for them to dwell in, and they were kept in check by my name. Their companies were very numerous, like hundreds of thousands. I assessed every one of them for taxes yearly, in

apparel and wheat from the stores and granaries. I crushed
the Saara and the tribes of the Shasu (nomad shepherds).
I carried off their tents from their men, and the equipment
thereof, and their flocks and herds likewise, which were
without number. They were put in fetters and brought along
as captives, as offerings to Egypt, and I gave them to the
Nine Gods as slaves for their temples.

Behold, I will also make you know concerning the other
schemes that have been carried out in Ta-mera during my
reign. The Labu (Libyans) and the Mashuashau had made
their dwelling in Egypt, for they had captured the towns
on the west bank of the Nile from Hetkaptah (Memphis)
to Qarabana. They had occupied also both banks of the
'Great River,' and they had been in possession of the towns
(or villages) of Kutut (perhaps the district of Canopus) for
very, very many years whilst they were [lords] over Egypt.
Behold, I crushed them and slaughtered them at one time
(i.e. in one engagement). I overthrew the Mashuashau, the
Libyans, the Asbatau, the Qaiqashau, the Shaiu, the Hasau,
and the Baqanau. [I] slaughtered them in their blood, and
they became piles of dead bodies. [Thus] I drove them away
from marching over the border of Egypt. The rest of them
I carried away, a vast multitude of prisoners, trussed like
geese in front of my horses, their women and their children
in tens of thousands, and their flocks and herds in hundreds
of thousands. I allotted fortresses to their chiefs, and they
lived there under my name. I made them officers of the
bowmen, and captains of the tribes; they were branded
with my name and became my slaves; their wives and their
children were likewise turned into slaves. Their flocks and

herds I brought into the House of Amen, and they became his live-stock forever.

I made a very large well in the desert of Aina. It had a girdle wall like a mountain of basalt(?), with twenty buttresses(?) in the foundation [on] the ground, and its height was thirty cubits, and it had bastions. The framework and the doors were cut out of cedar, and the bolts thereof and their sockets were of copper. I cut out large sea-going boats, with smaller boats before them, and they were manned with large crews, and large numbers of serving-men. With them were the officers of the bowmen of the boats, and there were trained captains and mates to inspect them. They were loaded with the products of Egypt which were without number, and they were in very large numbers, like tens of thousands. These were despatched to the Great Sea of the water of Qett (i.e. the Red Sea), they arrived at the lands of Punt, no disaster followed them, and they were in an effective state and were awe-inspiring. Both the large boats and the little boats were laden with the products of the Land of the God, and with all kinds of wonderful and mysterious things which are produced in those lands, and with vast quantities of the *anti* (myrrh) of Punt, which was loaded on to them by tens of thousands [of measures] that were without number. The sons of the chief of the Land of the God went in front of their offerings, their faces towards Egypt. They arrived and were sound and well at the mountain of Qebtit (Coptos; i.e. the part at the Red Sea end of the Valley of Hammamat), they moored their boats in peace, with the things which they had brought as offerings. To cross the desert they were loaded upon asses and on [the backs of] men, and they were [re]loaded into river-barges at the quay of Coptos. They were despatched down the river, they arrived during a festival, and some of the most wonderful of the offerings were carried into the presence of [My Majesty]. The children of their chiefs adored my face, they smelt the earth before my face, and rolled on the ground. I gave them to all the gods of this land to propitiate the two gods in front of me every morning.

I despatched my envoys to the desert of Aataka to the great copper workings that are in this place. Their sea-going boats were laden with [some of] them, whilst those who went through the desert rode on asses. Such a thing as this was never heard of before, from the time when kings began to reign. Their copper workings were found, and they were full of copper, and the metal was loaded by ten thousands [of measures] into their sea-going boats. They were despatched with their faces towards Egypt, and they arrived safely. The metal was lifted out and piled up under the veranda in the form of blocks (or ingots) of copper, vast numbers of them, as it were tens of thousands. They were in colour like gold of three refinings. I allowed everybody to see them, as they were wonderful things.

I despatched inspectors and overseers to the turquoise desert (i.e. Sinai) of my mother, the goddess Hathor, the lady of the turquoise. [They] carried to her silver, gold, byssus, fine (?) linen, and many things as numerous as the sand-grains, and laid them before her. And there were brought to me most wonderfully fine turquoises, real stones, in large numbers of bags, and laid out before me. The like had never been seen before – since kings began to reign.

I caused the whole country to be planted with groves of trees and with flowering shrubs, and I made the people to sit under the shade thereof. I made it possible for an Egyptian woman to walk with a bold step to the place whither she wished to go; no strange man attacked her, and no one on the road. I made the foot-soldiers and the charioteers sit down in my time, and the Shartanau and the Qehequ were in their towns lying at full length on their backs; they were unafraid, for there was no fighting man [to come] from Kash (Nubia), [and no] enemy from Syria. Their bows and their weapons of war lay idle in their barracks, and they ate their fill and drank their fill with shouts of joy. Their wives were with them, [their] children were by their side; there was no need to keep their eyes looking about them, their hearts were bold, for I was with them as strength and protection for their bodies. I kept alive (i.e. fed) the whole country, aliens, artisans, gentle and simple, men and women. I delivered a man from his foe and I gave him air. I rescued him from the strong man, him who was more honourable than the strong man. I made all men to have their rightful positions in their towns. Some I made to live [taking them] in the very chamber of the Tuat (the sick and needy who were at death's door). Where the land was bare I covered it over again; the land was well filled during my reign. I performed deeds of beneficence towards the gods as well as towards men; I had no property that belonged to the people. I served my office of king upon earth, as Governor of the Two Lands, and you were slaves under my feet without [complaint ?]. You were satisfactory to my heart, as were your good actions, and you performed my decrees and my words.

Behold, I have set in Akert (the Other World) like my father Ra. I am among the Great Companies of the gods of heaven, earth, and the Tuat. Amen-Ra has established my son upon my throne, he has received my rank in peace, as Governor of the Two Lands, and he is sitting upon the throne of Horus as Lord of the Two Nile-banks. He has put on himself the Atef crown like Ta-Tenn, UsermaatRa-setep-en-Amen, life, strength, health [be to him!], the eldest-born son of Ra, the self-begotten, Rameses (IV)-heqmaat-meri-Amen, life, strength, health [be to him!], the divine child, the son of Amen, who came forth from his body, rising as the Lord of the Two Lands, like Ta-Tenn. He is like a real son, favoured for his father's sake. Tie you yourselves to his sandals. Smell the earth before him. Do homage to him. Follow him at every moment. Praise him. Worship him. Magnify his beneficent actions as you do those of Ra every morning. Present before him your offerings [in] his Great House (i.e. palace), which is holy. Carry to him the 'blessings' (?) of the [tilled] lands and the deserts. Be strong to fulfil his words and the decrees that are uttered among you. Follow (?) his utterances, and you shall be safe under his Souls. Work all together for him in every work. Haul monuments for him, excavate canals for him, work for him in the work of your hands, and there will accrue to you his favour as well as his food daily. Amen has decreed for him his sovereignty upon earth, he has made this period of his life twice as long as that of any other king, the King of the South and North, the Lord of the Two Lands, UsermaatRa-setep-en-Amen, life, strength, health [be to him!], the son of Ra, the lord of crowns, Rameses

(IV)-heqmaat-meri-Amen, life, strength, health [be to him!], who is endowed with life forever.

THE INVASION AND CONQUEST OF EGYPT BY PIANKHI

The text describing the invasion and conquest of Egypt by Piankhi, King of Nubia, dated in the twenty-first year of the king's reign, is a very fine work. The king says:

'Listen to [the account of] what I have done more than my ancestors. I am a king, the emanation of the god, the living offspring of the god Tem, who at birth was ordained the Governor whom princes were to fear.'

His mother knew before his birth that he was to be the Governor, he the beneficent god, the beloved of the gods, the son of Ra who was made by his (the god's) hands, Piankhi-meri-Amen. One came and reported to His Majesty that the great prince Tafnekht had taken possession of all the country on the west bank of the Nile in the Delta, from the swamps even to Athi-taui (a fortress a few miles south of Memphis), that he had sailed up the river with a large force, that all the people on both sides of the river had attached themselves to him, and that all the princes and governors and heads of temple-towns had flocked to him, and that they were 'about his feet like dogs'. No city had shut its gates before him, on the contrary, Mer-Tem, Per-sekhem-kheper-Ra, Het-neter-Sebek, Per-Metchet, Thekansh, and all the towns in the west had opened their gates to him. In the east Het-benu, Taiutchait, Het-suten, and Pernebtepahet had opened to him, and he had besieged Hensu (Herakleopolis) and closely invested it. He had enclosed it like a serpent with its tail in its mouth. 'Those who would come out he will not allow to come out, and those who would go in he will not allow to go in, by reason of the fighting that takes place every day. He has thrown soldiers round about it everywhere.' Piankhi listened to the report undismayed, and he smiled, for his heart was glad. Presently further reports of the uprising came, and the king learned that Nemart, another great prince, had joined his forces to those of Tafnekht. Nemart had thrown down the fortifications of Nefrus, he had laid waste his own town, and had thrown off his allegiance to Piankhi completely.

Then Piankhi sent orders to Puarma and Las(?)-mer-sekni, the Nubian generals stationed in Egypt, and told them to assemble the troops, to seize the territory of Hermopolis, to besiege the city itself, to seize all the people, and cattle, and the boats on the river, and to stop all the agricultural operations that were going on; these orders were obeyed.

At the same time he despatched a body of troops to Egypt, with careful instructions as to the way in which they were to fight, and he bade them remember that they were fighting under the protection of Amen. He added, 'When you arrive at Thebes, opposite the Apts (i.e. the temples of Karnak and Luxor), go into the waters of the river and wash yourselves, then array yourselves in your finest apparel, unstring your bows, and lay down your spears. Let no chief imagine that he is as strong as the Lord of strength (i.e. Amen), for without him there is no strength. The weak of arm he makes strong of arm. Though the enemy be many they shall turn their backs in flight before the weak man, and one shall take captive a thousand. Wet yourselves with the water of his altars, smell the earth before him, and say: Oh make a way for us! Let us fight under the shadow of your sword, for a child, if he be but sent forth by you, shall vanquish multitudes when he attacks.' Then the soldiers threw themselves flat on their faces before His Majesty, saying, 'Behold, your name breeds strength in us. Your counsel guides your soldiers into port (i.e. to success). Your bread is in our bodies on every road, your beer quenches our thirst. Behold, your bravery has given us strength, and at the mere mention of your name there shall be victory. The soldiers who are led by a coward cannot stand firm. Who is like you? You are the mighty king who works with your hands, you are a master of the operations of war.'

Then the soldiers set out on their journey, and they sailed down the river and arrived at Thebes, and they did everything according to His Majesty's commands. And again they set out, and they sailed down the river, and they met many large boats sailing up the river, and they were full of soldiers and sailors, and mighty captains from the North land, every one fully armed to fight, and the soldiers of His Majesty inflicted a great defeat on them; they killed a very large but unknown number, they captured the boats, made the soldiers prisoners, whom they brought alive to the place where His Majesty was. This done they proceeded on their way to the region opposite Herakleopolis, to continue the battle. Again the soldiers of Piankhi attacked the troops of the allies, and defeated and routed them utterly, and captured their boats on the river. A large number of the enemy succeeded in escaping, and landed on the west bank of the river at Per-pek. At dawn these were attacked by Piankhi's troops, who slew large numbers of them, and [captured] many horses; the remainder, utterly terror-stricken, fled northwards, carrying with them the news of the worst defeat which they had ever experienced.

Nemart, one of the rebel princes, fled up the river in a boat, and landed near the town of Un (Hermopolis), wherein he took refuge. The Nubians promptly beleaguered the town with such rigour that no one could go out of it or come in. Then they reported their action to Piankhi, and when he had read their report, he growled like a panther, and said, 'Is it possible that they have permitted any of the Northmen to live and escape to tell the tale of his flight, and have not killed them to the very last man? I swear by my life, and by my love for Ra, and by the grace which Father Amen has bestowed upon me, that I will myself sail down the river, and destroy what the enemy has done, and I will make him retreat from the fight forever.' Piankhi also declared his intention of stopping at Thebes on his way down the river, so that he might assist at the Festival of the New Year, and might look upon the face of the god Amen in his shrine at Karnak and, said he, 'After that I will make the Lands of the North taste my fingers.' When the soldiers in Egypt heard of their lord's wrath, they attacked Per-Metchet (Oxyrrhynchus), and they 'overran it like a water-flood'; a report of the success was sent to Piankhi, but he was not satisfied. Then they attacked Ta-tehen (Tehnah?), which was filled with northern soldiers. The Nubians built a tower with a battering ram and breached the walls, and they poured into the town and slew everyone they found. Among the dead was the son of the rebel prince Tafnekht. This success was also reported to Piankhi, but still he was not satisfied. Het-Benu was also captured, and still he was not satisfied.

In the middle of the summer Piankhi left Napata (Gebel Barkal) and sailed down to Thebes, where he celebrated the New Year Festival. From there he went down the river to Un (Hermopolis), where he landed and mounted his war chariot; he was furiously angry because his troops had not destroyed the enemy utterly, and he growled at them like a panther. Having pitched his camp to the south-west of the city, he began to besiege it. He threw up a mound round about the city, he built wooden stages on it which he filled with archers and slingers, and these succeeded in killing the people of the city daily. After three days 'the city stank,' and envoys came bearing rich gifts to sue for peace. With the envoys came the wife of Nemart and her ladies, who cast themselves flat on their faces before the ladies of Piankhi's palace, saying, 'We come to you, Oh royal wives, royal daughters, and royal sisters. Pacify for us Horus (i.e. the King), the Lord of the Palace, whose Souls are mighty, and whose word of truth is great.'

A break of fifteen lines occurs in the text here, and the words that immediately follow the break indicate that Piankhi is upbraiding Nemart for his folly and wickedness in destroying his country, wherein 'not a full-grown son is seen with his father, all the districts round about being filled with children.' Nemart acknowledged his folly, and then swore fealty to Piankhi, promising to give him more gifts than any other prince in the country. Gold, silver, lapis-lazuli, turquoise, copper, and precious stones of all kinds were then presented, and Nemart himself led a horse with his right hand, and held a sistrum made of gold and lapis-lazuli in his left.

Piankhi then arose and went into the temple of Thoth, and offered up oxen, and calves, and geese to the god, and to the Eight Gods of the city. After this he went through Nemart's palace, and then visited the stables 'where the horses were, and the stalls of the young horses, and he perceived that they had been suffering from hunger. And he said, 'I swear by my own life, and by the love which I have for Ra, who renews the breath of life in my nostrils, that, in my opinion, to have allowed my horses to suffer hunger is the worst of all the evil things which you have done in the perversity of your heart.' A list was made of the goods that were handed over to Piankhi, and a portion of them was reserved for the temple of Amen at Thebes.

The next prince to submit was the Governor of Herakleopolis, and when he had laid before Piankhi his gifts he said: 'Homage to you, Horus, mighty king, Bull, conqueror of bulls. I was in a pit in hell. I was sunk deep in the depths of darkness, but now light shines on me. I had no friend in the evil day, and none to support me in the day of battle. You only, Oh mighty king, who have rolled away the darkness that was on me [art my friend]. Henceforward I am your servant, and all my possessions are yours. The city of Hensu shall pay tribute to you. You are the image of Ra, and are the master of the imperishable stars. He was a king, and you are a king; he perished not, and you shall not perish.'

From Hensu, Piankhi went down to the canal leading to the Fayyum and to Illahun and found the town gates shut in his face. The inhabitants, however, speedily changed their minds, and opened the gates to Piankhi, who entered with his troops, and received tribute, and slew no one. Town after town submitted as Piankhi advanced northwards, and none barred his progress until he reached Memphis, the gates of which were shut fast. When Piankhi saw this he sent a message to the Memphites, saying: 'Shut not your gates, and fight not in the city that has belonged to Shu (the son of Khepera, or Tem, or Nebertcher) forever. He who wishes to enter may do so, he who wishes to come out may do so, and he who wishes to travel about may do so. I will make an offering to Ptah and the gods of White Wall (Memphis). I will perform the ceremonies of Seker in the Hidden Shrine. I will look upon the god of his South Wall (i.e. Ptah), and I will sail down the river in peace. No man of Memphis shall be harmed, not a child shall cry out in distress. Look at the homes of the South! None has been slain except those who blasphemed the face of the god, and only the rebels have suffered at the block.' These pacific words of Piankhi were not believed, and the people of Memphis not only kept their gates shut, but manned the city walls with soldiers, and they were foolish enough to slay a small company of Nubian artisans and boatmen whom they found on the quay of Memphis. Tafnekht, the rebel prince of Sais, entered Memphis by night, and addressed eight thousand of his troops who were there, and encouraged them to resist Piankhi. He said to them: 'Memphis is filled with the bravest men of war in all the Northland, and its granaries are filled with wheat, barley, and grain of all kinds. The arsenal is full of weapons. A wall goes round the city, and the great fort is as strong as the mason could make it. The river flows along the east side, and no attack can be made there. The byres are full of cattle, and the treasury is well filled with gold, silver, copper, apparel, incense, honey, and unguents.... Defend the city till I return.' Tafnekht mounted a horse and rode away to the north.

At daybreak Piankhi went forth to reconnoitre, and he found that the waters of the Nile were lapping the city walls on the north side of the city, where the sailing craft were tied up. He also saw that the city was extremely well fortified, and that there was no means whereby he could effect an entrance into the city through the walls. Some of his officers advised him to throw up a mound of earth about the city, but this counsel was rejected angrily by Piankhi, for he had thought out a simpler plan. He ordered all his boats and barges to be taken to the quay of Memphis, with their bows towards the city wall; as the water lapped the foot of the wall, the boats were able to come quite close to it, and their bows were nearly on a level with the top of the wall. Then Piankhi's men crowded into the boats, and, when the word of command was given, they jumped from the bows of the boats on to the wall, entered the houses built near it, and then poured into the city. They rushed through the city like a waterflood, and large numbers of the natives were slain, and large numbers taken prisoners.

Next morning Piankhi set guards over the temples to protect the property of the gods, then he went into the great temple of Ptah and reinstated the priests, and they purified the holy place with natron and incense, and offered up many offerings. When the report of the capture of Memphis spread abroad, numerous local chiefs came to Piankhi, and did homage, and gave him tribute.

From Memphis he passed over to the east bank of the Nile to make an offering to Temu of Heliopolis. He bathed his face in the water of the famous 'Fountain of the Sun', he offered white bulls to Ra at Shaiqaem-Anu, and he went into the great temple of the Sun god. The chief priest welcomed him and blessed him; 'he performed the ceremonies of the Tuat chamber, he girded on the *seteb* garment, he censed himself, he was sprinkled with holy water, and he offered (?) flowers in the chamber in which the stone, wherein the spirit of the Sun god abode at certain times, was preserved. He went up the step leading to the shrine to look upon Ra, and stood there. He broke the seal, unbolted and opened the doors of the shrine, and looked upon Father Ra in Het-benben. He paid adoration to the two Boats of Ra (Matet and Sektet), and then closed the doors of the shrine and sealed them with his own seal.'

Piankhi returned to the west bank of the Nile, and pitched his camp at Kaheni, from where came a number of princes to tender their submission and offer gifts to him. After a time it was reported to Piankhi that Tafnekht, the head of the rebellion, had laid waste his town, burnt his treasury and his boats, and had entrenched himself at Mest with the remainder of his army. Thereupon Piankhi sent troops to Mest, and they slew all its inhabitants. Then Tafnekht sent an envoy to Piankhi asking for peace, and he said, 'Be at peace [with me]. I have not seen your face during the days of shame. I cannot resist your fire, the terror of you has conquered me. Behold, you are Nubti (the war-god of Ombos in Upper Egypt), the Governor of the South, and Menth (the war-god of Hermonthis in Upper Egypt), the Bull with strong arms. You did not find your servant in any town towards which you have turned your face. I went as far as the swamps of the Great Green (i.e. the Mediterranean), because I was afraid of your Souls, and because your word is a fire that works evil for me. Is not the heart of your Majesty cooled by reason of what you have done to me? Behold, I am indeed a most wretched man. Punish me not according to my abominable deeds, weigh them not in a balance as against weights; your punishment of me is already threefold. Leave the seed, and you shall find it again in due season. Dig not up the young root which is about to put forth shoots. Your Ka and the terror of you are in my body, and the fear of you is in my bones. I have not sat in the house of drinking beer, and no one has brought to me the harp. I have only eaten the bread which hunger demanded, and I have only drunk the water needed [to slake] my thirst. From the day in which you did hear my name misery has been in my bones, and my head has lost its hair. My apparel shall be rags until Neith (the chief goddess of Saïs, the city of Tafnekht) is at peace with me. You have brought on me the full weight of misery; Oh turn you your face towards me, for, behold, this year has separated my Ka from me. Purge your servant of his rebellion. Let my goods be received into your treasury, gold, precious stones of all kinds, and the finest of my horses, and let these be my indemnity to you for everything. I beseech you to send an envoy to me quickly, so that he may make an end of the fear that is in my heart. Verily I will go into the temple, and in his presence I will purge myself, and swear an oath of allegiance to you by the God.'

And Piankhi sent to him General Puarma and General Petamennebnesttaui, and Tafnekht loaded them with gold, and silver, and raiment, and precious stones, and he went into the temple and took an oath by the God that he would never again disobey the king, or make war on a neighbour, or invade his territory without Piankhi's knowledge. So Piankhi was satisfied and forgave him. After this the town of Crocodilopolis tendered its submission, and Piankhi was master of all Egypt. Then two Governors of the South and two Governors of the North came and smelt the ground before Piankhi, and these were followed by all the kings and princes of the North, 'and their legs were [weak] like those of women.' As they were uncircumcised and were eaters of fish they could not enter the king's palace; only one, Nemart, who was ceremonially pure, entered the palace. Piankhi was now tired of conquests, and he had all the loot which he had collected loaded on his barges, together with goods from Syria and the Land of the God, and he sailed up the river towards Nubia. The people on both banks rejoiced at the sight of His Majesty, and they sang hymns of praise to him as he journeyed southwards, and acclaimed him as the Conqueror of Egypt. They also invoked blessings on his father and mother, and wished him long life. When he returned to Gebel Barkal (Napata) he had the account of his invasion and conquest of Egypt cut upon a large grey granite stele about 1.8 metres (6 feet) high and 1.4 metres

(4 feet 8 inches) wide, and set up in his temple, among the ruins of which it was discovered accidentally by an Egyptian officer who was serving in the Egyptian Sudan in 1862.

AUTOBIOGRAPHICAL LITERATURE

Attention has already been called to the very great importance of the autobiographies of the military and administrative officials of the pharaohs, and a selection of them will now be given. They are, in many cases, the only sources of information which we possess about certain wars and about the social conditions of the periods during which they were composed, and they often describe events about which official Egyptian history is altogether silent.

Most of these autobiographies are found cut upon the walls of tombs, and, though according to modern notions their writers may seem to have been very conceited, and their language exaggerated and bombastic, the inscriptions bear throughout the impression of truth, and the facts recorded in them have therefore special value. The narratives are usually simple and clear, and as long as they deal with matters of fact they are easily understood, but when the writers describe their own personal characters and their moral excellences their meaning is sometimes not plain. Such autobiographies are sometimes very useful in settling the chronology of a doubtful period of history – for example, Ptah-shepses, a distinguished man born in the reign of MenkauRa, lived under eight kings, and so his inscription makes it possible to arrange their reigns in correct chronological order.

THE AUTOBIOGRAPHY OF UNA

This inscription was found cut in hieroglyphs upon a slab of limestone fixed in Una's tomb at Abydos; it is now in the Egyptian Museum in Cairo. It reads:

The Duke, the Governor of the South, the judge belonging to Nekhen, prince of Nekheb, the *smer uat* vassal of Osiris Khenti Amenti, Una, says: 'I was a child girded with a girdle under the Majesty of King Teta. My rank was that of overseer of tillage (?), and I was deputy inspector of the estates of Pharaoh.... I was chief of the *teb* chamber under the Majesty of Pepi. His Majesty gave me the rank of *smer* and deputy priest of his pyramid-town. Whilst I held the rank of ... His Majesty made me a "judge belonging to Nekhen". His heart was more satisfied with me than with any other of his servants. Alone I heard every kind of private case, there being with me only the Chief Justice and the Governor of the town ... in the name of the king, of the royal household, and of the Six Great Houses. The heart of the king was more satisfied with me than with any other of his high officials, or any of his nobles, or any of his servants. I asked the Majesty of [my] Lord to permit a white stone sarcophagus to be brought for me from Raau. His Majesty made the keeper of the royal seal, assisted by a body of workmen, bring this sarcophagus over from Raau in a barge, and he came bringing with it in a large boat, which was the property of the king, the cover of the sarcophagus, the slabs for the door, and the slabs for the setting of the stele, and a pair of stands for censers (?), and a tablet for offerings. Never before was the like of this done for any servant. [He did this for me] because I was perfect in the heart of His Majesty, because I was acceptable to the heart of His Majesty, and because the heart of His Majesty was satisfied with me.

'Behold, I was "judge belonging to Nekhen" when His Majesty made me a *smer uat*, and overseer of the estates of Pharaoh, and ... of the four overseers of the estate of Pharaoh who were there. I performed my duties in such a way as to secure His Majesty's approval, both when the Court was in residence and when it was travelling, and in appointing officials for duty. I acted in such a way that His Majesty praised me for my work above everything. During the secret inquiry which was made in the king's household concerning the Chief Wife Amtes, His Majesty made me enter to hear the case by myself. There was no Chief Justice there, and no Town Governor, and no nobleman, only myself, and this was because I was able and acceptable to the heart of His Majesty, and because the heart of His Majesty was filled with me. I did the case into writing, I alone, with only one judge belonging to Nekhen, and yet my rank was only that of overseer of the estates of Pharaoh. Never before did a man of my rank hear the case of a secret of the royal household, and His Majesty only made me hear it because I was more perfect to the heart of His Majesty than any officer of his, or any nobleman of his, or any servant of his.

'His Majesty had to put down a revolt of the Aamu dwellers on the sand (i.e. the nomads on the Marches of the Eastern Desert). His Majesty collected an army of many thousands strong in the South everywhere, beyond Abu (Elephantine) and northwards of Aphroditopolis, in the

Northland (Delta) everywhere, in both halves of the region, in Setcher, and in the towns like Setcher, in Arthet of the Blacks, in Matcha of the Blacks, in Amam of the Blacks, in Uauat of the Blacks, in Kaau of the Blacks, and in the Land of Themeh. His Majesty sent me at the head of this army. Behold, the dukes, the royal seal-bearers, the *smer uats* of the palace, the chiefs, the governors of the forts (?) of the South and the North, the *smeru*, the masters of caravans, the overseers of the priests of the South and North, and the overseers of the stewards, were commanding companies of the South and the North, and of the forts and towns which they ruled, and of the Blacks of these countries, but it was I who planned tactics for them, although my rank was only that of an overseer of the estates of Pharaoh of.... No one quarrelled with his fellow, no one stole the food or the sandals of the man on the road, no one stole bread from any town, and no one stole a goat from any encampment of people. I despatched them from North Island, the gate of Ihetep, the Uart of Heru-neb-Maat. Having this rank ... I investigated (?) each of these companies (or regiments); never had any servant investigated (?) companies in this way before. This army returned in peace, having raided the Land of the dwellers on sand. This army returned in peace, having thrown down the fortresses thereof. This army returned in peace, having cut down its fig-trees and vines. This army returned in peace, having set fire [to the temples] of all its gods. This army returned in peace, having slain the soldiers there in many tens of thousands. This army returned in peace, bringing back with it vast numbers of the fighting men thereof as living prisoners. His Majesty praised me for this exceedingly. His Majesty sent me to lead this army five times, to raid the Land of the dwellers on sand, whensoever they rebelled with these companies. I acted in such a way that His Majesty praised me exceedingly. When it was reported that there was a revolt among the wild desert tribes of the Land of Shert (a part of Syria possibly) ... I set out with these warriors in large transports, and sailed until I reached the end of the high land of Thest, to the north of the Land of the dwellers on sand, and when I had led the army up I advanced and attacked the whole body of them, and I slew every rebel among them.

'I was the ... of the Palace, and bearer of the [royal] sandals, when His Majesty the King of the South and North, MerenRa, my ever living Lord, made me Duke and Governor of the South land beyond Abu (Elephantine) and of the district north of Aphroditopolis, because I was perfect to the heart of His Majesty, because I was acceptable to the heart of His Majesty, and because the heart of His Majesty was satisfied with me. I was ... [of the Palace], and sandal-bearer when His Majesty praised me for displaying more watchfulness (or attention) at Court in respect of the appointment of officials for duty than any of his princes, or nobles, or servants. Never before was this rank bestowed on any servant. I performed the duties of Governor of the South to the satisfaction [of every one]. No one complained of (or quarrelled with) his neighbour; I carried out work of every kind. I counted everything that was due to the Palace in the South twice, and all the labour that was due to the Palace in the South I counted twice. I served the office of Prince, ruling as a Prince ought to rule in the

South; the like of this was never before done in the South. I acted in such a way that His Majesty praised me for it. His Majesty sent me to the Land of Abhat to bring back a sarcophagus, "the lord of the living one", with its cover, and a beautiful and magnificent pyramidion for the Queen's pyramid [which is called] Khanefer MerenRa. His Majesty sent me to Abu to bring back a granite door and its table for offerings, with slabs of granite for the stele door and its framework, and to bring back granite doors and tables for offerings for the upper room in the Queen's pyramid, Khanefer MerenRa. I sailed down the Nile to the pyramid Khanefer MerenRa with six lighters, and three barges, and three floats(?), accompanied by one war boat. Never before had any [official] visited Abhat and Abu with [only] one war boat since kings have reigned. Whensoever His Majesty gave an order for anything to be done I carried it out thoroughly according to the order which His Majesty gave concerning it.

'His Majesty sent me to Het-nub to bring back a great table for offerings of *rutt* stone (quartzite sandstone?) of Het-nub. I made this table for offerings reach him in seventeen days. It was quarried in Het-nub, and I caused it to float down the river in a lighter. I cut out the planks for him in acacia wood, sixty cubits long and thirty cubits broad; they were put together in seventeen days in the third month (May-June) of the Summer Season. Behold, though there was no water in the basins (?) it arrived at the pyramid Khanefer MerenRa in peace. I performed the work throughout in accordance with the order which the Majesty of my Lord had given to me. His Majesty sent me to excavate five canals in the South, and to make three lighters, and four barges of the acacia wood of Uauat. Behold, the governors of Arthet, Uauat, and Matcha brought the wood for them, and I finished the whole of the work in one year. [When] they were floated they were loaded with huge slabs of granite for the pyramid Khanefer MerenRa; moreover, all of them were passed through these five canals ... because I ascribed more majesty, and praise (?), and worship to the Souls of the King of the South and North, MerenRa, the ever living, than to any of the gods.... I carried out everything according to the order which his divine Ka gave me.

'I was a person who was beloved by his father, and praised by his mother, and gracious to his brethren, I the Duke, a real Governor of the South, the vassal of Osiris, Una.'

THE AUTOBIOGRAPHY OF HERKHUF

This inscription is cut in hieroglyphs upon a slab of stone, which was originally in the tomb of Herkhuf at Aswân, and is now in the Egyptian Museum in Cairo and upon parts of the walls of his tomb. Herkhuf was a Duke, a *smer uat*, a Kher-heb priest, a judge belonging to Nekhen, the Lord of Nekheb, a bearer of the royal seal, the shekh of the caravans, and an administrator of very high rank in the South. All these titles, and the following lines, together with prayers for offerings, are cut above the door of his tomb. He says:

'I came this day from my town. I descended from my nome. I built a house and set up doors. I dug a lake and

I planted sycamore trees. The King praised me. My father made a will in my favour. I am perfect.... [I am a person] who is beloved by his father, praised by his mother, whom all his brethren loved. I gave bread to the hungry man, raiment to the naked, and him who had no boat I ferried over the river. Oh living men and women who are on the earth, who shall pass by this tomb in sailing down or up the river, and who shall say, "A thousand bread-cakes and a thousand vessels of beer to the lord of this tomb", I will offer them for you in Khert Nefer (the Other World). I am a perfect spirit, equipped [with spells], and a Kher-heb priest whose mouth has knowledge. If any young man shall come into this tomb as if it were his own property I will seize him like a goose, and the Great God shall pass judgment on him for it. I was a man who spoke what was good, and repeated what was loved. I never uttered any evil word concerning servants to a man of power, for I wished that I might stand well with the Great God. I never gave a decision in a dispute between brothers which had the effect of robbing a son of the property of his father.'

Herkhuf, the Duke, the *smer uat*, the chamberlain, the Judge belonging to Nekhen, the Lord of Nekheb, bearer of the royal seal, the *smer uat*, the Kher-heb priest, the governor of the caravans, the member of council for the affairs of the South, the beloved of his Lord, Herkhuf, who brings the things of every desert to his Lord, who brings the offering of royal apparel, governor of the countries of the South, who sets the fear of Horus in the lands, who does what his lord applaudeth, the vassal of Ptah-seker, says:

'His Majesty MerenRa, my Lord, sent me with my father Ara, the *smer uat* and Kher-heb priest, to the land of Amam to open up a road into this country. I performed the journey in seven months. I brought back gifts of all kinds from that place, making beautiful the region (?); there was very great praise to me for it. His Majesty sent me a second time by myself. I started on the road of Abu (Elephantine), I came back from Arthet, Mekher, Terres, Artheth, in a period of eight months. I came back and I brought very large quantities of offerings from this country. Never were brought such things to this land. I came back from the house of the Chief of Setu and Arthet, having opened up these countries. Never before had any *smer* or governor of the caravan who had appeared in the country of Amam opened up a road. Moreover, His Majesty sent me a third time to Amam. I started from ... on the Uhat road, and I found the Governor of Amam was then marching against the Land of Themeh, to fight the Themeh, in the western corner of the sky. I set out after him to the Land of Themeh, and made him to keep the peace, whereupon he praised all the gods for the King (of Egypt). [Here follow some broken lines.] I came back from Amam with three hundred asses laden with incense, ebony, *heknu*, grain, panther skins, ivory, ... boomerangs, and valuable products of every kind. When the Chief of Arthet, Setu, and Uauat saw the strength and great number of the warriors of Amam who had come back with me to the Palace, and the soldiers who had been sent with me, this chief brought out and gave to me bulls, and sheep, and goats. And he guided me on the roads of the plains of Arthet, because I was more perfect, and more watchful (or alert) than any other *smer* or governor of a caravan who had ever been despatched to Amam. And when the servant (i.e. Herkhuf) was sailing down the river to the capital (or Court) the king made the duke, the *smer uat*, the overseer of the bath, Khuna (or Una) sail up the river with boats loaded with date wine, *mesuq* cakes, bread-cakes, and beer.' (Herkhuf's titles are here repeated.)

Herkhuf made a fourth journey into the Sudan, and when he came back he reported his successes to the new king, Pepi II, and told him that among other remarkable things he had brought back from Amam a dancing dwarf, or pygmy. The king then wrote a letter to Herkhuf and asked him to send the dwarf to him in Memphis. The text of this letter Herkhuf had cut on the front of his tomb, and it reads thus:

Royal seal. The fifteenth day of the third month of the Season Akhet (September-October) of the second year. Royal despatch to the *smer uat*, the Kher-heb priest, the governor of the caravan, Herkhuf. I have understood the words of this letter which you have made to the king in his chamber to make him know that you have returned in peace from Amam, together with the soldiers who were with you. You say in this your letter that there have been brought back by you great and beautiful offerings of all kinds, which Hathor, the Lady of Ammaau, has given to the divine Ka of the King of the South and North, NeferkaRa, the everliving, forever.

You say in this your letter that there has been brought back by you [also] a pygmy (or dwarf) who can dance the dance of the god, from the Land of the Spirits, like the pygmy whom the seal-bearer of the god Baurtet brought back from Punt in the time of Assa. You say to [my] Majesty, 'The like of him has never been brought back by any other person who has visited Amam.' Behold, every year you perform what your Lord wishes and praises. Behold, you pass your days and your nights meditating about doing what your Lord orders, and wishes, and praises. And His Majesty will confer on you so many splendid honours, which shall give renown to your grandson forever, that all the people shall say when they have heard what [my] Majesty has done for you, 'Was there ever anything like this that has been done for the *smer uat* Herkhuf when he came back from Amam because of the sagacity (or attention) which he displayed in doing what his Lord commanded, and wished for, and praised?'

Come down the river at once to the Capital. Bring with you this pygmy whom you have brought from the Land of the Spirits, alive, strong, and healthy, to dance the dance of the god, and to cheer and gratify the heart of the King of the South and North, NeferkaRa, the everliving. When he comes down with you in the boat, cause trustworthy men to be about him on both sides of the boat, to prevent him from falling into the water. When he is asleep at night cause trustworthy men to sleep by his side on his bedding. See [that he is there] ten times [each] night. [My] Majesty wishes to see this pygmy more than any offering of the countries of Ba and Punt. If when you arrive at the Capital, this pygmy who is with you is alive, and strong, and in good health, [My] Majesty will confer upon you a greater honour than that which was conferred upon the bearer of the seal Baurtet in the time of Assa, and as great is the wish of [My]

Majesty to see this pygmy orders have been brought to the *smer*, the overseer of the priests, the governor of the town ... to arrange that rations for him shall be drawn from every station of supply, and from every temple without....

THE AUTOBIOGRAPHY OF AMENI AMENEMHAT

This inscription is cut in hieroglyphs on the doorposts of the tomb of Ameni at Beni-hasan in Upper Egypt. It is dated in the forty-third year of the reign of Usertsen I, a king of the twelfth dynasty, about 2400 BCE After giving the date and a list of his titles, Ameni says:

'I followed my Lord when he sailed to the South to overthrow his enemies in the four countries of Nubia. I sailed to the south as the son of a duke, and as a bearer of the royal seal, and as a captain of the troops of the Nome of Mehetch, and as a man who took the place of his aged father, according to the favour which he enjoyed in the king's house and the love that was his at Court. I passed through Kash in sailing to the South. I set the frontier of Egypt further southwards, I brought back offerings, and the praise of me reached the skies. His Majesty set out and overthrew his enemies in the vile land of Kash. I returned, following him as an alert official. There was no loss among my soldiers.

'[And again] I sailed to the South to fetch gold ore for the Majesty of the King of the South, the King of the North, KheperkaRa (Usertsen I), the ever living. I sailed to the south with the Erpa and Duke, the eldest son of the king, of his body Ameni (he afterwards reigned as Amenemhat II). I sailed to the south with a company of four hundred chosen men from my troops; they returned in safety, none of them having been lost. I brought back the gold which I was expected to bring, and I was praised for it in the house of the king; the prince [Ameni] praised God for me. [And again] I sailed to the south to bring back gold ore to the town of Qebti (Coptos) with the Erpa, the Duke, the governor of the town, and the chief officer of the Government, Usertsen, life, strength, health [be to him!]. I sailed to the south with a company of six hundred men, every one being a mighty man of war of the Nome of Mehetch. I returned in peace, with all my soldiers in good health (or safe), having performed everything which I had been commanded to do.

'I was a man who was of a conciliatory disposition, one whose love [for his fellows] was abundant, and I was a governor who loved his town. I passed [many] years as governor of the Mehetch Nome. All the works (i.e. the forced labour) due to the palace were performed under my direction. The overseers of the chiefs of the districts of the herdsmen of the Nome of Mehetch gave me three thousand bulls, together with their gear for ploughing, and I was praised because of it in the king's house every year of making [count] of the cattle. I took over all the products of their works to the king's house, and there were no liabilities against me in any house of the king. I worked the Nome of Mehetch to its farthest limit, travelling frequently [through it]. No peasant's daughter did I harm, no widow did I wrong, no field labourer did I oppress, no herdsman did I repulse. I did not seize the men of any master of five field labourers for the forced labour (corvée). There was no man in abject want during the period of my rule, and there was no man hungry in my time. When years of hunger came, I rose up and had ploughed all the fields of the Nome of Mehetch, as far as it extended to the south and to the north, [thus] keeping alive its people, and providing the food thereof, and there was no hungry man therein. I gave to the widow as to the woman who possessed a husband. I made no distinction between the elder and the younger in whatsoever I gave. When years of high Nile floods came, the lords (i.e. the producers) of wheat and barley, the lords of products of every kind, I did not cut off (or deduct) what was due on the land [from the years of low Nile floods], I Ameni, the vassal of Horus, the Smiter of the Rekhti, generous of hand, stable of feet, lacking avarice because of his love for his town, learned in traditions (?), who appears at the right moment, without thought of guile, the vassal of Khnemu, highly favoured in the king's house, who bows before ambassadors, who performs the behests of the nobles, speaker of the truth, who judges righteously between two litigants, free from the word of deceit, skilled in the methods of the council chamber, who discovers the solution of a difficult question, Ameni.'

THE AUTOBIOGRAPHY OF THETHA

This inscription is cut in hieroglyphs upon a large rectangular slab of limestone now preserved in the British Museum (No. 100). It belongs to the period of the eleventh dynasty, when texts of the kind are very rare, and was made in the reign of Uahankh, or Antef. It reads:

Thetha, the servant in truth of the Horus Uahankh, the King of the South, the King of the North, the son of Ra, Antef, the doer of beneficent acts, living like Ra forever, beloved by him from the bottom of his heart, holder of the chief place in the house of his lord, the great noble of his heart, who knows the matters of the heart of his lord, who attends him in all his goings, one in heart with His Majesty in very truth, the leader of the great men of the house of the king, the bearer of the royal seal in the seat of confidential affairs, keeping close the counsel of his lord more than the chiefs, who makes rejoice the Horus (i.e. the king) through what he wishes, the favourite of his Lord, beloved by him as the mouth of the seal, the president of the place of confidential affairs, whom his lord loves, the mouth of the seal, the chief after the king, the vassal, says:

I was the beloved one of his Lord, I was he with whom he was well pleased all day and every day. I passed a long period of my life [that is] years, under the Majesty of my Lord, the Horus, Uahankh, the King of the South and North, the son of the Sun, Antef. Behold, this country was subject to him in the south as far as Thes, and in the north as far as Abtu of Then (Abydos of This). Behold, I was in the position of body servant of his, and was an actual chief under him. He magnified me, and he made my position to be one of great prominence, and he set me in the place beloved (?) for the affairs of his heart, in his palace. Because of the singleness [of my heart] he appointed me to be a bearer of the royal seal, and the deputy of the registrary (?). [I] selected the good things of all kinds of the offerings brought to the Majesty of my Lord, from the South and from the North land whensoever a taxing was made, and I made him to rejoice at the assessment which was made everywhere throughout the country. Now His Majesty had been afraid that the tribute, which was brought to His Majesty, my Lord, from the princes who were the overlords of the Red Country (Lower Egypt), would dwindle away in this country, and he had been afraid that the same would be the case in the other countries also. He committed to me these matters, for he knew that my administration was able. I rendered to him information about them, and because of my great knowledge of affairs never did anything escape that was not replaced. I was one who lived in the heart of his Lord, in very truth, and I was a great noble after his own heart. I was as cool water and fire in the house of my Lord. The shoulders of the great ones bent [before me]. I did not thrust myself in the train of the wicked, for which men are hated. I was a lover of what was good, and a hater of what was evil. My disposition was that of one beloved in the house of my Lord. I carried out every course of action in accordance with the urgency that was in the heart of my Lord. Moreover, in the matter of every affair which His Majesty caused me to follow out, if any official obstructed me in truth I overthrew his opposition. I neither resisted his order, nor hesitated, but I carried it out in very truth. In making any computation which he ordered, I made no mistake. I did not set one thing in the place of another. I did not increase the flame of his wrath in its strength. I did not filch property from an inheritance. Moreover, as concerning all that His Majesty commanded to set before him in respect of the royal household (or *harim*), I kept accounts of everything which His Majesty desired, and I gave them to him, and I made satisfactory all their statements. Because of the greatness of my knowledge nothing ever escaped me.

I made a *mekha* boat for my town, and a *sehi* boat, so that I might attend in the train of my Lord, and I was one of the number of the great ones on every occasion when travel or journeying had to be performed, and I was held in great esteem, and entreated most honourably. I provided my own equipment from the possessions which His Majesty, the Horus Uahankh, the King of the South, the King of the North, the son of the Sun, Antef, who lives like Ra forever, gave to me because of the greatness of his love for me, until he departed in peace to his horizon (i.e. the tomb). And when his son, that is to say, the Horus Nekhtneb-Tepnefer, the King of the South, the King of the North, the son of Ra, Antef, the producer of beneficent acts, who lives forever like Ra, entered his house, I followed him as his body-companion into all his beautiful places that rejoiced [his] heart, and because of the greatness of my knowledge there was never anything wanting (?). He committed to me and gave into my hand every duty that had been mine in the time of his father, and I performed it effectively under His Majesty; no matter connected with any duty escaped me. I lived the [remainder] of my days on the earth near the King, and was the chief of his body-companions. I was great and strong under His Majesty, and I performed everything which he decreed. I was one who was pleasing to his Lord all day and every day.

THE AUTOBIOGRAPHY OF AAHMES (AMASIS), SURNAMED PEN-NEKHEB

This inscription is cut in hieroglyphs upon the walls of the tomb of Aahmes at Al-Kab in Upper Egypt. Aahmes was a contemporary of Aahmes the transport officer, and served under several of the early kings of the eighteenth dynasty. The text reads:

The Erpa, the Duke, the bearer of the seal, the man who took prisoners with his own hands, Aahmes, says: I accompanied the King of the South, the King of the North, NebpehtiRa (Amasis I), whose word is truth, and I captured for him in Tchah (Syria) one prisoner alive and one hand. I accompanied the King of the South, the King of the North, TcheserkaRa, whose word is truth, and I captured for him in Kash (Nubia) one prisoner alive. On another occasion, I captured for him three hands to the north of Aukehek. I accompanied the King of the South, the King of the North, whose word is truth, and I captured for him two prisoners alive, in addition to the three other prisoners who were alive, and who escaped (?) from me in Kash, and were not counted by me. And on another occasion, I laboured for him, and I captured for him in the country of Neherina (Mesopotamia) twenty-one hands, one horse, and one chariot. I accompanied the King of the South, the King of the North, AakheperenRa, whose word is law, and I brought away as tribute a very large number of the Shasu (the nomads of the Syrian desert) alive, but I did not count them. I accompanied the Kings of the South, the Kings of the North, [those great] gods, and I was with them in the countries of the South and North, and in every place where they went, namely, King NebpehtiRa (Amasis I), King TcheserkaRa (Amenhetep I), AakheperkaRa (Thothmes I), AakheperenRa (Thothmes II), and this beneficent god MenkheperRa (Thothmes III), who is endowed with life forever. I have reached a good old age, I have lived with kings, I have enjoyed favours under their Majesties, and affection has been shown to me in the Palace, life, strength, health [be to them!]. The divine wife, the chief royal wife MaatkaRa, whose word is truth, showed several favours to me. I held in my arms her eldest daughter, the Princess NeferuRa, whose word is law, when she was a nursling, I the bearer of the royal seal, who captured my prisoners, Aahmes, who am surnamed Pen-Nekheb, did this. I was never absent from the king at the time of fighting, beginning with NebpehtiRa (Amasis I), and continuing until the reign of MenkheperRa (Thothmes III). TcheserkaRa (Amenhetep I) gave me in gold two rings, two collars, one armlet, one dagger, one fan, and one pectoral (?). AakheperkaRa (Thothmes I) gave me in gold four hand rings, four collars, one armlet, six flies, three lions, two axe-heads. AakheperenRa gave me in gold four hand rings, six collars, three armlets (?), one plaque, and in silver two axe-heads.

THE AUTOBIOGRAPHY OF TEHUTI, THE ERPA

The autobiographies given up to here are those of soldiers, sailors, and officials who in the performance of their duties travelled in Nubia, the Egyptian Sudan, the Eastern

Sudan, the Red Sea Littoral, Sinai, and Western Asia. The following autobiography is that of one of the great nobles, who in the eighteenth dynasty assisted in carrying out the great building schemes of Queen Hatshepset and Thothmes III. Tehuti was an hereditary chief (*erpa*), and a Duke, and the Director of the Department of the Government in which all the gold and silver that were brought to Thebes as tribute were kept, and he controlled the distribution of the same in connection with the Public Works Department. The text begins with the words of praise to Amen-Ra for the life of Hatshepset and of Thothmes III, thus:

Thanks be to Amen-Ra, the King of the Gods], and praise be to His Majesty when he rises in the eastern sky for the life, strength, and health of the King of the South, the King of the North, MaatkaRa (Hatshepset), and of the King of the South, the King of the North, MenkheperRa (Thothmes III), who are endowed with life, stability, serenity, and health like Ra forever.

I performed the office of chief mouth (i.e. director), giving orders. I directed the artificers who were engaged on the work of the great boat of the head of the river [called] Userhatamen. It was inlaid (or overlaid) with the very best gold of the mountains, the splendour of which illumined all Egypt, and it was made by the King of the South, the King of the North, MaatkaRa (this queen frequently ascribed to herself male attributes), in connection with the monuments which he made for his father Amen-Ra, Lord of the Thrones of the Two Lands, who is endowed with life like Ra forever.

I performed the office of chief mouth, giving orders. I directed the artificers who were engaged on the work of the

God-house, the horizon of the god, and on the work of the great throne, which was [made] of the very best silver-gold of the mountains, and of perfect work to last forever, which was made by MaatkaRa in connection with the monuments which he made for his father Amen-Ra, etc.

I performed the office of chief mouth, giving orders. I directed the artificers who were engaged on the work of the shrine (?) of Truth, the framework of the doors of which was of silver-gold, made by MaatkaRa, etc.

I performed the office of chief mouth, giving orders. I directed the artificers who were engaged on the works of Tcheser-Tcheseru (the 'Holy of Holies', the name of Hatshepset's temple at Deir el-Bahari), the Temple of Millions of Years, the great doors of which were made of copper inlaid with figures in silver-gold, which was made by MaatkaRa, etc.

I performed the office of chief mouth, giving orders. I directed the artificers who were engaged on the work of Khakhut, the great sanctuary of Amen, his horizon in Amen-tet, whereof all the doors [were made] of real cedar wood inlaid (or overlaid) with bronze, made by MaatkaRa, etc.

I performed the office of chief mouth, giving orders. I directed the artificers who were engaged on the works of the House of Amen, it shall flourish to all eternity! whereof the pavement was inlaid with blocks of gold and silver, and its beauties were like those of the horizon of heaven, made by MaatkaRa, etc.

I performed the office of chief mouth, giving orders. I directed the artificers who were engaged on the work of the great shrine, which was made of ebony from Kenset

(Nubia), with a broad, high base, having steps, made of translucent alabaster [from the quarry] of Het-nub, made by MaatkaRa, etc.

I performed the office of chief mouth, giving orders. I directed the artificers who were engaged on the works of the Great House of the god, which was plated with silver in which figures were inlaid in gold – its splendour lighted up the faces of all who beheld it – made by MaatkaRa, etc.

I performed the office of chief mouth, giving orders. I directed the artificers who were engaged on the work of the great broad, high doors of the temple of Karnak, which were covered with plates of copper inlaid with figures in silver-gold, made by MaatkaRa, etc.

I performed the office of chief mouth, giving orders. I directed the artificers who were engaged on the work of the holy necklaces and pectorals, and on the large talismans of the great sanctuary, which were made of silver-gold and many different kinds of precious stones, made by MaatkaRa, etc.

I performed the office of chief mouth, giving orders. I directed the artificers who were engaged on the works in connection with the two great obelisks, [each of which] was one hundred and eight cubits in height (about 50 metres/162 feet) and was plated with silver-gold, the brilliance whereof filled all Egypt, made by MaatkaRa, etc.

I performed the office of chief mouth, giving orders. I directed the artificers who were engaged on the work of the holy gate [called] 'Amen-shefit', which was made of a single slab of copper, and of the images (?) that belonged thereto, made by MaatkaRa, etc. I directed the artificers who were engaged on the work of the altar-stands of Amen. These were made of an incalculable quantity of silver-gold, set with precious stones, by MaatkaRa, etc. I directed the artificers who were engaged on the work of the store-chests, which were plated with copper and silver-gold and inlaid with precious stones, made by MaatkaRa, etc. I directed the artificers who were engaged on the works of the Great Throne, and the God-house, which is built of granite and shall last like the firmly fixed pillars of the sky, made by MaatkaRa, etc

And as for the wonderful things, and all the products of all the countries, and the best of the wonderful products of Punt, which His Majesty presented to Amen, Lord of the Apts, for the life, strength, and health of His Majesty, and with which he filled the house of this holy god, for Amen had given him Egypt because he knew that he would rule it wisely (?), behold, it was I who registered them, because I was of strict integrity. My favour was permanent before [His Majesty], it never diminished, and he conferred more distinctions on me than on any other official about him, for he knew my integrity in respect of him. He knew that I carried out works, and that I covered my mouth (i.e. held my tongue) concerning the affairs of his palace. He made me the director of his palace, knowing that I was experienced in affairs. I held the seal of the Two Treasuries, and of the store of all the precious stones of every kind that were in the God-house of Amen in the Apts (the temples of Karnak and Luxor), which were filled up to their roofs with the tribute paid to the god. Such a thing never happened before, even from the time of the primeval god.

His Majesty commanded to be made a silver-gold ... for the Great Hall of the festivals. [The metal] was weighed by the *heqet* measure for Amen, before all the people, and it was estimated to contain 88½ *heqet* measures, which were equal to 8592½ *teben* (the teben = 90.959 grams). It was offered to the god for the life, strength, and health of MaatkaRa, the ever living. I received the *sennu* offerings which were made to Amen-Ra, Lord of the Apts; these things, all of them, took place in very truth, and I exaggerate not. I was vigilant, and my heart was perfect in respect of my lord, for I wish to rest in peace in the mountain of the spirit-bodies who are in the Other World (Khert-Neter). I wish my memory to be perpetuated on the earth. I wish my soul to live before the Lord of Eternity. I wish that the doorkeepers of the gates of the Tuat (Other World) may not repulse my soul, and that it may come forth at the call of him that shall lay offerings in my tomb, that it may have bread in abundance and ale in full measure, and that it may drink of the water from the source of the river. I would go in and come out like the Spirits who do what the gods wish, that my name may be held in good repute by the people who shall come in after years, and that they may praise me at the two seasons (morning and evening) when they praise the god of my city.

THE AUTOBIOGRAPHY OF THAIEMHETEP

This remarkable inscription is found on a stele which is preserved in the British Museum (No. 1027), and which was made in the ninth year of King Ptolemy Philopator

Philadelphus (71 BCE). The text opens with a prayer to all the great gods of Memphis for funerary offerings, and after a brief address to her husband's colleagues, Thaiemhetep describes in detail the principal incidents of her life, and gives the dates of her birth, death, etc., which are rarely found on the funerary stelae of the older period. Thaiemhetep, the daughter of HeRankh, was an important member of the semi-royal, great high-priestly family of Memphis, and her funerary inscription throws much light on the theology of the Ptolemaic Period.

Suten-ta-hetep ('the king gives an offering'), may Seker-Osiris, at the head of the House of the Ka of Seker, the great god in Raqet; and Hap-Asar (Serapis), at the head of Amentet, the king of the gods, King of Eternity and Governor of everlastingness; and Isis, the great Lady, the mother of the god, the eye of Ra, the Lady of heaven, the mistress of all the gods; and Nephthys, the divine sister of Horus, the avenger of his father, the great god in Raqetit; and Anubis, who is on his hill, the dweller in the chamber of embalmment, at the head of the divine hall; and all the gods and goddesses who dwell in the mountain of Amentet the beautiful of Hetkaptah (Memphis), give the offerings that come forth at the word, beer, and bread, and oxen, and geese, and incense, and unguents, and suits of apparel, and good things of all kinds upon their altars, to the Ka of the Osiris, the great princess, the one who is adorned, the woman who is in the highest favour, the possessor of pleasantness, beautiful of body, sweet of love in the mouth of every man, who is greatly praised by her kinsfolk, the youthful one, excellent of disposition, always ready to speak her words of sweetness, whose counsel is excellent, Thaiemhetep, whose word (or voice) is truth, the beloved daughter of the royal kinsman, the priest of Ptah, libationer of the gods of White Wall (Memphis), priest of Menu (or Amsu), the Lord of Senut (Panopolis), and of Khnemu, the Lord of Smen-Heru (Ptolemais), priest of Horus, the Lord of Sekhem (Letopolis), chief of the mysteries in Aat-Beqt, chief of the mysteries in Sekhem, and in It, and in Kha-Hap; the daughter of the beautiful sistrum bearer of Ptah, the great one of his South Wall, the Lord of Ankh-taui, HeRankh, she says:

'Hail, all judges and all men of learning, and all high officials, and all nobles, and all people, when you enter into this tomb, come, I pray, and listen to what befell me.

'The ninth day of the fourth month (October-November) of the season Akhet of the ninth year under the Majesty of the King of the Two Lands, the god Philopator, Philadelphus, Osiris the Young, the Son of Ra, the lord of the Crowns of the South and of the North, Ptolemy, the ever living, beloved of Ptah and Isis, [was] the day whereon I was born.

'On the ... day of the third month (May-June) of the season Shemu of the twenty-third year under the Majesty of this same Lord of the Two Lands, my father gave me as wife to the priest of Ptah, the scribe of the library of divine books, the priest of the Tuat Chamber (the Hall of Offerings in the tomb), the libationer of the gods of the Wall, the superintendent of the priests of the gods and goddesses of the North and South, the two eyes of the King of Upper Egypt, the two ears of the King of Lower Egypt, the second of the king in raising up the Tet pillar, the staff of the king [when] brought into the temples, the Erpa in the throne chamber of Keb, the Kher-heb (precentor) in the seat of Thoth, the repeater (or herald) of the tillage of the Ram-god, who turns aside the Utchat (sacred eye), who approachs the Utchat by the great Ram of gold (?), who sees the setting of the great god [who] is born when it is fettered, the Ur-kherp-hem (the official title of the high-priest of Memphis), Pa-sher-en-Ptah, the son of a man who held like offices, Peta-Bast, whose word (or voice) is truth, born of the great decorated sistrum bearer and tambourine woman of Ptah, the great one of his South Wall, the Lord of Ankh-taui, whose word (or voice) is truth.

'And the heart of the Ur-kherp-hem rejoiced in her exceedingly. I bore to him a child three times, but I did not bear a man child besides these three daughters. And I and the Ur-kherp-hem prayed to the Majesty of this holy god, who [works] great wonders and bestows happiness (?), who gives a son to him that has one not, and Imhetep, the son of Ptah, listened to our words, and he accepted his prayers. And the Majesty of this god came to this Ur-kherp-hem during [his] sleep, and said to him, "Let there be built a great building in the form of a large hall [for the lord of] Ankh-taui, in the place where his body is wrapped up (or concealed), and in return for this I will give you a man child." And the Ur-kherp-hem woke up out of his sleep after these [words], and he smelt the ground before this holy god. And he laid them (i.e. the words) before the priests, and the chief of the mysteries, and the libationers, and the artisans of the House of Gold, at one time, and he despatched them to make the building perfect in the form of a large, splendid funerary hall. And they did everything according as he had said. And he performed the ceremony of "Opening the Mouth" for this holy god, and he made to him a great offering of the beautiful offerings of every kind, and he bestowed upon him sculptured images for the sake of this god, and he made happy their hearts with offerings of all kinds in return for this [promise].

'Then I conceived a man child, and I brought him forth on the fifteenth day of the third month (May-June) of the season Shemu of the sixth year, at the eighth hour of the day, under the Majesty of the Queen, the Lady of the Two Lands, Cleopatra, Life, Strength, Health [be to her!], [the day] of the festival of "things on the altar" of this holy god, Imhetep, the son of Ptah, his form being like that of the son of Him that is south of his wall (i.e. Ptah), great rejoicings on account of him were made by the inhabitants of White Wall (Memphis), and there were given to him his name of Imhetep and the surname of Peta-Bast, and all the people rejoiced in him.

'The sixteenth day of the second month (December-January) of the season Pert of the tenth year was the day on which I died. My husband, the priest and divine father of Ptah, the priest of Osiris, Lord of Rastau, the priest of the King of the South, the King of the North, the Lord of the Two Lands, Ptolemy, whose word is truth, the chief of the mysteries of the House of Ptah, the chief of the mysteries of heaven, earth, and the Other World, the chief of the mysteries of Rastau, the chief of the mysteries of Raqet, the Ur-kherp-hem, Pa-sher-en-Ptah, placed me in Am-urtet, he performed for me all the rites and ceremonies which are [performed] for the dead who are buried in a fitting manner, he had me made into a beautiful mummy, and caused me to be laid to rest in his tomb behind Raqet.

'Hail, brother, husband, friend! Oh Ur-kherp-hem, cease not to drink, to eat, to drink wine, to enjoy the love of women, and to pass your days happily; follow your heart (or desire) day and night. Set not sorrow in your heart, for oh, are the years [which we pass] so many on the earth [that we should do this]? For Amentet is a land where black darkness cannot be pierced by the eye, and it is a place of restraint (or misery) for him that dwells therein. The holy ones [who are there] sleep in their forms. They wake not up to look upon their friends, they see not their fathers [and] their mothers, and their heart has no desire for their wives [and] their children. The living water of the earth is for those who are on it, stagnant water is for me. It comes to him that is upon the earth. Stagnant is the water which is for me. I know not the place wherein I am. Since I arrived at this valley of the dead I long for running water. I say, "Let not my attendant remove the pitcher from the stream." Oh that one would turn my face to the north wind on the bank of the stream, and I cry out for it to cool the pain that is in my heart. He whose name is 'Arniau' (the great Death-god) calls everyone to him, and they come to him with quaking hearts, and they are terrified through their fear of him. By him is no distinction made between gods and men, with him princes are even as men of no account. His hand is not turned away from all those who love him, for he snatches away the babe from his mother's [breast] even as he does the aged man. He goes about on his way, and all men fear him, and [though] they make supplication before him, he turns not his face away from them. Useless is it to make entreaty to him, for he hearkens not to him that makes supplication to him, and even though he shall present to him offerings and funerary gifts of all kinds, he will not regard them.

'Hail, all you who arrive in this funeral mountain, present to me offerings, cast incense into the flame and pour out libations at every festival of Amentet.'

The scribe and sculptor, the councillor, the chief of the mysteries of the House of Shent in Tenen, the priest of Horus, Imhetep, the son of the priest Kha-Hap, whose word (or voice) is truth, cut this inscription.

TALES OF TRAVEL AND ADVENTURE

Here we provide three tales of adventure. The text of the very interesting 'Story of Sanehat' is found written in the hieratic character upon papyri which are preserved in Berlin. The narrative describes events which are said to have taken place under one of the kings of the twelfth dynasty, and it is very possible that the foundation of this story is historical.

The text of 'The Story of the Educated Peasant Khuenanpu' is written in the hieratic character on papyri which are preserved in the British Museum and in the Royal Library in Berlin. It is generally thought that the story is the product of the period that immediately followed the twelfth dynasty. The text of 'The Journey of the Priest Unu-Amen into Syria' is written in the hieratic character upon a papyrus preserved in St. Petersburg; it gives an excellent description of the troubles that befell the priest Unu-Amen during his journey into Syria ('to buy cedar wood to make a new boat for Amen-Ra') in the second half of the eleventh century before Christ.

THE STORY OF SANEHAT

The hero is himself supposed to relate his own adventures thus:

The Erpa, the Duke, the Chancellor of the King of the North, the *smer uati*, the judge, the Antchmer of the marches, the King in the lands of the Nubians, the veritable royal kinsman loving him, the member of the royal bodyguard, Sanehat, says: I am a member of the bodyguard of his lord, the servant of the King, and of the house of Neferit, the feudal chieftainess, the Erpat princess, the highly favoured lady, the royal wife of Usertsen, whose word is truth in Khnemetast, the royal daughter of Amenemhat, whose word is truth in Qanefer. On the seventh day of the third month of the season Akhet, in the thirtieth year [of his reign], the god drew nigh to his horizon, and the King of the South, the King of the North, SehetepabRa (i.e. Amenemhat II), ascended into heaven, and was invited to the Disk, and his divine members mingled with those of him that made him. The King's House was in silence, hearts were bowed down in sorrow, the two Great Gates were shut fast, the officials sat motionless, and the people mourned.

Now behold, [before his death] His Majesty had despatched an army to the Land of the Themehu, under the command of his eldest son, the beautiful god Usertsen. And he went and raided the desert lands in the south, and captured slaves from the Thehenu (Libyans), and he was at that moment returning and bringing back Libyan slaves and innumerable beasts of every kind. And the high officers of the Palace sent messengers into the western country to inform the King's son concerning what had taken place in the royal abode. And the messengers found him on the road, and they came to him by night and asked him if it was not the proper time for him to hasten his return, and to set out with his bodyguard without letting his army in general know of his departure. They also told him that a message had been sent to the princes who were in command of the soldiers in his train not to proclaim [the matter of the King's death] to anyone else.

Sanehat continues: When I heard his voice speaking I rose up and fled. My heart was cleft in twain, my arms dropped by my side, and trembling seized all my limbs. I ran about distractedly, hither and thither, seeking a hiding-place. I went into the thickets in order to find a place wherein I could travel without being seen. I made my way upstream, and I decided not to appear in the Palace, for I did not know but that deeds of violence were taking place there. And I did not say, 'Let life follow it', but I went on my way to the district of the Sycamore. Then I came to the Lake (or Island) of Seneferu, and I passed the whole day there on the edge of the plain. On the following morning I continued my journey, and a man rose up immediately in front of me on the road, and he cried for mercy; he was afraid of me. When the night fell I walked into the village of Nekau, and I crossed the river in an *usekht* boat without a rudder, by the help of the wind from the west. And I travelled eastwards of the district of Aku, by the pass of the goddess Herit, the Lady of the Red Mountain. Then I allowed my feet to take the road downstream, and I travelled on to Anebuheq, the fortress that had been built to drive back the Satiu (nomad marauders), and to hold in check the tribes that roamed the desert. I crouched down in the scrub during the day to avoid being seen by the watchmen on the top of the fortress. I set out again on the march, when the night fell, and when daylight fell on the earth I arrived at Peten, and I rested myself by the Lake of Kamur. Then thirst came upon me and overwhelmed me. I suffered torture. My throat was burnt up, and I said, 'This indeed is the taste of death.' But I took courage, and collected my members (i.e. myself), for I heard the sounds that are made by flocks and herds. Then the Satiu of the desert saw me, and the master of the caravan who had been in Egypt recognised me. And he rose up and gave me some water, and he warmed milk [for me], and I travelled with the men of his caravan, and thus I passed through one country after the other [in safety]. I avoided the land of Sunu and I journeyed to the land of Qetem, where I stayed for a year and a half.

And Ammuiansha, the Shekh of Upper Thennu, took me aside and said to me, 'You will be happy with me, for you will hear the language of Egypt.' Now he said this because he knew what manner of man I was, for he had heard the people of Egypt who were there with him bear testimony concerning my character. And he said to me, 'Why and wherefore have you come here? Is it because the departure of King SehetepabRa from the Palace to the horizon has taken place, and you did not know what would be the result of it?' Then I spoke to him with words of deceit, saying, 'I was among the soldiers who had gone to the land of Themeh. My heart cried out, my courage failed me utterly, it made me follow the ways over which I fled. I hesitated, but felt no regret. I did not listen to any evil counsel, and my name was not heard on the mouth of the herald. How I came to be brought into this country I know not; it was, perhaps, by the Providence of God.'

And Ammuiansha said to me, 'What will become of the land without that beneficent god the terror of whom passed through the lands like the goddess Sekhmet in a year of pestilence?' Then I made answer to him, saying, 'His son shall save us. He has entered the Palace, and has taken possession of the heritage of his father. Moreover, he is the god who has no equal, and no other can exist beside him, the lord of wisdom, perfect in his plans, of good will when he passes decrees, and one comes forth and goes in according to his ordinance. He reduced foreign lands to submission whilst his father [sat] in the Palace directing him in the matters which had to be carried out. He is mighty of valour, he slays with his sword, and in bravery he has no compeer. One should see him attacking the nomads of the desert, and pouncing upon the robbers of the highway! He beats down opposition, he smites arms helpless, his enemies cannot be made to resist him. He takes vengeance, he cleaves skulls, none can stand up before him. His strides are long, he slays him that flees, and he who turns his back upon him in flight never reaches his goal. When attacked his courage stands firm. He attacks again and again, and he never yields. His heart is bold when he sees the battle array, he permits none to sit down behind. His face is fierce [as] he rushes on the attacker. He rejoices when he takes captive the chief of a band of desert robbers. He seizes his shield, he rains blows upon him, but he has no need to repeat his attack, for he slays his foe before he can hurl his spear at him. Before he draws his bow the nomads have fled, his arms are like the souls of the Great Goddess. He fights, and if he reaches his object of attack he spars not, and he leaves no remnant. He is beloved, his pleasantness is great, he is the conqueror, and his town loves him more than herself; she rejoices in him more than in her god, and men throng about him with rejoicings. He was king and conqueror before his birth, and he has worn his crowns since he was born. He has multiplied births, and he it is whom God has made to be the joy of this land, which he has ruled, and the boundaries of which he has enlarged. He has conquered the Lands of the South, shall he not conquer the Lands of the North? He has been created to smite the hunters of the desert, and to crush the tribes that roam the sandy waste....' Then the Shekh of Upper Thennu said to me, 'Assuredly Egypt is a happy country in that it knows his vigour. Verily, as long as you tarry with me I will do good to you.'

And he set me before his children, and he gave me his eldest daughter as wife, and he made me to choose for myself a very fine territory which belonged to him, and which lay on the border of a neighbouring country, and this beautiful region was called Aa. In it there are figs, and wine is more abundant than water. Honey is plentiful, oil exists in large quantities, and fruits of every kind are on the trees thereof. Wheat, barley, herds of cattle, and flocks of sheep and goats are there in untold numbers. And the Shekh showed me very great favour, and his affection for me was so great that he made me Shekh of one of the best tribes in his country. Bread-cakes were made for me each day, and each day wine was brought to me with roasted flesh and wild fowl, and the wild creatures of the plain that were caught were laid before me, in addition to the game which my hunting dogs brought in. Food of all kinds was made for me, and milk was prepared for me in various ways. I passed many years in this manner, and my children grew up into fine strong men, and each one of them ruled his tribe. Every ambassador on his journey to and from Egypt visited me. I was kind to people of every class. I gave water to the thirsty man. I suppressed the highway robber. I directed the operations of the bowmen of the desert, who marched long distances to suppress the hostile Shekhs, and to reduce their power, for the Shekh of Thennu had appointed me General of his soldiers many years before this. Every country against which I marched I terrified into submission. I seized the crops by the wells, I looted the flocks and herds, I carried away the people and their slaves who ate their bread, I slew the men there. Through my sword and bow, and through my well-organised campaigns, I was highly esteemed in the mind of the Shekh, and he loved me, for he knew my bravery, and he set me before his children when he saw the bravery of my arms.

Then a certain mighty man of valour of Thennu came and reviled me in my tent; he was greatly renowned as a man of war, and he was unequalled in the whole country, which he had conquered. He challenged me to combat, being urged to fight by the men of his tribe, and he believed that he could conquer me, and he determined to take my flocks and herds as spoil. And the Shekh took counsel with me about the challenge, and I said, 'I am not an acquaintance of his, and I am by no means a friend of his. Have I ever visited him in his domain or entered his door, or passed through his compound? [Never!] He is a man whose heart becomes full of evil thoughts, whensoever he ses me, and he wishs to carry out his fell design and plunder me. He is like a wild bull seeking to slay the bull of a herd of tame cattle so that he may make the cows his own. Or rather he is a mere braggart who wishs to seize the property which I have collected by my prudence, and not an experienced warrior. Or rather he is a bull that loves to fight, and that loves to make attacks repeatedly, fearing that otherwise some other animal will prove to be his equal. If, however, his heart be set upon fighting, let him declare [to me] his intention. Is God, Who knows everything, ignorant of what he has decided to do?'

And I passed the night in stringing my bow, I made ready my arrows of war, I unsheathed my dagger, and I put all my weapons in order. At daybreak the tribes of the land of Thennu came, and the people who lived on both sides of it gathered themselves together, for they were greatly concerned about the combat, and they came and stood up round about me where I stood. Every heart burned for my success, and both men and women uttered cries (or exclamations), and every heart suffered anxiety on my behalf, saying, 'Can there exist possibly any man who is a mightier fighter and more doughty a man of war than he?' Then my adversary grasped his shield, and his battle-axe, and his spears, and after he had hurled his weapons at me, and I had succeeded in avoiding his short spears, which arrived harmlessly one after the other, he became filled with fury, and making up his mind to attack me at close quarters he threw himself upon me. And I hurled my javelin at him, which remained fast in his neck, and he uttered a long cry and fell on his face, and I slew him with his own weapons. And as I stood upon his back I shouted the cry of victory, and every Aamu man (i.e. Asiatic) applauded me, and I gave thanks to Menthu (the War-god of Thebes); and the slaves of my opponent mourned for their lord. And the Shekh Ammuiansha took me in his arms and embraced me. I carried off his (i.e. the opponent's) property. I seized his cattle as spoil, and what he meditated doing to me I did to him. I took possession of the contents of his tent, I stripped his compound, I became rich, I increased my store of goods, and I added greatly to the number of my cattle.

Thus did God prosper the man who made Him his support. Thus that day was washed (i.e. satisfied) the heart of the man who was compelled to make his escape from his own into another country. Thus that day the integrity of the man who was once obliged to take to flight as a miserable fugitive was proven in the sight of all the Court. Once I was a wanderer wandering about hungry, and now I can give bread to my neighbours. Once I had to flee naked from my country, and now I am the possessor of splendid raiment, and of apparel made of the finest byssus. Once I was obliged to do my own errands and to fetch and carry for myself, and now I am the master of troops of servants. My house is beautiful, my estate is spacious, and my name is repeated in the Great House. Oh Lord of the gods, who has ordered my goings, I will offer propitiatory offerings to you: I beseech you to restore me to Egypt, and Oh be You pleased most graciously to let me once again look upon the spot where my mind dwells for hours [at a time]! How great a boon would it be for me to cleanse my body in the land of my birth! Let, I pray, a period of happiness attend me, and may God give me peace. May He dispose events in such a way that the close of the career of the man who has suffered misery, whose heart has seen sorrow, who has wandered into a strange land, may be happy. Is He not at peace with me this day? Surely He shall hearken to him that is afar off.... Let the King of Egypt be at peace with me, and may I live upon his offerings. Let me salute the Mistress of the Land (i.e. the Queen) who is in his palace, and let me hear the greetings of her children. Oh would that my members could become young again! For now old age is stealing on me. Infirmity overtakes me. Mine eyes refuse to see, my hands fall helpless, my knees shake, my heart stands still, the funerary mourners approach and they will bear me away to the City of Eternity, wherein I shall become a follower of Nebertcher. She will declare to me the beauties of her children, and they shall traverse it with me.

Behold now, the Majesty of the King of Egypt, KheperkaRa, whose word is truth, having spoken concerning the various things that had happened to me, sent a messenger to me bearing royal gifts, such as he would send to the king of a foreign land, with the intention of making glad the heart of your servant now [speaking], and the princes of his palace made me to hear their salutations. And here is a copy of the document, which was brought to your servant [from the King] instructing him to return to Egypt:

'The royal command of the Horus, Ankh-mestu, Lord of Nekhebet and Uatchet, Ankh-mestu, King of the South, King of the North, KheperkaRa, the son of Ra, Amenemhat, the everliving, to my follower Sanehat. This royal order is despatched to you to inform you. You have travelled about everywhere, in one country after another, having set out from Qetem and reached Thennu, and you have journeyed from place to place at your own will and pleasure. Observe now, what you have done [to others, making them obey you], shall be done to you. Make no excuses, for they shall be set aside; argue not with [my] officials, for your arguments shall be refuted. Your heart shall not reject the plans which your mind has formulated. Your Heaven (i.e. the Queen), who is in the Palace, is stable and flourishing at this present time, her head is crowned with the sovereignty of the earth, and her children are in the royal chambers of the Palace. Lay aside the honours which you have, and your life of abundance (or luxury), and journey to Egypt. Come and look upon your native land, the land where you were born, smell the earth (i.e. do homage) before the Great Gate, and associate with the nobles thereof. For at this time you are beginning to be an old man, and you can no longer produce sons, and you have [ever] in your mind the day of [your] burial, when you will assume the form of a servant [of Osiris]. The unguents for your embalmment on the night [of mummification] have been set apart for you, together with your mummy swathings, which are the work of the hands of the goddess Tait. Your funerary procession, which will march on the day of your union with the earth, has been arranged, and there are prepared for you a gilded mummy-case, the head whereof is painted blue, and a canopy made of *mesket* wood. Oxen shall draw you [to the tomb], the wailing women shall precede you, the funerary dances shall be performed, those who mourn you shall be at the door of your tomb, the funerary offerings dedicated to you shall be proclaimed, sacrifices shall be offered for you with your oblations, and your funerary edifice shall be built in white stone, side by side with those of the princes and princesses. Your death must not take place in a foreign land, the Aamu folk shall not escort you [to your grave], you shall not be placed in the skin of a ram when your burial is effected; but at your burial there shall be ... and the smiting of the earth, and when you departest lamentations shall be made over your body.'

When this royal letter reached me, I was standing among the people of my tribe, and when it had been read to me I threw myself face downwards on the ground, and bowed until my head touched the dust, and I clasped the document reverently to my breast. Then [I rose up] and walked to and fro in my abode, rejoicing and saying, 'How can these things possibly be done to your servant who is now speaking, whose heart made him to fly into foreign lands [where dwell] peoples who stammer in their speech? Assuredly it is a good and gracious thought [of the King] to deliver me from death [here], for your Ka (i.e. double) will make my body end [its existence] in my native land.'

Here is a copy of the reply that was made by the servant of the Palace, Sanehat, to the above royal document:

'In peace the most beautiful and greatest! your Ka knows of the flight which your servant, who is now speaking, made when he was in a state of ignorance, Oh you beautiful god, Lord of Egypt, beloved of Ra, favoured of Menthu, the Lord of Thebes. May Amen-Ra, lord of the thrones of the Two Lands, and Sebek, and Ra, and Horus, and Hathor, and Tem and his Company of the Gods, and Neferbaiu, and Semsuu, and Horus of the East, and Nebt-Amehet, the goddess who is joined to your head, and the Tchatchau gods who preside over the Nile flood, and Menu, and Heru-khenti-semti, and Urrit, the Lady of Punt, and Nut, and Heru-ur (Haroeris), and Ra, and all the gods of Tamera (Egypt), and of the Islands of the Great Green Sea (i.e. Mediterranean), bestow upon you a full measure of their good gifts, and grant life and serenity to your nostrils, and may they grant to you an eternity which has no limit, and everlastingness which has no bounds! May your fear penetrate and extend into all countries and mountains, and mayest you be the possessor of all the region which the sun encircles in his course. This is the prayer which your servant who now speaks makes on behalf of his lord who has delivered him from Ament.

'The lord of knowledge who knows men, the Majesty of the Setepsa abode (i.e. the Palace), knows well that his servant who is now speaking was afraid to declare the matter, and that to repeat it was a great thing. The great god (i.e. the King), who is the counterpart of Ra, has done wisely in what he has done, and your servant who now speaks has meditated upon it in his mind, and has made himself to conform to his plans. Your Majesty is like Horus, and the victorious might of your arms has conquered the whole world. Let your Majesty command that Maka [chief of] the country of Qetma, and Khentiaaush [chief of] Khent-Keshu, and Menus [chief of] the lands of the Fenkhu, be brought hither, and these Governors will testify that these things have come to pass at the desire of your Ka (i.e. double), and that Thenu does not speak words of overboldness to

you, and that she is as [obedient as] your hunting dogs.
Behold, the flight, which your servant who is now speaking
made, was made by him as the result of ignorance; it was not
wilful, and I did not decide upon it after careful meditation.
I cannot understand how I could ever have separated myself
from my country. It seems to me now to have been the
product of a dream wherein a man who is in the swamps
of the Delta imagins himself to be in Abu (Elephantine,
or Syene), or of a man who whilst standing in fertile fields
imagines himself to be in the deserts of the Sudan. I fear
nothing and no man can make with truth [accusations]
against me. I have never turned my ear to disloyal plottings,
and my name has never been in the mouth of the crier [of
the names of proscribed folk]; though my members quaked,
and my legs shook, my heart guided me, and the God who
ordained this flight of mine led me on. Behold, I am not
a stiff-necked man (or rebel), nay, I held in honour [the
King], for I knew the land of Egypt and that Ra has made
your fear to exist everywhere in Egypt, and the awe of you to
permeate every foreign land. I beseech you to let me enter
my native land. I beseech you to let me return to Egypt.
You are the apparel of the horizon. The Disk (i.e. the Sun)
shines at your wish. One drinks the water of the river Nile
at your pleasure. One breathes the air of heaven when you
give the word of command. Your servant who now speaks
will transfer the possessions which he has gotten in this
land to his kinsfolk. And as for the embassy of your Majesty
which has been despatched to the servant who now speaks,
I will do according to your Majesty's desire, for I live by the
breath which you give, Oh you beloved of Ra, Horus, and

Hathor, and your holy nostrils are beloved of Menthu, Lord of Thebes; may you live forever!'

And I tarried one day in the country of Aa in order to transfer my possessions to my children. My eldest son attended to the affairs of the people of my settlement, and the men and women thereof (i.e. the slaves), and all my possessions were in his hand, and all my children, and all my cattle, and all my fruit trees, and all my palm plantations and groves.

Then your servant who is now speaking set out on his journey and travelled towards the South. When I arrived at Heruuatu, the captain of the frontier patrol sent a messenger to inform the Court of my arrival. His Majesty sent a courteous overseer of the servants of the Palace, and following him came large boats laden with gifts from the King for the soldiers of the desert who had escorted me and guided me to the town of Heruuatu. I addressed each man among them by name and every toiler had that which belonged to him.

I continued my journey, the wind bore me along, food was prepared for me and drink made ready for me, and the best of apparel (?), until I arrived at Athettaui. On the morning of the day following my arrival, five officials came to me, and they bore me to the Great House, and I bowed low until my forehead touched the ground before him. And the princes and princesses were standing waiting for me in the *umtet* chamber, and they advanced to meet me and to receive me, and the *smeru* officials conducted me into the hall, and led me to the privy chamber of the King, where I found His Majesty [seated] upon the Great Throne in the *umtet* chamber of silver-gold. I arrived there, I raised myself up after my prostrations, and I knew not that I was in his presence. Then this god (i.e. the King) spoke to me harshly, and I became like a man who is confounded in the darkness; my intelligence left me, my limbs quaked, my heart was no longer in my body, and I knew not whether I was dead or alive. Then His Majesty said to one of his high officials, 'Raise him, and let him speak to me.' And His Majesty said to me, 'You have come then! You have smitten foreign lands and you have travelled, but now weakness has vanquished you, you have become old, and the infirmities of your body are many. The warriors of the desert shall not escort you [to your grave] ... will you not speak and declare your name?' And I was afraid to contradict him, and I answered him about these matters like a man who was stricken with fear. Thus did my Lord speak to me.

And I answered and said, 'The matter was not of my doing, for, behold, it was done by the hand of God; bodily terror made me to flee according to what was ordained. But, behold, I am here in your presence! You are life. Your Majesty does as you please.' And the King dismissed the royal children, and His Majesty said to the Queen, 'Look now, this is Sanehat who comes in the guise of an Asiatic, and who has turned himself into a nomad warrior of the desert.' And the Queen laughed a loud hearty laugh, and the royal children cried out with one voice before His Majesty, saying, 'Oh Lord King, this man cannot really be Sanehat'; and His Majesty said, 'It is indeed!'

Then the royal children brought their instruments of music, their *menats* and their sistra, and they rattled their sistra, and they passed backwards and forwards before His Majesty, saying, 'Thy hands perform beneficent acts, Oh King. The graces of the Lady of Heaven rest [upon you]. The goddess Nubt gives life to your nostrils, and the Lady of the Stars joins herself to you, as you sail to the South wearing the Crown of the North, and to the North wearing the Crown of the South. Wisdom is established in the mouth of your Majesty, and health is on your brow. You strike terror into the miserable wretches who entreat your mercy. Men propitiate you, Oh Lord of Egypt, [as they do] Ra, and you are acclaimed with cries of joy like Nebertcher. Your horn conquers, your arrow slays, [but] you give breath to him that is afflicted. For our sakes graciously give a boon to this traveller Sanehat, this desert warrior who was born in Tamera (Egypt). He fled through fear of you, and he departed to a far country because of his terror of you. Does not the face that gazes on your blench? Does not the eye that gazes into your feel terrified?'

Then His Majesty said, 'Let him fear not, and let him not utter a sound of fear. He shall be a *smer* official among the princes of the palace, he shall be a member of the company of the *shenit* officials. Get gone to the refectory of the palace, and see to it that rations are provided for him.'

Thereupon I came forth from the privy chamber of the King, and the royal children clasped my hands, and we passed on to the Great Door, and I was lodged in the house of one of the King's sons, which was beautifully furnished. In it there was a bath, and it contained representations of the heavens and objects from the Treasury. And there [I found] apparel made of royal linen, and myrrh of the finest quality which was used by the King, and every chamber was in charge of officials who were favourites of the King, and every officer had his own appointed duties. And [there] the years were made to slide off my members. I cut and combed my hair, I cast from me the dirt of a foreign land, together with the apparel of the nomads who live in the desert. I arrayed myself in apparel made of fine linen, I anointed my body with costly ointments, I slept upon a bedstead [instead of on the ground], I left the sand to those who dwelt on it, and the crude oil of wood wherewith they anoint themselves.

I was allotted the house of a nobleman who had the title of *smer*, and many workmen laboured upon it, and its garden and its groves of trees were replanted with plants and trees. Rations were brought to me from the palace three or four times each day, in additions to the gifts which the royal children gave me unceasingly. And the site of a stone pyramid among the pyramids was marked out for me. The surveyor-in-chief to His Majesty chose the site for it, the director of the funerary designers drafted the designs and inscriptions which were to be cut upon it, the chief of the masons of the necropolis cut the inscriptions, and the clerk of the works in the necropolis went about the country collecting the necessary funerary furniture.

I made the building flourish, and provided everything that was necessary for its upkeep. I acquired land round about it. I made a lake for the performance of funerary ceremonies, and the land about it contained gardens, and groves of trees, and I provided a place where the people on the estate might dwell similar to that which is provided for a *smeru* nobleman of the first rank. My statue, which was made for me by His Majesty, was plated with gold, and the tunic thereof was of silver-gold. Not for any ordinary person did he do such things. May I enjoy the favour of the King until the day of my death shall come!

Here ends the book; [given] from its beginning to its end, as it has been found in writing.

THE STORY OF THE EDUCATED PEASANT KHUENANPU

Once upon a time there lived a man whose name was Khuenanpu, a peasant of Sekhet-hemat (a district to the west of Cairo now known as Wadi an-Natrun), and he had a wife whose name was Nefert. This peasant said to this wife of his, 'Behold, I am going down into Egypt in order to bring back food for my children. Go you and measure up the grain which remains in the granary, [and see how many] measures [there are].' Then she measured it, and there were eight measures. Then this peasant said to this wife of his, 'Behold, two measures of grain shall be for the support of yourself and your children, but of the other six you shall make bread and beer whereon I am to live during the days on which I shall be travelling.'

And this peasant went down into Egypt, having laden his asses with *aaa* plants, and *retmet* plants, and soda and salt, and wood of the district of ..., and *aunt* wood of the Land of Oxen (the Oasis of Farafrah), and skins of panthers and wolves, and *neshau* plants, and *anu* stones, and *tenem*

plants, and *kheperur* plants, and *sahut*, and *saksut* seeds
(?), and *masut* plants, and *sent* and *abu* stones, and *absa*
and *anba* plants, and doves and *naru* and *ukes* birds, and
tebu, *uben* and *tebsu* plants, and *kenkent* seeds, and the
plant 'hair of the earth', and *anset* seeds, and all kinds of
beautiful products of the land of Sekhet-hemat.

And when this peasant had marched to the south, to
Hensu (the Khanes of the Hebrews and Herakleopolis
of the Greeks, the modern Ahnas al-Madinah), and had
arrived at the region of Perfefa, to the north of Metnat,
he found a man standing on the river bank whose name
was Tehutinekht, who was the son of a man whose name
was Asri; both father and son were serfs of Rensi, the son
of Meru the steward. When this man Tehutinekht saw the
asses of this peasant, of which his heart approved greatly,
he said, 'Would that I had any kind of god with me to help
me to seize for myself the goods of this peasant!'

Now the house of this Tehutinekht stood upon the
upper edge of a sloping path along the river bank, which
was narrow and not wide. It was about as wide as a sheet
of linen cloth, and upon one side of it was the water of
the stream, and on the other was a growing crop. Then
this Tehutinekht said to his slave, 'Run and bring me a
sheet of linen out of my house'; and it was brought to him
immediately. Then he shook out the sheet of linen over
the narrow sloping path in such a way that its upper edge
touched the water, and the fringed edge the growing crop.
And when this peasant was going along the public path,
this Tehutinekht said to him, 'Be careful, peasant, would
you walk upon my clothes?' And this peasant said, 'I will do

as you please; my way is good.' And when he turned to the
upper part of the path, this Tehutinekht said, 'Is my corn
to serve as a road for you, Oh peasant?' Then this peasant
said, 'My way is good. The river-bank is steep, and the
road is covered up with your corn, and you have blocked
up the path with your linen garment. Do you really intend
not to let us pass? Has it come to pass that he dares to say
such a thing?'

[At that moment] one of the asses bit off a large
mouthful of the growing corn, and this Tehutinekht said,
'Behold, your ass is eating my corn! Behold, he shall come
and tread it out.' Then this peasant said, 'My way is good.
Because one side of the road was made impassable [by you],
I led my ass to the other side (?), and now you have seized
my ass because he bit off a large mouthful of the growing
corn. However, I know the master of this estate, which
belongs to Rensi, the son of Meru. There is no doubt that
he has driven every robber out of the whole country, and
shall I be robbed on his estate?' And this Tehutinekht said,
'Is not this an illustration of the proverb which the people
use, "The name of the poor man is only mentioned because
of his master?" It is I who speak to you, but it is the steward
[Rensi, the son of Meru] of whom you are thinking.'

Then Tehutinekht seized a cudgel of green tamarisk
wood, and beat cruelly with it every part of the peasant's
body, and took his asses from him and carried them off
into his compound. And this peasant wept and uttered loud
shrieks of pain because of what was done to him. And this
Tehutinekht said, 'Howl not so loudly, peasant, or verily
[you shall depart] to the domain of the Lord of Silence.'

Then this peasant said, 'You have beaten me, and robbed me of my possessions, and now you wish to steal even the very complaint that comes out of my mouth! Lord of Silence indeed! Give me back my goods. Do not make me utter complaints about your fearsome character.'

And this peasant spent ten whole days in making entreaties to this Tehutinekht [for the restoration of his goods], but Tehutinekht paid no attention to them whatsoever. At the end of this time this peasant set out on a journey to the south, to the city of Hensu, in order to lay his complaint before Rensi, the son of Meru, the steward, and he found him just as he was coming forth from the door in the courtyard of his house which opened on the river bank, to embark in his official boat on the river. And this peasant said, 'I earnestly wish that it may happen that I may make glad your heart with the words which I am going to say! Perhaps you will allow someone to call your confidential servant to me, in order that I may send him back to you thoroughly well informed as to my business.' Then Rensi, the son of Meru, the steward, caused his confidential servant to go to this peasant, who sent him back to him thoroughly well informed as to his business. And Rensi, the son of Meru, the steward, made inquiries about this Tehutinekht from the officials who were immediately connected with him, and they said to him, 'Lord, the matter is indeed only one that concerns one of the peasants of Tehutinekht who went [to do business] with another man near him instead of with him. And, as a matter of fact, [officials like Tehutinekht] always treat their peasants in this manner whenever they go to do business

249

with other people instead of with them. Would you trouble yourself to inflict punishment upon Tehutinekht for the sake of a little soda and a little salt? [It is unthinkable.] Just let Tehutinekht be ordered to restore the soda and the salt and he will do so [immediately].' And Rensi, the son of Meru, the steward, held his peace; he made no answer to the words of these officials, and to this peasant he made no reply whatsoever.

And this peasant came to make his complaint to Rensi, the son of Meru, the steward, and on the first occasion he said, 'Oh my lord steward, greatest one of the great ones, guide of the things that are not and of these that are, when you go down into the Sea of Truth (the name of a lake in the Other World), and sail thereon, may the attachment (?) of your sail not tear away, may your boat not drift (?), may no accident befall your mast, may the poles of your boat not be broken, may you not run aground when you would walk on the land, may the current not carry you away, may you not taste the calamities of the stream, may you never see a face of fear, may the timid fish come to you, and mayest you obtain fine, fat waterfowl. Oh you who are the father of the orphan, the husband of the widow, the brother of the woman who has been put away by her husband, and the clother of the motherless, grant that I may place your name in this land in connection with all good law. Guide in whom there is no avarice, great man in whom there is no meanness, who destroys falsehood and make what is true exist, who come to the word of my mouth, I speak that you may hear. Perform justice, Oh you who are praised, to whom those who are most worthy of praise give praise. Do away the oppression that weighs me down. Behold, I am weighted with sorrow, behold, I am sorely wronged. Try me, for behold, I suffer greatly.'

Now this peasant spoke these words in the time of the King of the South, the King of the North, NebkauRa, whose word is truth. And Rensi, the son of Meru, the steward, went into the presence of His Majesty, and said, 'My Lord, I have found one of these peasants who can really speak with true eloquence. His goods have been stolen from him by an official who is in my service, and behold, he has come to lay before me a complaint concerning this.' His Majesty said to Rensi, the son of Meru, the steward, 'If you would see me in a good state of health, keep him here, and do not make any answer at all to anything which he shall say, so that he may continue to speak. Then let that which he shall say be written down, and brought to us, so that we may hear it. Take care that his wife and his children have food to live on, and see that one of these peasants goes to remove want from his house. Provide food for the peasant himself to live on, but you shall make the provision in such a way that the food may be given to him without letting him know that it is you who have given it to him. Let the food be given to his friends and let them give it to him.' So there were given to him four bread-cakes and two pots of beer daily. These were provided by Rensi, the son of Meru, the steward, and he gave them to a friend, and it was this friend who gave them to the peasant. And Rensi, the son of Meru, the steward, sent instructions to the governor of [the Oasis of] Sekhet-hemat to supply the wife of the peasant with daily rations, and there were given to her regularly the bread-cakes that were made from three measures of corn.

Then this peasant came a second time to lay his complaint [before Rensi], and he found him as he was coming out from the ..., and he said, 'Oh steward, my lord, the greatest of the great, you richest of the rich, whose greatness is true greatness, whose riches are true riches, you rudder of heaven, you pole of the earth, you measuring rope for heavy weights (?)! Oh rudder, slip not, Oh pole, topple not, Oh measuring rope, make no mistake in measuring! The great lord takes away from her that has no master (or owner), and steals from him that is alone [in the world]. Your rations are in your house – a pot of beer and three bread-cakes. What do you spend in satisfying those who depend upon you? Shall he who must die die with his people? Will you be a man of eternity (i.e. will you live forever?) Behold, are not these things evils, namely, the balance that leans side-ways, the pointer of the balance that does not show the correct weight, and an upright and just man who departs from his path of integrity? Observe! The truth goes badly with you, being driven out of her proper place, and the officials commit acts of injustice. He who ought to estimate a case correctly gives a wrong decision. He who ought to keep himself from stealing commits an act of robbery. He who should be strenuous to arrest the man who breaks the word (i.e. law) in its smallest point, is himself guilty of departing therefrom. He who should give breath stifles him that could breathe. The land that ought to give repose drives repose away. He who should divide in fairness has become a robber. He who should blot out the oppressor gives him the command to turn the town into a waste of water. He who should drive away evil himself commits acts of injustice.'

Then Rensi, the son of Meru, the steward, said [to the peasant], 'Does your case appear in your heart so serious that I must have my servant [Tchutinekht] seized on your account?' This peasant said, 'He who measures the heaps of corn filches from them for himself, and he who fills [the measure] for others robs his neighbours. Since he who should carry out the behests of the law gives the order to rob, who is to repress crime? He who should do away with offences against the law himself commits them. He who should act with integrity behaves crookedly. He who does acts of injustice is applauded. When will you find yourself able to resist and to put down acts of injustice? [When] the ... comes to his place of yesterday the command comes: "Do a [good] deed in order that one may do a [good] deed [to you]", that is to say, "Give thanks to everyone for what he does". This is to drive back the bolt before it is shot, and to give a command to the man who is already overburdened with orders. Would that a moment of destruction might come, wherein your vines should be laid low, and your geese diminished, and your waterfowl be made few in number! [Thus] it comes that the man who ought to see clearly has become blind, and he who ought to hear distinctly has become deaf, and he who ought to be a just guide has become one who leads into error.

Observe! You are strong and powerful. Your arm is able to do deeds of might, and [yet] your heart is avaricious. Compassion has removed itself from you. The wretched man whom you have destroyed cries aloud in his anguish.

You are like the messenger of the god Henti (the Crocodile-god). Set not out [to do evil] for the Lady of the Plague (i.e. Sekhmet).... As there is nothing between you and her for a certain purpose, so there is nothing against you and her. If you will not do it [then] she will not show compassion. The beggar has the powerful owner of possessions (or revenues) robbed, and the man who has nothing has the man who has secreted [much] stolen goods. To steal anything at all from the beggar is an absolute crime on the part of the man who is not in want, and [if he does this] shall his action not be inquired into? You are filled full with your bread, and are drunken with your beer, and you are rich [beyond count]. When the face of the steersman is directed to what is in front of him, the boat falls out of its course, and sails wherever it pleases. When the King [remains] in his house, and when you work the rudder, acts of injustice take place round about you, complaints are widespread, and the loss (?) is very serious. And one says, "What is taking place?" You should make yourself a place of refuge [for the needy]. Your quay should be safe. But observe! your town is in commotion. Your tongue is righteous, make no mistake [in judgment]. The abominable behaviour of a man is, as it were, [one of] his members. Speak no lies yourself, and take good heed that your high officials do not do so. Those who assess the dues on the crops are like a ..., and to tell lies is very dear to their hearts. You who have knowledge of the affairs of all the people, do you not understand my circumstances? Observe, you who relieves the wants of all who have suffered by water, I am on the path of him that has no boat. Oh you who bring every drowning man to land, and who saves the man whose boat has foundered, are you going to let me perish?'

And this peasant came a third time to lay his complaint [before Rensi], and he said, 'Oh my Lord Rensi, the steward! You are Ra, the lord of heaven with your great chiefs. The affairs of all men [are ruled by you]. You are like the water-flood. You are Hep (the Nile-god) who makes green the fields, and who makes the islands that are deserts become productive. Exterminate the robber, be you the advocate of those who are in misery, and be not towards the petitioner like the water-flood that sweeps him away. Take heed to yourself likewise, for eternity comes, and behave in such a way that the proverb, "Righteousness (or truth) is the breath of the nostrils", may be applicable to you. Punish those who are deserving of punishment, and then these shall be like you in dispensing justice. Do not the small scales weigh incorrectly? Does not the large balance incline to one side? In such cases is not Thoth merciful? When you do acts of injustice you become the second of these three, and if these be merciful you also may be merciful. Answer not good with evil, and do not set one thing in the place of another. Speech flourishes more than the *senmit* plants, and grows stronger than the smell of the same. Make no answer to it whilst you pour out acts of injustice, to make grow apparel, which three ... will cause him to make. [If] you work the steering pole against the sail (?), the flood shall gather strength against the doing of what is right. Take good heed to yourself and set yourself on the mat (?) on the look-out place. The equilibrium of the earth is maintained by the doing of what is right. Tell not lies, for you are a great man. Act not in a light manner, for you are a man of solid worth. Tell not lies, for you are a pair of scales. Make no mistake [in your weighing], for you are a correct reckoner (?). Observe! You are all of a piece with the pair of scales. If they weigh incorrectly, you also shall act falsely. Let not the boat run aground when you are working the steering pole ... the look-out place. When you have to proceed against one who has carried off something, take you nothing, for behold, the great man ceases to be a great man when he is avaricious. Your tongue is the pointer of the scales; your heart is the weight; your lips are the two arms of the scales. If you cover your face so as not to see the doer of violent deeds, who is there [left] to repress lawless deeds? Observe! You are like a poor man for the man who washes clothes, who is avaricious and destroys kindly feeling (?). He who forsakes the friend who endows him for the sake of his client is his brother, who has come and brought him a gift. Observe! You are a ferryman who ferries over the stream only the man who possesses the proper fare, whose integrity is well attested (?). Observe! You are like the overseer of a granary who does not at once permit to pass him that comes empty. Observe! You are among men like a bird of prey that lives upon weak little birds. Observe! You are like the cook whose sole joy is to kill, whom no creature escapes. Observe! You are like a shepherd who is careless about the loss of his sheep through the rapacious crocodile; you never count [your sheep]. Would that you would make evil and rapacious men be fewer! Safety has departed from [every] town throughout the land. You should hear, but most assuredly you hear not! Why have you not heard that I have this day driven back the rapacious man? When the crocodile pursues.... How long is this condition of yours to last? Truth which is concealed shall be found, and falsehood shall perish. Do not imagine that you are master of tomorrow, which has not yet come, for the evils which it may bring with it are unknown.'

And behold, when this peasant had said these things to Rensi, the son of Meru, the steward, at the entrance to the hall of the palace, Rensi caused two men with leather whips to seize him, and they beat him in every member of his body. Then this peasant said: 'The son of Meru has made a mistake. His face is blind in respect of what he sees, he is deaf in respect of what he hears, and he is forgetting that which he ought to remember. Observe! You are like a town that has no governor, and a community that has no chief, and a ship that has no captain, and a body of men who have no guide. Observe! You are like a high official who is a thief, a governor of a town who takes [bribes], and the overseer of a province who has been appointed to suppress robbery, but who has become the captain of those who practise it.'

And this peasant came a fourth time to lay his complaint before Rensi, and he met him as he was coming out from the door of the temple of the god Herushefit, and said, 'Oh you who are praised, the god Herushefit, from whose house you come forth, praises you. When well-doing perishes, and there is none who seeks to prevent its destruction, falsehood makes itself seen boldly in the land. If it happens that the ferry-boat is not brought for you to cross the

stream in, how will you be able to cross the stream? If you
have to cross the stream in your sandals, is your crossing
pleasant? Assuredly it is not! What man is there who
continues to sleep until it is broad daylight? [This habit]
destroys the marching by night, and the travelling by day,
and the possibility of a man profiting by his good luck, in
very truth. Observe! One cannot tell you sufficiently often
that 'Compassion has departed from you.' And behold, how
the oppressed man whom you have destroyed complains!
Observe! You are like a man of the chase who would satisfy
his craving for bold deeds, who determines to do what he
wishes, to spear the hippopotamus, to shoot the wild bull,
to catch fish, and to catch birds in his nets. He who is
without hastiness will not speak without due thought. He
whose habit is to ponder deeply will not be light-minded.
Apply your heart earnestly and you shall know the truth.
Pursue diligently the course which you have chosen, and
let him that hears the plaintiff act rightly. He who follows
a right course of action will not treat a plaintiff wrongly.
When the arm is brought, and when the two eyes see,
and when the heart is of good courage, boast not loudly
in proportion to your strength, in order that calamity may
not come to you. He who passes by [his] fate halts between
two opinions. The man who eats tastes [his food], the
man who is spoken to answers, the man who sleeps sees
visions, but nothing can resist the presiding judge when he
is the pilot of the doer [of evil]. Observe, Oh stupid man,
you are apprehended. Observe, Oh ignorant man, you are
freely discussed. Observe, too, that men intrude upon your
most private moments. Steersman, let not your boat run

aground. Nourisher [of men], let not men die. Destroyer [of men], let not men perish. Shadow, let not men perish through the burning heat. Place of refuge, let not the crocodile commit ravages. It is now four times that I have laid my complaint before you. How much more time shall I spend in doing this?'

This peasant came a fifth time to make his complaint, and said, 'Oh my lord steward, the fisherman with a *khut* instrument ..., the fisherman with a ... kills *i*-fish, the fisherman with a harpoon spears the *aubbu* fish, the fisherman with a *tchabhu* instrument catches the *paqru* fish, and the common fishermen are always drawing fish from the river. Observe! You are even as they. Wrest not the goods of the poor man from him. The helpless man you know him. The goods of the poor man are the breath of his life; to seize them and carry them off from him is to block up his nostrils. You are committed to the hearing of a case and to the judging between two parties at law, so that you may suppress the robber; but, verily, what you do is to support the thief. The people love you, and yet you are a law-breaker. You have been set as a dam before the man of misery, take heed that he is not drowned. Verily, you are like a lake to him, Oh you who flows quickly.'

This peasant came the sixth time to lay his complaint [before Rensi], and said, 'Oh my lord steward ... who makes truth, who makes happiness (or, what is good), who destroys [all evil]; you are like the satiety that comes to put an end to hunger, you are like the raiment that comes to do away nakedness; you are like the heavens that become calm after a violent storm and refresh with warmth those who are cold; you are like the fire that cooks that which is raw, and you are like the water that quenches the thirst. Yet look round about you! He who ought to make a division fairly is a robber. He who ought to make everyone satisfied has been the cause of the trouble. He who ought to be the source of healing is one of those who cause sicknesses. The transgressor diminishes the truth. He who fills well the right measure acts rightly, provided that he gives neither too little nor too much. If an offering be brought to you, do you share it with your brother (or neighbour), for that which is given in charity is free from after-thought (?). The man who is dissatisfied induces separation, and the man who has been condemned brings on schisms, even before one can know what is in his mind. When you have arrived at a decision delay not in declaring it. Who keeps within him that which he can eject?... When a boat comes into port it is unloaded, and the freight thereof is landed everywhere on the quay. It is [well] known that you have been educated, and trained, and experienced, but behold, it is not that you may rob [the people]. Nevertheless, you do [rob them] just as other people do, and those who are found about you are thieves (?). You who should be the most upright man of all the people are the greatest transgressor in the whole country. [You are] the wicked gardener who waters his plot of ground with evil deeds in order to make his plot tell lies, so that he may flood the town (or estate) with evil deeds (or calamities).'

This peasant came the seventh time in order to lay his complaint [before Rensi], and said, 'Oh my lord steward, you are the steering pole of the whole land, and the land sails according to your command. You are the second (or counterpart) of Thoth, who judges impartially. My lord, permit you a man to appeal to you in respect of his cause which is righteous. Let not your heart fight against it, for it is unseemly for you to do so; [if you do this] you of the broad face will become evil-hearted. Curse not the thing that has not yet taken place, and rejoice not over that which has not yet come to pass. The tolerant judge rejoices in showing kindness, and he withholds all action concerning a decision that has been given, when he knows not what plan was in the heart. In the case of the judge who breaks the law, and overthrows uprightness, the poor man cannot live [before him], for the judge plunders him, and the truth salutes him not. But my body is full, and my heart is overloaded, and the expression thereof comes forth from my body by reason of the condition of the same. [When] there is a breach in the dam the water pours out through it: even so is my mouth opened and it utters speech. I have now emptied myself, I have poured out what I had to pour out, I have unburdened my body, I have finished washing my linen. What I had to say before you is said, my misery has been fully set out before you; now what have you to say in excuse (or apology)? your lazy cowardice has been the cause of your sin, your avarice has rendered you stupid, and your gluttony has been your enemy. Do you think that you will never find another peasant like me? If he has a complaint to make do you think that he will not stand, if he is a lazy man, at the door of his house? He whom you force to speak will not remain silent. He whom you force to wake up will not remain asleep. The faces which you make keen will not remain stupid. The mouth which you open will not remain closed. He whom you make intelligent will not remain ignorant. He whom you instruct will not remain a fool. These are they who destroy evils. These are the officials, the lords of what is good. These are the crafts-folk who make what exists. These are they who put on their bodies again the heads that have been cut off.'

This peasant came the eighth time to lay his complaint [before Rensi], and said, 'Oh my lord steward, a man falls because of covetousness. The avaricious man has no aim, for his aim is frustrated. Your heart is avaricious, which befitt you not. You plunder, and your plunder is no use to you. And yet formerly you did permit a man to enjoy that to which he had good right! your daily bread is in your house, your belly is filled, grain overflows [in your granaries], and the overflow perishes and is wasted. The officials who have been appointed to suppress acts of injustice have been rapacious robbers, and the officials who have been appointed to stamp out falsehood have become hiding-places for those who work iniquity. It is not fear of you that has driven me to make my complaint to you, for you do not understand my mind (or heart). The man who is silent and who turns back in order to bring his miserable state [before you] is not afraid to place it before you, and his brother does not bring [gifts] from the interior of [his quarter]. Your estates are in the fields, your food is on [your] territory, and your bread is in the storehouse, yet the officials make gifts to you and you seize them. Are you not then a robber? Will not the men who plunder hasten with you to the divisions of the fields? Perform the truth for the Lord of Truth, who possesses the real truth. You writing reed, you roll of papyrus, you palette, you Thoth, you are remote from acts of justice. Oh Good One, you are still goodness. Oh Good One, you are truly good. Truth endures forever. It goes down to the grave with those who perform truth, it is laid in the coffin and is buried in the earth; its name is never removed from the earth, and its name is remembered on earth for good (or blessing). That is the ordinance of the word of God. If it be a matter of a hand-balance it never goes askew; if it be a matter of a large pair of scales, the standard thereof never inclines to one side. Whether it be I who come, or another, verily you must make speech, but do not answer whether you speak to one who ought to hold his peace, or whether you seize one who cannot seize you. You are not merciful, you are not considerate. You have not withdrawn yourself, you have not gone afar off. But you have not in any way given in respect of me any judgment in accordance with the command, which came forth from the mouth of Ra himself, saying, "Speak the truth, perform the truth, for truth is great, mighty, and everlasting. When you perform the truth you will find its virtues (?), and it will lead you to the state of being blessed (?). If the hand-balance is askew, the pans of the balance, which perform the weighing, hang crookedly, and a correct weighing cannot be carried out, and the result is a false one; even so the result of wickedness is wickedness.'"

This peasant came the ninth time to lay his complaint [before Rensi], and said, 'The great balance of men is their tongues, and all the rest is put to the test by the hand balance. When you punish the man who ought to be punished, the act tells in your favour. [When he does not this] falsehood becomes his possession, truth turns away from before him, his goods are falsehood, truth forsakes him, and supports him not. If falsehood advances, she makes a mistake, and goes not over with the ferry-boat [to the Island of Osiris]. The man with whom falsehood prevails has no children and no heirs upon the earth. The man in whose boat falsehood sails never reaches land, and his boat never comes into port. Be not heavy, but at the same time do not be too light. Be not slow, but at the same time be not too quick. Rage not at the man who is listening to you. Cover not over your face before the man with whom you are acquainted. Make not blind your face towards the man who is looking at you. Thrust not aside the suppliant as you go down. Be not indolent in making known your decision. Do [good] to him that will do [good] to you. Do not listen to the cry of the mob, who say, "A man will assuredly cry out when his case is really righteous." There is no yesterday for the indolent man, there is no friend for the man who is deaf to [the words of] truth, and there is no day of rejoicing for the avaricious man. The informer becomes a poor man, and the poor man becomes a beggar, and the unfriendly man becomes a dead person. Observe now, I have laid my complaint before you, but you will not listen to it; I shall now depart, and make my complaint against you to Anubis.'

Then Rensi, the son of Meru, the steward, caused two of his servants to go and bring back the peasant. Now this peasant was afraid, for he believed that he would be beaten severely because of the words which he had spoken to him. And this peasant said, 'This is [like] the coming of the thirsty man to salt tears, and the taking of the mouth of the suckling child to the breast of the woman that is dry. That the sight of which is longed for comes not, and only death approaches.'

Then Rensi, the son of Meru, the steward, said, 'Be not afraid, Oh peasant, for behold, you shall dwell with me.' Then this peasant swore an oath, saying, 'Assuredly I will eat of your bread, and drink of your beer forever.' Then Rensi, the son of Meru, the steward, said, 'Come here, however, so that you may hear your petitions'; and he caused to be [written] on a roll of new papyrus all the complaints which this peasant had made, each complaint according to its day. And Rensi, the son of Meru, the steward, sent the papyrus to the King of the South, the King of the North, NebkauRa, whose word is truth, and it pleased the heart of His Majesty more than anything else in the whole land. And His Majesty said, 'Pass judgment on yourself, Oh son of Meru.' And Rensi, the son of Meru, the steward, despatched two men to bring him back. And he was brought back, and an embassy was despatched to Sekhet Hemat.... Six persons, besides ... his grain, and his millet, and his asses, and his dogs.... [The remaining lines are mutilated, but the words which are visible make it certain that Tehutinekht the thief was punished, and that he was made to restore to the peasant everything which he had stolen from him.]

THE JOURNEY OF THE PRIEST UNU-AMEN INTO SYRIA

On the eighteenth day of the third month of the season of the Inundation, of the fifth year, Unu-Amen, the senior priest of the Hait chamber of the house of Amen, the Lord of the thrones of the Two Lands, set out on his journey to bring back wood for the great and holy Boat of Amen-Ra, the King of the Gods, which is called 'User-hat', and floats on the canal of Amen.

On the day wherein I arrived at Tchan (Tanis or Zoan), the territory of Nessubanebtet (i.e. King Smendes) and Thent-Amen, I delivered to them the credentials which I had received from Amen-Ra, the King of the Gods, and when they had had my letters read before them, they said, 'We will certainly do whatsoever Amen-Ra, the King of the Gods, our Lord, commands.' And I lived in that place until the fourth month of the season of the Inundation, and I abode in the palace at Zoan. Then Nessubanebtet and Thent-Amen despatched me with the captain of the large ship called Menkabuta, and I set sail on the sea of Kharu (Syria) on the first day of the fourth month of the Season of the Inundation. I arrived at Dhir, a city of Tchakaru, and Badhilu, its prince, made his servants bring me bread-cakes by the ten thousand, and a large jar of wine, and a leg of beef. And a man who belonged to the crew of my boat ran away, having stolen vessels of gold that weighed five *teben*, and four vessels of silver that weighed twenty *teben*, and silver in a leather bag that weighed eleven *teben*; thus he stole five *teben* of gold and thirty-one *teben* of silver.

On the following morning I rose up, and I went to the place where the prince of the country was, and I said to him, 'I have been robbed in your port. Since you are the prince of this land, and the leader thereof, you must make search and find out what has become of my money. I swear to you that the money [once] belonged to Amen-Ra, King

of the Gods, the Lord of the Two Lands; it belonged to
Nessubanebtet, it belonged to my lord Her-Heru, and to the
other great kings of Egypt, but it now belongs to Uartha,
and to Makamaru, and to Tchakar-Bal, Prince of Kepuna
(Byblos).' And he said to me, 'Be angry or be pleased, [as
you like], but, behold, I know absolutely nothing about the
matter of which you speak to me. Had the thief been a man
who was a subject of mine, who had gone down into your
ship and stolen your money, I would in that case have made
good your loss from the moneys in my own treasury, until
such time as it had been found out who it was that robbed
you, and what his name was, but the thief who has robbed
you belongs to your own ship. Yet tarry here for a few days,
and stay with me, so that I may seek him out.' So I tarried
there for nine days, and my ship lay at anchor in his port.
And I went to him and I said to him, 'Verily you have not
found my money, [but I must depart] with the captain of
the ship and with those who are travelling with him.' ...

[The text here is mutilated, but from the fragments of
the lines that remain it seems clear that Unu-Amen left
the port of Dhir, and proceeded in his ship to Tyre. After
a short stay there he left Tyre very early one morning
and sailed to Kepuna (Byblos), so that he might have an
interview with the governor of that town, who was called
Tchakar-Bal. During his interview with Tchakar-Bal the
governor of Tyre produced a bag containing thirty *teben*
of silver, and Unu-Amen promptly seized it, and declared
that he intended to keep it until his own money which had
been stolen was returned to him. Whilst Unu-Amen was
at Byblos he buried in some secret place the image of the

god Amen and the amulets belonging to it, which he had
brought with him to protect him and to guide him on his
way. The name of this image was 'Amen-ta-mat'. The text
then proceeds in a connected form thus:]

And I passed nineteen days in the port of Byblos, and
the governor passed his days in sending messages to me
each day, saying, 'Get you gone out of my harbour.' Now
on one occasion when he was making an offering to his
gods, the god took possession of a certain young chief of
his chiefs, and he caused him to fall into a fit of frenzy,
and the young man said, 'Bring up the god (i.e. the figure
of Amen-ta-mat). Bring the messenger who has possession
of him. Make him set out on his way. Make him depart
immediately.' Now the man who had been seized with the
fit of divine frenzy continued to be moved by the same
during the night. And I found a certain ship, which was
bound for Egypt, and when I had transferred to it all my
property, I cast a glance at the darkness, saying, 'If the
darkness increases I will transfer the god to the ship also,
and not permit any other eye whatsoever to look upon
him.' Then the superintendent of the harbour came to me,
saying, 'Tarry you here until tomorrow morning, according
to the orders of the governor.' And I said to him, 'Are not
you yourself he who has passed his days in coming to me
daily and saying, 'Get you gone out of my harbour?' Do you
not say, 'Tarry here,' so that I may let the ship which I have
found [bound for Egypt] depart, when you will again come
and say, 'Haste you to be gone'?'

And the superintendent of the harbour turned away and
departed, and told the governor what I had said. And the

governor sent a message to the captain of the ship bound for Egypt, saying, 'Tarry till the morning; these are the orders of the governor.' And when the morning had come, the governor sent a messenger, who took me to the place where offerings were being made to the god in the fortress wherein the governor lived on the sea coast. And I found him seated in his upper chamber, and he was reclining with his back towards an opening in the wall, and the waves of the great Syrian sea were rolling in from seawards and breaking on the shore behind him. And I said to him, 'The grace of Amen [be with you]!' And he said to me, 'Including this day, how long is it since you came from the place where Amen is?' And I said to him, 'Five months and one day, including today.' And he said to me, 'Verily if that which you sayest is true, where are the letters of Amen which ought to be in your hand? Where are the letters of the high priest of Amen which ought to be in your hand?'

And I said to him, 'I gave them to Nessubanebtet and Thent-Amen.' Then was he very angry indeed, and he said to me, 'Verily, there are neither letters nor writings in your hands for us! Where is the ship made of acacia wood which Nessubanebtet gave to you? Where are his Syrian sailors? Did he not hand you over to the captain of the ship so that after you had started on your journey they might kill you and cast you into the sea? Whose permission did they seek to attack the god? And indeed whose permission were they seeking before they attacked you?' This is what he said to me.

And I said to him, 'The ship [wherein I sailed] was in very truth an Egyptian ship, and it had a crew of Egyptian sailors who sailed it on behalf of Nessubanebtet. There were no Syrian sailors placed on board of it by him.' He said to me, 'I swear that there are twenty ships lying in my harbour, the captains of which are in partnership with Nessubanebtet. And as for the city of Sidon, to where you wish to travel, I swear that there are there ten thousand other ships, the captains of which are in partnership with Uarkathar, and they are sailed for the benefit of his house.' At this grave moment I held my peace. And he answered and said to me, 'On what matter of business have you come hither?' And I said to him, 'The matter concerning which I have come is wood for the great and holy Boat of Amen-Ra, the King of the Gods. What your father did [for the god], and what your father's father did for him, do you also.' That was what I said to him. And he said to me, 'They certainly did do work for it (i.e. the boat). Give me a gift for my work for the boat, and then I also will work for it. Assuredly my father and my grandfather did do the work that was demanded of them, and Pharaoh, life, strength, and health be to him! caused six ships laden with the products of Egypt to come here, and the contents thereof were unloaded into their storehouses. Now, you must most certainly cause some goods to be brought and given to me for myself.'

Then he caused to be brought the books which his father had kept day by day, and he had them read out before me, and it was found that one thousand *teben* of silver of all kinds were [entered] in his books. And he said to me, 'If the Ruler of Egypt had been the lord of my possessions, and if I had indeed been his servant, he would never have had silver and gold brought [to pay my father and my father's father] when he told them to carry out the commands of Amen. The instructions which they (i.e. Pharaoh) gave to my father were by no means the command of one who was their king. As for me, I am assuredly not your servant, and indeed I am not the servant of him that made you to set out on your way. If I were to cry out now, and to shout to the cedars of Lebanon, the heavens would open, and the trees would be lying spread out on the sea-shore. I ask you now to show me the sails which you have brought to carry your ships which shall be loaded with your timber to Egypt. And show me also the tackle with which you will transfer to your ships the trees which I shall cut down for you for.... [Unless I make for you the tackle] and the sails of your ships, the tops will be too heavy, and they will snap off, and you will perish in the midst of the sea, [especially if] Amen utters his voice in the sky (i.e. if there is thunder), and he unfetters Sutekh (the Storm-god) at the moment when he rages. Now Amen has assumed the overlordship of all lands, and he has made himself their master, but first and foremost he is the overlord of Egypt, whence you have come. Excellent things have come forth from Egypt, and have reached even to this place wherein I am; and moreover, knowledge (or learning) has come forth therefrom, and has reached even this place where I am. But of what use is this beggarly journey of yours which you have been made to take?'

And I said to him, 'What a shameful thing [to say]! It is not a beggarly journey on which I have been despatched by those among whom I live. And besides, assuredly there is not a single boat that floats that does not belong to Amen. To him belong the sea and the cedars of Lebanon, concerning which you say, "They are my property." In Lebanon grows [the wood] for the Boat Amen-userhat, the lord of boats. Amen-Ra, the King of the Gods, spoke and told Her-Heru, my lord, to send me forth; and therefore he caused me to set out on my journey together with this great god (i.e. the figure of Amen). Now behold, you have caused this great god to pass nine and twenty days here in a boat that is lying at anchor in your harbour, for most assuredly you did know that he was resting here. Amen is now what he has always been, and yet you would dare to stand up and haggle about the [cedars of] Lebanon with the god who is their lord! And as concerning what you have spoken, saying, "The kings of Egypt in former times caused silver and gold to be brought [to my father and father's father", you are mistaken], since they had bestowed upon them life and health, they would never have caused gold and silver to be brought to them; but they might have caused gold and silver to be brought to your fathers instead of life and health. And Amen-Ra, the King of the Gods, is the Lord of life and health. He was the god of your fathers, and they served him all their lives, and made offerings to him, and indeed you yourself are a servant of Amen. If now you will say to Amen, "I will perform your commands, I will perform your commands", and will bring this business to a prosperous ending, you shall live, you shall be strong, you shall be healthy, and you shall rule your country to its uttermost limits wisely and well, and you shall do good to your people. But take good heed that you love not the possessions of Amen-Ra, the King of the Gods, for the lion loves the things that belong to him. And now, I pray you to allow my scribe to be summoned to me, and I will send him to Nessubanebtet and Thent-Amen, the local governors whom Amen has appointed to rule the northern portion of his land, and they will send to me everything which I shall tell them to send to me, saying, "Let such and such a thing be brought", until such time as I can make the journey to the South (i.e. to Egypt), when I will have your miserable dross brought to you, even to the uttermost portion thereof, in very truth.' That was what I said to him.

And he gave my letter into the hand of his ambassador. And he loaded up on a ship wood for the fore part and wood for the hind part [of the Boat of Amen], and four other trunks of cedar trees which had been cut down, in all seven trunks, and he despatched them to Egypt. And his ambassador departed to Egypt, and he returned to me in Syria in the first month of the winter season (November-December). And Nessubanebtet and Thent-Amen sent to me five vessels of gold, five vessels of silver, ten pieces of byssus, each sufficiently large to make a suit of raiment, five hundred rolls of fine papyrus, five hundred hides of oxen, five hundred ropes, twenty sacks of lentils, and thirty vessels full of dried fish. And for my personal use they sent to me five pieces of byssus, each sufficiently large to make a suit of raiment, a sack of lentils, and five vessels full of dried fish. Then the Governor was exceedingly glad and rejoiced greatly, and he sent three hundred men and three hundred oxen [to

Lebanon] to cut down the cedar trees, and he appointed overseers to direct them. And they cut down the trees, the trunks of which lay there during the whole of the winter season. And when the third month of the summer season had come, they dragged the tree trunks down to the sea-shore. And the Governor came out of his palace, and took up his stand before the trunks, and he sent a message to me, saying, 'Come.' Now as I was passing close by him, the shadow of his umbrella fell upon me, whereupon Pen-Amen, an officer of his bodyguard, placed himself between him and me, saying, 'The shadow of Pharaoh, life, strength, and health, be to him! your Lord, falls upon you.' And the Governor was angry with Pen-Amen, and he said, 'Let him alone.' Therefore I walked close to him.

And the Governor answered and said to me, 'Behold, the orders [of Pharaoh] which my fathers carried out in times of old, I also have carried out, notwithstanding the fact that you have not done for me what your fathers were wont to do for me. However, look for yourself, and take note that the last of the cedar trunks has arrived, and here it lies. Do now whatsoever you please with them, and take steps to load them into ships, for assuredly they are given to you as a gift. I beg you to pay no heed to the terror of the sea voyage, but if you persist in contemplating [with fear] the sea voyage, you must also contemplate [with fear] the terror of me [if you tarry here]. Certainly I have not treated you as the envoys of Kha-em-Uast (Rameses IX) were treated here, for they were made to pass seventeen (or fifteen) years in this country, and they died here.'

Then the Governor spoke to the officer of his bodyguard, saying, 'Lay hands on him, and take him to see the tombs wherein they lie.' And I said to him, 'Far be it from me to look upon such [ill-omened] things! As concerning the messengers of Kha-em-Uast, the men whom he sent to you as ambassadors were merely [officials] of his, and there was no god with his ambassadors, and so you say, 'Hasten to look upon your colleagues.' Behold, would you not have greater pleasure, and should you not [instead of saying such things] cause to be made a stele whereon should be said by you:

'Amen-Ra, the King of the Gods, sent to me Amen-ta-mat, his divine ambassador, together with Unu-Amen, his human ambassador, in quest of trunks of cedar wood for the Great and Holy Boat of Amen-Ra, the King of the Gods. And I cut down cedar trees, and I loaded them into ships. I provided the ships myself, and I manned them with my own sailors, and I made them to arrive in Egypt that they might bespeak [from the god for me] ten thousand years of life, in addition to the span of life which was decreed for me. And this petition has been granted.

'[And would you not rather] that, after the lapse of time, when another ambassador came from the land of Egypt who understood this writing, he should utter your name which should be on the stele, and pray that you should receive water in Amentet, even like the gods who subsist?'

And he said to me, 'These words which you have spoken to me are of a certainty a great testimony.' And I said to him, 'Now, as concerning the multitude of words which you have spoken to me: As soon as I arrive at the place where the First Prophet (i.e. Her-Heru) of Amen dwells, and he knows [how you have] performed the commands of the God [Amen], he will cause to be conveyed to you [a gift of] certain things.' Then I walked down to the beach, to the place where the trunks of cedar had been lying, and I saw eleven ships [ready] to put out to sea; and they belonged to Tchakar-Bal. [And the governor sent out an order] saying, 'Stop him, and do not let any ship with him on board [depart] to the land of Egypt.' Then I sat myself down and wept. And the scribe of the Governor came out to me, and said to me, 'What ails you?' And I said to him, 'Consider the *kashu* birds that fly to Egypt again and again! And consider how they flock to the cool water brooks! Until the coming of whom must I remain cast aside hither? Assuredly you see those who have come to prevent my departure a second time.'

Then [the scribe] went away and told the Governor what I had said; and the Governor shed tears because of the words that had been repeated to him, for they were full of pain. And he caused the scribe to come out to me again, and he brought with him two skins [full] of wine and a goat. And he caused to be brought out to me Thentmut, an Egyptian singing woman who lived in his house, and he said to her, 'Sing to him, and let not the cares of his business lay hold upon his heart.' And to me he sent a message, saying, 'Eat and drink, and let not business lay hold upon your heart. You shall hear everything which I have to say to you tomorrow morning.'

And when the morning had come, he caused [the inhabitants of the town] to be assembled on the quay, and having stood up in their midst, he said to the Tchakaru, 'For what purpose have you come here?' And they said to him, 'We have come here seeking for the ships which have been broken and dashed to pieces, that is to say, the ships which you did despatch to Egypt, with our unfortunate fellow-sailors in them.' And he said to them, 'I know not how to detain the ambassador of Amen in my country any longer. I beg of you to let me send him away, and then do pursue him, and prevent him [from escaping].' And he made me embark in a ship, and sent me forth from the sea-coast, and the winds drove me ashore to the land of Alasu (Cyprus?). And the people of the city came forth to slay me, and I was dragged along in their midst to the place where their queen Hathaba lived; and I met her when she was coming forth from one house to go into another. Then I cried out in entreaty to her, and I said to the people who were standing about her, 'Surely there must be among you someone who understands the language of Egypt.' And one of them said, 'I understand the speech [of Egypt].' Then I said to him, 'Tell my Lady these words: I have heard it said far from here, even in the city of [Thebes], the place where Amen dwells that wrong is done in every city, and that only in the land of Alasu (Cyprus?) is right done. And yet wrong is done here every day!' And she said, 'What is it that you really wish to say?' I said to her, 'Now that the angry sea and the winds have cast me up on the land wherein you dwell, you will surely not permit these men who have received me to slay me! Moreover, I am an ambassador of Amen. And consider carefully, for I am a man who will be searched for every day. And as for the sailors of Byblos whom they wish to kill, if their lord finds ten of your sailors he will assuredly slay them.' Then she caused her people to be called off me, and they were made to stand still, and she said to me, 'Lie down and sleep....' [The rest of the narrative is missing].

FAIRY TALES

One of the most interesting tales that have come down to us in Egyptian dress is the tale commonly called the 'Tale of the Two Brothers'. It is found written in the hieratic character upon a papyrus preserved in the British Museum (D'Orbiney, No. 10,183), and the form which the story has there is that which was current under the nineteenth dynasty, about 1300 BCE.

The two principal male characters in the story, Anpu and Bata, were originally gods, but in the hands of the Egyptian storyteller they became men, and their deeds were treated in such a way as to form an interesting fairy story. It is beyond the scope of this little book to treat of the mythological ideas that underlie certain parts of the narrative, and we therefore proceed to give a rendering of this very curious and important 'fairy tale'.

Under the heading of this chapter may well be included 'The Story of the Shipwrecked Traveller'. The text of this remarkable story is written in the hieratic character upon a roll of papyrus, which is preserved in the Imperial Library in St. Petersburg. It is probable that a layer of facts underlies the story, but the form in which we have it justifies us in assigning to it a place among the fairy stories of Ancient Egypt.

THE TALE OF THE TWO BROTHERS

It is said that there were two brothers, [the children] of one mother and of one father; the name of the elder was Anpu, and Bata was the name of the younger. Anpu had a house and a wife, and Bata lived with him like a younger brother. It was Bata who made the clothes; he tended and herded his cattle in the fields, he ploughed the land, he did the hard work during the time of harvest, and he kept the account of everything that related to the fields. And Bata was a most excellent farmer, and his like there was not in the whole country-side; and behold, the power of the God was in him.

And very many days passed during which Anpu's young brother tended his flocks and herds daily, and he returned to his house each evening loaded with field produce of every kind. And when he had returned from the fields, he set [food] before his elder brother, who sat with his wife drinking and eating, and then Bata went out to the byre and [slept] with the cattle. On the following morning as soon as it was day, Bata took bread-cakes newly baked, and set them before Anpu, who gave him food to take with him to the fields. Then Bata drove out his cattle into the fields to feed, and [as] he walked behind them they said to him, 'The pasturage is good in such and such a place,' and he listened to their voices, and took them where they wished to go. Thus the cattle in Bata's charge became exceedingly fine, and their calves doubled in number, and they multiplied exceedingly. And when it was the season for ploughing Anpu said to Bata, 'Come, let us get our teams

ready for ploughing the fields, and our implements, for the
ground has appeared, and it is in the proper condition for
the plough. Go to the fields and take the seed-corn with you
today, and at daybreak tomorrow we will do the ploughing';
this is what he said to him. And Bata did everything which
Anpu had told him to do. The next morning, as soon as it
was daylight, the two brothers went into the fields with
their teams and their ploughs, and they ploughed the land,
and they were exceedingly happy as they ploughed, from
the beginning of their work to the very end thereof.

Now when the two brothers had been living in this way
for a considerable time, they were in the fields one day
[ploughing], and Anpu said to Bata, 'Run back to the farm
and fetch some [more] seed corn.' And Bata did so, and
when he arrived there he found his brother's wife seated
dressing her hair. And he said to her, 'Get up and give me
some seed corn that I may hurry back to the fields, for Anpu
ordered me not to loiter on the way.' Anpu's wife said to
him, 'Go yourself to the grain shed, and open the bin, and
take out from it as much corn as you wishest; I could fetch
it for you myself, only I am afraid that my hair would fall
down on the way.' Then the young man went to the bin,
and filled a very large jar full of grain, for it was his desire
to carry off a large quantity of seed corn, and he lifted up
on his shoulders the pot, which was filled full of wheat and
barley, and came out of the shed with it. And Anpu's wife
said to him, 'How much grain have you on your shoulders?'
And Bata said to her, 'Three measures of barley and two
measures of wheat, in all five measures of grain; that is
what I have on my shoulders.' These were the words which

he spoke to her. And she said to him, 'How strong you are! I have been observing your vigorousness day by day.' And her heart inclined to him, and she entreated him to stay with her, promising to give him beautiful apparel if he would do so. Then the young man became filled with fury like a panther of the south because of her words, and when she saw how angry he was she became terribly afraid. And he said to her, 'Verily you are to me as my mother, and your husband is as my father, and being my elder brother he has provided me with the means of living. You have said to me what ought not to have been said, and I pray you not to repeat it. On my part I shall tell no man of it, and on your you must never declare the matter to man or woman.' Then Bata took up his load on his shoulders, and departed to the fields. And when he arrived at the place where his elder brother was they continued their ploughing and laboured diligently at their work.

And when the evening came the elder brother returned to his house. And having loaded himself with the products of the fields, Bata drove his flocks and herds back to the farm and put them in their enclosures. And behold, Anpu's wife was smitten with fear, because of the words which she had spoken to Bata, and she took some grease and a piece of linen, and she made herself appear like a woman who had been assaulted, and who had been violently beaten by her assailant, for she wished to say to her husband, 'Your young brother has beaten me sorely.' And when Anpu returned in the evening according to his daily custom, and arrived at his house, he found his wife lying on the ground in the condition of one who had been assaulted with violence. She did not [appear to] pour water over his hands according to custom, she did not light a light before him; his house was in darkness, and she was lying prostrate and sick. And her husband said to her, 'Who has been talking to you?' And she said to him, 'No one has been talking to me except your young brother. When he came to fetch the seed corn he found me sitting alone, and he spoke words of love to me, and he told me to tie up my hair. But I would not listen to him, and I said to him, 'Am I not like your mother? Is not your elder brother like your father?' Then he was greatly afraid, and he beat me to prevent me from telling you about this matter. Now, if you do not kill him I shall kill myself, for since I have complained to you about his words, when he comes back in the evening what he will do [to me] is manifest.'

Then the elder brother became like a panther of the southern desert with wrath. And he seized his dagger, and sharpened it, and went and stood behind the stable door, so that he might slay Bata when he returned in the evening and came to the byre to bring in his cattle. And when the sun was about to set Bata loaded himself with products of the field of every kind, according to his custom, [and returned to the farm]. And as he was coming back the cow that led the herd said to Bata as she was entering the byre, 'Verily your elder brother is waiting with his dagger to slay you; flee you from before him'; and Bata hearkened to the words of the leading cow. And when the second cow as she was about to enter into the byre spoke to him even as did the first cow, Bata looked under the door of the byre, and saw the feet of his elder brother as he stood behind the door with his dagger in his hand. Then he set down his load upon the ground, and he ran away as fast as he could run, and Anpu followed him grasping his dagger. And Bata cried out to Ra-Harmakhis (the Sun god) and said, 'Oh my fair Lord, you are he who judges between the wrong and the right.' And the god Ra listened to all his words, and he caused a great stream to come into being, and to separate the two brothers, and the water was filled with crocodiles. Now Anpu was on one side of the stream and Bata on the other, and Anpu wrung his hands together in bitter wrath because he could not kill his brother. Then Bata cried out to Anpu on the other bank, saying, 'Stay where you are until daylight, and until the Disk (i.e. the Sun god) rises. I will enter into judgment with you in his presence, for it is he who sets right what is wrong. I shall never more live with you, and I shall never again dwell in the place where you are. I am going to the Valley of the Acacia.'

And when the day dawned, and there was light on the earth, and Ra-Harmakhis was shining, the two brothers looked at each other. And Bata spoke to Anpu, saying, 'Why have you pursued me in this treacherous way, wishing to slay me without first hearing what I had to say? I am your brother, younger than you are, and you are as a father and your wife is as a mother to me. Is it not so? When you did send me to fetch seed corn for our work, it was your wife who said, 'I pray you to stay with me,' but behold, the facts have been misrepresented to you, and the reverse of what happened has been put before you.' Then Bata explained everything to Anpu, and made him understand exactly what had taken place between him and his brother's wife.

And Bata swore an oath by Ra-Harmakhis, saying, 'By Ra-
Harmakhis, to lie in wait for me and to pursue me, with
your knife in your hand ready to slay me, was a wicked and
abominable thing to do.' And Bata took [from his side] the
knife which he used in cutting reeds, and drove it into his
body, and he sank down fainting upon the ground. Then
Anpu cursed himself with bitter curses, and he lifted up
his voice and wept; and he did not know how to cross
over the stream to the bank where Bata was because of the
crocodiles. And Bata cried out to him, saying, 'Behold, you
are ready to remember against me one bad deed of mine,
but you do not remember my good deeds, or even one of
the many things that have been done for you by me. Shame
on you! Get you back to your house and tend your own
cattle, for I will no longer stay with you. I will depart to
the Valley of the Acacia. But you shall come to minister
to me, therefore take heed to what I say. Now know that
certain things are about to happen to me. I am going to
cast a spell on my heart, so that I may be able to place it
on a flower of the Acacia tree. When this Acacia is cut
down my heart shall fall to the ground, and you shall come
to seek for it. You shall pass seven years in seeking for it,
but let not your heart be sick with disappointment, for you
shall find it. When you find it, place it in a vessel of cold
water, and verily my heart shall live again, and shall make
answer to him that attacks me. And you shall know what
has happened to me [by the following sign]. A vessel of
beer shall be placed in your hand, and it shall froth and
run over; and another vessel with wine in it shall be placed
[in your hand], and it shall become sour. Then make no

tarrying, for indeed these things shall happen to you.' So the younger brother departed to the Valley of the Acacia, and the elder brother departed to his house. And Anpu's hand was laid upon his head, and he cast dust upon himself [in grief for Bata], and when he arrived at his house he slew his wife, and threw her to the dogs, and he sat down and mourned for his young brother.

And when many days had passed, Bata was living alone in the Valley of the Acacia, and he spent his days in hunting the wild animals of the desert; and at night he slept under the Acacia, on the top of the flowers of which rested his heart. And after many days he built himself, with his own hand, a large house in the Valley of the Acacia, and it was filled with beautiful things of every kind, for he delighted in the possession of a house. And as he came forth [one day] from his house, he met the Company of the Gods, and they were on their way to work out their plans in their realm. And one of them said to him, 'Hail, Bata, you Bull of the gods, have you not been living here alone since the time when you did forsake your town through the wife of your elder brother Anpu? Behold, his wife has been slain [by him], and moreover you have made an adequate answer to the attack which he made upon you'; and their hearts were very sore indeed for Bata. Then Ra-Harmakhis said to Khnemu (the god who fashioned the bodies of men), 'Fashion a wife for Bata, so that you, Oh Bata, may not dwell alone.' And Khnemu made a wife to live with Bata, and her body was more beautiful than the body of any other woman in the whole country, and the essence of every god was in her; and the Seven Hathor Goddesses came to her, and they said, 'She shall die by the sword.' And Bata loved her most dearly, and she lived in his house, and he passed all his days in hunting the wild animals of the desert so that he might bring them and lay them before her. And he said to her, 'Go not out of the house lest the River carry you off, for I know not how to deliver you from it. My heart is set upon the flower of the Acacia, and if any man finds it I must do battle with him for it'; and he told her everything that had happened concerning his heart.

And many days afterwards, when Bata had gone out hunting as usual, the young woman went out of the house and walked under the Acacia tree, which was close by, and the River saw her, and sent its waters rolling after her; and she fled before them and ran away into her house. And the River said, 'I love her', and the Acacia took to the River a lock of her hair, and the River carried it to Egypt, and cast it up on the bank at the place where the washermen washed the clothes of Pharaoh, life, strength, health [be to him]! And the odour of the lock of hair passed into the clothing of Pharaoh. Then the washermen of Pharaoh quarrelled among themselves, saying, 'There is an odour [as of] perfumed oil in the clothes of Pharaoh.' And quarrels among them went on daily, and at length they did not know what they were doing. And the overseer of the washermen of Pharaoh walked to the river bank, being exceedingly angry because of the quarrels that came before him daily, and he stood still on the spot that was exactly opposite to the lock of hair as it lay in the water. Then he sent a certain man into the water to fetch it, and when he brought it back, the overseer, finding that it had an exceedingly sweet odour, took it to Pharaoh. And the scribes and the magicians were summoned into the presence of Pharaoh, and they said to him, 'This lock of hair belongs to a maiden of Ra-Harmakhis, and the essence of every god is in her. It comes to you from a strange land as a salutation of praise to you. We therefore pray you send ambassadors into every land to seek her out. And as concerning the ambassador to the Valley of the Acacia, we beg you to send a strong escort with him to fetch her.' And His Majesty said to them, 'What we have decided is very good,' and he despatched the ambassadors.

And when many days had passed by, the ambassadors who had been despatched to foreign lands returned to make a report to His Majesty, but those who had gone to the Valley of the Acacia did not come back, for Bata had slain them, with the exception of one who returned to tell the matter to His Majesty. Then His Majesty despatched foot-soldiers and horsemen and charioteers to bring back the young woman, and there was also with them a woman who had in her hands beautiful trinkets of all kinds, such as are suitable for maidens, to give to the young woman. And this woman returned to Egypt with the young woman, and everyone in all parts of the country rejoiced at her arrival. And His Majesty loved her exceedingly, and he paid her homage as the Great August One, the Chief Wife. And he spoke to her and made her tell him what had become of her husband, and she said to His Majesty, 'I pray you to cut down the Acacia Tree and then to destroy it.' Then the King caused men and bowmen to set out with axes to cut down the Acacia, and when they arrived in the Valley of the Acacia, they cut down the flower on which was the heart of Bata, and he fell down dead at that very moment of evil.

And on the following morning when the light had come upon the earth, and the Acacia had been cut down, Anpu, Bata's elder brother, went into his house and sat down, and he washed his hands; and one gave him a vessel of beer, and it frothed up, and the froth ran over, and one gave him another vessel containing wine, and it was sour. Then he grasped his staff, and [taking] his sandals, and his apparel, and his weapons which he used in fighting and hunting, he set out to march to the Valley of the Acacia. And when he arrived there he went into Bata's house, and he found his young brother there lying dead on his bed; and when he looked upon his young brother he wept on seeing that he was dead. Then he set out to seek for the heart of Bata, under the Acacia where he was wont to sleep at night, and he passed three years in seeking for it but found it not. And when the fourth year of his search had begun, his heart craved to return to Egypt, and he said, 'I will depart there tomorrow morning'; that was what he said to himself. And on the following day he walked about under the Acacia all day long looking for Bata's heart, and as he was returning [to the house] in the evening, and was looking about him still searching for it, he found a seed, which he took back with him, and behold, it was Bata's heart. Then he fetched a vessel of cold water, and having placed the seed in it, he sat down according to his custom. And when the night came, the heart had absorbed all the water; and Bata [on his bed] trembled in all his members, and he looked at Anpu, whilst his heart remained in the vessel of water. And Anpu took

up the vessel wherein was his brother's heart, which had
absorbed the water. And Bata's heart ascended its throne
[in his body], and Bata became as he had been before, and
the two brothers embraced each other, and each spoke to
the other.

And Bata said to Anpu, 'Behold, I am about to take the
form of a great bull, with beautiful hair, and a disposition
(?) which is unknown. When the sun rises, mount on my
back, and we will go to the place where my wife is, and
I will make answer [for myself]. Then shall you take me
to the place where the King is, for he will bestow great
favours upon you, and he will heap gold and silver upon you
because you will have brought me to him. For I am going to
become a great and wonderful thing, and men and women
shall rejoice because of me throughout the country.' And
on the following day Bata changed himself into the form
of which he had spoken to his brother. Then Anpu seated
himself on his back early in the morning, and when he had
come to the place where the King was, and His Majesty
had been informed concerning him, he looked at him, and
he had very great joy in him. And he made a great festival,
saying, 'This is a very great wonder which has happened';
and the people rejoiced everywhere throughout the whole
country. And Pharaoh loaded Anpu with silver and gold,
and he dwelt in his native town, and the King gave him
large numbers of slaves, and very many possessions, for
Pharaoh loved him very much, far more than any other
person in the whole land.

And when many days had passed by the bull went into
the house of purification, and he stood up in the place

where the August Lady was, and said to her, 'Look upon me, I am alive in very truth.' And she said to him, 'Who are you?' And he said to her, 'I am Bata. When you did cause the Acacia which held my heart to be destroyed by Pharaoh, well did you know that you would kill me. Nevertheless, I am alive indeed, in the form of a bull. Look at me!' And the August Lady was greatly afraid because of what she had said concerning her husband [to the King]; and the bull departed from the place of purification. And His Majesty went to tarry in her house and to rejoice with her, and she ate and drank with him; and the King was exceedingly happy. And the August Lady said to His Majesty, 'Say these words: "Whatsoever she says I will listen to for her sake," and swear an oath by God that you will do them.' And the King listened to everything which she spoke, saying, 'I beseech you to give me the liver of this bull to eat, for he is wholly useless for any kind of work.' And the King cursed many, many times the request which she had uttered, and Pharaoh's heart was exceedingly sore.

On the following morning, when it was day, the King proclaimed a great feast, and he ordered the bull to be offered up as an offering, and one of the chief royal slaughterers of His Majesty was brought to slay the bull. And after the knife had been driven into him, and whilst he was still on the shoulders of the men, the bull shook his neck, and two drops of blood from it fell by the jambs of the doorway of His Majesty, one by one jamb of Pharaoh's door, and the other by the other, and they became immediately two mighty acacia trees, and each was of the greatest magnificence. Then one went and reported to His Majesty, saying, 'Two mighty acacia trees, whereat His Majesty will marvel exceedingly, have sprung up during the night by the Great Door of His Majesty.' And men and women rejoiced in them everywhere in the country, and the King made offerings to them. And many days after this His Majesty put on his tiara of lapis-lazuli, and hung a wreath of flowers of every kind about his neck, and he mounted his chariot of silver-gold, and went forth from the Palace to see the two acacia trees. And the August Lady came following after Pharaoh [in a chariot drawn by] horses, and His Majesty sat down under one acacia, and the August Lady sat under the other. And when she had seated herself the Acacia spoke to his wife, saying, 'Oh woman, who are full of guile, I am Bata, and I am alive even though you have treated me evilly. Well did you know when you did make Pharaoh cut down the Acacia that held my heart that you would kill me, and when I transformed myself into a bull you did cause me to be slain.'

And several days after this the August Lady was eating and drinking at the table of His Majesty, and the King was enjoying her society greatly, and she said to His Majesty, 'Swear to me an oath by God, saying, I will listen to whatsoever the August Lady shall say to me for her sake; let her say on.' And he listened to everything which she said, and she said, 'I entreat you to cut down these two acacia trees, and to let them be made into great beams'; and the King listened to everything which she said. And several days after this His Majesty made cunning wood-men to go and cut down the acacia trees of Pharaoh, and whilst the August Lady was standing and watching their being cut down, a splinter flew from one of them into her mouth, and she knew that she had conceived, and the King did for her everything which her heart desired. And many days after this happened she brought forth a man child, and one said to His Majesty, 'A man child has been born to you'; and a nurse was found for him and women to watch over him and tend him, and the people rejoiced throughout the whole land. And the King sat down to enjoy a feast, and he began to call the child by his name, and he loved him very dearly, and at that same time the King gave him the title of 'Royal son of Kash' (i.e. Prince of Kash, or Viceroy of the Sudan). Some time after this His Majesty appointed him 'Erpa' (i.e. hereditary chief, or heir) of the whole country. And when he had served the office of Erpa for many years, His Majesty flew up to heaven (i.e. he died). And the King (i.e. Bata) said, 'Let all the chief princes be summoned before me, so that I may inform them about everything which has happened to me.' And they brought his wife, and he entered into judgment with her, and the sentence which he passed upon her was carried out. And Anpu, the brother of the King, was brought to His Majesty, and the King made him Erpa of the whole country. When His Majesty had reigned over Egypt for twenty years, he departed to life (i.e. he died), and his brother Anpu took his place on the day in which he was buried.

Here ends the book happily [in] peace.

THE STORY OF THE SHIPWRECKED TRAVELLER

Prefixed to the narrative of the shipwrecked traveller is the following: 'A certain servant of wise understanding has said, Let your heart be of good cheer, Oh prince. Verily we have arrived at [our] homes. The mallet has been grasped, and the anchor-post has been driven into the ground, and the bow of the boat has grounded on the bank. Thanksgivings have been offered up to God, and every man has embraced his neighbour. Our sailors have returned in peace and safety, and our fighting men have lost none of their comrades, even though we travelled to the uttermost parts of Uaut (Nubia), and through the country of Senmut (Northern Nubia). Verily we have arrived in peace, and we have reached our own land [again]. Hearken, Oh prince, to me, even though I be a poor man. Wash yourself, and let water run over your fingers. I would that you should be ready to return an answer to the man who addresses you, and to speak to the King [from] your heart, and assuredly you must give your answer promptly and without hesitation. The mouth of a man delivers him, and his words provide a covering for [his] face. Act you according to the promptings of your heart, and when you have spoken [you will have made him] be at rest.'

The shipwrecked traveller then narrates his experiences in the following words: I will now speak and give you a description of the things that [once] happened to me myself [when] I was journeying to the copper mines of the king. I went down into the sea in a ship that was one hundred and fifty cubits in length, and forty cubits in breadth, and it was manned by one hundred and fifty sailors who were chosen from among the best sailors of Egypt. They had looked upon the sky, they had looked upon the land, and their hearts were more understanding than the hearts of lions. Now although they were able to say beforehand when a tempest was coming, and could tell when a squall was going to rise before it broke upon them, a storm actually overtook us when we were still on the sea. Before we could make the land the wind blew with redoubled violence, and it drove before it upon us a wave that was eight cubits [high]. A plank was driven towards me by it, and I seized it; and as for the ship, those who were therein perished, and not one of them escaped.

Then a wave of the sea bore me along and cast me up upon an island, and I passed three days there by myself, with none but mine own heart for a companion; I laid me down and slept in a hollow in a thicket, and I hugged the shade. And I lifted up my legs (i.e. I walked about), so that I might find out what to put in my mouth, and I found there figs and grapes, and all kinds of fine large berries; and there were there gourds, and melons, and pumpkins as large as barrels (?), and there were also there fish and water-fowl. There was no [food] of any sort or kind that did not grow in this island. And when I had eaten all I could eat, I laid the remainder of the food upon the ground, for it was too much for me [to carry] in my arms. I then dug a hole in the ground and made a fire, and I prepared pieces of wood and a burnt-offering for the gods.

And I heard a sound [as of] thunder, which I thought to be [caused by] a wave of the sea, and the trees rocked and the earth quaked, and I covered my face. And I found [that the sound was caused by] a serpent that was coming

towards me. It was thirty cubits in length, and its beard
was more than two cubits in length, and its body was
covered with [scales of] gold, and the two ridges over its
eyes were of pure lapis-lazuli (i.e. they were blue); and
it coiled its whole length up before me. And it opened
its mouth to me, now I was lying flat on my stomach in
front of it, and it said to me, 'Who has brought you here?
Who has brought you here, Oh miserable one? Who has
brought you here? If you do not immediately declare to
me who has brought you to this island, I will make you
know what it is to be burnt with fire, and you will become
a thing that is invisible. You speak to me, but I cannot
hear what you say; I am before you, do you not know me?'
Then the serpent took me in its mouth, and carried me off
to the place where it was wont to rest, and it set me down
there, having done me no harm whatsoever; I was sound
and whole, and it had not carried away any portion of my
body. And it opened its mouth to me whilst I was lying
flat on my stomach, and it said to me, 'Who has brought
you here? Who has brought you here, Oh miserable one?
Who has brought you to this island of the sea, the two
sides of which are in the waves?'

Then I made answer to the serpent, my two hands
being folded humbly before it, and I said to it, 'I am one
who was travelling to the mines on a mission of the king
in a ship that was one hundred and fifty cubits long, and
fifty cubits in breadth, and it was manned by a crew of
one hundred and fifty men, who were chosen from among
the best sailors of Egypt. They had looked upon the sky,
they had looked upon the earth, and their hearts were

more understanding than the hearts of lions. They were able to say beforehand when a tempest was coming, and to tell when a squall was about to rise before it broke. The heart of every man among them was wiser than that of his neighbour, and the arm of each was stronger than that of his neighbour; there was not one weak man among them. Nevertheless it blew a gale of wind whilst we were still on the sea and before we could make the land. A gale rose, which continued to increase in violence, and with it there came upon [us] a wave eight cubits [high]. A plank of wood was driven towards me by this wave, and I seized it; and as for the ship, those who were therein perished and not one of them escaped alive [except] myself. And now behold me by your side! It was a wave of the sea that brought me to this island.'

And the serpent said to me, 'Have no fear, have no fear, Oh little one, and let not your face be sad, now that you have arrived at the place where I am. Verily, God has spared your life, and you have been brought to this island where there is food. There is no kind of food that is not here, and it is filled with good things of every kind. Verily, you shall pass month after month on this island, until you have come to the end of four months, and then a ship shall come, and there shall be therein sailors who are acquaintances of thine, and you shall go with them to your country, and you shall die in your native town.' [And the serpent continued,] 'What a joyful thing it is for the man who has experienced evil fortunes, and has passed safely through them, to declare them! I will now describe to you some of the things that have happened to me on this island. I used to live here with my brethren, and with my children who dwelt among them; now my children and my brethren together numbered seventy-five. I do not make mention of a little maiden who had been brought to me by fate. And a star fell [from heaven], and these (i.e. his children, and his brethren, and the maiden) came into the fire which fell with it. I myself was not with those who were burnt in the fire, and I was not in their midst, but I [well-nigh] died [of grief] for them. And I found a place wherein I buried them all together. Now, if you are strong, and your heart flourishes, you shall fill both your arms (i.e. embrace) with your children, and you shall kiss your wife, and you shall see your own house, which is the most beautiful thing of all, and you shall reach your country, and you shall live therein again together with your brethren, and dwell therein.'

Then I cast myself down flat upon my stomach, and I pressed the ground before the serpent with my forehead, saying, 'I will describe your power to the King, and I will make him understand your greatness. I will cause to be brought to you the unguent and spices called *aba*, and *hekenu*, and *inteneb*, and *khasait*, and the incense that is offered up in the temples, whereby every god is propitiated. I will relate [to him] the things that have happened to me, and declare the things that have been seen by me through your power, and praise and thanksgiving shall be made to you in my city in the presence of all the nobles of the country. I will slaughter bulls for you, and will offer them up as burnt-offerings, and I will pluck feathered fowl in your [honour]. And I will cause to come to you boats laden with all the most costly products of the land of Egypt, even according to what is done for a god who is beloved by men and women in a land far away, whom they know not.' Then the serpent smiled at me, and the things which I had said to it were regarded by it in its heart as nonsense, for it said to me, 'You have not a very great store of myrrh [in Egypt], and all that you have is incense. Behold, I am the Prince of Punt, and the myrrh which is therein belongs to me. And as for the *heken* which you have said you will cause to be brought to me, is it not one of the chief [products] of this island? And behold, it shall come to pass that when you have once departed from this place, you shall never more see this island, for it shall disappear into the waves.'

And in due course, even as the serpent had predicted, a ship arrived, and I climbed up to the top of a high tree, and I recognised those who were in it. Then I went to announce the matter to the serpent, but I found that it had knowledge thereof already. And the serpent said to me, 'A safe [journey], a safe [journey], Oh little one, to your house. You shall see your children [again]. I beseech you that my name may be held in fair repute in your city, for verily this is the thing which I desire of you.'

Then I threw myself flat upon my stomach, and my two hands were folded humbly before the serpent. And the serpent gave me a [ship-] load of things, namely, myrrh, *heken*, *inteneb*, *khasait*, *thsheps* and *shaas* spices, eye-paint (antimony), skins of panthers, great balls of incense, tusks of elephants, greyhounds, apes, monkeys, and beautiful and costly products of all sorts and kinds.

And when I had loaded these things into the ship, and had thrown myself flat upon my stomach in order to give thanks to it for the same, it spoke to me, saying, 'Verily you shall travel to [your] country in two months, and you shall fill both your arms with your children, and you shall renew your youth in your coffin.' Then I went down to the place on the sea-shore where the ship was, and I hailed the bowmen who were in the ship, and I spoke words of thanksgiving to the lord of this island, and those who were in the ship did the same. Then we set sail, and we journeyed on and returned to the country of the King, and we arrived there at the end of two months, according to all that the serpent had said. And I entered into the presence of the King, and I took with me for him the offerings which I had brought out of the island. And the King praised me and thanked me in the presence of the nobles of all his country, and he appointed me to be one of his bodyguard, and I received my wages along with those who were his [regular] servants.

Cast you your glance then upon me [Oh Prince], now that I have set my feet on my native land once more, having seen and experienced what I have seen and experienced. Listen to me, for verily it is a good thing to listen to men. And the Prince said to me, 'Make not yourself out to be perfect, my friend! Does a man give water to a fowl at daybreak which he is going to kill during the day?'

Here ends [The Story of the Shipwrecked Traveller], which has been written from the beginning to the end thereof according to the text that has been found written in an [ancient] book. It has been written (i.e. copied) by Ameni-Amen-aa, a scribe with skilful fingers. Life, strength, and health be to him!

EGYPTIAN HYMNS
TO THE GODS

In this chapter are given translations of hymns that were sung in the temples in honour of the great gods of Egypt between 1600 BCE and 900 BCE, and of hymns that were used by kings and private individuals. The 'Hymn to Amen-Ra' is found in a papyrus preserved in the Egyptian Museum in Cairo. The extract from the 'Hymn to Amen' is taken from a work in which the power and glory of Amen are described in a long series of Chapters; the papyrus in which it is written is in Leyden. The extracts from hymns to the sun god and Osiris are written in the hieratic character upon slices of limestone now preserved in the Egyptian Museum in Cairo. The 'Hymn to Shu', written in the hieratic character, is found in the Magical Papyrus (Harris, No. 501), which is preserved in the British Museum.

HYMN TO AMEN-RA

I. **A Hymn to Amen-Ra**, the Bull, dweller in Anu, chief of all the gods, the beneficent god, beloved one, giving the warmth of life to all beautiful cattle.

II. Homage to you, Amen-Ra, Lord of the throne of Egypt. Master of the Apts (Karnak). Kamutef at the head of his fields. The long-strider, Master of the Land of the South. Lord of the Matchau (Nubians), Governor of Punt, King of heaven, first-born son of earth, Lord of things that are, establisher of things (i.e. the universe), establisher of all things.

III. One in his actions, as with the gods, Beneficent Bull of the Company of the Gods (or of the Nine Gods), Chief of all the gods, Lord of Truth, father of the gods, maker of men, creator of all animals, Lord of things that are, creator of the staff of life, Maker of the herbage that sustains the life of cattle.

IV. Power made by Ptah, Beautiful child of love. The gods ascribe praises to him. Maker of things celestial [and] of things terrestrial, he illumins Egypt, Traverser of the celestial heights in peace. King of the South, King of the North, Ra, whose word is truth, Chief of Egypt. Mighty in power, lord of awe-inspiring terror, Chief, creator of everything on earth, Whose dispensations are greater than those of every other god.

V. The gods rejoice in his beautiful acts. They acclaim him in the Great House (i.e. the sky). They crown him with crowns in the House of Fire. They love the odour of him, when he comes from Punt (Southern and Eastern Sudan). Prince of the dew, he traverss the lands of the Nubians. Beautiful of face, [he] comes from the Land of the God (Somaliland and Southern Arabia).

VI. The gods fall down awestruck at his feet, when they recognise His Majesty their Lord. Lord of terror, great one of victory, Great one of Souls, mighty one of crowns. He makes offerings abundant, [and] creates food. Praise be to you, creator of the gods. Suspender of the sky, who hammered out the earth.

VII. Strong Watcher, Menu-Amen, Lord of eternity, creator of everlastingness, Lord of praises, chief of the Apts (Karnak and Luxor), firm of horns, beautiful of faces.

VIII. Lord of the Urrt Crown, with lofty plumes, Whose diadem is beautiful, whose White Crown is high. Mehen and the Uatchti serpents belong to his face. His apparel (?) is in the Great House, the double crown, the *nemes* bandlet, and the helmet. Beautiful of face, he receives the Atef crown. Beloved of the South and North. Master of the double crown he receives the *ames* sceptre. He is the Lord of the Mekes sceptre and the whip.

IX. Beautiful Governor, crowned with the White Crown, Lord of light, creator of splendour, The gods ascribe to him praises. He gives his hand to him that loves him. The flame destroys his enemies. His eye overthrows the Seba devil. It casts forth its spear, which pierces the sky, and makes Nak vomit (?) what it has swallowed.

X. Homage to you, Ra, Lord of Truth. Hidden is the shrine of the Lord of the gods. Khepera in his boat gives the order, and the gods come into being. [He is] Tem, maker of the Rekhit beings, however many be their forms he makes them to live, distinguishing one kind from another.

XI. He hears the cry of him that is oppressed. He is gracious of heart to him that appeals to him. He delivers the timid man from the man of violence. He regards the poor man and considers [his] misery.

XII. He is the lord Sa (i.e. Taste); abundance is his utterance. The Nile comes at his will. He is the lord of graciousness, who is greatly beloved. He comes and sustains mankind. He sets in motion everything that is made. He works in the Celestial Water, making to be the pleasantness of the light. The gods rejoice in [his] beauties, and their hearts live when they see him.

XIII. He is Ra who is worshipped in the Apts. He is the one of many crowns in the House of the Benben Stone (the abode of the Spirit of Ra). He is the god Ani, the lord of the ninth-day festival. The festival of the sixth day and the Tenat festival are kept for him. He is King, life, strength, and health be to him! and the Lord of all the gods. He makes himself be seen in the horizon, Chief of the beings of the Other World. His name is hidden from the gods who are his children, in his name of 'Amen' (Amen means 'hidden.')

XIV. Homage to you, dweller in peace. Lord of joy of heart, mighty one of crowns, lord of the Urrt Crown with the lofty plumes, with a beautiful tiara and a lofty White Crown. The gods love to behold you. The double crown is established on your head. your love passes throughout Egypt. You send out light, you rises with [your] two beautiful eyes. The Pat beings [faint] when you appear in the sky, animals become helpless under your rays. your loveliness is in the southern sky, your graciousness is in the northern sky. your beauties seize upon hearts, your loveliness makes the arms weak, your beautiful operations make the hands idle, hearts become weak at the sight of you.

XV. [He is] the Form One, the creator of everything that is. The One only, the creator of things that shall be. Men and women proceeded from his two eyes. His utterance became the gods. He is the creator of the pasturage wherein herds and flocks live, [and] the staff of life for mankind. He gives life to the fish in the river, and the geese and the feathered fowl of the sky. He gives air to the creature that is in the egg. He nourishes the geese in their pens. He gives life to the water-fowl, and the reptiles and every insect that flies. He provides food for the mice in their holes, he nourishes the flying creatures on every bough.

XVI. Homage to you, Oh creator of every one of these creatures, the One only whose hands are many. He watches over all those who lie down to sleep, he seeks the well-being of his animal creation, Amen, establisher of every thing, Temu-Herukhuti. They all praise you with their words, adorations be to you because you rest among us, we smell the earth before you because you have fashioned us.

XVII. All the animals cry out, 'Homage to you.' Every country adores you, to the height of heaven, to the breadth of the earth, to the depths of the Great Green Sea. The gods bend their backs in homage to your Majesty, to exalt the Souls of their Creator, they rejoice when they meet their begetter. They say to you, 'Welcome, Oh father of the fathers of all the gods, suspender of the sky, beater out of the earth, maker of things that are, creator of things that shall be, King, life, strength, and health be to you! Chief of the gods, we praise your Souls, inasmuch as you have created us. You work for us your children, we adore you because you rest among us.'

XVIII. Homage to you, Oh maker of everything that is. Lord of Truth, father of the gods, maker of men, creator of animals, lord of the divine grain, making to live the wild animals of the mountains. Amen, Bull, Beautiful Face, Beloved one in the Apts, great one of diadems in the House of the Benben Stone, binding on the tiara in Anu (On), judge of the Two Men (i.e. Horus and Set) in the Great Hall.

XIX. Chief of the Great Company of the gods, One only, who has no second, President of the Apts, Ani, President of his Company of the gods, living by Truth every day, Khuti, Horus of the East. He has created the mountains, the gold [and] the real lapis-lazuli by his will, the incense and the natron that are mixed by the Nubians, and fresh myrrh for your nostrils. Beautiful Face, coming from the Nubians, Amen-Ra, lord of the throne of Egypt, President of the Apts, Ani, President of his palace.

XX. King, One among the gods. [His] names are so many, how many cannot be known. He rises in the eastern horizon, he sets in the western horizon.

XXI. He overthrows his enemies at dawn, when he is born each day. Thoth exalts his two eyes. When he sets in his splendour the gods rejoice in his beauties, and the Apes (i.e. dawn spirits) exalt him. Lord of the Sektet Boat and of the Antet Boat, they transport you [over] Nu in peace. your sailors rejoice when they see you overthrowing the Seba fiend, [and] stabbing his limbs with the knife. The flame devours him, his soul is torn out of his body, the feet (?) of this serpent Nak are carried off.

XXII. The gods rejoice, the sailors of Ra are satisfied. Anu rejoices, the enemies of Temu are overthrown. The Apts are in peace. The heart of the goddess Nebt-ankh is happy, [for] the enemies of her Lord are overthrown. The gods of Kher-aha make adorations [to him]. Those who are in their hidden shrines smell the earth before him, when they see him mighty in his power.

XXIII. [Oh] Power of the gods, [lord of] Truth, lord of the Apts, in your name of 'Maker of Truth'. Lord of food, bull of offerings, in your name of 'Amen-Ka-mutef', Maker of human beings, maker to be of ..., creator of everything that is in your name of 'Temu Khepera'.

XXIV. Great Hawk, making the body festal. Beautiful Face, making the breast festal, Image ... with the lofty Mehen crown. The two serpent-goddesses fly before him. The hearts of the Pat beings leap towards him. The Hememet beings turn to him. Egypt rejoices at his appearances. Homage to you, Amen-Ra, Lord of the throne of Egypt. His town [Thebes] loves him when he riseth.

HYMN TO AMEN

'He [Amen], drives away evils and scatters diseases. He is the physician who heals the eye without [the use of] medicaments. He opens the eyes, he drives away inflammation (?)... He delivers whom he pleases, even from the Tuat (the Other World). He saves a man from what is ordained for him at the dictates of his heart.

'To him belong both eyes and ears, [he is] on every path of him whom he loves. He hears the petitions of him that appeals to him. He comes from afar to him that calls [before] a moment has passed. He makes high (i.e. long) the life [of a man], he cuts it short. To him whom he loves he gives more than has been fated for him.

'[When] Amen casts a spell on the water, and his name is on the waters, if this name of his be uttered the crocodile (?) has no power. The winds are driven back, the hurricane is repulsed. At the remembrance of him the wrath of the angry man dies down. He speaks the gentle word at the moment of strife. He is a pleasant breeze to him that appeals to him. He delivers the helpless one. He is the wise (?) god whose plans are beneficent.... He is more helpful than millions to the man who has set him in his heart. One warrior [who fights] under his name is better than hundreds of thousands. Indeed he is the beneficent strong one. He is perfect [and] seizes his moment; he is irresistible....

'All the gods are three, Amen, Ra and Ptah, and there are none like them. He whose name is hidden is Amen. Ra belongs to him as his face, and his body is Ptah. Their cities are established upon the earth forever, [namely,] Thebes, Anu (Heliopolis), and Hetkaptah (Memphis). When a message is sent from heaven it is heard in Anu, and is repeated in Memphis to the Beautiful Face (i.e. Ptah). It is written, in the letters of Thoth (i.e. hieroglyphs), and despatched to the City of Amen (i.e. Thebes), with their things. The matters are answered in Thebes....

'His heart is Understanding, his lips are Taste, his Ka is all the things that are in his mouth. He enters, the two caverns are beneath his feet. The Nile appears from the hollow beneath his sandals. His soul is Shu, his heart is Tefnut. He is Heru-Khuti in the upper heaven. His right eye is day. His left eye is night. He is the leader of faces on every path. His body is Nu. The dweller in it is the Nile, producing everything that is, nourishing all that is. He breathes breath into all nostrils. The Luck and the Destiny of every man are with him. His wife is the earth, he unites with her, his seed is the tree of life, his emanations are the grain.'

HYMN TO THE SUN GOD

'**Well do you watch**, Oh Horus, who sails over the sky, you child who proceeds from the divine father, you child of fire, who shines like crystal, who destroys the darkness and the night. You child who grows rapidly, with gracious form, who rests in your eye.

'You wake up men who are asleep on their beds, and the reptiles in their nests. Your boat sails on the fiery Lake Neserser, and you traverse the upper sky by means of the winds thereof. The two daughters of the Nile-god crush for you the fiend Neka, Nubti (i.e. Set) pierces him with his arrows. Keb seizes (?) him by the joint of his back, Serqet grips him at his throat. The flame of this serpent that is over the door of your house burns him up. The Great Company of the Gods are angry with him, and they rejoice because he is cut to pieces. The Children of Horus grasp their knives, and inflict very many gashes in him. Hail! your enemy has fallen, and Truth stands firm before you.

'When you again transform yourself into Tem, you give your hand to the Lords of Akert (i.e. the dead), those who lie in death give thanks for your beauties when your light falls upon them. They declare to you what is their hearts' wish, which is that they may see you again. When you have passed them by, the darkness covers them, each one in his coffin. You are the lord of those who cry out (?) to you, the god who is beneficent forever. You are the Judge of words and deeds, the Chief of chief judges, who establishes truth, and does away sin. May he who attacks me be judged rightly, behold, he is stronger than I am; he has seized upon my office, and has carried it off with falsehood. May it be restored to me.'

HYMN TO OSIRIS

'**P**raise be to you, Oh you who extends your arms, who lie asleep on your side, who lie on the sand, the Lord of the earth, the divine mummy....

'You are the Child of the Earth Serpent, of great age. Your head ... and goes round over your feet. Ra-Khepera shines upon your body, when you lie on your bed in the form of Seker, so that he may drive away the darkness that shrouds you, and may infuse light in your two eyes. He passes a long period of time shining upon you, and sheds tears over you. The earth rests upon your shoulders, and its corners rest upon you as far as the four pillars of heaven. If you move yourself, the earth quakes, for you are greater than....

'[The Nile] appears out of the sweat of your two hands. You breathe forth the air that is in your throat into the nostrils of men; divine is that thing whereon they live. Through your nostrils (?) subsist the flowers, the herbage, the reeds, the flags (?), the barley, the wheat, and the plants whereon men live. If canals are dug ... and houses and temples are built, and great statues are dragged along, and lands are ploughed up, and tombs and funerary monuments are made, they [all] rest upon you. It is you who make them. They are upon your back. They are more than can be written (i.e. described). There is no vacant space on your back, they all lie on your back, and yet [you say] not, "I am [over] weighted therewith. You are the father and mother of men and women, they live by your breath, they eat the flesh of your members. 'Pautti' (i.e. Primeval God) is your name.'"

The writer of this hymn says in the four broken lines that remain that he is unable to understand the nature (?) of Osiris, which is hidden (?), and his attributes, which are sublime.

HYMN TO SHU

'**H**omage to you, Oh flesh and bone of Ra, you first-born son who did proceed from his members, who was chosen to be the chief of those who were brought forth, you mighty one, you divine form, who are endowed with strength as the lord of transformations. You overthrow the Seba fiends each day.

'The divine boat has the wind [behind it], your heart is glad. Those who are in the Antti Boat utter loud cries of joy when they see Shu, the son of Ra, triumphant, [and] driving his spear into the serpent fiend Nekau. Ra sets out to sail over the heavens at dawn daily. The goddess Tefnut is seated on your head, she hurls her flames of fire against your enemies, and destroys them utterly.

'You are equipped by Ra, you are mighty through his words of power, you are the heir of your father upon his throne, and your Doubles rest in the Doubles of Ra, even as the taste of what has been in the mouth remains therein. A will has been written by the lord of Khemenu (Thoth), the scribe of the library of Ra-Harmakhis, in the hall of the divine house (or temple) of Anu (Heliopolis), established, perfected, and made permanent in hieroglyphs under the feet of Ra-Harmakhis, and he shall transmit it to the son of his son forever and ever.

'Homage to you, Oh son of Ra, who was begotten by Temu himself. You did create yourself, and you had no mother. You are Truth, the lord of Truth, you are the Power, the ruling power of the gods. You conduct the Eye of your father Ra. They give gifts to you into your own hands. You make the Great Goddess be at peace, when storms are passing over her. You stretch out the heavens on high, and establish them with your own hands. Every god bows in homage before you, the King of the South, the King of the North, Shu, the son of Ra, life, strength and health be to you!

'You, Oh great god Pautti, are furnished with the brilliance of the Eye [of Ra] in Heliopolis, to overthrow the Seba fiends on behalf of your father. You make the divine Boat sail onwards in peace. The mariners who are therein exult, and all the gods shout for joy when they hear your divine name. Greater, yea greater (i.e. twice great) are you than the gods in your name of Shu, son of Ra.'

MORAL AND PHILOSOPHICAL LITERATURE

Side by side with the great mass of literature of a magical and religious character that flourished in Egypt under the Ancient Empire, we find that there existed also a class of writings that are remarkably like those contained in the Book of Proverbs, which is attributed to Solomon, the King of Israel, and in 'Ecclesiasticus', and the 'Book of Wisdom'. The priests of Egypt took the greatest trouble to compose Books of the Dead and Guides to the Other World in order to help the souls of the dead to traverse in safety the region that lay between this world and the next, or Dead Land, and the high officials who flourished under the pharaohs of the early dynasties drew up works, the object of which was to enable the living man to conduct himself in such a way as to satisfy his social superiors, to please his equals, and to content his inferiors, and at the same time to advance to honours and wealth himself. These works represent the experience, and shrewdness, and knowledge which their writers had gained at the Court of the Pharaohs, and are full of sound worldly wisdom and high moral excellence. They were written to teach young men of the royal and aristocratic classes to fear God, to honour the king, to do their duty efficiently, to lead strictly moral, if not exactly religious, lives, to treat every man with the respect due to his position in life, to cultivate home life, and to do their duty to their neighbours, both to those who were rich and those who were poor.

THE PRECEPTS OF PTAH-HETEP

The oldest Egyptian book of Moral Precepts, or Maxims, or Admonitions, is that of Ptah-hetep, governor of the town of Memphis, and high confidential adviser of the king; he flourished in the reign of Assa, a king of the fifth dynasty, about 3500 BCE. The following extracts will illustrate the piety and moral worth, and the sagacity and experience of the shrewd but kindly 'man of the world' who undertook to guide the young prince of his day. The sage begins his work with a lament about the evil effects that follow old age in a man:

'Depression seizes upon him every day, his eyesight fails, his ears become deaf, his strength declines, his heart has no rest, the mouth becomes silent and speaks not, the intelligence diminishes, and it is impossible to remember today what happened yesterday. The bones are full of pain, the pursuit that was formerly attended with pleasure is now fraught with pain, and the sense of taste departs. Old age is the worst of all the miseries that can befall a man. The nose becomes stopped up and one cannot smell at all.'

At this point Ptah-hetep asks, rhetorically, 'Who will give me authority to speak? Who is it that will authorise me to repeat to the prince the Precepts of those who had knowledge of the wise counsels of the learned men of old?' In answer to these questions the king replies to Ptah-hetep, 'Instruct you my son in the words of wisdom of olden time. It is instruction of this kind alone that forms the character of the sons of noblemen, and the youth who listens to such instruction will acquire a right understanding and the faculty of judging justly, and he will not feel weary of his duties.'

Immediately following these words come the 'Precepts of beautiful speech' of Ptah-hetep, whose full titles are given, viz. the Erpa, the Duke, the father of the god (i.e. the king), the friend of God, the son of the king. Governor of Memphis, confidential servant of the king. These Precepts instruct the ignorant, and teach them to understand fine speech; among them are the following:

'Be not haughty because of your knowledge. Converse with the ignorant man as well as with him that is educated.

'Do not terrify the people, for if you do, God will punish you. If any man says that he is going to live by these means, God will make his mouth empty of food. If a man says that he is going to make himself powerful (or rich) thereby, saying, "I shall reap advantage, having knowledge", and if he says, "I will beat down the other man", he will arrive at the result of being able to do nothing. Let no man terrify the people, for the command of God is that they shall enjoy rest.

'If you are one of a company seated to eat in the house of a man who is greater than yourself, take what he gives you [without remark]. Set it before you. Look at what is before you, but not too closely, and do not look at it too often. The man who rejects it is an ill-mannered person. Do not speak to interrupt when he is speaking, for one knows not when he may disapprove. Speak when he addresses you, and then your words shall be acceptable. When a man has wealth, he orders his actions according to his own dictates. He does what he will.... The great man can effect by the mere lifting up of his hand what a [poor] man cannot. Since the eating of bread is according to the dispensation of God, a man cannot object thereto.

'If you are a man whose duty it is to enter into the presence of a nobleman with a message from another nobleman, take care to say correctly and in the correct way what you are sent to say; give the message exactly as he said it. Take great care not to spoil it in delivery and so to set one nobleman against another. He who wrests the truth in transmitting the message, and only repeats it in words that give pleasure to all men, gentleman or common man, is an abominable person.

'If you are a farmer, till the field which the great God has given you. Eat not too much when you are near your neighbours.... The children of the man who, being a man of substance, seizes [prey] like the crocodile in the presence of the field labourers, are cursed because of his behaviour, his father suffers poignant grief, and as for the mother who bore him, every other woman is happier than she. A man who is the leader of a clan (or tribe) that trusts him and follows him becomes a god.

'If you humble yourself and obey a wise man, your behaviour will be held to be good before God. Since you know who are to serve, and who are to command, let not your heart magnify itself against the latter. Since you know who has the power, hold in fear him that has it....

'Be diligent at all times. Do more than is commanded. Waste not the time wherein you can labour; he is an abominable man who makes a bad use of his time. Lose no chance day by day in adding to the riches of your house. Work produces wealth, and wealth endures not when work is abandoned.

'If you are a wise man, beget a son who shall be pleasing to God.

'If you are a wise man, be master of your house. Love your wife absolutely, give her food in abundance, and raiment for her back; these are the medicines for her body. Anoint her with unguents, and make her happy as long as you live. She is your field, and she reflects credit on her possessor. Be not harsh in your house, for she will be more easily moved by persuasion than by violence. Satisfy her wish, observe what she expects, and take note of that whereon she has fixed her gaze. This is the treatment that will keep her in her house; if you repel her advances, it is ruin for you. Embrace her, call her by fond names, and treat her lovingly.

'Treat your dependants as well as you are able, for this is the duty of those whom God has blessed.

'If you are a wise man, and if you have a seat in the council chamber of your lord, concentrate your mind on the business [so as to arrive at] a wise decision. Keep silence, for this is better than to talk overmuch. When you speak you must know what can be urged against your words. To speak in the council chamber [needs] skill and experience.

'If you have become a great man having once been a poor man, and have attained to the headship of the city, study not to take the fullest advantage of your situation. Be not harsh in respect of the grain, for you are only an overseer of the food of God.

'Think much, but keep your mouth closed; if you do not how can you consult with the nobles? Let your opinion coincide with that of your lord. Do what he says, and then he shall say of you to those who are listening, "This is my son."'

THE MAXIMS OF ANI

T he Precepts of Ptah-hetep were drawn up for the guidance of highly-placed young men, and have little to do with practical, every-day morality. But whilst the Egyptian scribes who lived under the Middle and New Empires were ready to pay all honour to the writings of an earlier age, they were not slow to perceive that the older Precepts did not supply advice on every important subject, and they therefore proceeded to write supplementary Precepts. A very interesting collection of such Precepts is found in a papyrus preserved in the Egyptian Museum, Cairo. They are generally known as the 'Maxims of Ani' and the following examples will illustrate their scope and character:

'Celebrate you the festival of your God, and repeat the celebration thereof in its appointed season. God is angry with the transgressor of this law. Bear testimony [to Him] after your offering....

'The opportunity having passed, one seeks [in vain] to seize another.

'God will magnify the name of the man who exalts His Souls, who sings His praises, and bows before Him, who offers incense, and does homage [to Him] in his work.

'Enter not into the presence of the drunkard, even if his acquaintance be an honour to you.

'Beware of the woman in the street who is not known in her native town. Follow her not, nor any woman who is like her. Do not make her acquaintance. She is like a deep stream the windings of which are unknown.

'Go not with common men, lest your name be made to stink.

'When an inquiry is held, and you are present, multiply not speech; you will do better if you hold your peace. Act not the part of the chatterer.

'The sanctuary of God abhors noisy demonstrations. Pray you with a loving heart, and let your words be hidden (or secret). Do this, and He will do your business for you. He will listen to your words, and He will receive your offering.

'Place water before your father and your mother who rest in their tombs.... Forget not to do this when you are outside your house, and as you do for them so shall your son do for you.

'Frequent not the house where men drink beer, for the words that fall from your mouth will be repeated, and it is a bad thing for you not to know what you did really say. You will fall down, your bones may be broken, and there will be no one to give you a hand [to help you]. Your boon companions who are drinking with you will say, 'Throw this drunken man out of the door.' When your friends come to look for you, they will find you lying on the ground as helpless as a babe.

'When the messenger of [death] comes to carry you away, let him find you prepared. Alas, you will have no opportunity for speech, for verily his terror will be before you. Say not, "You are carrying me off in my youth." You know not when your death will take place. Death comes, and he seizes the babe at the breast of his mother, as well as the man who has arrived at a ripe old age. Observe this, for I speak to you good advice which you shall meditate upon in your heart. Do these things, and you will be a good man, and evils of all kinds shall remove themselves from you.

'Remain not seated whilst another is standing, especially if he be an old man, even though your social position (or rank) be higher than his.

'The man who utters ill-natured words must not expect to receive good-natured deeds.

'If you journey on a road [made by] your hands each day, you will arrive at the place where you would like to be.

'What ought people to talk about every day? Administrators of high rank should discuss the laws, women should talk about their husbands, and every man should speak about his own affairs.

'Never speak an ill-natured word to any visitor; a word dropped some day when you are gossiping may overturn your house.

'If you are well-versed in books, and have gone into them, set them in your heart; whatsoever you then utter will be good. If the scribe be appointed to any position, he will converse about his documents. The director of the treasury has no son, and the overseer of the seal has no heir. High officials esteem the scribe, whose hand is his position of honour, which they do not give to children....

'The ruin of a man rests on his tongue; take heed that you harm not yourself.

'The heart of a man is [like] the store-chamber of a granary that is full of answers of every kind; choose you those that are good, and utter them, and keep those that are bad closely confined within you. To answer roughly is like the brandishing of weapons, but if you will speak kindly and quietly you will always [be loved].

'When you offer up offerings to your God, beware lest you offer the things that are an abomination [to Him]. Chatter not [during] his journeyings (or processions), seek not to prolong (?) his appearance, disturb not those who carry him, chant not his offices too loudly, and beware lest you.... Let your eye observe his dispensations. Devote yourself to the adoration of his name. It is he who gives souls to millions of forms, and he magnifies the man who magnifies him....

'I gave you your mother who bore you, and in bearing you she took upon herself a great burden, which she bore without help from me. When after some months you were born, she placed herself under a yoke, for three years she suckled you.... When you were sent to school to be educated, she brought bread and beer for you from her house to your master regularly each day. You are now grown up, and you have a wife and a house of your own. Keep your eye on your child, and bring him up as your mother brought you up. Do nothing whatsoever that will cause her (i.e. your mother) to suffer, lest she lift up her hands to God, and He hear her complaint, [and punish you].

'Eat not bread, whilst another stands by, without pointing out to him the bread with your hand....

'Devote yourself to God, take heed to yourself daily for the sake of God, and let tomorrow be as today. Work you [for him]. God sees him that works for Him, and He esteems lightly the man who esteems Him lightly.

'Follow not after a woman, and let her not take possession of your heart.

'Answer not a man when he is angry, but remove yourself from him. Speak gently to him that has spoken in anger, for soft words are the medicine for his heart.

'Seek silence for yourself.'

TALK OF A MAN WHO WAS TIRED OF LIFE WITH HIS SOUL

For the study of the moral character of the ancient Egyptian, a document, of which a mutilated copy is found on a papyrus preserved in the Royal Library in Berlin, is of peculiar importance. As the opening lines are wanting it is impossible to know what the title of the work was, but because the text records a conversation that took place between a man who had suffered grievous misfortunes, and was weary of the world and of all in it, and wished to kill himself, it is generally called the 'Talk of a man who was tired of life with his soul'.

The general meaning of the document is clear. The man weary of life discusses with his soul, as if it were a being wholly distinct from himself, whether he shall kill himself or not. He is willing to do so, but is only kept from his purpose by his soul's observation that if he does there will be no one to bury him properly, and to see that the funerary ceremonies are duly performed. This shows that the man who was tired of life was alone in the world, and that all his relations and friends had either forsaken him, or had been driven away by him.

His soul then advised him to destroy himself by means of fire, probably, as has been suggested, because the ashes of a burnt body would need no further care. The man accepted the advice of his soul, and was about to follow it literally, when the soul itself drew back, being afraid to undergo the sufferings inherent in such a death for the body.

The man then asked his soul to perform for him the last rites, but it absolutely refused to do so, and told him that it objected to death in any form, and that it had no desire at all to depart to the kingdom of the dead. The soul supports its objection to suffer by telling the man who is tired of life that the mere remembrance of burial is fraught with mourning, and tears, and sorrow. It means that a man is torn away from his house and thrown out upon a hill, and that he will never go up again to see the sun. And after all, what is the good of burial? Take the case of those who have had granite tombs, and funerary monuments in the form of pyramids made for them, and who lie in them in great state and dignity. If we look at the slabs in their tombs, which have been placed there on purpose to receive offerings from the kinsfolk and friends of the deceased, we shall find that they are just as bare as are the tablets for offerings of the wretched people who belong to the Corvée, of whom some die on the banks of the canals, leaving one part of their bodies on the land and the other in the water, and some fall into the water altogether and are eaten by the fish, and others under the burning heat of the sun become bloated and loathsome objects. Because men receive fine burials it does not follow that offerings of food, which will enable them to continue their existence, will be made by their kinsfolk.

Finally the soul ends its speech with the advice that represented the view of the average Egyptian in all ages, 'Follow after the day of happiness, and banish care,' that is to say, spare no pains in making yourself happy at all times, and let nothing that concerns the present or the future trouble you.

This advice, which is well expressed by the words which the rich man spoke to his soul, 'Take your ease, eat, drink, and be merry' (St. Luke xii. 19), was not acceptable to the man who was tired of life, and he at once addressed to his soul a series of remarks, couched in rhythmical language, in which he made it clear that, so far as he was concerned, death would be preferable to life. He begins by saying that his name is more detested than the smell of birds on a summer's day when the heavens are hot, and the smell of a handler of fish newly caught when the heavens are hot, and the smell of water-fowl in a bed of willows wherein geese collect, and the smell of fishermen in the marshes where fishing has been carried on, and the stench of crocodiles, and the place where crocodiles do congregate.

In a second group of rhythmical passages the man who was tired of life goes on to describe the unsatisfactory and corrupt condition of society, and his wholesale condemnation of it includes his own kinsfolk. Each passage begins with the words, 'To whom do I speak this day?' and he says, 'Brothers are bad, and the friends of today lack love. Hearts are shameless, and every man seizes the goods of his neighbour. The meek man goes to ground (i.e. is destroyed), and the audacious man makes his way into all places. The man of gracious countenance is wretched, and the good are everywhere treated as contemptible. When a man stirs you up to wrath by his wickedness, his evil acts make all people laugh. One robs, and everyone steals the possessions of his neighbour. Disease is continual, and the brother who is with it becomes an enemy. One remembers not yesterday, and one does nothing ... in this hour. Brothers are bad.... Faces disappear, and each has a worse aspect than that of his brother. Hearts are shameless, and the man upon whom one leans has no heart. There are no righteous men left, the earth is an example of those who do evil. There is no true man left, and each is ignorant of what he has learnt. No man is content with what he has; go with the man [you believe to be contented], and he is not [to be found]. I am heavily laden with misery, and I have no true friend. Evil has smitten the land, and there is no end to it.'

The state of the world being thus, the man who was tired of life is driven to think that there is nothing left for him but death; it is hopeless to expect the whole state of society to change for the better, therefore death must be his deliverer. To his soul he says, 'Death stands before me this day, [and is to me as] the restoration to health of a man who has been sick, and as the coming out into the fresh air after sickness. Death stands before me this day like the smell of myrrh, and the sitting under the sail of a boat on a day with a fresh breeze. Death stands before me this day like the smell of lotus flowers, and like one who is sitting on the bank of drunkenness (i.e. sitting on a seat in a tavern built on the river bank). Death stands before me this day like a brook filled with rain water, and like the return of a man to his own house from the ship of war. Death stands before me this day like the brightening of the sky after a storm, and like one.... Death stands before me this day as a man who wishes to see his home once again, having passed many years as a prisoner.'

The three rhythmical passages that follow show that the man who was tired of life looked beyond death to a happier state of existence, in which wrong would be righted, and he who had suffered on this earth would be abundantly rewarded. The place where justice reigned supreme was ruled over by Ra, and the man does not call it 'heaven', but merely 'there'. He says, 'He who is there shall indeed be like a loving god, and he shall punish him that does wickedness. He who is there shall certainly stand in the Boat of the Sun, and shall bestow upon the temples the best [offerings]. He who is there shall indeed become a man of understanding who cannot be resisted, and who prays to Ra when he speaks.'

The arguments in favour of death of the man who was tired of life are superior to those of the soul in favour of life, for he saw beyond death the 'there' which the soul apparently had not sufficiently considered. The value of the discussion between the man and his soul was great in the opinion of the ancient Egyptian because it showed, with almost logical emphasis, that the incomprehensible things of 'here' would be made clear 'there'.

THE LAMENT OF KHAKHEPERSENB

The man who was tired of life did not stand alone in his discontent with the surroundings in which he lived, and with his fellow-man, for from a board inscribed in hieratic in the British Museum (No. 5645) we find that a priest of Heliopolis called Khakhepersenb, who was surnamed Ankhu, shared his discontent, and was filled with disgust at the widespread corruption and decadence of all classes of society that were everywhere in the land.

In the introduction to this description of society as he saw it, he says that he wishes he possessed new language in which to express himself, and that he could find phrases that were not trite in which to utter his experience. He says that men of one generation are very much like those of another, and have all done and said the same kind of things. He wishes to unburden his mind, and to remove his moral sickness by stating what he has to say in words that have not before been used.

He then goes on to say, 'I ponder on the things that have taken place, and the events that have occurred throughout the land. Things have happened, and they are different from those of last year. Each year is more wearisome than the last. The whole country is disturbed and is going to destruction. Justice (or right) is thrust out, injustice (or sin) is in the council hall, the plans of the gods are upset, and their behests are set aside. The country is in a miserable state, grief is in every place, and both towns and provinces lament. Everyone is suffering through wrong-doing. All respect of persons is banished. The lords of quiet are set in commotion. When daylight comes each day [every] face turns away from the sight of what has happened [during the night].... I ponder on the things that have taken place. Troubles flow in today, and tomorrow [tribulations] will not cease. Though all the country is full of unrest, none will speak about it. There is no innocent man [left], everyone works wickedness. Hearts are bowed in grief. He who gives orders is like the man to whom orders are given, and their hearts are well pleased. Men wake daily [and find it so], yet they do not abate it. The things of yesterday are like those of today, and in many respects both days are alike. Men's faces are stupid, and there is none capable of understanding, and none is driven to speak by his anger.... My pain is keen and protracted. The poor man has not the strength to protect himself against the man who is stronger than he. To hold the tongue about what one hears is agony, but to reply to the man who does not understand causes suffering. If one protests against what is said, the result is hatred; for the truth is not understood, and every protest is resented. The only words which any man will now listen to are his own. Everyone believes in his own.... Truth has forsaken speech altogether.'

THE LAMENT OF APUUR

Another Egyptian writer, called Apuur, who probably flourished a little before the rule of the kings of the twelfth dynasty, also depicts the terrible state of misery and corruption into which Egypt had fallen in his time, but his despair is not so deep as that of the man who was tired of his life or that of the priest Khakhepersenb. On the contrary, he has sufficient hope of his country to believe that the day will come when society shall be reformed, and when wickedness and corruption shall be done away, and when the land shall be ruled by a just ruler. He says:

'The guardians of houses say, 'Let us go and steal.' The snarers of birds have formed themselves into armed bands. The peasants of the Delta have provided themselves with bucklers. A man regards his son as his enemy. The righteous man grieves because of what has taken place in the country. A man goes out with his shield to plough. The man with a bow is ready [to shoot], the wrongdoer is in every place. The inundation of the Nile comes, yet no one goes out to plough. Poor men have gotten costly goods, and the man who was unable to make his own sandals is a possessor of wealth. The hearts of slaves are sad, and the nobles no longer participate in the rejoicings of their people. Men's hearts are violent, there is plague everywhere, blood is in every place, death is common, and the mummy wrappings call to people before they are used. Multitudes are buried in the river, the stream is a tomb, and the place of mummification is a canal.

The gentle folk weep, the simple folk are glad, and the people of every town say, 'Come, let us blot out these who have power and possessions among us.' Men resemble the mud-birds, filth is everywhere, and everyone is clad in dirty garments. The land spins round like the wheel of the potter. The robber is a rich man, and [the rich man] is a robber. The poor man groans and says, 'This is calamity indeed, but what can I do?' The river is blood, and men drink it; they cease to be men who thirst for water.

Gates and their buildings are consumed with fire, yet the palace is stable and nourishing. The boats of the peoples of the South have failed to arrive, the towns are destroyed, and Upper Egypt is desert. The crocodiles are sated with their prey, for men willingly go to them. The desert has covered the land, the Nomes are destroyed, and there are foreign troops in Egypt. People come here [from everywhere], there are no Egyptians left in the land. On the necks of the women slaves [hang ornaments of] gold, lapis-lazuli, silver, turquoise, carnelian, bronze, and *abhet* stone. There is good food everywhere, and yet mistresses of houses say, 'Would that we had something to eat.' The skilled masons who build pyramids have become hinds on farms, and those who tended the Boat of the god are yoked together [in ploughing]. Men do not go on voyages to Kepuna (Byblos in Syria) today. What shall we do for cedar wood for our mummies, in coffins of which priests are buried, and with the oil of which men are embalmed? They come no longer. There is no gold, the handicrafts languish. What is the good of a treasury if we have nothing to put in it?

Everything is in ruins. Laughter is dead, no one can laugh. Groaning and lamentation are everywhere in the land. Egyptians have turned into foreigners. The hair has fallen out of the head of every man. A gentleman cannot be distinguished from a nobody. Every man says, 'I would that I were dead,' and children say, '[My father] ought not to have begotten me.' Children of princes are dashed against the walls, the children of desire are cast out into the desert, and Khnemu (the god who fashioned the bodies of men) groans in sheer exhaustion. The Asiatics have become workmen in the Delta. Noble ladies and slave girls suffer alike. The women who used to sing songs now sing dirges. Female slaves speak as they like, and when their mistress commands they are aggrieved. Princes go hungry and weep. The hasty man says, 'If I only knew where God was I would make offerings to Him.'

The hearts of the flocks weep, and the cattle groan because of the condition of the land. A man strikes his own brother. What is to be done? The roads are watched by robbers, who hide in the bushes until a benighted traveller comes, when they rob him. They seize his goods, and beat him to death with cudgels.

Would that the human race might perish, and there be no more conceiving or bringing to the birth! If only the earth could be quiet, and revolts cease! Men eat herbs and drink water, and there is no food for the birds, and even

the swill is taken from the mouths of the swine. There
is no grain anywhere, and people lack clothes, unguents,
and oil. Every man says, 'There is none.' The storehouse
is destroyed, and its keeper lies prone on the ground.
The documents have been filched from their august
chambers, and the shrine is desecrated. Words of power are
unravelled, and spells made powerless. The public offices
are broken open and their documents stolen, and serfs
have become their own masters. The laws of the court-
house are rejected, men trample on them in public, and
the poor break them in the street. Things are now done
that have never been done before, for a party of miserable
men have removed the king. The secrets of the Kings of the
South and of the North have been revealed. The man who
could not make a coffin for himself has a large tomb. The
occupants of tombs have been cast out into the desert, and
the man who could not make a coffin for himself has now
a treasury. He who could not build a hut for himself is now
master of a habitation with walls. The rich man spends his
night athirst, and he who begged for the leavings in the
pots has now brimming bowls. Men who had fine raiment
are now in rags, and he who never wore a garment at all
now dresses in fine linen. The poor have become rich, and
the rich poor. Noble ladies sell their children for beds.
Those who once had beds now sleep on the ground. Noble
ladies go hungry, whilst butchers are sated with what was
once prepared for them. A man is slain by his brother's
side, and that brother flees to save his own life.'

Apuur next, in a series of five short exhortations,
entreats his bearers to take action of some sort; each

exhortation begins with the words, 'Destroy the enemies of the sacred palace (or Court).' These are followed by a series of sentences, each of which begins with the word 'Remember', and contains one exhortation to his hearers to perform certain duties in connection with the service of the gods. Thus they are told to burn incense and to pour out libations each morning, to offer various kinds of geese to the gods, to eat natron, to make white bread, to set up poles on the temples and stelae inside them, to make the priest purify the temples, to remove from his office the priest who is unclean, etc. After many breaks in the text we come to the passage in which Apuur seems to foretell the coming of the king who is to restore order and prosperity to the land. He is to make cool that which is hot. He is to be the 'shepherd of mankind', having no evil in his heart. When his herds are few [and scattered], he will devote his time to bringing them together, their hearts being inflamed.

The passage continues, 'Would that he had perceived their nature in the first generation (of men), then he would have repressed evils, he would have stretched forth (his) arm against it, he would have destroyed their seed (?) and their inheritance.... A fighter (?) goes forth, that (he?) may destroy the wrongs that (?) have been wrought. There is no pilot (?) in their moment. Where is he (?) today? Is he sleeping? Behold, his might is not seen.'

Many of the passages in the indictment of Apuur resemble the descriptions of the state of the land of Israel and her people which are found in the writings of the Hebrew Prophets, and the 'shepherd of mankind', i.e. of the Egyptians, forcibly reminds us of the appeal to the 'Shepherd of Israel' in Psalm lxxx. 1.

EGYPTIAN POETIC COMPOSITIONS

The poetry of the Egyptians is wholly unlike that of Western nations, but closely resembles the rhythmical compositions of the Hebrews, with their parallelism of members, with which we may be familiar in the Book of Psalms, the Song of Solomon, etc. The most important collection of Egyptian Songs known to us is contained in the famous papyrus in the British Museum, No. 10,060, more commonly known as 'Harris 500'. This papyrus was probably written in the thirteenth century BCE, but many of the songs belong to a far earlier date. Though dealing with a variety of subjects, there is no doubt that all of them must be classed under the heading of 'Love Songs'. In them the lover compares the lady of his choice to many beautiful flowers and plants, and describes at considerable length the pain and grief which her absence causes him. The lines of the strophes are short, and the construction is simple, and it seems certain that the words owed their effect chiefly to the voice of the singer, who then, as now, employed many semitones and thirds of tones, and to the skill with which he played the accompaniment on his harp. A papyrus at Leyden, which was written a little later than the 'Love Songs', contains three very curious compositions sung in the voices of various fruit trees. More interesting than any of those songs is the so-called 'Song of the Harper', of which two copies are known: the first is found in the papyrus Harris 500, already mentioned, and the second in a papyrus at Leyden. Extracts of this poem are also found on the walls of the tomb of Nefer-hetep at Thebes. Here we reproduce the copy in the papyrus.

SONG OF THE HARPER

'The poem** that is in the hall of the tomb of [the King of the South, the King of the North], Antuf (one of the kings of the eleventh dynasty), whose word is truth, [and is cut] in front of the Harper:

> Oh good prince, it is a decree,
> And what has been ordained thereby is well,
> That the bodies of men shall pass away and disappear,
> Whilst others remain.
>
> Since the time of the oldest ancestors,
> The gods who lived in olden time,
> Who lie at rest in their sepulchres,
> The Masters and also the Shining Ones,
> Who have been buried in their splendid tombs,
> Who have built sacrificial halls in their tombs,
> Their place is no more.
> Consider what has become of them!
>
> I have heard the words of Imhetep and Herutataf,
> Which are treasured above everything
> because they uttered them.
> Consider what has become of their tombs!

Their walls have been thrown down;
Their places are no more;
They are just as if they had never existed.

Not one [of them] comes from where they are.
[Who can describe to us their form (or, condition),
Who can describe to us their surroundings,
Who can give comfort to our hearts,
And can act as our guide
To the place whereto they have departed?

Give comfort to your heart,
And let your heart forget these things;
What is best for you to do is
To follow your heart's desire as long as you live.

Anoint your head with scented unguents.
Let your apparel be of byssus
Dipped in costly [perfumes],
In the veritable products (?) of the gods.

Enjoy yourself more than you have ever done before,
And let not your heart pine for lack of pleasure.

Pursue your heart's desire and your own happiness.
Order your surroundings on earth in such a way
That they may minister to the desire of your heart;
[For] at length that day of lamentation shall come,
Wherein he whose heart is still shall
not hear the lamentation.

Never shall cries of grief cause
To beat [again] the heart of a man who is in the grave.

Therefore occupy yourself with your pleasure daily,
And never cease to enjoy yourself.

Behold, a man is not permitted
To carry his possessions away with him.
Behold, there never was any one who, having departed,
Was able to come back again.

A GLOSSARY OF
MYTH & FOLKLORE

Aaru Heavenly paradise where the blessed go after death.

Ab Heart or mind.

Abiku (Yoruba) Person predestined to die. Also known as ogbanje.

Absál Nurse to Saláman, who died after their brief love affair.

Achilles The son of Peleus and the sea-nymph Thetis, who distinguished himself in the Trojan War. He was made almost immortal by his mother, who dipped him in the River Styx, and he was invincible except for a portion of his heel which remained out of the water.

Acropolis Citadel in a Greek city.

Adad-Ea Ferryman to Ut-Napishtim, who carried Gilgamesh to visit his ancestor.

Adapa Son of Ea and a wise sage.

Adar God of the sun, who is worshipped primarily in Nippur.

Aditi Sky goddess and mother of the gods.

Adityas Vishnu, children of Aditi, including Indra, Mitra, Rudra, Tvashtar, Varuna and Vishnu.

Aeneas The son of Anchises and the goddess Aphrodite, reared by a nymph. He led the Dardanian troops in the Trojan War According to legend, he became the founder of Rome.

Aengus Óg Son of Dagda and Boann (a woman said to have given the Boyne river its name), Aengus is the Irish god of love whose stronghold is reputed to have been at New Grange. The famous tale 'Dream of Aengus' tells of how he fell in love with a maiden he had dreamt of. He eventually discovered that she was to be found at the Lake of the Dragon's Mouth in Co. Tipperary, but that she lived every alternate year in the form of a swan. Aengus thus plunged into the lake transforming himself also into the shape of a swan. Then the two flew back together to his palace on the Boyne where they lived out their days as guardians of would-be lovers.

Aesir Northern gods who made their home in Asgard; there are twelve in number.

Afrásiyáb Son of Poshang, king of Túrán, who led an army against the ruling shah Nauder. Afrásiyáb became ruler of Persia on defeating Nauder.

Afterlife Life after death or paradise, reached only by the process of preserving the body from decay through embalming and preparing it for reincarnation.

Agamemnon A famous King of Mycenae. He married Helen of Sparta's sister Clytemnestra. When Paris abducted Helen, beginning the Trojan War, Menelaus called on Agamemnon to raise the Greek troops. He had to sacrifice his daughter Iphigenia in order to get a fair wind to travel to Troy.

Agastya A rishi (sage). Leads hermits to Rama.

Agemo (Yoruba) A chameleon who aided Olorun in outwitting Olokun, who was angry at him for letting Obatala create life on her lands without her permission. Agemo outwitted Olokun by changing colour, letting her think that he and Olorun were better cloth dyers than she was. She admitted defeat and there was peace between the gods once again.

Aghasur A dragon sent by Kans to destroy Krishna.

Aghríras Son of Poshang and brother of Afrásiyáb, who was killed by his brother.

Agni The god of fire.

Agora Greek marketplace.

Ahura-Mazda Supreme god of the Persians, god of the sky. Similar to the Hindu god Varuna.

Ajax Ajax the Greater was the bravest, after Achilles, of all warriors at Troy, fighting Hector in single combat and distinguishing himself in the Battle of the Ships. He was not chosen as the bravest warrior and eventually went mad.

Ajax of Locris Another warrior at Troy. When Troy was captured, he committed the ultimate sacrilege by seizing Cassandra from her sanctuary with the Palladium.

Aje (Igbo) Goddess of the earth and the underworld.

Aje (Yoruba) Goddess of the River Niger, daughter of Yemoja.

Akhet Season of the year when the River Nile traditionally flooded.

Akkadian Person of the first Mesopotamian empire, centred in Akkad.

Akwán Diw An evil spirit who appeared as a wild ass in the court of Kai-khosráu. Rustem fought and defeated the demon, presenting its head to Kai-khosráu.

Alba Irish and Scottish Gaelic word for Scotland.

Alberich King of the dwarfs.

Alcinous King of the Phaeacians.

Alf-heim Home of the elves, ruled by Frey.

All Hallowmass All Saints' Day.

Allfather Another name for Odin; Yggdrasill was created by Allfather.

Alsvider Steed of the moon (Mani) chariot.

Alsvin Steed of the sun (Sol) chariot.

Amado Outer panelling of a dwelling, usually made of wood.

Ama-no-uzume Goddess of the dawn, meditation and the arts, who showed courage when faced with a giant who scared the other deities, including Ninigi. Also known as Uzume.

Amaterasu Goddess of the sun and daughter of Izanagi after Izanami's death; she became ruler of the High Plains of Heaven on her father's withdrawal from the world. Sister of Tsuki-yomi and Susanoo.

Ambalika Daughter of the king of Benares.

Ambika Daughter of the king of Benares.

Ambrosia Food of the gods.

Amemet Eater of the dead, monster who devoured the souls of the unworthy.

Amen Original creator deity.

Amen-Ra A being created from the fusion of Ra and Osiris. He champions the poor and those in trouble. Similar to the Greek god Zeus.

Ananda Disciple of Buddha.

Anansi One of the most popular African animal myths, Anansi the spider is a clever and shrewd character who outwits his fellow animals to get his own way. He is an entertaining but morally dubious character. Many African countries tell Anansi stories.

Ananta Thousand-headed snake that sprang from Balarama's mouth, Vishnu's attendant, serpent of infinite time.

Andhrímnir Cook at Valhalla.

Andvaranaut Ring of Andvari, the King of the dwarfs.

Angada Son of Vali, one of the monkey host.

Anger-Chamber Room designated for an angry queen.

Angurboda Loki's first wife, and the mother of Hel, Fenris and Jormungander.

Aniruddha Son of Pradyumna.

Anjana Mother of Hanuman.

Anunnaki Great spirits or gods of Earth.

Ansar God of the sky and father of Ea and Anu. Brother-husband to Kishar. Also known as Anshar or Asshur.

Anshumat A mighty chariot fighter.

Anu God of the sky and lord of heaven, son of Ansar and Kishar.

Anubis Guider of souls and ruler of the underworld before Osiris; he was one of the divinities who brought Osiris back to life. He is portrayed as a canid, African wolf or jackal.

Apep Serpent and emblem of chaos.

Apollo One of the twelve Olympian gods, son of Zeus and Leto. He is attributed with being the god of plague, music, song and prophecy.

Apsaras Dancing girls of Indra's court and heavenly nymphs.

Apsu Primeval domain of fresh water, originally part of Tiawath with whom he mated to have Mummu. The term is also used for the abyss from which creation came.

Aquila The divine eagle.

Arachne A Lydian woman with great skill in weaving. She was challenged in a competition by the jealous Athene who destroyed her work and when she killed herself, turned her into a spider destined to weave for eternity.

Aralu Goddess of the underworld, also known as Eres-ki-Gal. Married to Nergal.

Ares God of War, 'gold-changer of corpses', and the son of Zeus and Hera.

Argonauts Heroes who sailed with Jason on the ship Argo to fetch the golden fleece from Colchis.

Ariki A high chief, a leader, a master, a lord.

Arjuna The third of the Pandavas.

Aroha Affection, love.

Artemis The virgin goddess of the chase, attributed with being the moon goddess and the primitive mother-goddess. She was daughter of Zeus and Leto.

Arundhati The Northern Crown.

Asamanja Son of Sagara.

Asclepius God of healing who often took the form of a snake. He is the son of Apollo by Coronis.

Asgard Home of the gods, at one root of Yggdrasill.

Ashvatthaman Son of Drona.

Ashvins Twin horsemen, sons of the sun, benevolent gods and related to the divine.

Ashwapati Uncle of Bharata and Satrughna.

Asipû Wizard.

Asopus The god of the River Asopus.

Assagai Spear, usually made from hardwood tipped with iron and used in battle.

Astrolabe Instrument for making astronomical measurements.

Asuras Titans, demons, and enemies of the gods with magical powers.

Atef crown White crown made up of the Hedjet, the white crown of Upper Egypt, and red feathers.

Atem The first creator-deity, he is also thought to be the finisher of the world. Also known as Tem.

Athene Virgin warrior-goddess, born from the forehead of Zeus when he swallowed his wife Metis. Plays a key role in the travels of Odysseus, and Perseus.

Atlatl Spear-thrower.

Atua A supernatural being, a god.

Atua-toko A small carved stick, the symbol of the god whom it represents. It was stuck in the ground whilst holding incantations to its presiding god.

Augeas King of Elis, one of the Argonauts.

Augsburg Tyr's city.

Avalon Legendary island where Excalibur was created and where Arthur went to recover from his wounds. It is said he will return from Avalon one day to reclaim his kingdom.

Ba Dead person or soul. Also known as ka.

Bairn Little child, also called bairnie.

Balarama Brother of Krishna.

Balder Son of Frigga; his murder causes Ragnarok. Also spelled as Baldur.

Bali Brother of Sugriva and one of the five great monkeys in the *Ramayana*.

Balor The evil, one-eyed King of the Fomorians and also grandfather of Lugh of the Long Arm. It was prophesied that Balor would one day be slain by his own grandson so he locked his daughter away on a remote island where he intended that she would never fall pregnant. But Cian, father of Lugh, managed to reach the island disguised as a woman, and Balor's daughter eventually bore him a child. During the second battle of Mag Tured (or Moytura), Balor was killed by Lugh who slung a stone into his giant eye.

Ban King of Benwick, father of Lancelot and brother of King Bors.

Bannock Flat loaf of bread, typically of oat or barley, usually cooked on a griddle.

Banshee Mythical spirit, usually female, who bears tales of imminent death. They often deliver the news by wailing or keening outside homes. Spelled *bean sí* in Gaelic.

Bard Traditionally a storyteller, poet or music composer whose work often focused on legends.

Barû Seer.

Basswood Any of several North American linden trees with a soft light-coloured wood.

Bastet Goddess of love, fertility and sex and a solar deity. She is often portrayed with the head of a cat.

Bateta (Yoruba) The first human, created alongside Hanna by the Toad and reshaped into human form by the Moon.

Bau Goddess of humankind and the sick, and known as the 'divine physician'. Daughter of Anu.

Bawn Fortified enclosure surrounding a castle.

Beaver Largest rodent in the United States of America, held in high esteem by Native American people. Although a land mammal, it spends a great deal of time in water and has a dense waterproof fur coat to protect it from harsh weather conditions.

Behula Daughter of Saha.

Bel Name for the god En-lil, the word is also used as a title meaning 'lord'.

Belus Deity who helped form the heavens and earth and created animals and celestial beings. Similar to Zeus in Greek mythology.

Benten Goddess of the sea and one of the Seven Divinities of Luck. Also referred to as the goddess of love, beauty and eloquence and as being the personification of wisdom.

Bere Barley.

Berossus Priest of Bel who wrote a history of Babylon.

Berserker Norse warrior who fights with a frenzied rage.

Bestla Giant mother of Aesir's mortal element.

Bhadra A mighty elephant.

Bhagavati Shiva's wife, also known as Parvati.

Bhagiratha Son of Dilipa.

Bharadhwaja Father of Drona and a hermit.

Bharata One of Dasharatha's four sons.

Bhaumasur A demon, slain by Krishna.

Bhima The second of the Pandavas.

Bhimasha King of Rajagriha and disciple of Buddha.

Bier Frame on which a coffin or dead body is placed before being carried to the grave.

Bifrost Rainbow bridge presided over by Heimdall.

Big-Belly One of Ravana's monsters.

Bilskirnir Thor's palace.

Bodach The term means 'old man'. The Highlanders believed that the Bodach crept down chimneys in order to steal naughty children. In other territories, he was a spirit who warned of death.

Bodkin Large, blunt needle used for threading strips of cloth or tape through cloth; short pointed dagger or blade.

Boer Person of Dutch origin who settled in southern Africa in the late seventeenth century. The term means 'farmer'. Boer people are often called Afrikaners.

Bogle Ghost or phantom; goblin-like creature.

Boliaun Ragwort, a weed with ragged leaves.

Book of the Dead Book for the dead, thought to be written by Thoth, texts from which were written on papyrus and buried with the dead, or carved on the walls of tombs, pyramids or sarcophagi.

Bors King of Gaul and brother of King Ban.

Bothy Small cottage or hut.

Brahma Creator of the world, mythical origin of colour (caste).

Brahmadatta King of Benares.

Brahman Member of the highest Hindu caste, traditionally a priest.

Bran In Scottish legend, Bran is the great hunting hound of Fionn Mac Chumail. In Irish mythology, he is a great hero.

Branstock Giant oak tree in the Volsung's hall; Odin placed a sword in it and challenged the guests of a wedding to withdraw it.

Brave Young warrior of Native American descent, sometimes also referred to as a 'buck'.

Bree Thin broth or soup.

Breidablik Balder's palace.

Brigit Scottish saint or spirit associated with the coming of spring.

Brisingamen Freyia's necklace.

Britomartis A Cretan goddess, also known as Dictynna.

Brocéliande Legendary enchanted forest and the supposed burial place of Merlin.

Brokki Dwarf who makes a deal with Loki, and who makes Miolnir, Draupnir and Gulinbursti.

Brollachan A shapeless spirit of unknown origin. One of the most frightening in Scottish mythology, it spoke only two words, 'Myself' and 'Thyself', taking the shape of whatever it sat upon.

Brownie A household spirit or creature which took the form of a small man (usually hideously ugly) who undertakes household chores, and mill or farm work, in exchange for a bowl of milk.

Brugh Borough or town.

Brunhilde A Valkyrie found by Sigurd.

Buddha Founder of buddhism, Gautama, avatar of Vishnu in Hinduism.

Buddhism Buddhism arrived in China in the first century BCE via the silk trading route from India and Central Asia. Its founder was Guatama Siddhartha (the Buddha), a religious teacher in northern India. Buddhist doctrine declared that by destroying the causes of all suffering, mankind could attain perfect enlightenment. The religion encouraged a new respect for all living things and brought with it the idea of reincarnation; i.e. that the soul returns to the earth after death in another form, dictated by the individual's behaviour in his previous life. By the fourth century, Buddhism was the dominant religion in China, retaining its powerful influence over the nation until the mid-ninth century.

Buffalo A type of wild ox, once widely scattered over the Great Plains of North America. Also known as a 'bison', the buffalo was an important food source for Native American tribes and its hide was also used in the construction of tepees and to make clothing. The buffalo was also sometimes revered as a totem animal, i.e. venerated as a direct ancestor of the tribesmen, and its skull used in ceremonial fashion.

Bull of Apis Sacred bull, thought to be the son of Hathor.

Bulu Sacrificial rite.

Bundles, sacred These bundles contained various venerated objects of the tribe, believed to have supernatural powers. Custody or ownership of the bundle was never lightly entered upon, but involved the learning of endless songs and ritual dances.

Bushel Unit of measurement, usually used for agricultural products or food.

Bushi Warrior.

Byre Barn for keeping cattle.

Byrny Coat of mail.

Cacique King or prince.

Cailleach Bheur A witch with a blue face who represents winter. When she is reborn each autumn, snow falls. She is mother of the god of youth (Angus mac Og).

Calabash Gourd from the calabash tree, commonly used as a bottle.

Calchas The seer of Mycenae who accompanied the Greek fleet to Troy. It was his prophecy which stated that Troy would never be taken without the aid of Achilles.

Calpulli Village house, or group or clan of families.

Calumet Ceremonial pipe used by Native Americans.

Calypso A nymph who lived on the island of Ogygia.

Camaxtli Tlascalan god of war and the chase, similar to Huitzilopochtli.

Camelot King Arthur's castle and centre of his realm.

Caoineag A banshee.

Caravanserai Traveller's inn, traditionally found in Asia or North Africa.

Carle Term for a man, often old; peasant.

Cat A black cat has great mythological significance, is often the bearer of bad luck, a symbol of black magic, and the familiar of a witch. Cats were also the totem for many tribes.

Cath Sith A fairy cat who was believed to be a witch transformed.

Cazi Magical person or influence.

Ceasg A Scottish mermaid with the body of a maiden and the tail of a salmon.

Ceilidh Party.

Cerberus The three-headed dog who guarded the entrance to the Underworld.

Chalchiuhtlicue Goddess of water and the sick or newborn, and wife of Tlaloc. She is often symbolized as a small frog.

Changeling A fairy substitute-child left by fairies in place of a human child they have stolen.

Channa Guatama's charioteer.

Chaos A state from which the universe was created – caused by fire and ice meeting.

Charon The ferryman of the dead who carries souls across the River Styx to Hades.

Charybdis *See* Scylla and Charybdis.

Chicomecohuatl Chief goddess of maize and one of a group of deities called Centeotl, who care for all aspects of agriculture.

Chicomoztoc Legendary mountain and place of origin of the Aztecs. The name means 'seven caves'.

Chinawezi Primordial serpent.

Chinvat Bridge Bridge of the Gatherer, which the souls of the righteous cross to reach Mount Alborz or the world of the dead. Unworthy beings who try to cross Chinvat Bridge fall or are dragged into a place of eternal punishment.

Chitambaram Sacred city of Shiva's dance.

Chrysaor Son of Poseidon and Medusa, born from the severed neck of Medusa when Perseus beheaded her.

Chryseis Daughter of Chryses who was taken by Agamemnon in the battle of Troy.

Chullasubhadda Wife of Buddha-elect (Sumedha).

Chunda A good smith who entertains Buddha.

Churl Mean or unkind person.

Circe An enchantress and the daughter of Helius. She lived on the island of Aeaea with the power to change men to beasts.

Citlalpol The Mexican name for Venus, or the Great Star, and one of the only stars they worshipped. Also known as Tlauizcalpantecutli, or Lord of the Dawn.

Cleobis and Biton Two men of Argos who dragged the wagon carrying their mother, priestess of Hera, from Argos to the sanctuary.

Clio Muse of history and prophecy.

Clytemnestra Daughter of Tyndareus, sister of Helen, who married Agamemnon but deserted him when he sacrificed Iphigenia, their daughter, at the beginning of the Trojan War.

Coatepetl Mythical mountain, known as the 'serpent mountain'.

Coatl Serpent.

Coatlicue Earth mother and celestial goddess, she gave birth to Huitzilopochtli and his sister, Coyolxauhqui, and the moon and stars.

Codex Ancient book, often a list with pages folded into a zigzag pattern.

Confucius (Kong Fuzi) Regarded as China's greatest sage and ethical teacher, Confucius (551–479 BCE) was not especially revered during his lifetime and had a small following of some three thousand people. After the Burning of the Books in 213 BCE, interest in his philosophies became widespread. Confucius believed that mankind was essentially good, but argued for a highly structured society, presided over by a strong central government which would set the highest moral standards. The individual's sense of duty and obligation, he argued, would play a vital role in maintaining a well-run state.

Coracle Small, round boat, similar to a canoe. Also known as curragh or currach.

Coyolxauhqui Goddess of the moon and sister to Huitzilopochtli, she was decapitated by her brother after trying to kill their mother.

Creel Large basket made of wicker, usually used for fish.

Crodhmara Fairy cattle.

Cronan Musical humming, thought to resemble a cat purring or the drone of bagpipes.

Crow Usually associated with battle and death, but many mythological figures take this form.

Cu Sith A great fairy dog, usually green and oversized.

Cubit Ancient measurement, equal to the approximate length of a forearm.

Cuculain Irish warrior and hero. Also known as Cuchulainn.

Cutty Girl.

Cyclopes One-eyed giants who were imprisoned in Tartarus by Uranus and Cronus, but released by Zeus, for whom they made thunderbolts. Also a tribe of pastoralists who live without laws, and on, whenever possible, human flesh.

Daedalus Descendant of the Athenian King Erechtheus and son of Eupalamus. He killed his nephew and apprentice. Famed for constructing the labyrinth to house the Minotaur, in which he was later imprisoned. He constructed wings for himself and his son to make their escape.

Dagda One of the principal gods of the Tuatha De Danann, the father and chief, the Celtic equivalent of Zeus. He was the god reputed to have led the People of Dana in their successful conquest of the Fir Bolg.

Dagon God of fish and fertility; he is sometimes described as a sea-monster or chthonic god.

Daikoku God of wealth and one of the gods of luck.

Daimyō Powerful lord or magnate.

Daksha The chief Prajapati.

Dana Also known as Danu, a goddess worshipped from antiquity by the Celts and considered to be the ancestor of the Tuatha De Danann.

Danae Daughter of Acrisius, King of Argos. Acrisius trapped her in a cave when he was warned that his grandson would be the cause of his ultimate death. Zeus came to her and Perseus was born.

Danaids The fifty daughters of Danaus of Argos, by ten mothers.

Daoine Sidhe The people of the Hollow Hills, or Otherworld.

Dardanus Son of Zeus and Electra, daughter of Atlas.

Dasharatha A Manu amongst men, King of Koshala, father of Santa.

Deianeira Daughter of Oeneus, who married Heracles after he won her in a battle with the River Achelous.

Deirdre A beautiful woman doomed to cause the deaths of three Irish heroes and bring war to the whole country. After a soothsayer prophesied her fate, Deidre's father hid her away from the world to prevent it. However, fate finds its way and the events come to pass before Deidre eventually commits suicide to remain with her love.

Demeter Goddess of agriculture and nutrition, whose name means earth mother. She is the mother of Persephone.

Demophoon Son of King Celeus of Eleusis, who was nursed by Demeter and then dropped in the fire when she tried to make him immortal.

Dervish Member of a religious order, often Sufi, known for their wild dancing and whirling.

Desire The god of love.

Deva A god other than the supreme God.

Devadatta Buddha's cousin, plots evil against Buddha.

Dhrishtadyumna Twin brother of Draupadi, slays Drona.

Dibarra God of plague. Also a demonic character or evil spirit.

Dik-dik Dwarf antelope native to eastern and southern Africa.

Dilipa Son of Anshumat, father of Bhagiratha.

Dionysus The god of wine, vegetation and the life force, and of ecstasy. He was considered to be outside the Greek pantheon, and generally thought to have begun life as a mortal.

Dioscuri Castor and Polydeuces, the twin sons of Zeus and Leda, who are important deities.

Distaff Tool used when spinning which holds the wool or flax and keeps the fibres from tangling.

Divan Privy council.

Divots Turfs.

Dog The dog is a symbol of humanity, and usually has a role helping the hero of the myth or legend. Fionn's Bran and Grey Dog are two examples of wild beasts transformed to become invaluable servants.

Dōshin Government official.

Dossal Ornamental altar cloth.

Doughty Persistent and brave person.

Dragon Important animal in Japanese culture, symbolizing power, wealth, luck and success.

Draiglin' Hogney Ogre.

Draupadi Daughter of Drupada.

Draupnir Odin's famous ring, fashioned by Brokki.

Drona A Brahma, son of the great sage Bharadwaja.

Druid An ancient order of Celtic priests held in high esteem who flourished in the pre-Christian era. The word 'druid' is derived from an ancient Celtic one meaning 'very knowledgeable'. These individuals were believed to have mystical powers and in ancient Irish literature possess the ability to conjure up magical charms, to create tempests, to curse and debilitate their enemies and to perform as soothsayers to the royal courts.

Drupada King of the Panchalas.

Dryads Nymphs of the trees.

Dun A stronghold or royal abode surrounded by an earthen wall.

Durga Goddess, wife of Shiva.

Durk Knife. Also spelled as dirk.

Duryodhana One of Drona's pupils.

Dvalin Dwarf visited by Loki; also the name for the stag on Yggdrasill.

Dwarfie Stone Prehistoric tomb or boulder.

Dwarfs Fairies and black elves are called dwarfs.

Dwarkanath The Lord of Dwaraka; Krishna.

Dyumatsena King of the Shalwas and father of Satyavan.

Ea God of water, light and wisdom, and one of the creator deities. He brought arts and civilization to humankind. Also known as Oannes and Nudimmud.

Eabani Hero originally created by Aruru to defeat Gilgamesh, the two became friends and destroyed Khumbaba together. He personifies the natural world.

Each Uisge The mythical water-horse which haunts lochs and appears in various forms.

Ebisu One of the gods of luck. He is also the god of labour and fishermen.

Echo A nymph who was punished by Hera for her endless stories told to distract Hera from Zeus's infidelity.

Ector King Arthur's foster father, who raised Arthur to protect him.

Edda Collection of prose and poetic myths and stories from the Norsemen.

Eight Immortals Three of these are reputed to be historical: Han Chung-li, born in Shaanxi, who rose to become a Marshal of the Empire in 21 BCE. Chang Kuo-Lao, who lived in the seventh to eighth century CE, and Lü Tung-pin, who was born in 755 CE.

Einheriear Odin's guests at Valhalla.

Eisa Loki's daughter.

Ekake (Ibani) Person of great intelligence, which means 'tortoise'. Also known as Mbai (Igbo).

Ekalavya Son of the king of the Nishadas.

Electra Daughter of Agamemnon and Clytemnestra.

Eleusis A town in which the cult of Demeter is centred.

Elf Sigmund is buried by an elf; there are light and dark elves (the latter called dwarfs).

Elokos (Central African) Imps of dwarf-demons who eat human flesh.

Elpenor The youngest of Odysseus's crew who fell from the roof of Circe's house on Aeaea and visited with Odysseus at Hades.

Elysium The home of the blessed dead.

Emain Macha The capital of ancient Ulster.

Emma Dai-o King of hell and judge of the dead.

En-lil God of the lower world, storms and mist, who held sway over the ghostly animistic spirits, which at his bidding might pose as the friends or enemies of men. Also known as Bel.

Eos Goddess of the dawn and sister of the sun and moon.

Erichthonius A child born of the semen spilled when Hephaestus tried to rape Athene on the Acropolis.

Eridu The home of Ea and one of the two major cities of Babylonian civilization.

Erin Term for Ireland, originally spelled Éirinn.

Erirogho Magical mixture made from the ashes of the dead.

Eros God of Love, the son of Aphrodite.

Erpa Hereditary chief.

Erysichthon A Thessalian who cut down a grove sacred to Demeter, who punished him with eternal hunger.

Eshu (Yoruba) God of mischief. He also tests people's characters and controls law enforcement.

Eteocles Son of Oedipus.

Eumaeus Swineherd of Odysseus's family at Ithaca.

Euphemus A son of Poseidon who could walk on water. He sailed with the Argonauts.

Europa Daughter of King Agenor of Tyre, who was taken by Zeus to Crete.

Eurydice A Thracian nymph married to Orpheus.

Excalibur The magical sword given to Arthur by the Lady of the Lake. In some versions of the myths, Excalibur is also the sword that the young Arthur pulls from the stone to become king.

Fabulist Person who composes or tells fables.

Fafnir Shape-changer who kills his father and becomes a dragon to guard the family jewels. Slain by Sigurd.

Fairy The word is derived from 'Fays' which means Fates. They are immortal, with the gift of prophecy and of music, and their role changes according to the origin of the myth. They were often considered to be little people, with enormous propensity for mischief, but they are central to many myths and legends, with important powers.

Faro (Mali, Guinea) God of the sky.

Fates In Greek mythology, daughters of Zeus and Themis, who spin the thread of a mortal's life and cut it when his time is due. Called Norns in Viking mythology.

Fenris A wild wolf, who is the son of Loki. He roams the earth after Ragnarok.

Ferhad Sculptor who fell in love with Shireen, the wife of Khosru, and undertook a seemingly impossible task to clear a passage through the mountain of Beysitoun and join the rivers in return for winning Shireen's hand.

Fialar Red cock of Valhalla.

Fianna/Fenians The word 'fianna' was used in early times to describe young warrior-hunters. These youths evolved under the leadership of Finn Mac Cumaill as a highly skilled band of military men who took up service with various kings throughout Ireland.

Filheim Land of mist, at the end of one of Yggdrasill's roots.

Fingal Another name for Fionn Mac Chumail, used after MacPherson's Ossian in the eighteenth century.

Fionn Mac Chumail Irish and Scottish warrior, with great powers of fairness and wisdom. He is known not for physical strength but for knowledge, sense of justice, generosity and canny instinct. He had two hounds, which were later discovered to be his nephews transformed. He became head of the Fianna, or Féinn, fighting the enemies of Ireland and Scotland. He was the father of Oisin (also called Ossian, or other derivatives), and father or grandfather of Osgar.

Fir Bolg   One of the ancient, pre-Gaelic peoples of Ireland who were reputed to have worshipped the god Bulga, meaning god of lighting. They are thought to have colonized Ireland around 1970 BCE, after the death of Nemed and to have reigned for a short period of thirty-seven years before their defeat by the Tuatha De Danann.

Fir Chlis   Nimble men or merry dancers, who are the souls of fallen angels.

Flitch   Side of salted and cured bacon.

Folkvang   Freyia's palace.

Fomorians   A race of monstrous beings, popularly conceived as sea-pirates with some supernatural characteristics who opposed the earliest settlers in Ireland, including the Nemedians and the Tuatha De Danann.

Frey   Comes to Asgard with Freyia as a hostage following the war between the Aesir and the Vanir.

Freyia   Comes to Asgard with Frey as a hostage following the war between the Aesir and the Vanir. Goddess of beauty and love.

Frigga   Odin's wife and mother of gods; she is goddess of the earth.

Fuath   Evil spirits which lived in or near the water.

Fulla   Frigga's maidservant.

Furies   Creatures born from the blood of Cronus, guarding the greatest sinners of the Underworld. Their power lay in their ability to drive mortals mad. Snakes writhed in their hair and around their waists.

Furoshiki Cloths used to wrap things.

Gae Bolg Cuchulainn alone learned the use of this weapon from the woman-warrior, Scathach and with it he slew his own son Connla and his closest friend, Ferdia. Gae Bolg translates as 'harpoon-like javelin' and the deadly weapon was reported to have been created by Bulga, the god of lighting.

Gaea Goddess of Earth, born from Chaos, and the mother of Uranus and Pontus. Also spelled as Gaia.

Gage Object of value presented to a challenger to symbolize good faith.

Galahad Knight of the Round Table, who took up the search for the Holy Grail. Son of Lancelot, Galahad is considered the purest and most perfect knight.

Galatea Daughter of Nereus and Doris, a sea-nymph loved by Polyphemus, the Cyclops.

Gandhari Mother of Duryodhana.

Gandharvas Demi-gods and musicians.

Gandjharva Musical ministrants of the upper air.

Ganesha Elephant-headed god of scribes and son of Shiva.

Ganges Sacred river personified by the goddess Ganga, wife of Shiva and daughter of the mount Himalaya.

Gareth of Orkney King Arthur's nephew and knight of the Round Table.

Garm Hel's hound.

Garuda King of the birds and mount Vishnu, the divine bird, attendant of Narayana.

Gautama Son of Suddhodana and also known as Siddhartha.

Gawain Nephew of King Arthur and knight of the Round Table, he is best known for his adventure with the Green Knight, who challenges one of Arthur's knights to cut off his head, but only if he agrees to be beheaded in turn in a year and a day, if the Green Knight survives. Gawain beheads the Green Knight, who simply replaces his head. At the appointed time, they meet, and the Green Knight swings his axe but merely nicks Gawain's skin instead of beheading him.

Geisha Performance artist or entertainer, usually female.

Geri Odin's wolf.

Ghommid (Yoruba) Term for mythological creatures such as goblins or ogres.

Giallar Bridge in Filheim.

Giallarhorn Heimdall's trumpet – the final call signifies Ragnarok.

Giants In Greek mythology, a race of beings born from Gaea, grown from the blood that dropped from the castrated Uranus. Usually represent evil in Viking mythology.

Gilgamesh King of Erech known as a half-human, half-god hero similar to the Greek Heracles, and often listed with the gods. He is the personification of the sun and is protected by the god Shamash, who in some texts is described as his father. He is also portrayed as an evil tyrant at times.

Gillie Someone who works for a Scottish chief, usually as an attendant or servant; guide for fishing or hunting parties.

Gladheim Where the twelve deities of Asgard hold their thrones. Also called Gladsheim.

Gled Bird of prey.

Golden Fleece Fleece of the ram sent by Poseidon to substitute for Phrixus when his father was going to sacrifice him. The Argonauts went in search of the fleece.

Goodman Man of the house.

Goodwife Woman of the house.

Gopis Lovers of the young Krishna and milkmaids.

Gorgon One of the three sisters, including Medusa, whose frightening looks could turn mortals to stone.

Graces Daughters of Aphrodite by Zeus.

Gramercy Expression of surprise or strong feeling.

Great Head The Iroquois believed in the existence of a curious being known as Great Head, a creature with an enormous head poised on slender legs.

Great Spirit The name given to the Creator of all life, as well as the term used to describe the omnipotent force of the Creator existing in every living thing.

Great-Flank One of Ravana's monsters.

Green Knight A knight dressed all in green and with green hair and skin who challenged one of Arthur's knights to strike him a blow with an axe and that, if he survived, he would return to behead the knight in a year and a day. He turned out to be Lord Bertilak and was under an enchantment cast by Morgan le Fay to test Arthur's knights.

Gruagach Mythical creature, often a giant or ogre similar to a wild man of the woods. The term can also refer to other mythical creatures such as brownies or fairies. As a brownie, he is usually dressed in red or green as opposed to the traditional brown. He has great power to enchant the hapless, or to help mortals who are worthy (usually heroes). He often appears to challenge a boy-hero, during his period of education.

Gudea High priest of Lagash, known to be a patron of the arts and a writer himself.

Guebre Religion founded by Zoroaster, the Persian prophet.

Gugumatz Creator god who, with Huracan, formed the sky, earth and everything on it.

Guha King of Nishadha.

Guidewife Woman.

Guinevere Wife of King Arthur; she is often portrayed as a virtuous lady and wife, but is perhaps best known for having a love affair with Lancelot, one of Arthur's friends and knights of the Round Table. Her name is also spelled Guenever.

Gulistan *Rose Garden*, written by the poet Sa'di

Gungnir Odin's spear, made of Yggdrasill wood, and the tip fashioned by Dvalin.

Gylfi A wandering king to whom the Eddas are narrated.

Haab Mayan solar calendar that consisted of eighteen twenty-day months.

Hades One of the three sons of Cronus; brother of Poseidon and Zeus. Hades is King of the Underworld, which is also known as the House of Hades.

Haere-mai Maori phrase meaning 'come here, welcome.'

Haere-mai-ra, me o tatou mate Maori phrase meaning 'come here, that I may sorrow with you.'

Haere-ra Maori phrase meaning 'goodbye, go, farewell.'

Haji Muslim pilgrim who has been to Mecca.

Hakama Traditional Japanese clothing, worn on the bottom half of the body.

Hanuman General of the monkey people.

Harakiri Suicide, usually by cutting or stabbing the abdomen. Also known as seppuku.

Hari-Hara Shiva and Vishnu as one god.

Harmonia Daughter of Ares and Aphrodite, wife of Cadmus.

Hatamoto High-ranking samurai.

Hathor Great cosmic mother and patroness of lovers. She is portrayed as a cow.

Hati The wolf who pursues the sun and moon.

Hatshepsut Second female pharaoh.

Hauberk Armour to protect the neck and shoulders, sometimes a full-length coat of mail.

Hector Eldest son of King Priam who defended Troy from the Greeks. He was killed by Achilles.

Hecuba The second wife of Priam, King of Troy. She was turned into a dog after Troy was lost.

Heimdall White god who guards the Bifrost bridge.

Hel Goddess of death and Loki's daughter. Also known as Hela.

Helen Daughter of Leda and Tyndareus, King of Sparta, and the most beautiful woman in the world. She was responsible for starting the Trojan War.

Heliopolis City in modern-day Cairo, known as the City of the Sun and the central place of worship of Ra. Also known as Anu.

Helius The sun, son of Hyperion and Theia.

Henwife Witch.

Hephaestus or **Hephaistos** The Smith of Heaven.

Hera A Mycenaean palace goddess, married to Zeus.

Heracles An important Greek hero, the son of Zeus and Alcmena. His name means 'Glory of Hera'. He performed twelve labours for King Eurystheus, and later became a god.

Hermes The conductor of souls of the dead to Hades, and god of trickery and of trade. He acts as messenger to the gods.

Hermod Son of Frigga and Odin who travelled to see Hel in order to reclaim Balder for Asgard.

Hero and Leander Hero was a priestess of Aphrodite, loved by Leander, a young man of Abydos. He drowned trying to see her.

Hestia Goddess of the hearth, daughter of Cronus and Rhea.

Hieroglyphs Type of writing that combines symbols and pictures, usually cut into tombs or rocks, or written on papyrus.

Himalaya Great mountain and range, father of Parvati.

Hiordis Wife of Sigmund and mother of Sigurd.

Hoderi A fisher and son of Okuninushi.

Hodur Balder's blind twin; known as the personification of darkness.

Hoenir Also called Vili; produced the first humans with Odin and Loki, and was one of the triad responsible for the creation of the world.

Hōichi the Earless A biwa hōshi, a blind storyteller who played the biwa or lute. Also a priest.

Holger Danske Legendary Viking warrior who is thought to never die. He sleeps until he is needed by his people and then he will rise to protect them.

Homayi Phoenix.

Hoodie Mythical creature which often appears as a crow.

Hoori A hunter and son of Okuninushi.

Horus God of the sky and kinship, son of Isis and Osiris. He captained the boat that carried Ra across the sky. He is depicted with the head of a falcon.

Hotei One of the gods of luck. He also personifies humour and contentment.

Houlet Owl.

Houri Beautiful virgin from paradise.

Hrim-faxi Steed of the night.

Hubris Presumptuous behaviour which causes the wrath of the gods to be brought on to mortals.

Hueytozoztli Festival dedicated to Tlaloc and, at times, Chicomecohuatl or other deities. Also the fourth month of the Aztec calendar.

Hugin Odin's raven.

Huitzilopochtli God of war and the sun, also connected with the summer and crops; one of the principal Aztec deities. He was born a full-grown adult to save his mother, Coatlicue, from the jealousy of his sister, Coyolxauhqui, who tried to kill Coatlicue. The Mars of the Aztec gods. In some origin stories he is one of four offspring of Ometeotl and Omecihuatl.

Hurley A traditional Irish game played with sticks and balls, quite similar to hockey.

Hurons A tribe of Iroquois stock, originally one people with the Iroquois.

Huveane (Pedi, Venda) Creator of humankind, who made a baby from clay into which he breathed life. He is known as the High God or Great God. He is also known as a trickster god.

Hymir Giant who fishes with Thor and is drowned by him.

Iambe Daughter of Pan and Echo, servant to King Celeus of Eleusis and Metaeira.

Icarus Son of Daedalus, who plunged to his death after escaping from the labyrinth.

Ichneumon Mongoose.

Idunn Guardian of the youth-giving apples.

Ifa (Yoruba) God of wisdom and divination. Also the term for a Yoruban religion.

Ife (Yoruba) The place Obatala first arrived on Earth and took for his home.

Igigi Great spirits or gods of Heaven and the sky.

Igraine Wife of the duke of Tintagel, enemy of Uther Pendragon, who marries Uther when her first husband dies. She is King Arthur's mother.

Ile (Yoruba) Goddess of the earth.

Imhetep High priest and wise sage. He is sometimes thought to be the son of Ptah.

Imam Person who leads prayers in a mosque.

Imana (Banyarwanda) Creator or sky god.

In The male principle who, joined with Yo, the female side, brought about creation and the first gods. In and Yo correspond to the Chinese Yang and Yin.

Inari God of rice, fertility, agriculture and, later, the fox god. Inari has both good and evil attributes but is often presented as an evil trickster.

Indra The King of Heaven.

Indrajit Son of Ravana.

Indrasen Daughter of Nala and Damayanti.

Indrasena Son of Nala and Damayanti.

Inundation Annual flooding of the River Nile.

Iphigenia The eldest daughter of Agamemnon and Clytemnestra who was sacrificed to appease Artemis and obtain a fair wind for Troy.

Iris Messenger of the gods who took the form of a rainbow.

Iseult Princess of Ireland and niece of the Morholt. She falls in love with Tristan after consuming a love potion but is forced to marry King Mark of Cornwall.

Ishtar Goddess of love, beauty, justice and war, especially in Ninevah, and earth mother who symbolizes fertility. Married to Tammuz, she is similar to the Greek goddess Aphrodite. Ishtar is sometimes known as Innana or Irnina.

Isis Goddess of the Nile and the moon, sister-wife of Osiris. She and her son, Horus, are sometimes thought of in a similar way to Mary and Jesus. She was one of the most worshipped female

Egyptian deities and was instrumental in returning Osiris to life after he was killed by his brother, Set.

Istakbál Deputation of warriors.

Izanagi Deity and brother-husband to Izanami, who together created the Japanese islands from the Floating Bridge of Heaven. Their offspring populated Japan.

Izanami Deity and sister-wife of Izanagi, creator of Japan. Their children include Amaterasu, Tsuki-yomi and Susanoo.

Jade It was believed that jade emerged from the mountains as a liquid which then solidified after ten thousand years to become a precious hard stone, green in colour. If the correct herbs were added to it, it could return to its liquid state and when swallowed increase the individual's chances of immortality.

Jambavan A noble monkey.

Jason Son of Aeson, King of Iolcus and leader of the voyage of the Argonauts.

Jatayu King of all the eagle-tribes.

Jesseraunt Flexible coat of armour or mail.

Jimmo Legendary first emperor of Japan. He is thought to be descended from Hoori, while other tales claim him to be descended from Amaterasu through her grandson, Ninigi.

Jizo God of little children and the god who calms the troubled sea.

Jord Daughter of Nott; wife of Odin.

Jormungander The world serpent; son of Loki. Legends tell that when his tail is removed from his mouth, Ragnarok has arrived.

Jorō Geisha who also worked as a prostitute.

Jotunheim Home of the giants.

Ju Ju tree Deciduous tree that produces edible fruit.

Jurasindhu A rakshasa, father-in-law of Kans.

Jyeshtha Goddess of bad luck.

Ka Life power or soul. Also known as ba.

Kai-káús Son of Kai-kobád. He led an army to invade Mázinderán, home of the demon-sorcerers, after being persuaded by a demon. Known for his ambitious schemes, he later tried to reach Heaven by trapping eagles to fly him there on his throne.

Kaikeyi Mother of Bharata, one of Dasharatha's three wives.

Kai-khosrau Son of Saiawúsh, who killed Afrásiyáb in revenge for the death of his father.

Kai-kobád Descendant of Feridún, he was selected by Zál to lead an army against Afrásiyáb. Their powerful army, led by Zál and Rustem, drove back Afrásiyáb's army, who then agreed to peace.

Kailyard Kitchen garden or small plot, usually used for growing vegetables.

Kali The Black, wife of Shiva.

Kalindi Daughter of the sun, wife of Krishna.

Kaliya A poisonous hydra that lived in the jamna.

Kalki Incarnation of Vishnu yet to come.

Kalnagini Serpent who kills Lakshmindara.

Kal-Purush The Time-man, Bengali name for Orion.

Kaluda A disciple of Buddha.

Kalunga-ngombe (Mbundu) Death, also depicted as the king of the netherworld.

Kama God of desire.

Kamadeva Desire, the god of love.

Kami Spirits, deities or forces of nature.

Kamund Lasso.

Kans King of Mathura, son of Ugrasena and Pavandrekha.

Kanva Father of Shakuntala.

Kappa River goblin with the body of a tortoise and the head of an ape. Kappa love to challenge human beings to single combat.

Karakia Invocation, ceremony, prayer.

Karna Pupil of Drona.

Kaross Blanket or rug, also worn as a traditional garment. It is often made from the skins of animals which have been sewn together.

Kasbu A period of twenty-four hours.

Kashyapa One of Dasharatha's counsellors.

Kauravas or Kurus Sons of Dhritarashtra, pupils of Drona.

Kaushalya Mother of Rama, one of Dasharatha's three wives.

Kay Son of Ector and adopted brother to King Arthur, he becomes one of Arthur's knights of the Round Table.

Keb God of the earth and father of Osiris and Isis, married to Nut. Keb is identified with Kronos, the Greek god of time.

Kehua Spirit, ghost.

Kelpie Another word for each uisge, the water-horse.

Ken Know.

Keres Black-winged demons or daughters of the night.

Keshini Wife of Sagara.

Khalif Leader.

Khara Younger brother of Ravana.

Khepera God who represents the rising sun. He is portrayed as a scarab. Also known as Nebertcher.

Kher-heb Priest and magician who officiated over rituals and ceremonies.

Khnemu God of the source of the Nile and one of the original Egyptian deities. He is thought to be the creator of children and of other gods. He is portrayed as a ram.

Khosru King and husband to Shireen, daughter of Maurice, the Greek Emperor. He was murdered by his own son, who wanted his kingdom and his wife.

Khumbaba Monster and guardian of the goddess Irnina, a form of the goddess Ishtar. Khumbaba is likened to the Greek gorgon.

Kia‑ora Welcome, good luck. A greeting.

Kiboko Hippopotamus.

Kikinu Soul.

Kimbanda (Mbundu) Doctor.

Kimono Traditional Japanese clothing, similar to a robe.

King Arthur Legendary king of Britain who plucked the magical sword from the stone, marking him as the heir of Uther Pendragon and 'true king' of Britain. He and his knights of the Round Table defended Britain from the Saxons and had many adventures, including searching for the Holy Grail. Finally wounded in battle, he left Britain for the mythical Avalon, vowing to one day return to reclaim his kingdom.

Kingu Tiawath's husband, a god and warrior who she promised would rule Heaven once he helped her defeat the 'gods of light'. He was killed by Merodach who used his blood to make clay, from which he formed the first humans. In some tales, Kingu is Tiawath's son as well as her consort.

Kinnaras Human birds with musical instruments under their wings.

Kinyamkela (Zaramo) Ghost of a child.

Kirk Church, usually a term for Church of Scotland churches.

Kirtle One-piece garment, similar to a tunic, which was worn by men or women.

Kis Solar deity, usually depicted as an eagle.

Kishar Earth mother and sister-wife to Anshar.

Kist Trunk or large chest.

Kitamba (Mbundu) Chief who made his whole village go into mourning when his head-wife, Queen Muhongo, died. He also pledged that no one should speak or eat until she was returned to him.

Knowe Knoll or hillock.

Kojiki One of two myth-histories of Japan, along with the *Nihon Shoki*.

Ko-no-Hana Goddess of Mount Fuji, princess and wife of Ninigi.

Kore 'Maiden', another name for Persephone.

Kraal Traditional rural African village, usually consisting of huts surrounded by a fence or wall. Also an animal enclosure.

Krishna The Dark one, worshipped as an incarnation of Vishnu.

Kui-see Edible root.

Kumara Son of Shiva and Paravati, slays demon Taraka.

Kumbha-karna Ravana's brother.

Kunti Mother of the Pandavas.

Kura Red. The sacred colour of the Maori.

Kusha or Kusi One of Sita's two sons.

Kvasir Clever warrior and colleague of Odin. He was responsible for finally outwitting Loki.

Kwannon Goddess of mercy.

Labyrinth A prison built at Knossos for the Minotaur by Daedalus.

Lady of the Lake Enchantress who presents Arthur with Excalibur.

Laertes King of Ithaca and father of Odysseus.

Laestrygonians Savage giants encountered by Odysseus on his travels.

Laili In love with Majnun but unable to marry him, she was given to the prince, Ibn Salam, to marry. When he died, she escaped and found Majnun, but they could not be legally married. The couple died of grief and were buried together. Also known as Laila.

Laird Person who owns a significant estate in Scotland.

Lakshmana Brother of Rama and his companion in exile.

Lakshmi Consort of Vishnu and a goddess of beauty and good fortune.

Lakshmindara Son of Chand resurrected by Manasa Devi.

Lancelot Knight of the Round Table. Lancelot was raised by the Lady of the Lake. While he went on many quests, he is perhaps best known for his affair with Guinevere, King Arthur's wife.

Land of Light One of the names for the realm of the fairies. If a piece of metal welded by human hands is put in the doorway to their land, the door cannot close. The door to this realm is only open at night, and usually at a full moon.

Lang syne The days of old.

Lao Tzu (Laozi) The ancient Taoist philosopher thought to have been born in 571 BCE a contemporary of Confucius with whom, it is said, he discussed the tenets of Tao. Lao Tzu was an advocate of simple rural existence and looked to the Yellow Emperor and Shun as models of efficient government. His philosophies were recorded in the Tao Te Ching. Legends surrounding his birth suggest that he emerged from the left-hand side of his mother's body, with white hair and a long white beard, after a confinement lasting eighty years.

Laocoon A Trojan wiseman who predicted that the wooden horse contained Greek soldiers.

Laomedon The King of Troy who hired Apollo and Poseidon to build the impregnable walls of Troy.

Lava Son of Sita.

Leda Daughter of the King of Aetolia, who married Tyndareus. Helen and Clytemnestra were her daughters.

Legba (Dahomey) Youngest offspring of Mawu-Lisa. He was given the gift of all languages. It was through him that humans could converse with the gods.

Leman Lover.

Leprechaun Mythical creature from Irish folk tales who often appears as a mischievous and sometimes drunken old man.

Lethe One of the four rivers of the Underworld, also called the River of Forgetfulness.

Lif The female survivor of Ragnarok.

Lifthrasir The male survivor of Ragnarok.

Lil Demon.

Liongo (Swahili) Warrior and hero.

Lofty mountain Home of Ahura-Mazda.

Logi Utgard-loki's cook.

Loki God of fire and mischief-maker of Asgard; he eventually brings about Ragnarok. Also spelled as Loptur.

Lotus-Eaters A race of people who live a dazed, drugged existence, the result of eating the lotus flower.

Ma'at State of order meaning truth, order or justice. Personified by the goddess Ma'at, who was Thoth's consort.

Macha There are thought to be several different Machas who appear in quite a number of ancient Irish stories. For the purposes of this book, however, the Macha referred to is the wife of Crunnchu. The story unfolds that after her husband had boasted of her great athletic ability to the King, she was subsequently forced to run against his horses in spite of the fact that she was heavily pregnant. Macha died giving birth to her twin babies and with her dying breath she cursed Ulster for nine generations, proclaiming that it would suffer the weakness of a woman in childbirth in times of great stress. This curse had its most disastrous effect when Medb of Connacht invaded Ulster with her great army.

Machi-bugyō Senior official or magistrate, usually samurai.

Macuilxochitl God of art, dance and games, and the patron of luck in gaming. His name means 'source of flowers' or 'prince of flowers'. Also known as Xochipilli, meaning 'five-flower'.

Madake Weapon used for whipping, made of bamboo.

Maduma Taro tuber.

Mag Muirthemne Cuchulainn's inheritance. A plain extending from River Boyne to the mountain range of Cualgne, close to Emain Macha in Ulster.

Magni Thor's son.

Mahaparshwa One of Ravana's generals.

Maharaksha Son of Khara, slain at Lanka.

Mahasubhadda Wife of Buddha-select (Sumedha).

Majnun Son of a chief, who fell in love with Laili and followed her tribe through the desert, becoming mad with love until they were briefly reunited before dying.

Makaras Mythical fish-reptiles of the sea.

Makoma (Senna) Folk hero who defeated five mighty giants.

Mana Power, authority, prestige, influence, sanctity, luck.

Manasa Devi Goddess of snakes, daughter of Shiva by a mortal woman.

Manasha Goddess of snakes.

Mandavya Daughter of Kushadhwaja.

Man-Devourer One of Ravana's monsters.

Mandodari Wife of Ravana.

Mandrake Poisonous plant from the nightshade family which has hallucinogenic and hypnotic qualities if ingested. Its roots resemble the human form and it has supposedly magical qualities.

Mani The moon.

Manitto Broad term used to describe the supernatural or a potent spirit among the Algonquins, the Iroquois and the Sioux.

Man-Slayer One of Ravana's counsellors.

Manthara Kaikeyi's evil nurse, who plots Rama's ruin.

Mantle Cloak or shawl.

Manu Lawgiver.

Manu Mythical mountain on which the sun sets.

Mara The evil one, tempts Gautama.

Markandeya One of Dasharatha's counsellors.

Mashu Mountain of the Sunset, which lies between Earth and the underworld. Guarded by scorpion-men.

Matali Sakra's charioteer.

Mawu-Lisa (Dahomey) Twin offspring of Nana Baluka. Mawu (female) and Lisa (male) are often joined to form one being. Their own offspring populated the world.

Mbai (Igbo) Person of great intelligence, also known as Ekake (Ibani), which means 'tortoise'.

Medea Witch and priestess of Hecate, daughter of Aeetes and sister of Circe. She helped Jason in his quest for the Golden Fleece.

Medusa One of the three Gorgons whose head had the power to turn onlookers to stone.

Melpomene One of the muses, and mother of the Sirens.

Menaka One of the most beautiful dancers in Heaven.

Menat Amulet, usually worn for protection.

Mendicant Beggar.

Menelaus King of Sparta, brother of Agamemnon. Married Helen and called war against Troy when she eloped with Paris.

Menthu Lord of Thebes and god of war. He is portrayed as a hawk or falcon.

Mere-pounamu A native weapon made of a rare green stone.

Merlin Wizard and advisor to King Arthur. He is thought to be the son of a human female and an incubus (male demon). He brought about Arthur's birth and ascension to king, then acted as his mentor.

Merodach God who battled Tiawath and defeated her by cutting out her heart and dividing her corpse into two pieces. He used these pieces to divide the upper and lower waters once controlled by Tiawath, making a dwelling for the gods of light. He also created humankind. Also known as Marduk.

Merrow Mythical mermaid-like creature, often depicted with an enchanted cap called a cohuleen driuth which allows it to travel between land and the depths of the sea. Also known as murúch.

Metaneira Wife of Celeus, King of Eleusis, who hired Demeter in disguise as her nurse.

Metztli Goddess of the moon, her name means 'lady of the night'. Also known as Yohualtictl.

Michabo Also known as Manobozho, or the Great Hare, the principal deity of the Algonquins, maker and preserver of the earth, sun and moon.

Mictlan God of the dead and ruler of the underworld. He was married to Mictecaciuatl and is often represented as a bat. He is also the Aztec lord of Hades. Also known as Mictlantecutli. Mictlan is also the name for the underworld.

Midgard Dwelling place of humans (Earth).

Midsummer A time when fairies dance and claim human victims.

Mihrab Father of Rúdábeh and descendant of Zohák, the serpent-king.

Milesians A group of iron-age invaders led by the sons of Mil, who arrived in Ireland from Spain around 500 BCE and overcame the Tuatha De Danann.

Mimir God of the ocean. His head guards a well; reincarnated after Ragnarok.

Minos King of Crete, son of Zeus and Europa. He was considered to have been the ruler of a sea empire.

Minotaur A creature born of the union between Pasiphae and a Cretan Bull.

Minúchihr King who lives to be one hundred and twenty years old. Father of Nauder.

Miolnir *See* Mjolnir.

Mithra God of the sun and light in Iran, protector of truth and guardian of pastures and cattle. Alo known as Mitra in Hindu mythology and Mithras in Roman mythology.

Mixcoatl God of the chase or the hunt. Sometimes depicted as the god of air and thunder, he introduced fire to humankind. His name means 'cloud serpent'.

Mjolnir Hammer belonging to the Norse god of thunder, which is used as a fearsome weapon which always returns to Thor's hand, and as an instrument of consecration.

Mnoatia Forest spirits.

Moccasins One-piece shoes made of soft leather, especially deerskin.

Modi Thor's son.

Moly A magical plant given to Odysseus by Hermes as protection against Circe's powers.

Montezuma Great emperor who consolidated the Aztec Empire.

Mordred Bastard son of King Arthur and Morgawse, Queen of Orkney, who, unknown to Arthur, was his half-sister. Mordred becomes one of King Arthur's knights of the Round Table before betraying and fatally wounding Arthur, causing him to leave Britain for Avalon.

Morgan le Fay Enchantress and half-sister to King Arthur, Morgan was an apprentice of Merlin's. She is generally depicted as benevolent, yet did pit herself against Arthur and his knights on occasion. She escorts Arthur on his final journey to Avalon. Also known as Morgain le Fay.

Morholt The knight sent to Cornwall to force King Mark to pay tribute to Ireland. He is killed by Tristan.

Morongoe the brave (Lesotho) Man who was turned into a snake by evil spirits because Tau was jealous that he had married the beautiful Mokete, the chief's daughter. Morongoe was returned to human form after his son, Tsietse, returned him to their family.

Mosima (Bapedi) The underworld or abyss.

Mount Fuji Highest mountain in Japan, on the island of Honshū.

Mount Kunlun This mountain features in many Chinese legends as the home of the great emperors on Earth. It is written in the *Shanghaijing (The Classic of Mountains and Seas)* that this towering structure measured no less than 3300 miles in circumference and 4000 miles in height. It acted both as a central pillar to support the heavens, and as a gateway between Heaven and Earth.

Moving Finger Expression for taking responsibility for one's life and actions, which cannot be undone.

Moytura Translated as the 'Plain of Weeping', Mag Tured, or Moytura, was where the Tuatha De Danann fought two of their most significant battles.

Mua An old-time Polynesian god.

Muezzin Person who performs the Muslim call to prayer.

Mugalana A disciple of Buddha.

Muilearteach The Cailleach Bheur of the water, who appears as a witch or a sea-serpent. On land she grew larger and stronger by fire.

Mul-lil God of Nippur, who took the form of a gazelle.

Muloyi Sorcerer, also called mulaki, murozi, ndozi or ndoki.

Mummu Son of Tiawath and Apsu. He formed a trinity with them to battle the gods. Also known as Moumis. In some tales, Mummu is also Merodach, who eventually destroyed Tiawath.

Munin Odin's raven.

Murile (Chaga) Man who dug up a taro tuber that resembled his baby brother, which turned into a living boy. His mother killed the baby when she saw Murile was starving himself to feed it.

Murtough Mac Erca King who ruled Ireland when many of its people – including his wife and family – were converting to Christianity. He remained a pagan.

Muses Goddesses of poetry and song, daughters of Zeus and Mnemosyne.

Musha Expression, often of surprise.

Muskrat North American beaver-like, amphibious rodent.

Muspell Home of fire, and the fire-giants.

Mwidzilo Taboo which, if broken, can cause death.

Nabu God of writing and wisdom. Also known as Nebo. Thought to be the son of Merodach.

Nahua Ancient Mexicans.

Nakula Pandava twin skilled in horsemanship.

Nala One of the monkey host, son of Vishvakarma.

Nana Baluka (Dahomey) Mother of all creation. She gave birth to an androgynous being with two faces. The female face was Mawu, who controlled the night and lands to the west. The male face was Lisa and he controlled the day and the east.

Nanahuatl Also known as Nanauatzin. Presided over skin diseases and known as Leprous, which in Nahua meant 'divine'.

Nandi Shiva's bull.

Nanna Balder's wife.

Nannar God of the moon and patron of the city of Ur.

Naram-Sin Son or ancestor of Sargon and king of the Four Zones or Quarters of Babylon.

Narcissus Son of the River Cephisus. He fell in love with himself and died as a result.

Narve Son of Loki.

Nataraja Manifestation of Shiva, Lord of the Dance.

Natron Preservative used in embalming, mined from the Natron Valley in Egypt.

Nauder Son of Minúchihr, who became king on his death and was tyrannical and hated until Sám begged him to follow in the footsteps of his ancestors.

Nausicaa Daughter of Alcinous, King of Phaeacia, who fell in love with Odysseus.

Nebuchadnezzar Famous king of Babylon. Also known as Nebuchadrezzar.

Necromancy Communicating with the dead.

Nectar Drink of the gods.

Neith Goddess of hunting, fate and war. Neith is sometimes known as the creator of the universe.

Nemesis Goddess of retribution and daughter of night.

Neoptolemus Son of Achilles and Deidameia, he came to Troy at the end of the war to wear his father's armour. He sacrificed Polyxena at the tomb of Achilles.

Nephthys Goddess of the air, night and the dead. Sister of Isis and sister-wife to Seth, she is also the mother of Anubis.

Nereids Sea-nymphs who are the daughters of Nereus and Doris. Thetis, mother of Achilles, was a Nereid.

Nergal God of death and patron god of Cuthah, which was often known as a burial place. He is also known as the god of fire. Married to Aralu, the goddess of the underworld.

Nestor Wise King of Pylus, who led the ships to Troy with Agamemnon and Menelaus.

Neta Daughter of Shiva, friend of Manasa.

Ngai (Gikuyu) Creator god.

Ngaka (Lesotho) Witch doctor.

Niflheim The underworld In Norse mythology, ruled over by Hel.

Night Daughter of Norvi.

Nikumbha One of Ravana's generals.

Nila One of the monkey host, son of Agni.

Nin-Girsu God of fertility and war, patron god of Girsu. Also known as Shul-gur.

Ninigi Grandson of Amaterasu, Ninigi came to Earth bringing rice and order to found the Imperial family. He is known as the August Grandchild.

Niord God of the sea; marries Skadi.

Nippur The home of En-lil and one of the two major cities of Babylonian civilization.

Nirig God of war and storms, and son of Bel. Also known as Enu-Restu.

Nirvana Transcendent state and the final goal of Buddhism.

Nis Mythological creature, similar to a brownie or goblin, usually harmless or even friendly, but can be easily offended. They are often associated with Christmas or the winter solstice.

Noatun Niord's home.

Noisy-Throat One of Ravana's counsellors.

Noondah (Zanzibar) Cannibalistic cat which attacked and killed animals and humans.

Norns The fates and protectors of Yggdrasill. Many believe them to be the same as the Valkyries.

Norvi Father of the night.

Nott Goddess of night.

Nsasak bird Small bird who became chief of all small birds after winning a competition to go without food for seven days. The

Nsasak bird beat the Odudu bird by sneaking out of his home to feed.

Nü Wa   The Goddess Nü Wa, who in some versions of the Creation myths is the sole creator of mankind, and in other tales is associated with the God Fu Xi, also a great benefactor of the human race. Some accounts represent Fu Xi as the brother of Nü Wa, but others describe the pair as lovers who lie together to create the very first human beings. Fu Xi is also considered to be the first of the Chinese emperors of mythical times who reigned from 2953 to 2838 BCE.

Nuada   The first king of the Tuatha De Danann in Ireland, who lost an arm in the first battle of Moytura against the Fomorians. He became known as 'Nuada of the Silver Hand' when Diancecht, the great physician of the Tuatha De Danann, replaced his hand with a silver one after the battle.

Nunda   (Swahili, East Africa) Slayer that took the form of a cat and grew so big that it consumed everyone in the town except the sultan's wife, who locked herself away. Her son, Mohammed, killed Nunda and cut open its leg, setting free everyone Nunda had eaten.

Nut   Goddess of the sky, stars and astronomy. Sister-wife of Keb and mother of Osiris, Isis, Set and Nephthys. She often appears in the form of a cow.

Nyame   (Ashanti) God of the sky, who sees and knows everything.

Nymphs   Minor female deities associated with particular parts of the land and sea.

Obassi Osaw   (Ekoi) Creator god with his twin, Obassi Nsi. Originally, Obassi Osaw ruled the skies while Obassi Nsi ruled the Earth.

Obatala   (Yoruba) Creator of humankind. He climbed down a golden chain from the sky to the earth, then a watery abyss, and formed land and humankind. When Olorun heard of his success, he created the sun for Obatala and his creations.

Oberon Fairy king.

Odin Allfather and king of all gods, he is known for travelling the nine worlds in disguise and recognized only by his single eye; dies at Ragnarok.

Oduduwa (Yoruba) Divine king of Ile-Ife, the holy city of Yoruba.

Odur Freyia's husband.

Odysseus Greek hero, son of Laertes and Anticleia, who was renowned for his cunning, the master behind the victory at Troy, and known for his long voyage home.

Oedipus Son of Leius, King of Thebes and Jocasta. Became King of Thebes and married his mother.

Ogdoad Group of eight deities who were formed into four male-female couples who joined to create the gods and the world.

Ogham One of the earliest known forms of Irish writing, originally used to inscribe upright pillar stones.

Oiran Courtesan.

Oisin Also called Ossian (particularly by James Macpherson who wrote a set of Gaelic Romances about this character, supposedly garnered from oral tradition). Ossian was the son of Fionn and Sadbh, and had various brothers, according to different legends. He was a man of great wisdom, became immortal for many centuries, but in the end he became mad.

Ojibwe Another name for the Chippewa, a tribe of Algonquin stock.

Okuninushi Deity and descendant of Susanoo, who married Suseri-hime, Susanoo's daughter, without his consent. Susanoo tried to kill him many times but did not succeed and eventually forgave Okuninushi. He is sometimes thought to be the son or grandson of Susanoo.

Olokun (Yoruba) Most powerful goddess who ruled the seas and marshes. When Obatala created Earth in her domain, other gods began to divide it up between them. Angered at their presumption, she caused a great flood to destroy the land.

Olorun (Yoruba) Supreme god and ruler of the sky. He sees and controls everything, but others, such as Obatala, carry out the work for him. Also known as Olodumare.

Olympia Zeus's home in Elis.

Olympus The highest mountain in Greece and the ancient home of the gods.

Omecihuatl Female half of the first being, combined with Ometeotl. Together they are the lords of duality or lords of the two sexes. Also known as Ometecutli and Omeciuatl or Tonacatecutli and Tonacaciuatl. Their offspring were Xipe Totec, Huitzilopochtli, Quetzalcoatl and Tezcatlipoca.

Ometeotl Male half of the first being, combined with Omecihuatl.

Ometochtli Collective name for the pulque-gods or drink-gods. These gods were often associated with rabbits as they were thought to be senseless creatures.

Onygate Anyway.

Opening of the Mouth Ceremony in which mummies or statues were prayed over and anointed with incense before their mouths were opened, allowing them to eat and drink in the afterlife.

Oracle The response of a god or priest to a request for advice – also a prophecy; the place where such advice was sought; the person or thing from whom such advice was sought.

Oranyan (Yoruba) Youngest grandson of King Oduduwa, who later became king himself.

Orestes Son of Agamemnon and Clytemnestra who escaped following Agamemnon's murder to King Strophius. He later returned to Argos to murder his mother and avenge the death of his father.

Orpheus Thracian singer and poet, son of Oeagrus and a Muse. Married Eurydice and when she died tried to retrieve her from the Underworld.

Orunmila (Yoruba) Eldest son of Olorun, he helped Obatala create land and humanity, which he then rescued after Olokun flooded the lands. He has the power to see the future.

Osiris God of fertility, the afterlife and death. Thought to be the first of the pharaohs. He was murdered by his brother, Set, after which he was conjured back to life by Isis, Anubis and others before becoming lord of the afterworld. Married to Isis, who was also his sister.

Otherworld The world of deities and spirits, also known as the Land of Promise, or the Land of Eternal Youth, a place of everlasting life where all earthly dreams come to be fulfilled.

Owuo (Krachi, West Africa) Giant who personifies death. He causes a person to die every time he blinks his eye.

Palamedes Hero of Nauplia, believed to have created part of the ancient Greek alphabet. He tricked Odysseus into joining the fleet setting out for Troy by placing the infant Telemachus in the path of his plough.

Palermo Stone Stone carved with hieroglyphs, which came from the Royal Annals of ancient Egypt and contains a list of the kings of Egypt from the first to the early fifth dynasties.

Palfrey Docile and light horse, often used by women.

Palladium Wooden image of Athene, created by her as a monument to her friend Pallas who she accidentally killed. While in Troy it protected the city from invaders.

Pallas Athene's best friend, whom she killed.

Pan   God of Arcadia, half-goat and half-man. Son of Hermes. He is connected with fertility, masturbation and sexual drive. He is also associated with music, particularly his pipes, and with laughter.

Pan Gu   Some ancient writers suggest that this God is the offspring of the opposing forces of nature, the yin and the yang. The yin (female) is associated with the cold and darkness of the earth, while the yang (male) is associated with the sun and the warmth of the heavens. 'Pan' means 'shell of an egg' and 'Gu' means 'to secure' or 'to achieve'. Pan Gu came into existence so that he might create order from chaos.

Pandareus   Cretan King killed by the gods for stealing the shrine of Zeus.

Pandavas   Alternative name for sons of Pandu, pupils of Drona.

Pandora   The first woman, created by the gods, to punish man for Prometheus's theft of fire. Her dowry was a box full of powerful evil.

Papyrus   Paper-like material made from the pith of the papyrus plant, first manufactured in Egypt. Used as a type of paper as well as for making mats, rope and sandals.

Paramahamsa   The supreme swan.

Parashurama   Human incarnation of Vishnu, 'Rama with an axe'.

Paris   Handsome son of Priam and Hecuba of Troy, who was left for dead on Mount Ida but raised by shepherds. Was reclaimed by his family, then brought them shame and caused the Trojan War by eloping with Helen.

Parsa   Holy man. Also known as a zahid.

Parvati   Consort of Shiva and daughter of Himalaya.

Passion   Wife of desire.

Pavanarekha   Wife of Ugrasena, mother of Kans.

Peerie Folk Fairy or little folk.

Pegasus The winged horse born from the severed neck of Medusa.

Peggin Wooden vessel with a handle, often shaped like a tub and used for drinking.

Peleus Father of Achilles. He married Antigone, caused her death, and then became King of Phthia. Saved from death himself by Jason and the Argonauts. Married Thetis, a sea nymph.

Penelope The long-suffering but equally clever wife of Odysseus who managed to keep at bay suitors who longed for Ithaca while Odysseus was at the Trojan War and on his ten-year voyage home.

Pentangle Pentagram or five-pointed star.

Pentecost Christian festival held on the seventh Sunday after Easter. It celebrates the holy spirit descending on the disciples after Jesus's ascension.

Percivale Knight of the Round Table and original seeker of the Holy Grail.

Persephone Daughter of Zeus and Demeter who was raped by Hades and forced to live in the Underworld as his queen for three months of every year.

Perseus Son of Danae, who was made pregnant by Zeus. He fought the Gorgons and brought home the head of Medusa. He eventually founded the city of Mycenae and married Andromeda.

Pesh Kef Spooned blade used in the Opening the Mouth ceremony.

Phaeacia The Kingdom of Alcinous on which Odysseus landed after a shipwreck which claimed the last of his men as he left Calypso's island.

Pharaoh King or ruler of Egypt.

Philoctetes Malian hero, son of Poeas, received Heracles's bow and arrows as a gift when he lit the great hero's pyre on Mount Oeta. He was involved in the last part of the Trojan War, killing Paris.

Philtre Magic potion, usually a love potion.

Pibroch Bagpipe music.

Pintura Native manuscript or painting.

Pipiltin Noble class of the Aztecs.

Pismire Ant.

Piu-piu Short mat made from flax leaves and neatly decorated.

Po Gloom, darkness, the lower world.

Polyphemus A Cyclops, but a son of Poseidon. He fell in love with Galatea, but she spurned him. He was blinded by Odysseus.

Polyxena Daughter of Priam and Hecuba of Troy. She was sacrificed on the grave of Achilles by Neoptolemus.

Pooka Mythical creature with the ability to shapeshift. Often appears as a horse, but also as a bull, dog or in human form, and has the ability to talk. Also known as púca.

Popol Vuh Sacred 'book of counsel' of the Quiché or K'iche' Maya people.

Poseidon God of the sea, and of sweet waters. Also the god of earthquakes. His is brother to Zeus and Hades, who divided the earth between them.

Pradyumna Son of Krishna and Rukmini.

Prahasta (Long-Hand) One of Ravana's generals.

Prajapati Creator of the universe, father of the gods, demons and all creatures, later known as Brahma.

Priam King of Troy, married to Hecuba, who bore him Hector, Paris, Helenus, Cassandra, Polyxena, Deiphobus and Troilus. He was murdered by Neoptolemus.

Pritha Mother of Karna and of the Pandavas.

Prithivi Consort of Dyaus and goddess of the earth.

Proetus King of Argos, son of Abas.

Prometheus   A Titan, son of Iapetus and Themus. He was champion of mortal men, which he created from clay. He stole fire from the gods and was universally hated by them.

Prose Edda   Collection of Norse myths and poems, thought to have been compiled in the 1200s by Icelandic historian Snorri Sturluson.

Proteus   The old man of the sea who watched Poseidon's seals.

Psyche   A beautiful nymph who was the secret wife of Eros, against the wishes of his mother Aphrodite, who sent Psyche to perform many tasks in hope of causing her death. She eventually married Eros and was allowed to become partly immortal.

Ptah   Creator god and deity of Memphis who was married to Sekhmet. Ptah built the boats to carry the souls of the dead to the afterlife.

Puddock   Frog.

Pulque   Alcoholic drink made from fermented agave.

Purusha   The cosmic man, he was sacrificed and his dismembered body became all the parts of the cosmos, including the four classes of society.

Purvey   To provide or supply.

Pushkara   Nala's brother.

Pushpaka   Rama's chariot.

Putana   A rakshasi.

Pygmalion   A sculptor who was so lonely he carved a statue of a beautiful woman, and eventually fell in love with it. Aphrodite brought the image to life.

Quauhtli   Eagle.

Quern   Hand mill used for grinding corn.

Quetzalcoatl   Deity and god of wind. He is represented as a feathered or plumed serpent and is usually a wise and benevolent god. Offspring of Ometeotl and Omecihuatl, he is also known as Kukulkan.

Ra God of the sun, ruling male deity of Egypt whose name means 'sole creator'.

Radha The principal mistress of Krishna.

Ragnarok The end of the world.

Rahula Son of Siddhartha and Yashodhara.

Raiden God of thunder. He traditionally has a fierce and demonic appearance.

Rakshasas Demons and devils.

Ram of Mendes Sacred symbol of fatherhood and fertility.

Rama or **Ramachandra** A prince and hero of the *Ramayana*, worshipped as an incarnation of Vishnu.

Ra-Molo (Lesotho) Father of fire, a chief who ruled by fear. When trying to kill his brother, Tau the lion, he was turned into a monster with the head of a sheep and the body of a snake.

Rangatira Chief, warrior, gentleman.

Regin A blacksmith who educated Sigurd.

Reinga The spirit land, the home of the dead.

Reservations Tracts of land allocated to the Native American people by the United States Government with the purpose of bringing the many separate tribes under state control.

Rewati Daughter of Raja, marries Balarama.

Rhadha Wife of Adiratha, a gopi of Brindaban and lover of Krishna.

Rhea Mother of the Olympian gods. Cronus ate each of her children, but she concealed Zeus and gave Cronus a swaddled rock in his place.

Rill Small stream.

Rimu (Chaga) Monster known to feed off human flesh, which sometimes takes the form of a werewolf.

Rishis Sacrificial priests associated with the devas in Swarga.

Rituparna King of Ayodhya.

Rohini The wife of Vasudeva, mother of Balarama and Subhadra, and carer of the young Krishna. Another Rohini is a goddess and consort of Chandra.

Rōnin Samurai whose master had died or fallen out of favour.

Rubáiyát Collection of poems written by Omar Khayyám.

Rúdábeh Wife of Zál and mother of Rustem.

Rudra Lord of Beasts and disease, later evolved into Shiva.

Rukma Rukmini's eldest brother.

Rustem Son of Zál and Rúdábeh, he was a brave and mighty warrior who undertook seven labours to travel to Mázinderán to rescue Kai-káús. Once there, he defeated the White Demon and rescued Kai-káús. He rode the fabled stallion Rakhsh and is also known as Rustam.

Ryō Traditional gold currency.

Sabdh Mother of Ossian, or Oisin.

Sabitu Goddess of the sea.

Sagara King of Ayodhya.

Sahadeva Pandava twin skilled in swordsmanship.

Sahib diwan Lord high treasurer or chief royal executive.

Saiawúsh Son of Kai-káús, who was put through trial by fire when Sudaveh, Kai-káús's wife, told him that Saiawúsh had taken advantage of her. His innocence was proven when the fire did not harm him. He was eventually killed by Afrásiyáb.

Saithe Blessed.

Sajara (Mali) God of rainbows. He takes the form of a multi-coloured serpent.

Sake Japanese rice wine.

Sakuni Cousin of Duryodhana.

Salam Greeting or salutation.

Saláman Son of the Shah of Yunan, who fell in love with Absál, his nurse. She died after they had a brief love affair and he returned to his father.

Salmali tree Cotton tree.

Salmon A symbol of great wisdom, around which many Scottish legends revolve.

Sám Mighty warrior who fought and won many battles. Father of Zál and grandfather to Rustem.

Sambu Son of Krishna.

Sampati Elder brother of Jatayu.

Samurai Noblemen who were part of the military in medieval Japan.

Sanehat Member of the royal bodyguard.

Sango (Yoruba) God of war and thunder.

Sangu (Mozambique) Goddess who protects pregnant women, depicted as a hippopotamus.

Santa Daughter of Dasharatha.

Sarapis Composite deity of Apis and Osiris, sometimes known as Serapis. Thought to be created to unify Greek and Egyptian citizens under the Greek pharaoh Ptolemy.

Sarasvati The tongue of Rama.

Sarcophagus Stone coffin.

Sargon of Akkad Raised by Akki, a husbandman, after being hidden at birth. Sargon became King of Assyria and a great hero. He founded the first library in Babylon. Similar to King Arthur or Perseus.

Sarsar Harsh, whistling wind.

Sasabonsam (Ashanti) Forest ogre.

Sassun Scottish word for England.

Sati Daughter of Daksha and Prasuti, first wife of Shiva.

Satrughna One of Dasharatha's four sons.

Satyavan Truth speaker, husband of Savitri.

Satyavati A fisher-maid, wife of Bhishma's father, Shamtanu.

Satyrs Elemental spirits which took great pleasure in chasing nymphs. They had horns, a hairy body and cloven hooves.

Saumanasa A mighty elephant.

Scamander River running across the Trojan plain, and father of Teucer.

Scarab Dung beetle, often used as a symbol of the immortal human soul and regeneration.

Scylla and Charybdis Scylla was a monster who lived on a rock of the same name in the Straits of Messina, devouring sailors. Charybdis was a whirlpool in the Straits which was supposedly inhabited by the hateful daughter of Poseidon.

Seal Often believed that seals were fallen angels. Many families are descended from seals, some of which had webbed hands or feet. Some seals were the children of sea-kings who had become enchanted (selkies).

Seelie-Court The court of the Fairies, who travelled around their realm. They were usually fair to humans, doling out punishment that was morally sound, but they were quick to avenge insults to fairies.

Segu (Swahili, East Africa) Guide who informs humans where honey can be found.

Sekhmet Solar deity who led the pharaohs in war. She is goddess of healing and was sent by Ra to destroy humanity when people turned against the sun god. She is portrayed with the head of a lion.

Selene Moon-goddess, daughter of Hyperion and Theia. She was seduced by Pan, but loved Endymion.

Selkie Mythical creature which is seal-like when in water but can shed its skin to take on human form when on land.

Seneschal Steward of a royal or noble household.

Sensei Teacher.

Seriyut A disciple of Buddha.

Sessrymnir Freyia's home.

Set God of chaos and evil, brother of Osiris, who killed him by tricking him into getting into a chest, which he then threw in the Nile, before cutting Osiris's body into fourteen separate pieces. Also known as Seth.

Sgeulachd Stories.

Sháhnámeh *The Book of Kings* written by Ferdowsi, one of the world's longest epic poems, which describes the mythology and history of the Persian Empire.

Shaikh Respected religious man.

Shaivas or Shaivites Worshippers of Shiva.

Shakti Power or wife of a god and Shiva's consort as his feminine aspect.

Shaman Also known as the 'Medicine Men' of Native American tribes, it is the shaman's role to cultivate communication with the spirit world. They are endowed with knowledge of all healing herbs, and learn to diagnose and cure disease. They are believed to foretell the future, find lost property and have power over animals, plants and stones.

Shamash God of the sun and protector of Gilgamesh, the great Babylonian hero. Known as the son of Sin, the moon god, he is also portrayed as a judge of good and evil.

Shamtanu Father of Bhishma.

Shankara A great magician, friend of Chand Sadagar.

Shashti The Sixth, goddess who protects children and women in childbirth.

Sheen Beautiful and enchanted woman who casts a spell on Murtough, King of Ireland, causing him to fall in love with her and cast out his family. He dies at her hands, half burned and half drowned, but she then dies of grief as she returns his love. Sheen is known by many names, including Storm, Sigh and Rough Wind.

Shesh A serpent that takes human birth through Devaki.

Shi-en Fairy dwelling.

Shinto Indigenous religion of Japan, from the pre-sixth century to the present day.

Shireen Married to Khosru. Her beauty meant that she was desired by many, including Khosru's own son by his previous marriage. She killed herself rather than give in to her stepson.

Shitala The Cool One and goddess of smallpox.

Shiva One of the two great gods of post-Vedic Hinduism with Vishnu.

Shogun Military ruler or overlord.

Shoji Sliding door, usually a lattice screen of paper.

Shu God of the air and half of the first divine couple created by Atem. Brother and husband to Tefnut, father to Keb and Nut.

Shubistán Household.

Shudra One of the four fundamental colours (caste).

Shuttle Part of a machine used for spinning cloth, used for passing weft threads between warp threads.

Siddhas Musical ministrants of the upper air.

Sif Thor's wife; known for her beautiful hair.

Sigi Son of Odin.

Sigmund Warrior able to pull the sword from Branstock in the Volsung's hall.

Signy Volsung's daughter.

Sigurd Son of Sigmund, and bearer of his sword. Slays Fafnir the dragon.

Sigyn Loki's faithful wife.

Símúrgh Griffin, an animal with the body of a lion and the head and wings of an eagle. Known to hold great wisdom. Also called a symurgh.

Sin God of the moon, worshipped primarily in Ur.

Sindri Dwarf who worked with Brokki to fashion gifts for the gods; commissioned by Loki.

Sirens Sea nymphs who are half-bird, half-woman, whose song lures hapless sailors to their death.

Sisyphus King of Ephrya and a trickster who outwitted Autolycus. He was one of the greatest sinners in Hades.

Sita Daughter of the earth, adopted by Janaka, wife of Rama.

Skadi Goddess of winter and the wife of Niord for a short time.

Skanda Six-headed son of Shiva and a warrior god.

Skraeling Person native to Canada and Greenland. The name was given to them by Viking settlers and can be translated as 'barbarian'.

Skrymir Giant who battled against Thor.

Sleipnir Odin's steed.

Sluagh The host of the dead, seen fighting in the sky and heard by mortals.

Smote Struck with a heavy blow.

Sohráb Son of Rustem and Tahmineh, Sohráb was slain in battle by his own father, who killed him by mistake.

Sol The sun-maiden.

Soma A god and a drug, the elixir of life.

Somerled Lord of the Isles, and legendary ancestor of the Clan MacDonald.

Soothsayer Someone with the ability to predict or see the future, by the use of magic, special knowledge or intuition. Known as seanagal in Scottish myths.

Squaw A Native American woman or wife (now offensive).

Squint‑Eye One of Ramana's monsters.

Squire Shield- or armour-bearer of a knight.

Srutakirti Daughter of Kushadhwaja.

Stirabout Porridge made by stirring oatmeal into boiling milk or water.

Stone Giants A malignant race of stone beings whom the Iroquois believed invaded their territory, threatening the Confederation of the Five Nations. These fierce and hostile creatures lived off human flesh and were intent on exterminating the human race.

Stoorworm A great water monster which frequented lochs. When it thrust its great body from the sea, it could engulf islands and whole ships. Its appearance prophesied devastation.

Stot Bullock.

Styx River in Arcadia and one of the four rivers in the Underworld. Charon ferried dead souls across it into Hades, and Achilles was dipped into it to make him immortal.

Subrahmanian Son of Shiva, a mountain deity.

Sugriva The chief of the five great monkeys in the *Ramayana*.

Sukanya The wife of Chyavana.

Suman Son of Asamanja.

Sumantra A noble Brahman.

Sumati Wife of Sagara.

Sumedha A righteous Brahman who dwelt in the city of Amara.

Sumitra One of Dasharatha's three wives, mother of Lakshmana and Satrughna.

Suniti Mother of Dhruva.

Suparshwa One of Ravana's counsellors.

Supranakha A rakshasi, sister of Ravana.

Surabhi The wish-bestowing cow.

Surcoat Loose robe, traditionally worn over armour.

Surtr Fire-giant who eventually destroys the world at Ragnarok.

Surya God of the sun.

Susanoo God of the storm. He is depicted as a contradictory character with both good and bad characteristics. He was banished from Heaven after trying to kill his sister, Amaterasu.

Sushena A monkey chief.

Svasud Father of summer.

Swarga An Olympian paradise, where all wishes and desires are gratified.

Sweating A ritual customarily associated with spiritual purification and prayer practised by most tribes throughout North America prior to sacred ceremonies or vision quests. Steam was produced within a 'sweat lodge', a low, dome-shaped hut, by sprinkling water on heated stones.

Syrinx An Arcadian nymph who was the object of Pan's love.

Tablet of Destinies Cuneiform clay tablet on which the fates were written. Tiawath had given this to Kingu, but it was taken by Merodach when he defeated them. The storm god Zu later stole it for himself.

Taiaha A weapon made of wood.

Tailtiu One of the most famous royal residences of ancient Ireland. Possibly also a goddess linked to this site.

Tall One of Ravana's counsellors.

Tammuz Solar deity of Eridu who, with Gishzida, guards the gates of Heaven. Protector of Anu.

Tamsil Example or guidance.

Tangi Funeral, dirge. Assembly to cry over the dead.

Taniwha Sea monster, water spirit.

Tantalus Son of Zeus who told the secrets of the gods to mortals and stole their nectar and ambrosia. He was condemned to eternal torture in Hades, where he was tempted by food and water but allowed to partake of neither.

Taoism Taoism (or Daoism) came into being at roughly the same time as Confucianism, although its tenets were radically different and were largely founded on the philosophies of Lao Tzu (Laozi). While Confucius argued for a system of state discipline, Taoism strongly favoured self-discipline and looked upon nature as the architect of essential laws. A newer form of Taoism evolved after the Burning of the Books, placing great emphasis on spirit worship and pacification of the gods.

Tapu Sacred, supernatural possession of power. Involves spiritual rules and restrictions.

Tara Also known as Temair, the Hill of Tara was the popular seat of the ancient High-Kings of Ireland from the earliest times to the sixth century. Located in Co. Meath, it was also the place where great noblemen and chieftains congregated during wartime, or for significant events.

Tara Sugriva's wife.

Tartarus Dark region, below Hades.

Tau (Lesotho) Brother to Ra-Molo, depicted as a lion.

Taua War party.

Tefnut Goddess of water and rain. Married to Shu, who was also her brother. She, like Sekhmet, is portrayed with the head of a lion. Also known as Tefenet.

Telegonus Son of Odysseus and Circe. He was allegedly responsible for his father's death.

Telemachus Son of Odysseus and Penelope who was aided by Athene in helping his mother to keep away the suitors in Odysseus's absence.

Temu The evening form of Ra, the Sun god.

Tengu Goblin or gnome, often depicted as bird-like. A powerful fighter with weapons.

Tenochtitlán Capital city of the Aztecs, founded around 1350 CE and the site of the 'Great Temple'. Now Mexico City.

Teo-Amoxtli Divine book.

Teocalli Great temple built in Tenochtitlán, now Mexico City.

Teotleco Festival of the Coming of the Gods; also the twelfth month of the Aztec calendar.

Tepee A conical-shaped dwelling constructed of buffalo hide stretched over lodge-poles. Mostly used by Native American tribes living on the plains.

Tepeyollotl God of caves, desert places and earthquakes, whose name means 'heart of the mountain'. He is depicted as a jaguar, often leaping at the sun. Also known as Tepeolotlec.

Tepitoton Household gods.

Tereus King of Daulis who married Procne, daughter of Pandion King of Athens. He fell in love with Philomela, raped her and cut out her tongue.

Tezcatlipoca Supreme deity and Lord of the Smoking Mirror. He was also patron of royalty and warriors. Invented human sacrifice to the gods. Offspring of Ometeotl and Omecihuatl, he is known as the Jupiter of the Aztec gods.

Thalia Muse of pastoral poetry and comedy.

Theia Goddess of many names, and mother of the sun.

Theseus Son of King Aegeus of Athens. A cycle of legends has been woven around his travels and life.

Thetis Chief of the Nereids loved by both Zeus and Poseidon. They married her to a mortal, Peleus, and their child was Achilles. She tried to make him immortal by dipping him in the River Styx.

Thialfi Thor's servant, taken when his peasant father unwittingly harms Thor's goat.

Thiassi Giant and father of Skadi, he tricked Loki into bringing Idunn to him. Thrymheim is his kingdom.

Thomas the Rhymer Also called 'True Thomas', he was Thomas of Ercledoune, who lived in the thirteenth century. He met with the Queen of Elfland, and visited her country, was given clothes and a tongue that could tell no lie. He was also given the gift of prophecy, and many of his predictions were proven true.

Thor God of thunder and of war (with Tyr). Known for his huge size, and red hair and beard. Carries the hammer Miolnir. Slays Jormungander at Ragnarok.

Thoth God of the moon. Invented the arts and sciences and regulated the seasons. He is portrayed with the head of an ibis or a baboon.

Three-Heads One of Ravana's monsters.

Thrud Thor's daughter.

Thrudheim Thor's realm. Also called Thrudvang.

Thunder-Tooth Leader of the rakshasas at the siege of Lanka.

Tiawath Primeval dark ocean or abyss, Tiawath is also a monster and evil deity of the deep. She took the form of a dragon or sea serpent and battled the gods of light for supremacy over all living beings. She was eventually defeated by Merodach, who used her body to create Heaven and Earth.

Tiglath-Pileser I King of Assyria, who made it a leading power for centuries.

Tiki First man created, a figure carved of wood, or other representation of man.

Tirawa The name given to the Great Creator (*see* Great Spirit) by the Pawnee tribe who believed that four direct paths led from his house in the sky to the four semi-cardinal points: north-east, north-west, south-east and south-west.

Tiresias A Theban who was given the gift of prophecy by Zeus. He was blinded for seeing Athene bathing. He continued to use his prophetic talents after his death, advising Odysseus.

Tirfing Sword made by dwarves which was cursed to kill every time it was drawn, be the cause of three great atrocities, and kill Suaforlami (Odin's grandson), for whom it was made.

Tisamenus Son of Orestes, who inherited the Kingdom of Argos and Sparta.

Titania Queen of the fairies.

Tlaloc God of rain and fertility, so important to the people, because he ensured a good harvest, that the Aztec heaven or paradise was named Tlalocan in his honour.

Tlazolteotl Goddess of ordure, filth and vice. Also known as the earth-goddess or Tlaelquani, meaning 'filth-eater'. She acted as a confessor of sins or wrongdoings.

Tohu-mate Omen of death.

Tohunga A priest; a possessor of supernatural powers.

Toltec Civilization that preceded the Aztecs.

Tomahawk Hatchet with a stone or iron head used in war or hunting.

Tonalamatl Record of the Aztec calendar, which was recorded in books made from bark paper.

Tonalpohualli Aztec calendar composed of twenty thirteen-day weeks called trecenas.

Totec Solar deity known as Our Great Chief.

Totemism System of belief in which people share a relationship with a spirit animal or natural being with whom they interact. Examples include Ea, who is represented by a fish.

Toxilmolpilia The binding up of the years.

Tristan Nephew of King Mark of Cornwall, who travels to Ireland to bring Iseult back to marry his uncle. On the way, he and Iseult consume a love potion and fall madly in love before their story ends tragically.

Triton A sea-god, and son of Poseidon and Amphitrite. He led the Argonauts to the sea from Lake Tritonis.

Trojan War War waged by the Greeks against Troy, in order to reclaim Menelaus's wife Helen, who had eloped with the Trojan prince Paris. Many important heroes took part, and form the basis of many legends and myths.

Troll Unfriendly mythological creature of varying size and strength. Usually dwells in mountainous areas, among rocks or caves.

Truage Tribute or pledge of peace or truth, usually made on payment of a tax.

Tsuki-yomi God of the moon, brother of Amaterasu and Susanoo.

Tuat The other world or land of the dead.

Tupuna Ancestor.

Tvashtar Craftsman of the gods.

Tyndareus King of Sparta, perhaps the son of Perseus's daughter Grogphone. Expelled from Sparta but restored by Heracles. Married Leda and fathered Helen and Clytemnestra, among others.

Tyr Son of Frigga and the god of war (with Thor). Eventually kills Garm at Ragnarok.

Tzompantli Pyramid of Skulls.

Uayeb The five unlucky days of the Mayan calendar, which were believed to be when demons from the underworld could reach Earth. People would often avoid leaving their houses on uayeb days.

Ubaaner Magician, whose name meant 'splitter of stones', who created a wax crocodile that came to life to swallow up the man who was trying to seduce his wife.

Uile Bheist Mythical creature, usually some form of wild beast.

Uisneach A hill formation between Mullingar and Athlone said to mark the centre of Ireland.

uKqili (Zulu) Creator god.

Uller God of winter, whom Skadi eventually marries.

Ulster Cycle Compilation of folk tales and legends telling of the Ulaids, people from the northeast of Ireland, now named Ulster. Also known as the *Uliad Cycle*, it is one of four Irish cycles of mythology.

Unseelie Court An unholy court comprising a kind of fairies, antagonistic to humans. They took the form of a kind of Sluagh, and shot humans and animals with elf-shots.

Urd One of the Norns.

Urien King of Gore, husband of Morgan le Fey and father to Yvain.

Urmila Second daughter of Janaka.

Usha Wife of Aniruddha, daughter of Vanasur.

Ushas Goddess of the dawn.

Utgard-loki King of the giants. Tricked Thor.

Uther Pendragon King of England in sub-Roman Britain; father of King Arthur.

Utixo (Hottentot) Creator god.

Ut-Napishtim Ancestor of Gilgamesh, whom Gilgamesh sought out to discover how to prevent death. Similar to Noah in that he was sent a vision warning him of a great deluge. He built an ark in seven days, filling it with his family, possessions and all kinds of animals.

Uz Deity symbolized by a goat.

Vach Goddess of speech.

Vajrahanu One of Ravana's generals.

Vala Another name for Norns.

Valfreya Another name for Freyia.

Valhalla Odin's hall for the celebrated dead warriors chosen by the Valkyries.

Vali The cruel brother of Sugriva, dethroned by Rama.

Valkyries Odin's attendants, led by Freyia. Chose dead warriors to live at Valhalla. Also spelled as Valkyrs.

Vamadeva One of Dasharatha's priests.

Vanaheim Home of the Vanir.

Vanir Race of gods in conflict with the Aesir; they are gods of the sea and wind.

Varuna Ancient god of the sky and cosmos, later, god of the waters.

Vasishtha One of Dasharatha's priests.

Vassal Person under the protection of a feudal lord.

Vasudev Descendant of Yadu, husband of Rohini and Devaki, father of Krishna.

Vasudeva A name of Narayana or Vishnu.

Vavasor Vassal or tenant of a baron or lord who himself has vassals.

Vedic Mantras, hymns.

Vernandi One of the Norns.

Vichitravirya Bhishma's half-brother.

Vidar Slays Fenris.

Vidura Friend of the Pandavas.

Vigrid The plain where the final battle is held.

Vijaya Karna's bow.

Vikramaditya A king identified with Chandragupta II.

Vintail Moveable front of a helmet.

Virabhadra A demon that sprang from Shiva's lock of hair.

Viradha A fierce rakshasa, seizes Sita, slain by Rama.

Virupaksha The elephant who bears the whole world.

Vishnu The Preserver, Vedic sun god and one of the two great gods of post-Vedic Hinduism.

Vision Quest A sacred ceremony undergone by Native Americans to establish communication with the spirit set to direct them in life. The quest lasted up to four days and nights and was preceded by a period of solitary fasting and prayer.

Vivasvat The sun.

Vizier High-ranking official or adviser. Also known as vizir or vazir.

Volsung Family of great warriors about whom a great saga was spun.

Vrishadarbha King of Benares.

Vrishasena Son of Karna, slain by Arjuna.

Vyasa Chief of the royal chaplains.

Wairua Spirit, soul.

Wanjiru (Kikuyu) Maiden who was sacrificed by her village to appease the gods and make it rain after years of drought.

Weighing of the Heart Procedure carried out after death to assess whether the deceased was free from sin. If the deceased's heart weighed less than the feather of Ma'at, they would join Osiris in the Fields of Peace.

Whare Hut made of fern stems tied together with flax and vines, and roofed in with raupo (reeds).

White Demon Protector of Mázinderán. He prevented Kai-káus and his army from invading.

Withy Thin twig or branch which is very flexible and strong.

Wolverine Large mammal of the musteline family with dark, very thick, water-resistant fur, inhabiting the forests of North America and Eurasia.

Wroth Angry.

Wyrd One of the Norns.

Xanthus & Balius Horses of Achilles, immortal offspring of Zephyrus the west wind. A gift to Achilles's father Peleus.

Xipe Totec High priest and son of Ometeotl and Omecihuatl. Also known as the god of the seasons.

Xiupohualli Solar year, composed of eighteen twenty-day months. Also spelt Xiuhpōhualli.

Yadu A prince of the Lunar dynasty.

Yakshas Same as rakshasas.

Yakunin Government official.

Yama God of Death, king of the dead and son of the sun.

Yamato Take Legendary warrior and prince. Also known as Yamato Takeru.

Yashiki Residence or estate, usually of a daimyō.

Yasoda Wife of Nand.

Yemaya (Yoruba) Wife of Obatala.

Yemoja (Yoruba) Goddess of water and protector of women.

Yggdrasill The World Ash, holding up the Nine Worlds. Does not fall at Ragnarok.

Ymir Giant created from fire and ice; his body created the world.

Yo The female principle who, joined with In, the male side, brought about creation and the first gods. In and Yo correspond to the Chinese Yang and Yin.

Yomi The underworld.

Yudhishthira The eldest of the Pandavas, a great soldier.

Yuki-Onna The Snow-Bride or Lady of the Snow, who represents death.

Yvain Son of Morgan le Fay and knight of the Round Table, who goes on chivalric quests with a lion he rescued from a dragon.

Zahid Holy man.

Zál Son of Sám, who was born with pure white hair. Sám abandoned Zál, who was raised by the Símúrgh, or griffins. Zal became a great warrior, second only to his son, Rustem. Also known as Ním-rúz and Dustán.

Zephyr Gentle breeze.

Zeus King of gods, god of sky, weather, thunder, lightning, home, hearth and hospitality. He plays an important role as the voice of justice, arbitrator between man and gods, and among them. Married to Hera, but lover of dozens of others.

Zohák Serpent-king and figure of evil. Father of Mihrab.

Zu God of the storm, who took the form of a huge bird. Similar to the Persian símúrgh.

Zukin Head covering.